Carola Dunn is the author of several mysteries featuring
Daisy Dalrymple, as well as numerous historical novels.
Born and raised in England, she lives in Eugene, Oregon.

A Mourning Wedding

A Daisy Dalrymple Mystery

CAROLA DUNN

ROBINSON

Constable & Robinson Ltd
3 The Lanchesters
162 Fulham Palace Road
London W6 9ER
www.constablerobinson.com

First published in the US by St Martin's Press, 2004

This edition published in the UK by Robinson,
an imprint of Constable & Robinson Ltd, 2011

A copy of the British Library Cataloguing in
Publication Data is available from the British Library

ISBN: 978-1-84901-708-4

Typeset by TW Typesetting, Plymouth, Devon

Printed and bound in the UK

1 3 5 7 9 10 8 6 4 2

To Carole,
with fond memories of our trek around
the stately homes of East Anglia.
Thanks!

2nd EARL OF HAVERHILL

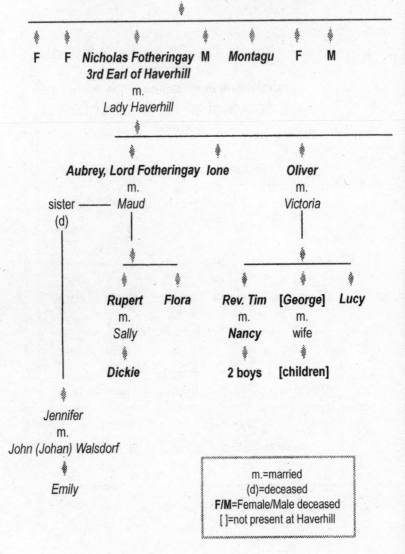

F F **Nicholas Fotheringay** M *Montagu* F M
3rd Earl of Haverhill
m.
Lady Haverhill

Aubrey, Lord Fotheringay *Ione* *Oliver*
m. m.
sister ——— *Maud* *Victoria*
(d)

Rupert **Flora** **Rev. Tim** **[George]** *Lucy*
m. m. m.
Sally **Nancy** wife

Dickie 2 boys [children]

Jennifer
m.
John (Johan) Walsdorf

Emily

m.=married
(d)=deceased
F/M=Female/Male deceased
[ ]=not present at Haverhill

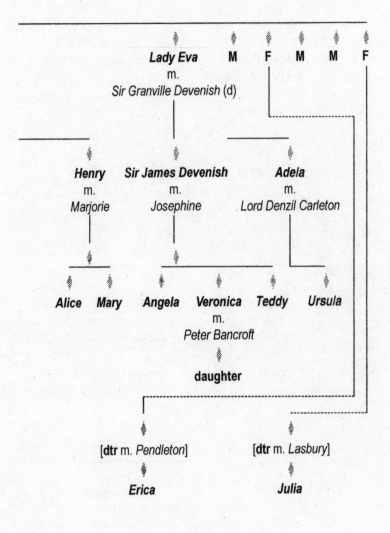

Prologue

Lady Eva Devenish capped her gold fountain pen and leant back with a sigh, flexing her beringed fingers. These days her hand was always stiff after writing. Sometimes she even felt the beginning of a cramp, but she wasn't going to let it stop her. Her writing was still tiny and neat, and her eyesight nearly as good as ever.

She pulled the heavy ledger-book towards her, blotted the ink, and reread the last paragraph she had written. The evidence seemed incontrovertible. She just hoped no one else would put the two snippets of gossip together.

It was really very naughty of her great-niece to spend the night with Lord Gerald. If Lucy had not been going to marry the man in just a couple of months, Lady Eva would have dealt with her severely. As the wedding date was set, least said soonest mended. Morals had started going downhill when the dear Queen died, and that dreadful German war seemed to have finished them off.

Besides, Lucy had always gone her own way. Look at that photography business! It would have been unthinkable in Lady Eva's youth. Yet, though she wouldn't dream of telling her so, she admired a certain independence in a girl, as long as the proprieties were observed.

She opened the right-hand bottom drawer of her desk and not without difficulty slid the heavy book into its place. Family – hers and her late husband's – she kept in the right drawer, others in the left. Others meant those less closely related than second cousin, for between them the Devenishes and the Fotheringays were connected to three-quarters of the aristocracy, by marriage if not by blood.

And Lady Eva knew more about them all than anyone else did. For decades she had collected rumours, checked them insofar as was practicable, and written them down. People would be amazed if they realized how much information she had stored away.

Some of them would be not merely amazed but shocked and horrified.

She locked the bottom right drawer and tucked the key away in the secret place at the back of the central drawer. In the wrong hands such information could be dangerous. It was rather like dynamite, though, quite harmless when properly handled, and of course Lady Eva knew just what she was doing.

CHAPTER 1

'Darling, I wish you hadn't planned a *morning* wedding. I'm getting the most frightful morning sickness these days. I'm more likely to need support than to be able to support you.' Daisy reached for another buttery toasted teacake.

'Bosh!' Blood-red nail varnish gleamed as Lucy deftly slid the willow-pattern plate on its lace doily across the dark oak table, away from Daisy. 'You're as healthy as a horse.'

'I'm eating for two,' Daisy protested. 'And making up for lost time, too. You haven't seen me between seven and eleven in the morning. I can barely manage to down a cup of tea for breakfast.'

'Too sickening, darling!' Lucy said sardonically, her clear soprano turning heads as it rang through the small tea-shop.

It was all very well for her. She never had the least difficulty keeping the straight-up-and-down figure – still fashionable in 1924, alas – which Daisy would never attain. But Lucy moved the plate back within Daisy's reach before pouring herself a second cup of Earl Grey.

Daisy didn't care for Earl Grey at the best of times. Now the musky scent gave her a twinge of incipient nausea. She hastily took another teacake, the smells of cinnamon and nutmeg bringing comfort to her queasy stomach. The Cosy Corner didn't put in as much spice as the Bluebell Tea Rooms used to, she thought regretfully, but after what happened at the Bluebell she'd never been quite brave enough to go back.

She turned her attention back to her friend. As always, Lucy was the epitome of the stylish young woman, from the feathered cloche perched on her dark, sleek bob to the fashionable knee-length hemline, flesh-coloured silk stockings, and strapped shoes below.

Usually cool, calm and collected, she was now fidgeting with her teaspoon, although she didn't take sugar in her tea. She regarded Daisy with uncharacteristic anxiety and lowered her voice to say, 'For a moment there you looked quite green. Darling, will it really be too much for you to come to Haverhill a few days early?'

'Everyone says morning sickness only lasts a month, or six weeks at most. The trouble is, they say it in that frightfully hearty, encouraging way that makes one sure they're conceal-ing the bad news.'

'The wedding's not for another month. I don't know how I'll cope without you to rely on for a breath of sanity, Daisy. All the family will be gathering, and besides the general fuss, some of my relations are utterly poisonous.'

'Her brothers and her cousins, whom she reckons up by dozens, her brothers and her cousins and her aunts!' Daisy misquoted HMS *Pinafore*. 'I suppose you're getting married at Haverhill rather than in town because Lord Haverhill's getting a bit creaky about the joints?'

'Actually, Grandfather may be eighty but he's as frisky as a spring lamb, and Grandmama too.'

'I can't imagine Lady Haverhill frisking!'

'No, much too Victorian, but she's healthy as a horse. They

both adore any excuse to gather the whole family at Haverhill. It's Uncle Aubrey who has a dicky heart, though I don't believe it's quite as bad as Aunt Maud likes to think.'

'I seem to remember Lady Fotheringay being a bit of a worrier.'

'Fussbox, more like,' said Lucy with an unladylike snort. 'Cosseting him makes her feel important.'

'It must be difficult playing second fiddle for decades,' Daisy said charitably. 'She'd like to be the Countess of Haverhill before your uncle pops off, I expect. It's only natural. I suppose Lady Eva will be there. She rather terrifies me. I'm always sure she's reading my mind.'

'Oh, Aunt Eva doesn't need supernatural means to collect her information. She's a bit of a bore but really quite a decent old trout.'

'I bet there are a lot of people who feel threatened by her curiosity. People who have something they desperately want to hide.'

'It's not as if she ever does anything with what she finds out. She just likes to know what everyone's up to. Our sort of people, I mean. She couldn't care less about Mr Bones the Butcher.'

'It wouldn't surprise me if she found out I was pregnant before I did! Or did she lose interest in me when I married a policeman?'

'It was touch and go,' Lucy said frankly, 'but your mother is still the Dowager Viscountess Dalrymple, and your sister's Lady John. In spite of which you might have been relegated to *hoi polloi* if Alec was an ordinary bobby, not a Detective Chief Inspector of Scotland Yard. His title may not be noble but it has a certain lustre.'

Daisy laughed. 'That's all that reconciled Mother to my marriage, insofar as she's ever reconciled to anything once she's decided to disapprove. At least your relatives, however poisonous, can't possibly disapprove of Binkie.'

'No,' Lucy agreed complacently, leaning back in the high-backed Windsor chair. 'The son of a marquis, even a younger son, is a creditable match.'

'Lucy, you do love him, don't you?'

'I. . . I think so. I'm pretty certain, actually. I'm not likely to find anyone else who's willing to let me keep up the photography business after we're married.'

'You can wind him around your little finger.' Disturbed by her friend's attitude, Daisy sighed.

'One can't ever be absolutely certain, can one?' Lucy pleaded.

'I am. Most of the time, anyway. Right-oh, darling, I'll come to Haverhill to hold your hand and cheer you on. Maybe I can get an article out of it for my American editor: "A Fashionable English Wedding", perhaps.'

'Thanks, darling.' Lucy took out her compact to powder her nose and refresh her crimson lip-salve. 'I've got to run. Lady Moresby wants yet another portrait, though I can't think why, considering her face. But she says I'm the only photographer who brings out her "inner being". By the way, not a word about the photography. The parents assume I'm going to give up the studio once I'm Lady Gerald Bincombe.'

'I'll be silent as the grave,' Daisy promised.

On a sunny afternoon in June, Lord Haverhill's dark blue Daimler sped between the flat, emerald green fields of

Cambridgeshire. Leaning back in the luxuriously soft leather seat she shared with a hamper from Fortnum and Mason, Daisy caught a glimpse to her right of their goal.

Her stepdaughter, Belinda, would love to see Haverhill, she thought. At this distance, the mansion resembled an exotic hybrid of a mediaeval castle and a Gothic cathedral. The sprawling mass, complete with towers and spires, turrets and battlements, oriels and arches, was a triumph of early Victorian neo-Gothic.

One of the two tallest spires belonged to the chapel where Lucy would be married. In Victorian times, the entire household, including throngs of servants, had gathered there for daily prayers. Nowadays it saw a Sunday service only when a clergyman was visiting, as the present Lord Haverhill had no private chaplain.

Turning off a narrow lane, the motorcar approached the mansion along an avenue of elms. The grounds visible between the trees were well-kept parkland with scattered trees and a spinney off to the right. None of the fallow deer Daisy remembered were visible.

The Daimler drew up before the broad flight of marble steps leading up to the cathedral-sized front door. The chauffeur came around to open Daisy's door.

She stepped out and paused to contemplate the vast façade. Not having visited for a while, she had forgotten how enormous the house was. From here, only the main block was visible, but that alone could have swallowed Alec's suburban semi-detached without a hiccup. Altogether, Haverhill was at least twice, perhaps three times, the size of Fairacres, Daisy's childhood home.

As she started up the steps, Lucy came out through a wicket in the great double door and hurried down to meet her. Elegant as ever in a simple summer frock of buttercup-yellow linen, belted at the hips with a white sash, she made Daisy feel crumpled and dusty. Behind her, a woman with mousy marcelled hair paused on the top step, watching.

'Darling, I hope the journey wasn't too frightfully tiresome. I managed to escape to the library . . .'

'The library? You?' Daisy said, laughing.

'. . . To watch out for you.' Lucy gestured at the windows to their left. 'No one but John is ever there – you know we're not a bookish family – but Sally saw me go in and followed. She's trying to persuade me to let her little darling carry my train. I'm supposed to make an exception because the brat will be Earl of Haverhill in fifty years or so.'

'Sally is your cousin Rupert's wife, I take it?'

'Yes. Then there are my sisters-in-law who think their offspring should have precedence, and Mummy, who agrees on no children in the wedding but wants me to carry tuberoses, which always make me sneeze, and . . .'

'Darling, you're babbling.'

'I'm well on the way to becoming a raving lunatic. Thank heaven you've come, Daisy.'

'Introduce me to Mrs Rupert and then you'll have to escort me to my room for a lie-down before tea. I'm quite exhausted from the journey.'

Lucy peered into her face, concerned. 'You don't look . . . Oh, you mean . . . Right-oh.' She raised her voice. 'Sally, I don't believe you've met my friend Daisy Fletcher.'

Mrs Rupert Fotheringay's tweed skirt, silk blouse, and pearls, though perfectly suitable for the country, looked formal beside Lucy's frock, and her tone was more formal than friendly as she said, 'Welcome to Haverhill, Mrs Fletcher.'

'I'm taking Daisy up to her room to rest after the journey.'

'That hardly seems necessary as your grandfather sent the Daimler for her.' The tone was distinctly chilly now. 'Those of us who came down by train—'

'Daisy's pregnant,' Lucy announced baldly. 'Her husband wouldn't let her come if she had to take the train.'

'The car didn't come just for me. It was crammed full of parcels for the wedding,' Daisy explained.

'Come on, darling, before you drop.' Lucy linked her arm through Daisy's and practically dragged her into the house. 'Sally is jealous,' she hissed, 'because this time I'm the bride who gets all the attention, and I'm getting a bigger show than she did. Heaven knows I could do without it! If I'd realized what a big family wedding entails, I'd have made Binkie elope to Gretna.'

The hall was cavernous, lit high above by windows in the octagonal base of the clock tower. Between the surrounding marble pillars lurked portraits by Van Dyck, Lely and Raeburn. Daisy and Lucy picked their way across the chequer-board marble floor between stacks of trestle tables and folding chairs.

'Good gracious, how many people are coming?'

'Six hundred to the breakfast, most of them relatives. My great-grandfather had thirteen children, all dead but three, but there's their children and children's children. Then there's Mummy's side of the family. And Binkie's mother's guest list was almost as long as ours. Grandfather's paying for the lot, the lamb, not expecting Daddy to cough up out of his own pocket.'

'That's jolly generous.'

'Oh, he has pots of money. In spite of – or perhaps because

of – all those children, my great-grandfather popped off before ruinous death duties came in.'

'Helpful of him!'

'Very. Mind you, Grandfather has plenty of expenses what with all the people battening on him. Not only those living here. Great-uncle Montagu gets enough income from the estate to live on. And Grandfather gives Uncle Henry and Daddy allowances, and Rupert too, because he's the eldest son of the eldest son. Girls are supposed to stay at home until they marry.'

'Don't I know it!' Daisy had been expected to reside with her mother or the cousin who inherited Fairacres when her father and brother died. Like Lucy, she had chosen to earn her own living, in her case with writing, and they had shared digs. 'It was fun, but I have to confess I did get fearfully tired of living on eggs and sardines and mousetrap cheese.'

'It's no fun without you, darling. But no more of that from now on. Binkie gets an allowance from his father, and he's doing surprisingly well in the City. You're all right with stairs, aren't you, darling?' Lucy asked as they reached the splendidly carved oak staircase, saved from the demolition of the ancient house which once stood on this spot. 'Grandmama told Jennifer to put you in the room next to mine. First floor, not too much climbing.'

'I'm perfectly well, now that the beastly morning sickness is over. But thanks all the same.'

'Lucy!' Lady Fotheringay came out of the dining room to their right. A short, plump, grey-haired lady, she was aflutter with gauzy draperies in a variety of pastel shades. 'Lucy, such a shame . . . Oh, it's Daisy Dalrymple isn't it? How lovely to see you again, my dear. But you're married now, aren't you. Perhaps I ought to call you Mrs Fletcher?'

'Daisy will do very well, Lady Fotheringay.'

'What was it you wanted to tell me, Aunt Maud?' Lucy demanded with barely concealed impatience.

'Oh yes. Your uncle is very much afraid he won't have any pineapples ripe by Saturday.'

'I'm sure there's plenty of other fruit, cherries and such, or you can send to London. Excuse us, please, Aunt. Daisy needs to rest before tea.'

Daisy glanced back with a smile of apology as Lucy bustled her up the stairs. Lady Fotheringay appeared undismayed by her niece's rudeness, but Daisy protested, 'Lucy, you're being quite as poisonous as any of your relatives can possibly be. I won't be turned into an invalid just so that you can avoid them.'

'Sorry, darling! I'll grovel to Aunt Maud, I promise, but not to Sally, who was foul to you first.'

'She was rather. Pineapples – Your uncle's still mad for his conservatories, I take it?'

'Yes. Uncle Aubrey's a dear old bird but mad is the word, quite potty, in fact. I told you he has a weak heart? Sometimes I wonder if his brain isn't getting enough blood. At least he sticks to his plants and doesn't fuss at me. Oh Lord, now here comes Grandmama!'

The Countess of Haverhill was a tall, upright old lady dressed in the black her generation considered suitable for the elderly. 'Welcome back to Haverhill, Mrs Fletcher,' she said. 'I trust you will be a calming influence on Lucy. Nerves were expected of a bride in my day, but I thought you modern young people were supposed to be above such weaknesses.'

'I dare say it takes everyone differently, Lady Haverhill.'

'No doubt.' She looked beyond Daisy and frowned slightly. 'What is it, Jennifer?'

'Mrs Oliver wants Lucy to try on her going-away costume, Lady Haverhill.' A woman came hurrying down the upper staircase, by no means so grand as the lower. Her slightly shabby clothes could have been Sally Fotheringay's cast-offs, and very likely were. A niece of Lady Fotheringay, she had married a penniless war refugee from somewhere in Europe.

'Again?' Lucy heaved a big sigh. 'In the sewing room? Tell Mummy I'll be along as soon as I've settled Daisy, will you, Jennifer?'

'Hello, Jennifer,' said Daisy.

'Hello, Daisy. Shall I show you your room while Lucy goes to her mother?'

Lucy opened her mouth to object, caught her grandmother's eye, sighed again, and acquiesced.

'I hope to see you at tea, Mrs Fletcher,' said Lady Haverhill, 'if you feel up to coming down.'

'I'll be there, never fear.' Daisy walked with Jennifer along the carpeted gallery and turned left into the west wing.

'I expect you're surprised that we're still living here,' Jennifer said with a touch of belligerence.

'Not surprised, exactly, though I do remember some talk last time I was here about you and Johan returning to ... Luxemburg, is it?'

'That's right, only my husband likes to be called John now. He went back for a visit and found everything quite devastated after the German occupation. He's decided to become a British subject, as much for Emily's sake as anything.'

'Oh yes, your baby. How is she?' Nowadays Daisy was genuinely interested in babies.

Jennifer's rather plain face lit up. 'She's just beginning to talk comprehensibly. Would you like to come and see her?'

'After tea, perhaps?'

'Anytime. Lady Haverhill's been terribly good about letting one of the housemaids play nursemaid for Emily sometimes, but of course I mostly look after her myself.'

'That must keep you busy.'

'It does, but I lend a hand with the housekeeping as well. The housekeeper's nearly as old as Lord Haverhill and won't be pensioned off. And John is acting as Lord Haverhill's secretary and cataloguing the library, so we are not living on charity, whatever Sally says. Here's Lucy's room, and this is yours next door. There's a bathroom in between, all the hot water you want, and the lav is just across the passage there.'

'Thank heaven the first Earl of Haverhill didn't insist on mediaeval plumbing to match the exterior!' said Daisy.

As the bride, Lucy had one of the better of the thirty or forty guest chambers, so Daisy's room was also spacious and comfortably furnished. There was a small writing table with paper, envelopes and an inkstand. A couple of easy chairs stood by the window, which looked over parkland to the lake and the folly on the low hill beyond. Daisy's bags had been sent up by the chauffeur, and a maid had already started unpacking.

Jennifer Walsdorf seemed disposed to stay and chat. Daisy didn't know her well but rather admired her for having the nerve to marry a foreigner in spite of family disapproval. They sat in the chairs by the window. Daisy asked who else had already arrived for the wedding.

'Lucy's parents. I expect you know them?'

'Yes. I used to call them Uncle Oliver and Aunt Vickie, but I expect that's inappropriate now I'm married. Who else?'

'Lady Eva Devenish, Lord Haverhill's sister. She often

comes down for the weekend, so she's just stayed on. I can't wait to see her hat for the wedding.'

'Yes, there's something to be said for those vast Edwardian hats she still goes in for.'

'Her son, Sir James, is here too, with Lady Devenish and Angela.'

'Angela?'

'Their unmarried daughter. Her brother, Teddy, is coming later. Their married sister – one of them – will be here tonight, I think, with husband and children. That's Veronica and Peter Bancroft. They sometimes come for the weekend when Lady Eva's here, and Emily likes their little girl. She's crazy about Dickie Fotheringay, too – Sally's little boy, who's already here. You know Sally, don't you? Colonel Rupert's wife?'

'I just met her. Rupert's not here yet?'

'No, he's on manoeuvres, if the Household Cavalry do anything so prosaic. Most of the men are coming down later. Uncle Montagu's here, though, and Lucy's brother Timothy, the clergyman, and family. He's going to perform the ceremony.'

'Yes, Lucy told me she'd asked him.'

'Then there's a variety of cousins – you don't want me to go into all the cousins and their spouses and children, do you? There will be over twenty for dinner tonight, and more swarms turning up throughout the week. I have a hard time keeping them straight, though most of them visit here quite often. You'll never manage it in four days.'

'No, you're right, I shan't try. Just thinking about them exhausts me. I think I'll put my feet up for a while.'

'You ought to have a footstool.'

'Oh, that's all right, the bed will do.'

'I'll send a footman up with a footstool later. Is there anything else I can get you?'

'No thanks, Jennifer. I'll see you later. Tea's in the Long Gallery, as usual?'

'Or out on the terrace if it stays warm. Quarter to five.'

The maid had finished unpacking and departed. Daisy took off her skirt and jacket and blouse and lay down on the bed in her petticoat. Next thing she knew, Lucy was shaking her shoulder.

'Darling, if you want tea – which I'm sure you do or I wouldn't wake you – you'd better get dressed.'

'Gosh, is it that late already? I'll be right down.'

CHAPTER 2

Five minutes later, thanking heaven for shingled hair which didn't have to be unpinned and brushed and pinned up again, Daisy hurried down to the Long Gallery.

It was her favourite room in the house. One long wall was devoted to panelling salvaged from the old house, elaborately carved with knights and musicians, birds and animals, flowers and trees, even ships and sea serpents. Along the wall stood marvellous old chests, some carved, some of marquetry, and a hideous table with ornate gilt legs and a green marble top inlaid with swirling patterns of multi-coloured marble.

The opposite wall was all windows and French doors opening to the terrace and the gardens beyond.

Outside, the marble benches along the balustrade had been supplemented by a scattering of chintz-cushioned wicker and wrought-iron chairs. With the dining room and drawing room wings protruding at either end, the south-facing terrace was sheltered from stray breezes. Summer frocks and shady hats flocked about a tea-table presided over by Lady Haverhill, though Jennifer was doing the actual pouring, Daisy noticed.

Of the few gentlemen present, for the most part the elder were in tweeds, the younger in flannels and blazers. Amongst this casual country attire, a dark blue pin-striped suit stood out.

Daisy recognized its wearer as the Honourable Montagu Fotheringay, the earl's younger brother, a very large gentleman fortunately seated on iron, not wicker. Montagu resided at his club in London, and though his forays to Haverhill were frequent, he never ventured further out of doors than the terrace.

With him at the small glass-topped table was his sister, Lady Eva Devenish. Her proportions were majestic rather than ample. So was her Edwardian cartwheel hat, which bore a veritable garden of rosebuds and a bird's worth of pink feathers. Her frock bloomed with cabbage roses – though widowed, unlike her sister-in-law she eschewed black. Even her stockings were pink to match the roses.

She and her brother had their heads together, deep in conversation. Daisy wondered how much of Lady Eva's purported vast fund of information about the aristocracy originated with her brother's fellow-clubmen's gossip.

According to Lucy, her great-aunt did not rely on rumour but always did her best to verify the facts. She was not herself a gossip; she simply enjoyed her omniscience.

All the same, Daisy was uneasy with someone who had all the facts about her life at her fingertips. If, as Lucy said, Lady Eva was still interested in her, no doubt she knew that Daisy had not only married a policeman but had managed to entangle herself in a number of his investigations.

So, on her way to get the cup of tea of which she was sorely in need, Daisy tried to pass the pair inconspicuously.

'Daisy!' Lady Eva's strident voice called her back. 'I suppose it's Mrs Fletcher now, but having known you since you were a schoolgirl . . .'

'Daisy is quite all right, Lady Eva. Good afternoon, Mr Fotheringay.'

Montagu, who had heaved himself to his feet, bowed courteously, if ponderously, and waved her to his seat. 'I'll fetch you a cup of tea, Mrs Fletcher. Eva's dying for a chat.'

'I see your sister has a girl this time,' Lady Eva started. 'Still, she's already produced two boys. It's a shame there's no title to be inherited. I know several families who'd be thrilled to have a son and heir. How is your mother?'

'Very well.' Her health was about the only thing the Dowager Viscountess Dalrymple never complained about.

'Still not reconciled to the present Lord Dalrymple, I hear. Pity she didn't have two sons.'

Daisy resented this casual reference to her only brother's death in the war. 'Unfortunately one has no choice in the matter,' she said coolly.

Ignoring her tone, Lady Eva got down to what she really wanted to talk about: 'Odd, this business of Westmoor's heir. Of course it's in the courts now and the rights of it are still to be decided, but I suppose what your mother told me is accurate?'

'I don't know what she told you, but I'd be very surprised if she made up a story for your benefit.'

'She said you—'

'Daisy!' Lucy came to the rescue. 'Excuse us, Aunt Eva. Grandfather wants a word with Daisy.'

'I'll talk to you later, Daisy,' Lady Eva promised – or threatened, depending on one's point of view. 'Lucy, has your uncle Aubrey come to tea?'

'I think he's still in the conservatory.'

'I'll go and rout him out. He ought to be more sociable at a time like this. His weak heart is mostly in Maud's imagination and he uses it as an excuse.' Lady Eva strode off around the side of the house, carrying her seventy-plus years and thirteen-plus stone lightly.

'Sorry to summon you like that.'

'I'm delighted, darling.'

'I thought you might be. The thing is, Grandfather's feeling rather rheumaticky. Old age seems to have pounced rather suddenly instead of creeping up in a decent manner.'

'What a shame. Your great-uncle Montagu was fetching me a cup of tea . . .'

'I'll redirect him. Oh, here comes Uncle Aubrey. Aunt Eva dashed off on a fruitless errand.'

Lord Fotheringay came out from the Long Gallery with his wife. Tall, thin, balding, stooped, with gold-rimmed glasses, he might have looked scholarly but for his sun-ruddy skin and disreputable clothes.

'I have washed my hands, Maud,' he was saying plaintively. 'You know the sap won't wash off. Oh, Miss Dalrymple!' he greeted Daisy with delight.

'Mrs Fletcher,' Lady Fotheringay corrected him. 'I told you.'

'It's been ages since you were here. I have some new specimens which will interest you, and any number of plants in bloom: tuberose, hibiscus, oleanders, gardenias, and some quite spectacular orchids. Shall we . . . ?'

'Daisy's dying for a cup of tea, Uncle Aubrey,' Lucy came to the rescue again, taking his arm and moving the group towards the tea table. 'I expect you are, too.'

'I usually have it in the conservatory,' he said doubtfully, glancing down at his baggy-kneed, earth-stained trousers. 'I'm not exactly dressed for company, but Maud told me . . .'

'I told you your mother expects you to turn out when we have so many people here for Lucy's wedding. And I told you no one would expect you to climb all those stairs to your dressing room to change your clothes, not in your state of health. It's all family, after all, except for Mrs Fletcher.'

'I'd love to see your flowers, Lord Fotheringay,' Daisy put in quickly. 'After tea, perhaps?' She remembered she was to visit Jennifer Walsdorf's little girl after tea. 'I've promised to pop into the nursery but I shan't stay more than half an hour, then I'll come and find you. And now I must go and say hello to Lord Haverhill.'

The old Earl was still an impressive figure, his silver hair and moustache as thick as ever. Daisy found him in a sardonic mood. 'I suppose Aubrey's been inviting you to take a look at his plants. When I'm gone, he'll no doubt turn the entire estate over to hothouses and conservatories.'

'I think it's admirable that Lord Fotheringay found an interest and has pursued it with such success.'

'Hmph. Well, he always was a sickly boy. I never thought he'd outlive me.'

Daisy couldn't think of any polite retort which would not imply that either Lord Haverhill or his son was facing imminent death, so she changed the subject. 'You're putting on a splendid do for Lucy's wedding.'

'She's the best of my grandchildren,' the Earl said gruffly. 'Standing on her own two feet, though it wouldn't have been countenanced in a girl in my young day. She's not forever running to me with her hand out. Pity she wasn't born a boy.'

'Never say that, Nick!' Montagu arrived bearing Daisy's cup of tea and a plate with an assortment of tiny sandwiches, biscuits and cake. He deposited the lot on the table between his elder brother and Daisy. 'Can't ever be too many lovely ladies in the world, eh, Mrs Fletcher?'

Another unanswerable comment. Daisy smiled and sipped her tea.

'You're a dolt, Montagu,' snapped Lord Haverhill. 'Mrs Fletcher is right, at least Aubrey has a respectable hobby.'

'And expectations. All he has to do is sit tight and Haverhill drops into his pocket,' said Montagu, his affability apparently undiminished.

'Ah yes,' said the Earl with a sneer, 'it was hard luck on you that Rupert dodged all the German bullets sent his way in the war, wasn't it? With Aubrey in poor health, you might have stepped into my shoes after all.'

'Are you insinuating . . . ? Sorry, Mrs Fletcher!' Montagu waved Daisy back to the seat from which she was rising. 'Don't go. Brother Nicholas and I rub each other the wrong way, as you can see. I'm off.'

Uncomfortably, Daisy settled back.

'My apologies, Mrs Fletcher,' said Lord Haverhill. 'I usually manage to muster more patience with fools, even my brother. I must be growing old! Tell me, what are you writing these days? I read your articles in *Town and Country* with great enjoyment.'

'And little else,' said a mournful voice. Johan – now John – Walsdorf bowed. He was a small, spare man, sandy-haired, wearing steel-rimmed glasses. His accent was barely detectable. 'Good afternoon, Mrs Fletcher,' he continued. 'I do not mean to disparage your articles, which are indeed delightful and well written. However, I could wish there were something of more substance in his lordship's library than bound copies of *Punch*, dating back to the inception of that excellent magazine, and a century's worth of popular novels.'

'Nonsense, my dear fellow. I distinctly recall my mother and my grandmother reading books of sermons.'

'There are sermons,' Mr Walsdorf acknowledged, a smile lighting his face. 'Also out-of-date books on agriculture and the peerage. Like the rest of your library, my lord, none are of any conceivable antiquarian interest.'

'We're a young family, Mrs Fletcher, about the same age as the house. Of no antiquarian interest, and without literary aspirations. The ancestors hanging in the hall are someone else's. But I expect you have heard the story?'

'No, actually.' The Dalrymples stretched back into the mists of time and Daisy had never been particularly interested in noble lineages. Moreover, the war had allowed her to avoid a young lady's usual introduction to Society: she had worked in a military hospital instead of attending balls and hunting a husband of her own class.

It was odd, she now realized, that Lucy, who was much more conscious of such things, had never talked about her own family's history.

'It all started,' said the Earl, 'with Eustace Fothers, who was a manufacturer of umbrella silk in the Suffolk town of Haverhill. You know it perhaps?'

'I don't recall it.'

'Unsurprising. It is a small and very dull town.'

Mr Eustace Fothers, it seemed, did rather well with his umbrella silk and quadrupled the resulting fortune by shrewd investment. The purchase of an estate (from a noble but impoverished family who had not soiled their hands with trade since the sixteenth century) scarcely dented his wealth.

Mr Fothers had torn down the house and, having built the present pile, renamed the place after the source of his fortune, then changed his own name to Fotheringay. His investments continuing to prosper, he had next made a very large donation to the political party then in power. His reward, not unexpected, was a viscountcy, soon raised to an earldom.

His son, the second Earl, had been lucky in both his investments and his marriage to a daughter of the old nobility.

'My mother,' said the third Lord Haverhill, 'did not cavil at the umbrella silk. By that time, fortunately, the taint of trade was no longer regarded as an insuperable obstacle.'

'A great deal more respectable than being a peer because a distant ancestor was Charles the Second's mistress,' said Daisy.

The Earl shouted with laughter. Heads turned. Mr Walsdorf looked faintly puzzled, as if he couldn't see what was funny in the ignoble origins of the English peerage. After all these years in England, all those bound volumes of *Punch* catalogued, he still did not quite fathom the English sense of humour. On the other hand, Daisy suspected Lucy would be equally unamused.

Smiling at Lord Haverhill, she set down her empty cup and saucer. 'If you'll excuse me, it's time I said hello to Lucy's parents.'

The Honourable Mr and Mrs Oliver Fotheringay were a staid, rather dull couple. He sat on the boards of a couple of companies, doubtless due to his courtesy title, and was a churchwarden. She pottered contentedly about the garden of their small manor house in a small Essex village, driving her gardener to distraction, and was sometimes asked to open church fêtes. Their two sons, Lucy's brothers Timothy and George, were both equally stodgy. Daisy had never understood how they could have produced a vivacious daughter like Lucy.

However, they had always been kind to Daisy, ever since her first visit from school, and she was fond of them. She was making her way towards them when Sally came up to her.

'I wonder what you said to amuse Grandfather?' she said. 'He's been feeling under the weather lately, I'm afraid. We are a little anxious for his health. I only hope laughing won't overtire him. I'd better see if he wants to go in and lie down.'

'A good laugh's more likely to do him good, if you ask me,' asserted a woman Daisy didn't recognize. 'I'm Angela Devenish, Mrs Fletcher. How d'ye do? It was splendid to hear my great-uncle laughing.'

Lady Eva's spinster granddaughter looked to be in her early thirties. Even in her youth, Daisy thought, she could never have been anything but plain. Her boyish figure was skinny rather than svelte. Her jumper was grubby and the hem of her tweed skirt had all too obviously been turned up to the newly fashionable knee length by an amateur seamstress – probably herself, and probably with more regard to convenience than fashion. Her boots suggested she had been a Land Girl during the war. A small dog of undistinguished parentage lurked at her heels.

Her grin was infectious. Daisy smiled at her and held out her hand to the dog. 'It looks a bit like our Nana.' The dog cowered.

'Tiddler's been badly treated,' Angela Devenish said gruffly, and added in a slightly belligerent tone, 'I work for the RSPCA.'

'Good for you. It must be rather upsetting at times.'

'You can't imagine. Not fit for tea-time conversation, my mother would say.'

'No, I expect not. But I'd like to talk to you about it sometime. I'm a journalist. Maybe I could write an article that would encourage people to help.'

Angela beamed. 'Jolly good show. Anytime.'

Daisy exchanged a few more words with her before resuming her pursuit of Lucy's parents, who had moved to the other side of the terrace. Sally, she saw, was bending solicitously over Lord Haverhill, who waved her away, looking irritable. Lord Fotheringay was contemplating a stone urn of geraniums and lobelia, plainly bored by such common-place plants.

Lucy stood at bay by the balustrade, surrounded by a swarm of giggling girls, cousins no doubt. She shot Daisy a look of desperate appeal. Daisy altered course. This, after all, was why she had been invited.

'Lucy, come and reintroduce me to your parents. I haven't seen them in such ages.'

'Coming! Daisy, these are my cousins Julia, Alice, Erica, Mary, Ursula. My bridesmaids. Girls, my friend Mrs Fletcher.' Linking arms, she hurried Daisy off with no time to respond to the chorus of 'How do you do.'

'I'll never remember which is which,' Daisy said.

'They're interchangeable. Were we ever so silly?'

'We never had the chance, darling. At that age, you were busy being the most elegant girl in the Land Army, and I was busy in a hospital office because I couldn't face being a nurse on the wards. I expect we'd have managed to be just as silly if we hadn't been otherwise engaged.'

'I might have. I doubt you would. Darling, thank you for rescuing me, but you don't really need me to help you tackle the parents.'

'Of course not. It was all I could think of on the spur of the moment when I saw you were drowning. Who is that heading our way?'

Lucy glanced round at the approaching woman and groaned.

'Aunt Josephine. Lady Devenish. Great-aunt Eva's daughter-in-law.'

'Angela's mother?'

'That's right.'

It was possible to imagine Lady Devenish in youth as a pretty, doll-like creature, but the years had added flabbiness to her short figure and discontent to her round face. 'I'll leave you to her,' said Daisy.

'If you must. She's bound to ask me yet again to give Angela a few hints about dressing decently. She simply can't believe the poor fish doesn't care two hoots. Angela won't spend a penny on clothes. It all goes on her wretched animals.'

Lucy turned away to intercept Lady Devenish, and Daisy at last caught up with Mr and Mrs Oliver Fotheringay. They thanked her for coming to support Lucy.

'I simply don't understand her,' said Mrs Fotheringay in bewilderment. 'A girl's wedding should be the most wonderful day of her life, but Lucy is utterly offhand about the whole thing. I'm trying to make it perfect for her, but nothing I do seems to be right.'

Daisy did her best to soothe the poor lady. Lady Haverhill came to join them, and Daisy found herself having to defend 'the modern young woman'.

Meanwhile Oliver Fotheringay wandered off to chat with his brother, Aubrey. Lord Fotheringay had descended the steps to the rose garden and was on his knees poking at the soil. Angela Devenish should have been Lord Fotheringay's daughter, Daisy decided. They would have understood each other.

Mrs Oliver and her mother-in-law agreed to blame the Germans for the shortcomings of the modern generation.

After a good night's sleep, Daisy was enjoying a warm, comfortable drowse when a maid brought morning tea, with two Bath Oliver biscuits. Since the end of her morning sickness she always woke ravenous. Before she even sat up in bed, she reached for a biscuit and bit into it.

So her mouth was full of crumbs when the screaming started.

CHAPTER 3

Daisy scrambled out of bed, reaching for her dressing-gown. A crumb went down the wrong way and the subsequent choking cough brought tears to her eyes. Unable to locate her slippers, she hurried out to the passage barefoot.

The housemaid who had brought her tea stood in a doorway further down the hall, facing into the room. Her hands were clapped over her ears as if to drown out her own shrill screams.

Daisy had been quick off the mark, but now doors started opening and heads popping out. Several people emerged a few steps from the safety of their rooms. From one room came another housemaid, an older woman. She marched up to the screaming girl, swung her around and slapped her face. The girl started sobbing.

'She's dead!' she gasped. 'Murdered!'

The head housemaid glanced into the room, turned pale, and swayed. As Daisy hurried towards them, the elder visibly pulled herself together. She shook the younger by the shoulders.

'Go and tell Mr Baines,' she ordered, giving the girl a shove towards the back stairs. 'Get along with you, right this minute.' Head averted, she fumbled behind her for the doorknob and pulled the door to, scraping shards of broken china into the corridor.

Montagu Fotheringay, massive in a crimson silk dressing-gown, advanced from the opposite direction. 'What the deuce is going on?' he demanded. 'That's Eva's room.'

Lady Eva! Of course, Daisy thought, if anyone in this house was going to be murdered, it would have to be Lady Eva Devenish, the collector of secrets. But perhaps the maid was mistaken. Perhaps the old lady was merely ill.

'Who screamed?' That was Nancy, Lucy's sister-in-law, pattering down the stairs from the second floor. 'Is someone hurt, Daisy? I was a VAD nurse in the war.'

'It's Lady Eva. I don't know . . . The maid seemed to think she's dead.'

'Her ladyship's dead,' the elder maid confirmed grimly, still very pale. 'And if you'll excuse me, madam, I'm going to sit down for a minute.' She sank to the floor beside the table where a tray of tea things awaited distribution to the bedrooms.

Nancy knelt beside her and forced her head between her knees. 'Breathe deeply, Merton,' she advised.

Montagu, frowning, reached for the doorknob. 'I'm going to—'

'No.' Stopping him was rather like tackling a tank but Daisy managed to hold him back. 'You mustn't go in there, Mr Fotheringay. Nancy, would you take a look at Lady Eva and make sure there's nothing we can do for her? No, Mr Fotheringay, you really must not. I'm afraid the girl spoke of . . . of murder.'

'M . . . m . . .' Montagu's mouth opened and closed but he couldn't get the word out.

Stepping over the smashed tea things, Nancy Fotheringay slipped past him into the room. She came out again after a few seconds, very white about the mouth. 'No question of it. Daisy, the police will have to be sent for.'

Obviously Lucy had told at least some of her family about Daisy's involvement with several of Alec's cases, Daisy realized with resignation. Now she was going to be expected to deal with the police. Well, she wasn't going to ring them up without being sure of her facts. It was too late to worry about fingerprints after the two maids and Nancy had all touched the handle. She opened the door Nancy had shut and peeked in.

For a moment all she saw was a snowstorm. A pillow had been ripped and feathers were all over the place, a few floating in the draught between the door and the open window. Amid the drifts, Lady Eva sprawled on her back, head and shoulders hanging over the side of the bed. Her face was purple, her tongue sticking out, eyes glaring. One hand was at her throat, as if plucking at something tied around it.

Feeling sick, Daisy turned her back on the dreadful sight. What she wanted to do was sit down beside the maid and put her head between her knees, but she knew from unhappy experience that action was the best antidote. She took the key from the inside of the door, closed the door again, and locked it. 'I'll ring the police. Absolutely no one must go in there till they come.'

She was not prepared to trust the stricken Montagu with the key, but several more people had arrived by now. Among them she saw Nancy's husband, the Reverend Timothy Fotheringay, in a brown flannel dressing-gown over blue-and-white pyjamas. His arm around his wife's shoulders, he was listening gravely to her quiet explanation. Daisy had always thought of him as stodgy; surely he would be reliable.

'Tim!' Her voice cut through the growing clamour of questions. 'Timothy, will you look after the key?'

'I think you should keep it, Daisy.'

'Oh no! People will say I'm taking altogether too much upon myself, and rightly so. I'm not family, after all.'

'Precisely.'

'No!' Did he not realize that his great-aunt's prying extended far beyond her family? As soon as the local police heard about Lady Eva's proclivity, Daisy was going to be as much a suspect as anyone else. 'Oh, here's Baines. I'll give the key to him.'

The butler surveyed the scene with unmistakable disapproval. He himself, not expecting to be on public display at this hour of the morning, was in his shirtsleeves and baize apron. The head housemaid was seated on the floor, surrounded by a gabbling crowd of ladies and gentlemen who ought to know better.

'The key, madam?' he enquired austerely.

'To Lady Eva's room.' Daisy handed it to him. 'Didn't the maid tell you?'

'I gathered through the girl's hysterics, madam, that something untoward had occurred. As you see, I came with all due haste.'

'Good for you. Lady Eva has been ... has met with an accident. I'm going to telephone the police but until they come the room must remain undisturbed.'

'The police, madam!' Baines was aghast.

'Yes, and I'd better ring up the local doctor, too, though I'm afraid it's too late for his help. What's his name?'

'Dr Arbuthnot, madam.'

'You understand that absolutely no one is to go in?'

'Indeed, madam.' The butler pocketed the key. 'I'll send a footman to stand at the door.'

'Good idea.' With one last glance around the assembled relatives, Daisy fled. Let the Reverend Timothy deal with them. Perhaps she ought to stay and watch the effect on them and on later arrivals on the scene, but the local police were unlikely to be interested in her impressions. How she wished Alec had come with her!

Not till she reached the bottom of the stairs and stepped onto the cold marble floor of the hall did she realize that she was still barefoot. She hesitated, then went on to the library, where she knew there was a telephone.

To her surprise, she found John Walsdorf there, already fully dressed at this early hour and busy at his desk at the far end of the long room. He stared at her in astonishment and dismay, not unnaturally, considering her half-clad, dishevelled state. Slipping the paper he had been writing on under the blotter, he rose courteously, and said, 'Good morning, Mrs Fletcher. You wish a novel to read? May I be of assistance?'

'No, thanks. Sorry to disturb you but something dreadful's happened and I have to ring the police.'

'The police! This is not for a lady to do.' As he spoke, Walsdorf moved a chair to the desk for her. 'Tell me what is to be reported and I will telephone.'

'Will you really?' Daisy dropped into the chair. 'I'd far rather not.'

'If there is urgency, I must warn you, the village is nearly two miles distant and Constable Fritch bicycles very slowly.'

'Then we had better get in touch with the Cambridgeshire

police directly.' What Daisy really wanted was a good excuse to phone Scotland Yard and talk to Alec. None came to mind. 'It's murder.'

'Murder!' Paling, Walsdorf hesitated as if afraid to ask. 'Who . . . ?'

'Lady Eva.'

A flicker of relief crossed his face. Daisy wondered whether he had something discreditable in his past – or present – that Lady Eva might have discovered.

'How?' He picked up the telephone.

'Strangulation.'

For a moment his command of English faltered. 'Please? Strangu . . . Ah, she was strangled?' Unhooking the receiver, he clicked the hook up and down to summon the operator. 'Put me through to the county police headquarters, miss. It is urgent.'

Daisy listened with one ear to Walsdorf's half of the ensuing conversation. She was trying to picture the group who had gathered in the hallway when the maid's screams shattered the morning peace. Montagu Fotheringay had been there of course, apparently stunned by his sister's death; Lucy's brother Tim and his level-headed wife, thank heavens; Lucy's parents? Just her father, Daisy thought.

The rest were a blur of four or five faces, but she was fairly certain the Haverhills had not turned up, nor Lord and Lady Fotheringay. Fortunately their rooms were in another wing of the house. Daisy didn't want to contemplate the effect of murder in the family on the aged earl and countess and their weak-hearted son, but at least it could be broken to them gently – by someone other than herself.

Other guests were sleeping in distant parts of the house, but one person who should have put in an appearance was missing:

Lucy. Her room was closer than Daisy's to Lady Eva's, so she must have heard the commotion. Why ... ?

'Mrs Fletcher, it is quite certainly murder I am reporting?'

She nodded. 'I saw her,' she said reluctantly.

One glance at Lady Eva's face would be enough to convince the most hardened sceptic. At least Daisy didn't have to waffle about unnatural death and try to persuade the police there had been foul play. *Of that there is no manner of doubt, No probable, possible shadow of doubt, No possible doubt whatever* – the tune from *The Gondoliers* ran through her head, almost obliterating the awful sight from her mind's eye.

'Mrs Fletcher.' Her name caught her attention. 'A guest of his lordship ... Yes, a most reliable witness, I am sure. I understand Mr Fletcher is a detective at New Scotland Yard.'

Daisy groaned. Her status as the wife of a Metropolitan Police detective would by no means dispose the Cambridge police to trust her as a reliable witness. More likely they would regard her with suspicion, afraid her presence would lead to the Yard interfering in their case. She should have refused to have anything to do with reporting to them, even through John Walsdorf.

'No, Mr Fletcher is not at Haverhill at present,' he was saying. 'I believe he is expected on Friday.'

With any luck at all, the local detectives would clear up the case before Alec arrived for the wedding.

'Oh gosh, the wedding!' Daisy exclaimed as Walsdorf rang off. 'It will have to be postponed, won't it? There will be a funeral instead. How ghastly! I must go and talk to Lucy. Mr Walsdorf, did the police say anything about sending for the local doctor?'

'No. Should I?'

Daisy hesitated in an agony of indecision. No more interference, said one part of her. The sooner a doctor saw the victim the better, argued another part. It might help establish the time of death, even the precise cause of death. The police surgeon might not arrive for ages. But would the local practitioner understand about not moving the body, not touching anything in the room?

Walsdorf was waiting for her instructions. Everyone seemed to think she should know what to do.

'Ring up Dr Arbuthnot. Explain what's happened and leave it to him to decide. No, on second thoughts, Lord Fotheringay may need him. I gather he has a weak heart, and the shock . . . You'd better ask the doctor to come. All right? I'm going to Lucy.'

Daisy scurried across the icy hall. The polished oak of the stairs was not much warmer to her feet, but she slowed down, trying to think how to break the news to Lucy.

Turning into the west wing, she was surprised to find it empty but for the footman Baines had posted at Lady Eva's door. She'd have expected people to stand about discussing the horror in their midst.

'Where is everyone?' she asked the footman.

'Gone to dress, ma'am.'

'Oh, of course.' Thoroughly chilled by now, Daisy was tempted to go and put on something warm. But, assuming no one had yet enlightened Lucy, she wanted to be the one to break the news.

She tapped on Lucy's door.

'Who is it?' Lucy sounded apprehensive.

'Just me, darling.' Daisy went in. Lucy was still in bed, her face naked and vulnerable without the light make-up she wore even in the country. 'Didn't you hear all that racket a bit ago?'

'Yes. I stuck my head under the pillow till it went away. You look frozen. Here, have my counterpane.'

Wrapping herself up, Daisy settled at the foot of the bed. 'Didn't you wonder what it was all about?'

'I assumed one of the maids had seen a spider, or something of the sort. I wasn't frightfully interested. But I expect you're going to tell me.' Both words and tone were flippant, but Daisy knew her friend very well and saw her brace herself for bad news.

'It's very bad.'

'Darling, I can tell that from your face. Spit it out.'

'It's your great-aunt.'

'Poor old Aunt Eva. She died in the night? What was it, heart attack?'

'It's worse than that, I'm afraid. Someone killed her.'

'Oh, Daisy, no!'

Daisy nodded. 'The police are on their way.'

'Alec's coming?' Lucy asked hopefully.

'No, the local chaps. Alec can't butt in without an invitation.'

'Then we'll just have to get him invited.' Lucy started to scramble out of bed. 'I'll talk to Grandfather.'

'Not so fast! For a start, as far as I know, no one has broken the news to Lord Haverhill yet. Do you want to be the one?'

'Gosh, no! I should think Timmy's the one for that, being the only clergyman in the family. Does he know?'

'Yes, both he and Nancy turned out. I think they're dressing. Your great-uncle was there too. He seemed pretty shaken.'

'He and Aunt Eva are . . . were thick as thieves. I can hardly believe she's gone, Daisy. She was years younger than Grandfather and always so full of pep. Uncle Montagu must be devastated.'

'He seemed pretty cut up.'

'Goodness knows how Uncle Aubrey will take it. The shock's bound to be bad for his heart, don't you think? Timmy will have to tell him, as well.'

'I wonder if I should go and suggest that he's the man for the job,' Daisy said reluctantly.

'I'd better. My brother – my family – and you're not dressed either. Wait here.'

Lucy slipped on a peacock silk kimono and her slippers and hurried out. She was much too matter-of-fact, Daisy thought, as if she hadn't really taken in the fact of murder. When it hit her, already ruffled as she was by the wedding preparations, it could be the last straw. Daisy had never seen Lucy distraught, and she didn't want to.

No more than a couple of minutes passed before Lucy returned. 'I hope you don't mind, darling, I rather implied you were falling apart and in need of my succour.'

'Rotter!'

'I'd never have got away, else. You know how Timmy bores on. But he's agreed to go and break it to Grandfather and Uncle Aubrey.'

'What about Sir James?'

'Heavens, I'd forgotten him! It's his mother who's been done in. Daisy, are you really quite certain she didn't just die naturally?'

That irreverent refrain from *The Gondoliers* passed unwanted through Daisy's mind: *No probable, possible shadow of doubt . . .* 'Quite certain,' she said. 'But even if it was natural, which it wasn't, the wedding would have to be postponed.'

Lucy stared at her blankly. 'I suppose so. Oh, Daisy, I simply can't go through all this again! All the fuss! I'm calling the whole thing off.'

'You mean you're not going to marry Binkie after all? Don't be ridiculous, darling, you can't just cast him off because getting married involves a lot of fuss.'

'No, I'm quite relieved, actually. I told you I wasn't certain ... It's not as if I'll be pinching pennies any longer. Aunt Eva told me she's leaving me four hundred a year.'

'Lady Eva's left you enough to live on? But Lucy, that gives you a motive for murdering her!'

'Darling, you don't think I'd ...'

'Don't be a blithering idiot, darling. But the police will.'

CHAPTER 4

The police had not yet arrived when Daisy went down to breakfast. She hadn't expected to be hungry but she was, after all, eating for two and the junior member of the pair had not lost his or her appetite.

She noticed that the others who preceded her or drifted in later did justice to the splendid array of dishes, hot and cold, on the buffet. Lord Haverhill's cook provided everything from kippers, kidneys and kedgeree to mushrooms, muffins and marmalade. One of his footmen, a bovine youth, was on duty to help serve and to pour and carry coffee or tea.

His lordship was not present to partake of his own largesse, though that was nothing out of the ordinary. Daisy remembered from past visits that he and Lord Fotheringay always breakfasted together in a small parlour in the family wing, while Lady Haverhill indulged in breakfast in bed. Lady Fotheringay usually joined their guests to play hostess, but this morning she was absent, presumably hovering over her husband.

Also missing were Montagu, Tim and Nancy, and Lucy. Daisy hoped Lucy wasn't busy trying to persuade her grandfather to send for Alec. Surely she had understood that any request for Scotland Yard's assistance had to come from the Chief Constable.

Sir James and Lady Devenish did not put in an appearance at the breakfast table. Someone must have told them the news of his mother's death. Daisy rather wished she'd been there to see their faces when they were informed. They surely had far greater expectations from Lady Eva's estate than Lucy and so must be considered suspects.

On the other hand, in the first place the Cambridgeshire police would not want to know her theories; in the second place, Lady Eva's penchant for collecting embarrassing facts enormously widened the field of suspects; and in the third place, Daisy didn't want to believe even a man dedicated to the slaughter of bird, beast and fish would contemplate strangling his mother. He might poison her, perhaps, or even shoot her, but not strangle her.

Those who did turn up for breakfast wore their drabbest clothes, in the case of the women mostly much too bright for mourning since they had, after all, been packed for a summer wedding.

When Daisy arrived, one of Lady Eva's grandchildren was already at the table. Daisy had been introduced to Veronica and her husband, Peter Bancroft, but didn't know them at all well. They sat together, appropriately long-faced, speaking to each other in low voices.

Not wanting to disturb them, Daisy took her egg and ham and toast to the far end of the table. As she sat down, Angela Devenish came in.

After helping herself at the buffet, Angela glanced at her sister and put the length of the room between them. 'Is anyone sitting here, Daisy?'

'No, do join me. I'm so sorry about your grandmother.'

'Isn't it frightful? She didn't approve of my work, you know, but she was jolly decent about it.'

'Mmm?' said Daisy encouragingly.

'She told Daddy and Mummy the world was changing and they couldn't stop me. And she promised to leave me enough in her will to buy a place where I can take in mistreated and abandoned dogs. That's what I really want to do. I've got my eye on a cottage in Yorkshire with a couple of acres that would be perfect.'

Angela went on to describe her plans in detail, so single-minded she seemed to have forgotten it was her grandmother's murder which would make it possible to carry them out. Daisy was prepared to accept this as evidence of innocent mono-mania, but the police might well take a different view. To them it would suggest either an overwhelming motive for murder or an attempt to mislead them by a show of unworldliness, depending on how tortuous their minds were.

Daisy was wondering whether to try to explain this to Angela when Lucy's parents joined them. Mrs Oliver Fotheringay was much more upset about the wedding postponement than anything else.

'It was terribly difficult to find a day to suit Lord Gerald's parents,' she lamented in her clear, carrying soprano, so like Lucy's. 'The Marquis is active in the government, you know, and Lady Tiverton is on countless committees. Now I shall have to start all over again.'

This was not the moment to mention that Lucy had decided not to marry Binkie after all, especially as she'd probably change her mind again. 'You have an awful lot of people to notify,' Daisy said. 'Is there anything I can do to help?'

'Thank you, dear, but Mr Walsdorf is taking care of everything of that sort, bless him.'

'Dashed foreigner,' muttered her husband. 'Wouldn't sur-prise me if he had a hand in this nasty business.'

'Why on earth should he?' Daisy asked.

'The man's as near a German as makes no odds. You must know what Aunt Eva was like, poking her nose in everywhere. Suppose she discovered he was a spy, during the war?'

'Then surely she would have gone to the authorities. It's not the sort of information anyone with a grain of patriotism would keep to herself. Anyway, it's six years since the Armistice. Mr Walsdorf would hardly wait till now to silence her if he thought her a threat.'

Mrs Oliver pursued her own thoughts. 'I don't know what the caterers will say when we cancel. And all the food ordered from Fortnum's! The dressmaker's coming for a final fitting this afternoon, and heavens, I've just remembered, Erica's getting married next month so her bridesmaid dress will go to waste. Though they'll have to postpone, too, come to think of it. I suppose we shall have to wait at least three months, Oliver, for decency's sake?'

'That's for Mother to decide,' Mr Fotheringay said irritably, dissecting his kipper with a jaundiced air. 'For pity's sake, leave me out of it, Vickie. I told you, I'll march Lucinda up the aisle. The rest is up to you.'

Meanwhile, Angela had been gobbling down her porridge and muffins. Now, pushing back her chair, she stood up. 'See you later, Daisy,' she said, and, with an abrupt nod to the Fotheringays, she departed.

'Such odd manners,' Mrs Fotheringay exclaimed as the footman removed Angela's dishes and reset the place, 'and my parlourmaid is better dressed! At least Lucinda is presentable. One isn't ashamed to be seen with her in public.'

'Has Lucy telephoned Binkie yet, Mrs Fotheringay?' Daisy asked. 'That's not something which can be left to Mr Walsdorf.'

'Goodness only knows. I've not seen hide nor hair of her this morning. She's been most uncooperative, Daisy. I wish you'd have a word with her. Oh, here's Sally, perhaps she knows. Sally, do you know where Lucinda has got to?'

'She was with her grandfather a few minutes ago, Aunt Victoria. I felt myself *de trop*, being a relative only by marriage.' Sally's face was pale and set. She might not feel much sorrow for the death of a relative by marriage whom she probably didn't know particularly well, but murder in the house was enough to upset anyone. 'Besides, as a soldier's wife, I must soldier on, and in the absence of those better qualified, I count myself temporarily your hostess. Excuse me a moment.'

She turned away and went to speak to the butler, who had popped in to check on his underling and the state of the buffet. Jennifer Walsdorf arrived just in time to beat her to it.

Daisy couldn't make out what was said, but she heard Sally's biting tone. Jennifer left. Sally exchanged a few words with Baines, helped herself to a single slice of toast, and returned to Daisy and the Oliver Fotheringays. A spot of angry colour burned in each cheek.

'That woman takes too much upon herself!' she snapped.

'She's just trying to help,' Daisy protested. 'Baines may be carrying on in true butlerian fashion but I'd be surprised if most of the servants aren't at sixes and sevens.'

Visibly simmering down, Sally forced a smile, and said, 'Yes, one ought to look on Mrs Walsdorf as simply a glorified housekeeper doing her job. I shouldn't have bitten her head off, but to tell the truth I'm feeling quite ill. It's too horrible to think of her ... of Lady Eva like that. I can't get the picture out of my head.'

'Nancy described what she saw?' Daisy was surprised. She herself had been doing her best to forget, and she would have expected Nancy to suppress the sickening details.

'I'm just being oversensitive, what Rupert would describe as "weak and womanish". I wish he were here. How one relies on a strong husband at a time like this!'

Much as she wished for the comfort of Alec's presence, Daisy would have kicked him if he'd called her 'weak and womanish'.

'You'd better go and lie down, Sally,' said a malicious voice. Lady Ione had sat down nearby, disregarded as always. 'I'm sure Jennifer Walsdorf is quite capable of managing without you.'

Her brother Oliver looked as astonished as Daisy felt. Not that she could claim to know Lady Ione as well as Oliver Fotheringay must, but it was like seeing a lapdog turn into a lion cub. Mrs Oliver seemed stunned as well.

Lady Ione's sallow cheeks coloured slightly. 'You look like a stuffed fish, Oliver. I have often thought so. Don't gape. Aunt Eva is dead,' she went on in a hard, tight voice, 'so I don't have to pretend any longer.' She turned her attention back to her kidneys wrapped in bacon.

'I think I shall go and lie down,' Sally said faintly, standing up, 'as Aunt Ione suggests.'

'What do you mean, Ione?' asked Mrs Oliver.

To Daisy's disappointment, Lady Ione showed no sign of having heard, let alone responding to her sister-in-law. Daisy was left wondering whether here lurked yet another motive for getting rid of Lady Eva.

Daisy had finished her breakfast. Another cup of coffee would give her an excuse to linger in the hope of further interesting revelations. The footman had come over to remove

Sally's plate and Daisy was about to ask him to refill her cup when Baines reappeared and came up behind her.

'Mrs Fletcher, his lordship asks if you will be so kind as to step upstairs for a word with him.'

'Of course.' Daisy was sure Lucy must have persuaded Lord Haverhill to send for Alec. She hoped she could persuade him that not even an earl could ring up Scotland Yard and order a Detective Chief Inspector as one rings the butcher to order a saddle of lamb.

She and the butler had nearly reached the door when the way was blocked by a stream of people entering. First came a couple Daisy recalled as Mr and Mrs Henry Fotheringay. They were the parents of two of the bridesmaids, she rather thought. The next couple were Lord and Lady Carleton, parents of a third bridesmaid.

Then came Miss Flora Fotheringay, Lord and Lady Fotheringay's eldest daughter, who owned and managed a successful interior decorating business. A positive model for Lucy, and perhaps for Angela, Flora was also a possible article subject for Daisy. She made a mental note to find time somehow to talk to her when the first furore over the murder had died down.

After these five flocked the five indistinguishable brides-maids, no longer giggling. Two looked frightened, two merely subdued. The fifth wore an aggrieved expression and an engagement ring, so she was Erica whose wedding, like Lucy's, must be postponed.

Or, in Lucy's case, cancelled. Poor Binkie!

Lucy was usually so decisive, Daisy thought, following the butler's dignified tread up the stairs. Why couldn't she make up her mind whether she wanted to marry Binkie? The reticent, unassuming Lord Gerald Bincombe had been her constant and obviously devoted escort for two or three years. A large, calm ex-rugger Blue, his taciturn disposition led some people to think him slow-witted. His success in the City, doing something with stocks and shares that neither Daisy nor Lucy understood, argued the contrary.

Admittedly, since the war eligible young men did not grow on trees, but Lucy had not lacked for other opportunities. In fact, she hinted that she had proposed to Binkie when that diffident young man muffed it for the third time. Why the change of heart?

'Here we are, madam.' Baines knocked on a door and opened it. 'Mrs Fletcher, my lord.'

The family sitting room Daisy entered was a complete contrast to the public rooms below. Instead of heavy Victorian stateliness, it was all cool green and silver accented with daffodil yellow, light and airy, modern without being faddish. Charmed, Daisy wondered whether Flora had designed it, but she had no time to study her surroundings.

'Daisy, darling!' Lucy came to meet her. 'Come and tell Grandfather how to set about getting Alec here. I told him he mustn't telephone the Home Secretary and requisition him.'

Lord Haverhill stood on the hearth with his back to a lively fire. His face was grave, but he didn't seem unduly disturbed by his sister's beastly death. Of all the people Daisy had seen this morning, only Montagu was really upset. Had no one else been truly fond of Lady Eva?

'My dear Mrs Fletcher, I shall welcome your advice,' said the Earl. 'I confess I do not care for the idea of our local force infesting the house and pestering the family. Lucy assures me I shall prefer to be interrogated by your husband.'

'It's up to the Chief Constable to call in Scotland Yard, Lord Haverhill. He won't want to do it unless his own men feel they can't cope with the case and ask for help. Alec says they're reluctant to go over the heads of their people. It makes for disgruntlement, as you can imagine.'

'I see.'

'The other possibility is when a case involves more than one police jurisdiction. But you're right in the middle of Cambridgeshire here so that won't work.'

'Aunt Eva lived in London, though,' Lucy pointed out. 'All her notes—'

'Lucy!' Age had robbed the Earl's tone of none of its authority.

So Lady Eva had not relied on her memory, Daisy thought. Whatever Lord Haverhill hoped for in the way of concealment, the police would find her memoranda sooner or later.

'Thank you, Mrs Fletcher, for your advice,' he went on. 'I feel certain your husband is the man for the job. I'm acquainted with our Chief Constable. I'll have a word with him on the telephone and see what can be arranged.'

He moved stiffly, even a little unsteadily, holding his faltering body together with an effort of his still strong will, towards an open connecting door. In the next room, Daisy could see a big rosewood desk with a reading lamp, inkstand and telephone. Beyond this a leather easy chair was visible, and part of a marble mantelpiece.

'Oh blast!' she said to Lucy in an undertone. 'I wish you hadn't talked him into this. Alec will kill me.'

'Not literally, I hope, darling. Yes, Baines?'

The butler had reappeared, the imperturbability unshaken by mere murder now visibly shaken. 'The police, miss. My lord,' he raised his voice.

Lord Haverhill turned back, frowning, steadying himself with a hand on the back of a chair.

Baines continued, 'I regret that one of the footmen was so ill-advised as to direct this person to find your lordship here. Meeting him upon the stair, I instructed him to return below to await your lordship's pleasure in the library, but I fear he persisted in following me. Inspector Crumble, my lord.'

'Crummle, that's Detective Inspector Crummle,' said the policeman irritably. He was a plump man with a pale, doughy face from which incongruously large, wintry blue eyes regarded the world with suspicion. They should have been small and black like currants in a suet pudding, Daisy felt. 'Pursuant to a report of murder, my lord, I proceeded here with my men, who are waiting below.' He spared a glare for Baines. 'Before instructing them to proceed with their duties, I wished to inform your lordship of my arrival and to ask whether you have any information which may enable me to bring this investigation to a rapid conclusion.'

'No.' Lord Haverhill's curt monosyllable cleft the tide of the policeman's verbosity.

'Then I shall proceed about my duty. I shall need a room in which to conduct my enquiries, preferably with a telephone.'

'You may use the library, Inspector.'

'Thank you, my lord.' Crummle bowed, subjected Daisy and Lucy to a rapid inspection, and departed.

'I am going to telephone the Chief Constable,' Lord Haverhill said grimly. He went through to his study.

'Not a good start,' said Daisy. 'How is your grandmother taking it, Lucy? And your Uncle Aubrey and Aunt Maud?'

'Grandmama and Aunt Maud are too busy fussing over Uncle Aubrey to get the wind up. You'd think they'd be really rattled with murder in the family. I suppose it must have been one of the family who did her in?'

'Well, it wasn't me. One of the servants, perhaps?'

'I shouldn't think so. As I told you, she wasn't interested in the peccadilloes of the lower classes. Besides, the doors between the servants' wing and the rest of the house are locked at night – a frightfully Victorian precaution against the sons of the house philandering with housemaids.'

'How on earth do you know that?'

'I heard Rupert sniggering about it once, years ago, not that I understood then what he was talking about. He said it was directed against Uncle Montie but now it was dashed inconvenient for him – for Rupert himself.'

'Oh, was he in that line?'

'Just big talk, I suspect. As far as I remember, he was only about fifteen.'

'All the same, I wonder whether Lady Eva had him written down as a womanizer.'

'He's not much use as a suspect, darling. He wasn't here last night. Manoeuvres on Salisbury Plain, perfectly grim! He won't be here till tomorrow. But with the servants out of things, no doubt the rest of us are for it.'

'Yes, sir, a request from the Chief Constable of Cambridgeshire, chap I've worked with in the past, Sir Leonard Crowe.'

'A request specifically for Fletcher?' growled the Assistant Commissioner (Crime).

'I'm afraid so,' apologized Superintendent Crane.

'You don't need to tell me, that woman is at it again!'

'Not exactly,' said Crane cautiously. 'The sister of the Earl of Haverhill, Lady Eva Devenish, was murdered last night at his lordship's home, also known as Haverhill. My information is that his lordship's granddaughter, a Miss Lucy Fotheringay, advised him to send for Fletcher. Now it happens that I remember Miss Fotheringay from Fletcher's wedding reception . . .'

'There, I knew it! If she's not an intimate friend of the former Honourable Daisy Dalrymple, I'll eat my hat. What's more, I'll bet you a fiver, Superintendent, that Mrs Fletcher is on the spot.'

'No takers, sir.'

'What the devil made me suppose that marrying her would allow Fletcher to keep her out of mischief?'

'He would if he could, sir,' said Crane, 'but he can't.'

CHAPTER 5

Daisy and Lucy were alone in the dining room when the summons came. Lucy had suddenly realized she was ravenous and, most unlike her usual abstemious self, had taken two sausages to go with her toast and coffee. Just to keep her company, Daisy had another cup of coffee and a piece of marmaladed toast. After all, she was eating for two.

An elderly uniformed constable with squeaky boots came in. 'Mrs Fletcher? Inspector Crummle wants to see you first, ma'am, in the liberry.'

'Me?' Maybe the unpromising Crumble had some sense after all and would listen to her suggestions.

'Well, ma'am, not strictly first, seeing he's talked to Mr Walsdorf as phoned up the station. But Mr Walsdorf says it was you as told him to ring up us instead of the local chap, and the Inspector says all right then he'll see you first.'

'Right-oh,' said Daisy, swallowing a last bite of toast.

'Darling, do you want me to come and hold your hand?' Lucy asked anxiously.

In front of the constable, Daisy didn't care to point out that she was quite used to being questioned by detectives. She had never actually confessed to Lucy just how often she inadvertently stumbled into police cases. If Lucy were present, she wouldn't be able to speak freely about the family, so she said, 'Thanks, darling, but they're not allowed to use the "third degree" *à l'américaine.* I'll be all right. Why don't you ring Binkie? You really mustn't put it off any longer.'

Lucy pulled a face. 'Yes, I'd better, though he'll be at the office so I shan't be able to talk to him properly. Right-oh. Good luck, Daisy.'

Accompanying her, the constable walked as if his feet hurt him.

'New boots?' Daisy asked sympathetically.

'Bought 'em last week. They pinch something chronic. I were just getting the old pair wore in nicely when the Inspector up and said they're a disgrace to the Force. And me retiring in a year and a half!' The constable was indignant. 'Won't hardly have time to wear 'em in.'

'Maybe you'll be able to use them for gardening.'

'Now there's a thought! The missus has been on about getting an allotment when I retire. The price of cabbages and taters has gone up something shocking since the war. Here we are, madam.' He opened the library door and ushered her in. 'Mrs Fletcher, sir.'

Detective Inspector Crummle did not so much as glance up from the papers he had scattered across Walsdorf's usually neat desk. Daisy decided she was being put in her place.

She wondered whether Lord Haverhill had persuaded the Chief Constable to get in touch with Scotland Yard. Lucy was right: Alec would be more acceptable to her family. What she probably had not considered was that he would also be better able to cope with them. They might intimidate Inspector Crummle, but not Chief Inspector Fletcher.

Daisy went over to the desk, sat down on the chair Walsdorf

had placed for her earlier, and waited. This did not bode well for her intention of helping Crummle. She realized the poor man was bound to feel rather out of his depth among lords and ladies, but being discourteous wasn't going to help him.

At last he looked up from his notebook.

Before he could speak, she asked kindly, 'What can I do for you, Inspector?'

Disconcerted, then affronted, he snapped, 'I'll ask the questions, madam. I understand you discovered the deceased?'

'Gosh, no! One of the maids was taking round morning tea. She started screaming murder and most of the people in the bedrooms on that passage came out to see what was up. Another maid looked in and said Lady Eva was dead. Mr Montagu Fotheringay, Lady Eva's brother, wanted to go in but I stopped him. I asked Nancy – Mrs Timothy Fotheringay – to go in and check, because she was a nurse during the war. She confirmed that Lady Eva had been murdered.'

'So you didn't even seen the cor— the deceased?'

'I did take a quick look before I went to telephone. I didn't want to be responsible for a false alarm. When I saw – well, I imagine you've seen for yourself. There's not really any question as to whether she was murdered, is there? – I locked the door and gave the key to the butler, Baines. Then I came down here to telephone.'

'You seem to have taken a great deal upon yourself, Mrs Fletcher.' The inspector scowled at her. 'I understood from Mr Walsdorf that you're a guest at Haverhill, not a member of the family. Yet you took charge and everyone followed your instructions?'

'Not exactly.' Daisy hesitated, extremely reluctant to explain her unorthodox credentials to the touchy detective.

Apparently the desk officer who took John Walsdorf's call hadn't told Crummle about Alec. With luck – lots of luck – he'd never have to find out. 'I suppose they turned to me because I'm not one of the family, so I'm able to view the tragedy with a clearer head.'

'Hmph.' His pale blue eyes held nothing but scepticism.

More to stop him pursuing that line of thought than for any other reason, Daisy said, 'There's one more thing I ought to tell you. Lady Eva was an inveterate collector of gossip and scandal. I believe she kept records at her place in London of all the information she gathered.'

'London!'

'Have to ask the Yard for help, sir,' observed the constable with malicious satisfaction.

Crummle looked as if he'd rather die the death of a thousand cuts. Daisy awaited his response with interest and a certain trepidation, but it never came. The door opened, a breezy voice said 'No need to announce me,' and a short, thin man limped in.

The inspector jumped to his feet. 'Sir!'

'Sit down, my dear chap, sit down. I see you're hard at work already?' He looked at Daisy.

'This is Mrs Fletcher, sir. She's helping me with my enquiries.'

'How do you do, Mrs Fletcher. Fletcher? Aha! Crowe's the name, Sir Leonard Crowe. I'm the Chief Constable of this county. You won't mind if I just interrupt for long enough to give the good inspector a bit of news?'

'Not at all, Sir Leonard.'

'Excellent!'

Daisy read complicity in his regard and knew what was coming. 'Perhaps I should leave?' she said hopefully.

'Oh, no, no, no, dear lady. Quite unnecessary.' Turning back to Crummle with a guilty air, Sir Leonard hesitated.

The inspector beat him to it. 'It is my duty to inform you, sir, that Mrs Fletcher here claims the deceased was a blackmailer.'

'I never said anything of the sort!'

'Pardon me, madam, but I have it down here in black and white.' He studied his notebook. 'Here: "veteran collector of scandal. Kept records."'

'Yes, but I'm sure she never used them to extort money. I can't think of anything less likely.'

'Good gracious, no!' The Chief Constable was horrified. 'My dear Inspector, a lady of the unhappy victim's social standing simply doesn't stoop to extortion.'

'There's other kinds of blackmail,' Crummle said obstinately, 'like making people do what you want. And there's just plain mischief-making, like telling a wife her husband's been seen in Brighton with a chorus girl. And I've known them that'll tell a person they know something just to enjoy watching them squirm.'

In spite of his curious syntax, the Inspector was making sense. 'But I don't think it was any of those,' Daisy said. 'I think she just enjoyed knowing. It gave her a feeling of power, though she would never use the knowledge.'

'Ah, you can say Lady Eva wouldn't stoop to it, madam, but you can't be sure. And no more could the people she found out about be sure she wouldn't tell. And to my mind, that's motive enough for murder, sir.'

Sir Leonard sighed. 'You may be right.'

'Mrs Fletcher here says the deceased kept her records at her house in London, sir. I'll have to send a man up to take a look.'

'Can't spare anyone,' Sir Leonard said with suspicious promptitude. 'Look here, my dear chap, we'd have to notify the Metropolitan Police before intruding upon their bailiwick. Why not just ask them to see what they can find at Lady Eva's? And once they're involved, why not ask 'em to give you a hand down here?'

'I've got everything well in hand,' Crummle protested, with no great conviction.

'What you've got is a whacking great house full of important people any number of whom may turn out to be suspects. They're not going to take kindly to being questioned. Now wouldn't you rather they vented their spleen at some London chappie, not at you?'

'You can be sure I'll do my duty, sir, without fear nor favour.'

'Naturally, naturally. I don't mean to suggest otherwise.' A note of desperation entered Sir Leonard's voice. 'The fact is, my dear fellow, I'm bound to take Lord Haverhill's wishes into account. As long as they don't run counter to my duty, of course! I hardly think a request for a detective from Scotland Yard can be regarded as beyond the pale.'

'His lordship wants a Yard man on the case?' Crummle demanded angrily.

''Fraid so. No reflection on your competence, Inspector, no reflection at all. But as a matter of fact, I've already been on to a chap I know, Superintendent Crane, and he's sending us one of his best men, a chief inspector.'

Sir Leonard had funked mentioning the chief inspector's name, Daisy noted. Or perhaps he was being tactful not mentioning it in her presence. With luck, Crummle would finish with her before he found out her husband was to take over his case.

Sir Leonard was making soothing noises about how much the London DCI would appreciate Crummle's groundwork as a strong basis for the investigation. 'Fingerprints, I suppose, and photographs and all that. Dr What's-his-name, the police surgeon, never can remember his name, he's been already, eh?'

'Yes, sir,' grunted Crummle, unsoothed. 'Dr Philpotts.'

'Good, good. Right you are. Now, who's going to telephone London and tell them about these mysterious records of Lady Eva's? Like me to do it, would you, my dear chap?'

'You'd better, sir, seeing I don't have your connections at the Yard. You'll be wanting me to assist this DCI, will you, then?'

'Yes indeed. He may bring down a sergeant, but they're bound to need your help.' Sir Leonard waved his hands at the spread of papers on the desk. 'All the information at your fingertips, eh? That's the stuff. I expect you have a list of everyone in the house?'

'Not yet,' Crurnmle admitted grudgingly.

'I expect Mrs Walsdorf can tell you, Sir Leonard,' Daisy suggested. 'She's Lady Fotheringay's niece but most of the business of running the household seems to land on her shoulders.'

'Sounds like a German name. Married a Jerry, eh?'

'No, he's from Luxemburg. He's Lord Haverhill's secretary.'

'Ah. Righty-ho, then, Mrs Walsdorf it shall be. I'll hand the list on to you, Inspector, when I'm done with it. Now I'm going to go and find a telephone elsewhere and leave you to finish your little chat with Mrs Fletcher.'

Turning, he bowed to Daisy with a wink which confirmed to her that his 'London DCI' was indeed Alec. As he limped out, she wondered how Alec felt about his summons to

Haverhill for a murder three days before he had been due to arrive for a wedding.

Alec stood in the doorway of Lady Eva's private sitting room in her house in Belgravia. His immediate impression was of luxury: brocades and velvets in rich colours, gleaming wood, thick-pile carpet, and everywhere photographs in silver frames.

Beside him, Lady Eva's housekeeper twittered on. 'Yes, the house belongs to the Devenish family, but her ladyship lives here alone – lived, I should say. I can't take it in she's gone, and that's a fact. Full of life, she was when last I saw her, looking forward to seeing Miss Lucy wed, that she's so fond of. What a nasty business! I don't know what the world's coming to, really I don't.'

'The Devenishes visited often, I suppose?'

'Well, not to say often. Sir James, that's her ladyship's son, he's a countryman through and through, if you know what I mean. Mr Edward, the young master, has his own flat in town he shares with friends, doesn't care to live with his gran, well that's natural, isn't it? He came to tea now and then, not as often as she'd've liked, I dare say. Lady Devenish comes up for shopping, and of course the young ladies had their presentations – before the war that was – and all married well enough, saving Miss Angela.'

'Miss Angela's not married?'

'Nor like to be. That's why my lady left most of her own money to her, and some to Miss Lucy. She liked an independent spirit in a young lady, she'd tell me, long as everything was quite proper.'

Dismayed to hear Lucy had a motive for doing in her

great-aunt, Alec glanced back to see if Ernie Piper was taking notes. The young detective constable's pencil was busy.

'Much money, is there?'

'No lack,' said the housekeeper complacently. 'No fussing about the price of coal in this house, I'm glad to say. Besides the income the late Sir Granville left her ladyship, she has her own fortune from an aunt that married well and had no children. There's a nice bit going to Miss Angela and Miss Lucy, and what's left over to the young master. Of course the house belongs to the master, Sir James. Part of the estate it is.'

'Lady Eva seems to have confided in you a good deal.'

'Bless you, sir, I've been with her ladyship thirty years. You can't live with someone that long without you learn something of their affairs, whether you will or no. A word or two here and a word or two there, if you know what I mean. And no fussing about the price of coal, like I said. Lordy, Lordy, I can hardly believe she's gone. There'll be changes around here, for sure. I only hope Sir James won't go and sell the house out from under me.'

'Is that likely?'

'He hasn't got any use for it himself, and it'd bring a pretty penny, I don't doubt.'

'No doubt.' Alec gestured towards a large kneehole desk on the other side of the room. 'Is that where Lady Eva kept her private papers?'

'That's right. Account book and receipts and chequebook top left, letters top right, everything in its place, she always says ... said. The middle drawer's just stationery and stamps and what-not. Second down, invitations on the right, and likely you'll find a copy of her will on the left. The bottom drawers are locked. She keeps . . . kept her big notebooks there, that she was always scribbling in.'

'Do you have a key, or know where she kept it?'

'Not me, and no more does Miss Parsons that's her maid,' the housekeeper said warily. '"It's Pandora's box," her lady-ship said once to Miss Parsons, "or rather, two Pandora's boxes. If anyone but me opens them, there's nothing but Trouble going to fly out, like in the old story. The key's in a safe place and nobody's going to find it."'

'Thank you, madam. You've been very helpful. Perhaps you wouldn't mind going downstairs now with Sergeant Tring and answering a few more questions, names and addresses, that sort of thing, just for the record?'

'I'll bet you've got a good memory,' Tom Tring said jovially. 'I've never known a housekeeper that didn't.'

She went off with him quite willingly. On hearing that they were heading for the abode of an earl, Tom had changed out of his robin's-egg blue-and-white check summer suit. In the dark suit he kept at the Yard for dealing with 'the nobs', he was the essence of respectability, as well as looking several sizes smaller. He'd have the housekeeper eating out of his hand in no time, in a way Alec couldn't hope to match.

Ernie Piper joined Alec at the desk. While Alec leafed through the contents of the second drawer on the left, Piper pulled the centre drawer all the way out and set it on the blotter on the desk-top. A twist and a click and he had in his hand a small brass key.

'Too easy,' he said, disappointed, returning the wide, shallow drawer to its place. He went down on one knee to unlock and open the bottom drawer on the right.

Alec peered into a large manilla envelope. 'Here's her will. What have you got there?'

'Several loose-leaf ledgers. Arranged by alphabet and date, looks like.' Piper took out the first ledger, balanced it on his knee, flipped it open and started to read. 'Whew! Looks like Mrs Fletcher's given us the goods again, Chief.'

'The Met was brought into the case at Lord Haverhill's request, nothing to do with Daisy,' Alec said firmly but without much belief in his own veracity. 'She just happens to be at his house. I was going down on Friday anyway, so I'm the obvious person to send. Checking Lady Eva's papers was the Chief Constable's suggestion.'

'I bet Mrs Fletcher put him up to it.' Piper's faith in Daisy was boundless. 'How would he know what her ladyship was up to? Listen to this! "Teddy escorted Genevieve Rendell to a house-party at the Varleys', not a month after her husband divorced her." Then there's brackets with "see 1924 R". Must be another book.'

'Who's Teddy?'

'No surname. Prob'ly one of the family. This book's A to D, and Lady Eva's a Devenish. Teddy'd be Edward, wouldn't he? There wasn't an Edward Devenish on the list the CC read to me over the phone.'

Alec didn't ask if he was sure. That was the sort of detail at which Ernie Piper excelled, and his fast, accurate shorthand was the reason he'd been put on the phone to take down the names of those staying at Haverhill.

He looked at his watch. 'Right-oh, there's just time for Tom and me to catch the next train if we hurry, so we'll leave you to it. You know what we want.'

'Anything recent on anyone on the list . . .'

'Six months, say.'

'That looks like they might kill to keep it quiet.'

'Yes, not the births, marriages and deaths, obviously.'

'Shouldn't be too hard if her system's as simple as it looks.'

'Good. Do a quick check around the house for anything else of interest, then come and join us. I gathered from the CC that the local inspector isn't too happy about our being called in. If he won't cooperate, we'll have our work cut out for us.'

On his way down to find Tom and the housekeeper, Alec contemplated with foreboding the investigation before him. An uncooperative local man would be merely an extra fly in the ointment. The aristocracy were always awkward to deal with, regarding the most innocuous questions as impertinence and expecting deference even as one delved into their sordid secrets. This time there was the added complication that in another few days he would have been the earl's guest. He wondered whether Lord Haverhill had asked for him, rather than for any DCI the Met chose to send, because he expected special treatment.

And then there was Daisy.

Reaching the kitchen, where he found Tom Tring enjoying a cup of tea and a piece of pie, Alec gladly postponed consideration of Daisy's place in the scheme of things.

CHAPTER 6

When Daisy emerged from the library, a dozen people were lurking in the hall. They converged on her, all talking at once. Everyone knew that Alec was coming and everyone knew that Daisy had talked to the local police and everyone wanted to talk to her.

Lord and Lady Carleton reached her first. Daisy had been introduced to them but she had never exchanged more than a few words with them and she had no idea where they came on the family tree.

Lady Carleton clasped Daisy's hand as if she were a long-lost friend. 'Mrs Fletcher, tell me they don't really believe Aunt Eva's death was murder! Some sort of horrible accident, I'm sure.'

'I'm afraid not. There seems to be no question of anything but murder.' Even as she spoke, Daisy regretted it. She should have denied any inside knowledge and referred them to Inspector Crummle. Now all those crowding around would expect her to answer their questions.

'They won't make us stay, will they?' Lady Carleton asked anxiously. 'Denzil says we won't be let go till they've arrested someone.'

'It must be one of us, must it not, Mrs Fletcher?' That was

Henry Fotheringay. The effect of his words was to make people glance around and move slightly apart from each other.

'That's for the police to decide.'

'But those of us who obviously didn't do it,' Lady Carleton persisted, 'they'll let us leave, won't they? Ursula is terribly sensitive, just a child still. I've sent her to the nursery but it's not at all good for her to stay in a house with such an unpleasant atmosphere.'

'Poor little Ursula,' Erica said sarcastically. 'I can't imagine why Lucy invited such a child to be a bridesmaid.'

'I can't think why she asked you, Erica,' said another bridesmaid.

'You're only a second cousin,' her sister seconded her, 'and you're getting married next month yourself.'

'That's enough, Alice, Mary!' snapped Mrs Henry. 'This is not the time or place for childish squabbles. You're not too old to be sent to the nursery yourselves.'

'I *was* getting married next month. My wedding's going to have to be postponed too,' Erica pointed out. 'Too tedious! Mrs Fletcher, I really need to go home right away and start notifying people.'

'I have to leave today.' That was Flora, Lord Fotheringay's unmarried daughter. She was dressed for the city, in a tailored black costume and white silk blouse. 'I only came down yesterday to advise Aunt Vickie on decorating the chapel. I have a meeting with an important client in town this afternoon. They won't stop me going, will they? They've no reason to suspect me.'

'It's not for me to say,' Daisy insisted. 'But I wouldn't advise anyone to leave without permission. It'd look very fishy.'

'Very fishy indeed.' Mr Henry agreed with apparent relish.

'We'll just have to wait for Mr Fletcher to arrive to separate the sheep from the goats, if you'll pardon the mixed metaphors.'

'How can you all be so petty, with poor Grandmama lying murdered upstairs?' Veronica Bancroft sniffed and dabbed at her eyes. 'Wanting to rush off as if she was a stranger who had inconvenienced you!'

'Hush, my dear.' Peter Bancroft put his arm around his wife's shoulders. 'You can't expect everyone to feel the horror as deeply as you do, close to your grandmother as you were.'

In fact, Daisy thought, no one she'd spoken to appeared heartbroken by Lady Eva's demise. Her brother Montagu seemed the most affected. Even Veronica Bancroft's eyes, though slightly reddened, were quite dry, for all her dabbing at them.

Her reproach was reasonable, however. Most of the others had beaten a retreat as she spoke. Only Oliver Fotheringay and Jennifer Walsdorf lingered, at a little distance.

'It's true, is it, Mrs Fletcher,' said Peter Bancroft, 'that your husband is going to be in charge of the case?'

'I believe so.'

'He'll soon find out we had nothing to gain. Lady Eva was aware that I am perfectly able to provide for Veronica and the children. She left practically everything to Angela, you know.'

'For her stupid dogs. Angela cares more for dogs than people. She'd do anything for her abandoned dogs, absolutely anything.'

'It's good to know someone's willing to help the poor things, isn't it?' said Daisy, wondering what could have caused such spite – worse than spite, if it was a deliberate attempt to suggest that Angela was capable of killing her grandmother for the sake of her dogs.

At least Daisy's response got rid of the Bancrofts. As they went off, Oliver Fotheringay came closer. He looked worried. 'Daisy – Mrs Fletcher, I should say—'

'Please go on calling me Daisy.'

He smiled. 'Then you'd better call me Oliver, without the "Uncle", since you're now a married lady. Daisy, Vickie is desperately concerned about Lucinda. She's saying now that she's not sure she's going to marry Bincombe after all, that perhaps it was all a mistake.'

Was Lucy wavering again, or just leading up gently to revealing her decision? 'To tell the truth,' Daisy said with caution, 'I think she just has cold feet, as well as being thoroughly fed up with all the pomp and circumstance.'

'Vickie's been trying so hard to give her a dream wedding.'

'Lucy's dream? Or her mother's?'

'In that case, why didn't Lucinda say long ago that she wanted something different?'

'Partly she didn't know exactly what she wanted, and partly she didn't want to disappoint her mother. That's my guess, anyway.'

'She's always had different ideas from the rest of us. We've never known just how to deal with her.' Oliver sighed. 'We'll try to understand. At least, I'll try to explain to Vickie. Perhaps it's just as well the whole thing must be postponed – not that I'd wish for poor Aunt Eva's death to be the cause! But I wouldn't want Lucinda to marry Bincombe if she's not sure.'

'Has Lucy telephoned him?'

'I don't know. She won't talk about it,' said Lucy's harassed father. 'Perhaps she'll tell you.'

'I expect so,' said Daisy. 'I'll go and look for her in a minute.' She looked enquiringly at Jennifer, still waiting in the background.

Becoming aware that someone else wanted to speak to Daisy, Oliver apologized for keeping her and excused himself.

'Daisy, you must be sick of people treating you as a surrogate for the police,' said Jennifer, 'but I'm not sure what I ought to do. Do you mind if I ask your advice?'

'Not if I can sit down while you ask! Marble is a very unfriendly surface to stand about on.'

'Come into the library.'

'Inspector Crummle . . .'

'He came out while you were talking to all those people.' Jennifer led the way. 'I think he went to interview the servants.'

Leaving the nobs for Alec to cope with, of course. 'A good move on his part.' Daisy sank into one of the comfortable leather chairs by the fireplace. 'He was frightfully annoyed by Sir Leonard's calling in Alec, but I'm quite sure he was feeling out of his depth, dealing with the aristocracy. Did Sir Leonard get a list of guests from you? Guests and residents?'

'Ye-es.'

'What's the trouble?'

'It's Aunt Ione. Baines told me she'd ordered a car to take her to the station. I went to look for her to tell her she'd better stick around just now, but she'd already gone. I don't know what's got into her. She never goes anywhere.'

'Oh dear!' Daisy had a sudden picture of the worm turning at breakfast this morning, of the meek, silent Lady Ione announcing that now Aunt Eva was dead she didn't have to pretend any longer. 'Did she take a suitcase?'

'Her maid says not. Daisy, ought I to tell the Inspector? Or Sir Leonard? Or wait till your husband arrives? Or hope she returns before anyone else finds out?'

'Do you know exactly when the car left? Assuming she was making for the station, would she have arrived by now? Could she have caught a train already?'

'Yes, if she's going to London. I suppose I'd better tell Inspector Crummle, but it would be too awful if he had her arrested when she gets to Liverpool Street!'

'Whatever I advise, Alec's liable to grind his teeth and accuse me of interfering. I'd say least said soonest mended, except that the servants will talk.'

'And the Inspector's with them now.'

'Oh yes, that's all right, then,' said Daisy, relieved. 'They'll tell him, and neither you nor I need have any hand in it.'

'Thank heaven! But I do wonder what on earth's come over her.'

'It's odd, if she usually doesn't go anywhere. But I doubt if she's done a bunk. She probably wouldn't know how. Where's John, by the way? I understood he was in charge of dealing with the wedding postponement, but Crummle's turned him out of the library.'

'Yes, he's taken all his stuff up to Lord Haverhill's study. He was too late to catch several people before they set out, so they'll be arriving sometime today.' Jennifer stood up. 'If they have any sense they'll turn right around and go home again, but I'd better make sure their rooms are ready.'

'And I'd better look for Lucy. Any idea where she's to be found?'

'Try the folly. I saw her heading for the park and it wouldn't surprise me if she's gone to earth there.'

'Good idea. I wouldn't mind a walk.' It would give her a chance to think about people and their attitudes towards Lady Eva.

Daisy followed Jennifer out to the hall. There she was pounced upon by Angela Devenish, the mongrel Tiddler at her heels as usual.

'Daisy, Mummy and Daddy want to see you. Would you mind awfully coming up to their room?'

The only possible reasons for the bereaved Sir James and Lady Devenish to ask for Daisy were to pick her brains about the police or to give her information to pass on to the police. Jennifer gave her a commiserating look and deserted her.

'I'll come,' said Daisy. 'Your father must be frightfully shocked by what's happened, Angela. Was your mother close to Lady Eva?'

'Not to say close. They rubbed along all right together. I say, Daisy, I've just remembered, Lucy said you're expecting a baby? I shouldn't rush you up the stairs like this.'

'I'm perfectly all right, honestly. I wish Lucy hadn't told everyone.'

'I expect she hoped they'd fuss over you instead of her,' said Angela with unexpected insight. 'Now poor Grandmother's murder has put everything else out of people's minds. Almost everything. Daddy wanted to go fishing, but Mummy won't let him, though he says he can mourn just as well with a rod in his hand. At least there's a few less fish suffering today. Daisy, do you think my grandmother suffered much?'

'No, I think it was very quick.' She did her best to suppress the memory of those desperate, bulging eyes, so horribly like a fish out of water gasping away its life. 'Lady Eva lived mostly in town, didn't she?'

'Yes. It wasn't because she'd quarrelled with Mummy or Daddy, or anything like that. She used to come down for weekends, but except for house-parties she found the country dull. Not enough gossip about the right sort of people. I expect you know about her collection?'

'It isn't exactly a secret.'

'No. She was quite open about her ferreting. Do you think someone killed her because of something she found out?'

'It's possible.' Daisy wondered whether Angela was trying to divert suspicion from herself She seemed the soul of candour, of an almost childlike frankness, but that would not sway Alec. He was bound to put her near the top of his list; just above Lucy, no doubt. 'It will be something Alec has to take into account.'

'I suppose he'll have to go through her memoranda, reading about people's beastly secrets. Almost as bad as seeing what they do to dumb, helpless creatures. Ugh! Here we are. Jennifer said we should use this room.'

The small sitting room set aside for the bereaved Devenishes was on the second floor at the front of the house. As Angela opened the door, Daisy heard Lady Devenish's discontented voice: 'I didn't bring a black dress, of course. Teddy, you must have brought a dark suit for church on Sunday.'

'I wasn't intending to stay on after the wedding on Saturday.'

The north-facing room was quite chilly, though a fire burned in the hearth. Lady Devenish was sitting in a chair by the fireplace, holding out her hands to the flames. Opposite her, a lissome young man lounged against the mantelpiece, his hands in his trouser pockets, looking both bored and sulky.

'Mummy, I've brought Daisy.'

Sir James, who appeared to have been pacing up and down the confined space, came eagerly to meet Daisy. 'Mrs Fletcher, can you tell us—'

Lady Devenish cut off her husband. 'So kind of you to come, Mrs Fletcher,' she said, her voice as chilly as the room.

'Please accept my condolences. It's a dreadful thing to happen.'

'Daisy, I don't think you know my brother, Teddy.'

'No, I don't believe we've met. How do you do, Mr Devenish.'

Edward Devenish was several years younger than his sisters Angela and Veronica, not much over twenty-one, Daisy guessed, and the spoilt baby of the family. Expensive, too: his sloppy posture did nothing to conceal the exquisite cut of his light grey tweeds. At least he had manners enough to straighten when he was introduced and take his hands out of his pockets.

'I hear you married a copper, Mrs Fletcher.'

His tone was so indifferent as to be almost offensive, but Daisy saw a spark of emotion in his eyes. Fear, perhaps; she couldn't be sure. He had not been at dinner last night, had not come into the drawing room before she went to bed. When did he arrive at Haverhill? Was he on the list Jennifer had given the Chief Constable?

'Won't you sit down, Mrs Fletcher?' Lady Devenish interrupted her thoughts. 'We wish to consult you. Angela informs us that Lord Haverhill has sent for your husband.' Her condescension was much more offensive than her son's ambiguous indifference.

The Dowager Vicountess Dalrymple, though in general she disapproved of her younger daughter, would have applauded the steel that entered Daisy's voice. 'I won't sit down, thank you. I can only spare you a few minutes. Uncle Oliver has asked me to . . . talk things over with Lucy.'

'Poor Lucy!' exclaimed Angela, much as if Lucy was an abandoned dog.

'What exactly is it you want to know, Sir James?'

He glanced at his wife. 'Josephine and I just wondered whether Mr Fletcher – Detective Inspector Fletcher—'

'Detective *Chief* Inspector, Daddy,' Angela corrected him.

This threw him off his stride, and his wife again took over. 'I suppose Mr Fletcher will want to ask a great many questions of everyone in the house?'

'Undoubtedly.'

'This places us in a thoroughly invidious position.'

'What the mater means,' said Teddy, 'is that being Grandmother's nearest and dearest, we are liable to be blamed for the whole show when people are asked questions they'd rather not answer. Worse, in newspaper reports and detective stories the immediate family are always the prime suspects, so everyone's going to avoid sitting next to us at lunch in case we put arsenic in the soup.'

His mother let him finish his rant before saying acidly, 'What I should like to know is how long we are to be subjected to such conditions. How long will it take the police to arrest the murderer?'

'That depends mostly on how much cooperation they get,' said Daisy, 'particularly from the immediate family. So when you're asked questions you'd rather not answer, I suggest you tell the truth, the whole truth, right away. And now, if you'll excuse me, Lucy needs me.'

As she turned to leave, Sir James hurried to open the door for her. 'Sorry,' he mumbled. 'Should be thinking of my poor mother, what?'

Daisy gave him a regal nod as she passed. Behind her she heard Lady Devenish again: 'I wonder if Maud has a black frock I could bear to wear.'

Angela followed her out. 'So put that in your pipe and smoke it!' she observed. 'Well said, Daisy. Of course what Mummy really wanted to ask, but didn't quite dare after you got on your high horse, is whether Mr Fletcher is going to think one of us did it.'

'You'll be on the list he starts with, at least. By the way, when did your brother arrive?'

'Last night, well after one. He motored over – he has a sporty little Lea Francis. He rang me up yesterday evening and asked me to go down and let him in at one, but I hung about on the terrace for ages, waiting for him. I didn't quite dare leave a door unlocked and go back to bed in case a burglar chose that moment to try all the handles.'

'You were wandering about the house in the middle of the night? Didn't you hear or see anything suspicious?'

'I went down the back stairs, nowhere near Grandmother's room. That's my room, there – Teddy spent the rest of the night with a couple of pillows and a bedspread on my floor – and that's the door to the stairs I used.' Angela pointed at a baize-padded swing door.

'All the way from the ground floor to the top?' Daisy asked.

'Yes, the Victorians liked their servants to be invisible. Hence all those ridiculous pillars in the entrance hall, for servants to hide behind with their mops and pails. Gosh, the murderer could have been right there when I crossed the hall. I don't know whether to be glad I didn't meet him creeping about or to wish I had. I might have been able to save Grandmother.'

'Or you might have been done in too,' said Daisy.

CHAPTER 7

'Would you mind awfully if Tiddler and I walked over to the folly with you?' Angela asked as she and Daisy reached the hall. She and her dog gazed at Daisy with their heads tilted to exactly the same angle and the same appeal in their eyes.

Daisy had intended to put her thoughts in order so that she would have a coherent tale to tell Alec when he arrived. She needed solitude to ponder which of Angela's relatives might have murdered Angela's grandmother, which wasn't the sort of thing one could decently say to Angela.

'I'm expecting to find Lucy in the folly and I rather wanted a private word with her.'

'Oh, that's all right. We'll sheer off when we get to the lake.'

'I wish I'd brought Nana. She'd love it here.'

Beneath a hazy blue sky, they walked down a gentle slope on a grassy track across parkland with scattered oaks and elms. Tiddler kept his nose to Angela's heels until a rabbit dashed across the path just in front of them. The little dog chased it for a few yards before returning to his usual post.

Angela was delighted. 'He's going to be all right. I was beginning to think he'd never recover his spirits.'

'But the rabbit had a terrible fright, even if the creature chasing it wasn't much bigger.'

'With different instincts. Predator and prey.'

'I was teasing.'

'One can't change the basic nature of animals,' Angela said seriously. 'Cats will always catch and torment mice and birds, and I expect people will always eat meat. But people can be taught not to inflict cruelty, deliberately or through negligence.'

Daisy encouraged her to talk about her job with the RSPCA. 'It would make an interesting article,' she decided. 'I'll make some notes on what you've told me and see if I can interest an editor. You wouldn't mind answering a lot of questions, maybe letting me trail around with you for a day?'

'Not at all. I'll do anything to further our work. Oh, but I may not keep the job much longer, if Grandmother's really left me enough money. I don't know how long it takes for probate and things like that.'

'Not long, I believe, if there are no challenges, or other difficulties.' Difficulties such as one or more of the heirs being arrested for murder, Daisy thought. Just how far would Angela go to further her work?

They had come to the bank of the artificial lake. The track continued around the water in both directions and across it by means of a stone bridge in the mediaeval style, just wide enough for a heavily laden packhorse. It even had niches on each side for pedestrians to get out of the way of a passing horse. It led to a wooded island, whence a similar bridge led to the farther shore.

Angela set off to circle the lake, while Daisy took the bridge. It was very quiet, with nothing but the song of birds and squirrels chattering in the trees.

Emerging from the island copse, Daisy saw the folly not far

ahead, at the top of a low rise. From her bedroom back at the house, it presented the appearance of a ruined cloister. Close to, it was obviously a comfortable gazebo in disguise, with open arches in front, arched windows at the back. Daisy remembered picnics held there during earlier visits with Lucy.

The gazebo was empty. Had she come all this way for nothing? At least the exercise was good for her, Daisy told herself.

'Lucy?' she called.

'Oh, it's you, darling. I'm here.' Lucy appeared, framed in one of the misleadingly ruinous arches. 'I thought it might be amusing to put together a book of follies,' she said gloomily. 'I've been taking photos.'

'What a good idea. Will you just label the pictures or would you like me to supply some text?'

'I don't suppose anything will come of it.' She stepped over the sill. The new short skirts certainly had their points. 'I shall just go on taking pictures of ugly society matrons till I die.'

'Bosh! You've done plenty of beautiful women and hand-some men, and with Lady Eva's legacy you'll be able to pick and choose your subjects. Even if you really don't marry Binkie. Have you talked to him?'

'Spoken to him. Not really talked. He was at the office and I didn't want to upset him.'

'It would have been a bit mean. Did you tell him about Lady Eva?'

'I just said something dreadful had happened. He's going to leave work early and drive down. It doesn't take long in the Alvis. I told him to meet me in the conservatory at five, when Uncle Aubrey's out of the way.'

'Lord Fotheringay might not join the rest for tea, now that there's a police investigation instead of a festive house-party.'

'Oh well, if he's still there, Binkie and I can always hide behind a potted palm or something. Or you could come with me and bear him off.'

'Right-oh,' said Daisy.

Alec had telephoned from Liverpool Street to give the Chief Constable the time of their arrival. Instead of the expected police car, Lord Haverhill's Daimler met him and Tom Tring at the station. In the back was Sir Leonard Crowe himself.

The sergeant settled his substantial bulk on the front seat, the Murder Bag nursed on his lap. His weight caused the massive car to shudder barely perceptibly. Unless the chauffeur was a confirmed misanthrope, by the time they reached Haverhill Tom would know exactly what the servants' hall thought about the murder. Understanding that, his later questions could be framed so as to elicit answers where a less sympathetic manner would fail.

Alec got in beside the Chief Constable.

'I was going to fetch you in my own motor,' said Sir Leonard, 'but Lord Haverhill insisted on sending his. My dear fellow, I'm very glad to see you. My chap is out of his depth, I fear. An excellent chap in his way, but unaccustomed to dealing with lords and ladies, don't you know. You're quite in the way of it, I gather?'

'I've had a number of cases involving the aristocracy, sir,' Alec said cautiously.

'Your wife being one of them. A charming lady, and with her wits very much about her, I should say. Haverhill told me her friend, Miss Lucy Fotheringay, has a very high opinion of your ability.'

Lucy had never given Alec that impression – rather the reverse – but she had never had need of his services before. 'It's going to be damned awkward,' he said, 'being both his lordship's guest and a detective investigating a murder in his family.'

'Neither fish, flesh, fowl nor good red herring, eh? Crane seems to think you're up to it. One of the best, is Birdy Crane.'

'I take it you were at school with the Superintendent, sir.' No one at the Yard dared pronounce that nickname aloud.

'Yes, yes, more years ago than I care to think about. Never thought we'd both end up in the same line of work. Not that I'd call myself a detective, mind you! Administration, that's my line, and cheering the fellows on. I won't be interfering with your investigation, don't worry about that.'

'Can you tell me, sir, is there any chance Lady Eva was killed by an intruder?'

Sir Leonard shook his head gloomily. 'No sign of a break-in. Nothing pinched. That's the sort of thing I'd trust Inspector Crummle for. And he's ruled out the servants, too, I'm afraid. You'll want to go over all that with him, of course.'

'Yes, but I'm glad to hear you trust his judgment. That'll make my job much easier. The cause of death was strangulation?'

'Even the medical Johnnies – family doctor and police surgeon – couldn't argue about that. A nasty sight. I'm very sorry Mrs Fletcher should have seen it.'

'So am I.' But if she would keep getting herself involved in murder investigations, she had only herself to blame. Alec was prepared to wager a substantial sum that there had been absolutely no real need of her looking at the body.

She knew the people involved, though. That was always her strong point. And people told her things. Those misleadingly ingenuous blue eyes drew out information no one would ever think of volunteering to the police. Alec sighed. He'd have to accept her help on this one, so he might as well do it graciously.

'I expect you'll want to talk to your wife first of all,' said Sir Leonard, apparently reading his mind. 'Reassure the little woman, and so on.'

Not reading his mind. Daisy would kill him if he tried to 'reassure the little woman'. An acknowledgment that she was needed was what she'd want. 'Yes, I'd better see Daisy,' he agreed.

'That reminds me, do you have the list of everyone who was in the house last night? The one I dictated to your young man on the telephone?'

'No. I left it with DC Piper. There was no time to make a copy.'

'Now where did I put it? Ah, here we are. This is the original. Your wife is on it, of course, my dear chap, though naturally she is not considered to be under suspicion, so I didn't mention her to Piper.'

'I'm glad you don't suspect her, sir, but if your inspector does I shall have to bow out of the case.'

'No, no, no question of that! His lordship wouldn't hear of it. I'll have a word with Crummle.'

Convenient, if highly irregular, Alec thought, scanning the list. Confusingly, a large proportion of the surnames were Fotheringay. There were lords, ladies and baronets, quite enough to give a provincial DI cold feet, especially with the addition of a few Honourables and a clergyman. He himself had the inestimable advantage of a wife who was herself an Hon., however little she used her courtesy title.

Of course, he also had the disadvantage of a wife who would refuse to believe in the possibility of Miss Lucy Fotheringay's guilt. Not that Alec was inclined to put Lucy high on his personal list, though he could imagine circumstances which might drive her to murder. However, so fastidious a young lady was unlikely to resort to strangulation when she had all sorts of lethal chemicals available in her dark-room.

Sir Leonard had maintained a diffident silence while Alec pondered, but now he burst out, 'I say, my dear fellow, nothing in this blackmail business, eh? Crummle would have it that while Lady Eva wouldn't extort money, she might have used this wretched information she collected in other ways.'

'It's quite possible, I'm afraid.' Actually, Alec was by no means so sure Lady Eva was above extorting money. If that were the case, Ernie Piper would surely find evidence, her ladyship having an obsession with written memoranda.

'Mrs Fletcher is of the opinion that Lady Eva simply enjoyed having all the facts at her fingertips, without any intention of making use of them.' The Chief Constable sighed. 'But Crummle pointed out that no one could be sure she wouldn't reveal her knowledge in a disastrous way. I'm afraid he's right.'

'Undoubtedly. Great Scott, is that Haverhill?'

'Quite a pile, isn't it? A bit too fantastic for my taste, I must confess. Rather like a fairy-tale palace – "Sleeping Beauty", or some such. On the large side, too, but several family members live there on a regular basis, and scores of servants, even since the war.'

'Pay well enough and one can still find domestic staff, I'm sure.' Alec mentally noted this evidence of prosperity, borne out by the excellent condition of the drive and the parkland on either side of the avenue.

He turned his attention back to the house itself as the Daimler approached that endless façade. An intimidating sight, he acknowledged. If Daisy's childhood home had been on this scale, he might never have dared propose to her.

The exterior of the fairy-tale palace – in Sir Leonard's unexpectedly whimsical phrase – looked as well maintained as the grounds. The upkeep must cost a small fortune annually. The Fotheringays were clearly not one of those noble families who had fallen on hard times after the war. Whether that fact had any bearing on the murder remained to be seen.

As the car stopped, Daisy came pattering down the steps. Jumping out, Alec called, 'Careful!'

'It's all right, darling, I'm not front-heavy yet.' But she slowed to a more decorous pace. 'I did my best to persuade Lucy not to persuade Lord Haverhill to ask Sir Leonard to call you in, but I'm jolly glad you're here, all the same. Hello, Mr Tring! Thank you for rushing to the rescue!'

Tom's bald dome gleamed as he doffed his hat. 'My pleasure, Mrs Fletcher.' His luxuriant moustache quite failed to hide a beam. Though not, like Piper, convinced of Daisy's infallibility, he had a very soft spot for her. 'The Chief'll soon have it all sorted out, I don't doubt.'

Sir Leonard came around the car. 'Well, I'll leave you to get on with it, Fletcher. You won't mind if I hang about a bit? I won't interfere with your doings, I promise.'

'I hope you'll introduce me to Detective Inspector Crummle, sir, in ten ...' Alec caught Daisy's eye. '... In a quarter of an hour or so. And later to Lord Haverhill.'

'Of course, of course. In the meantime, suppose I take your sergeant here to see Crummle?'

'I'd take it very kindly, sir,' said Tom tactfully.

They all went into the house. The enormous hall, inhabited only by ancestral portraits, made Alec think of the over-populated rabbit warrens of London's East End, through which he'd chased many a villain. In some ways, the challenge here was going to be entirely different. In some ways it would be much the same: a web of family loyalties, a confusion of lies concealing unimportant secrets, a motive turning on some variation of greed or fear.

Cui Bono? Who would profit from Lady Eva's death, whether financially or by freedom from dread of exposure?

'Come into the library, darling. Mr Walsdorf is the only person who ever uses it, and he's moved his theatre of operations up to Lord Haverhill's study. The poor chap's in charge of cancelling all the wedding arrangements.'

'Cancelling? Not postponing?'

'I'll come to that later. I have so much to tell you!'

Alec shut the library door behind them and kissed Daisy thoroughly. 'Are you all right, love? I hate to think of you having such a shock in your condition.'

'Whereas you don't mind a bit if I have a shock when I'm not pregnant?'

'You know very well I wish you'd never in your life come within a hundred miles of murder.'

'Then I'd never have met you.'

'True,' Alec admitted. 'That wouldn't have done at all.' He kissed her again before surveying his surroundings.

The library was another huge apartment, though without the lofty height of the hall. The only sign of mediaeval influence was the row of tall arched windows looking north onto the carriage sweep and avenue. Between the windows, bookshelves rose to the ceiling. Matching bookcases on the opposite wall were interspersed with more portraits, these of stalwart Victorian and Edwardian gentlemen with whiskers or beards and their ladies in crinolines, bustles or Grecian bends.

'These are the real family portraits,' said Daisy, noting the direction of his gaze. 'The ones in the hall are someone else's ancestors. Lord Haverhill told me the history of the Fotheringays.'

'Is it relevant?'

'I don't think so. I shan't waste time on it now, anyway. Come and sit down. You'll want to use the desk, won't you?'

'Yes. This looks like a good room for us to settle in, telephone and all.'

'I'm sure no one will mind. Right-oh, where shall I start? With the . . . the body?'

'No, I'll get all that from Crummle. Let's go through this list of who was here last night. Tell me a bit about each, which will no doubt lead to further revelations.'

'I suspect I have a revelation before we start. Is Edward, or Teddy, Devenish on your list?'

Something nagged at the back of Alec's mind as he ran his finger down the list. 'Edward Devenish? No. Are you saying he was in fact here?'

'He arrived in the wee small hours, I'm told. His sister let him in and he slept on her bedroom floor.'

'What's their relationship to the deceased?'

'Grandchildren. Teddy's the only male child of Sir James and Lady Devenish.'

'"The young master,"' Alec quoted Lady Eva's house-keeper. 'Ernie found a reference to his consorting with a divorcée. I left him going through the papers, by the way – and thanks for the tip. It might have taken us a while to get on to that stash of dynamite.'

'The relatives mightn't have been too happy to mention it,' Daisy agreed. 'Really rather an infra dig hobby for the daughter of an earl and widow of a baronet. I mean, gossip's one thing but digging around for it and writing it down is not at all the thing. Do you think the motive for her murder's there?'

'I'm not quite ready to pronounce on that. We'll see what else Ernie digs up.'

Daisy pounced on his pronoun. 'We? We'll see?'

'Tom and I, and possibly the local chap. It's no good looking so disconsolate, love. You don't really want to know all the naughty antics Lucy's family gets up to.'

'I suppose not,' she conceded reluctantly.

'Apart from other considerations, such as my professional integrity, it's dangerous knowledge.' He frowned. 'In fact, you'd better drop the odd disgruntled hint that I'm being close-mouthed. I don't want you suffering Lady Eva's fate, and you've the baby to think of now, too. Cheer up. I do need your help.'

'Noble of you to admit it for once, darling!'

'Back to Teddy Devenish. Do you know why he turned up in the early hours of the morning?'

'I haven't the foggiest. Angela – his sister – just told me he telephoned last night, and she went down to let him in at one. He was late and she had to hang about. I don't know what excuse he gave her. She's a bit naïve. She also told me she expects to inherit a fair amount from Lady Eva.'

'She must have known we'd see the will. As a matter of fact, I have it in my pocket.'

'But she could have pretended not to know about the bequest.'

'True, though since the housekeeper told me about the bequest, that wouldn't have washed. Tell me about her. I'm going to concentrate on the financial motive until I hear from Piper.'

Daisy complied, ending, 'I can't see anyone so determined to fight cruelty inflicting such a frightful death on any living being.'

'Unless for the greater good.'

'I don't believe she's that fanatical, but if she is, she'd surely have found a quick and painless way to do her grandmother in. I saw her face, Alec.'

He reached across the corner of the desk to squeeze Daisy's hand. 'Don't think about it, love. Let's move on to Teddy. He's the residuary legatee. What do you make of him?'

'Spoilt. By his mother, at least, and indulged by his sister, who lurked on the cold, dark terrace for ages waiting for him to put in an appearance.'

'And his father?'

'I suspect Sir James's opinions don't carry a great deal of weight. Lady Devenish rather squashed him. Perhaps that's why he's such an avid pursuer of game large and small. It gets him out of the house. Is he in the will?'

'Not exactly. But the town house belongs to the estate so he gains the free use of it by his mother's death. He could rent it out for income, or use it to escape from his wife. Would they have condoned Teddy's carrying on with a divorcée?'

'Who knows? Though I doubt their indulgence would stretch so far, even if she was technically the wronged party. Do you think Lady Eva might have threatened to tell his parents? Or to rewrite her will?'

'It seems rather more likely than that she should hold a discovery over the head of anyone less closely related. It would give him a double motive. So far, young Master Teddy is shaping up as my prime suspect. Daisy, I hate to tell you this, but Lucy figures largely in the will.'

'I know. She told me. But it was she who persuaded the Earl to ask the Chief Constable to ask for you. Besides, darling, can you imagine Lucy strangling someone? She's much too fastidious.'

'I must admit that's my feeling, but you know I can't go by my feelings. I'll have to treat her like the rest.'

'It's not really a woman's crime, is it? Besides being gruesomely grotesque, wouldn't it take a lot of strength? Lady Eva was pretty hefty.'

'Not if the victim was taken by surprise, in her sleep, say, as seems likely. By the time she awaked and realized what was happening it would be too late to struggle. Unconsciousness comes quite quickly.'

'Thank heaven for that.'

Daisy was looking pale again, but Alec failed to see how he could avoid the subject entirely, unless he cut her out of the investigation altogether. She'd be furious if he tried, and her views on the people involved, apart from Lucy, were too valuable to lose.

'Were you there when Lucy heard the news?' he asked. 'How did she react?'

'You have to understand that she was already in a blue funk over the wedding. When the maid who found the body started screaming, she hid her head under the pillow and pretended she . . . Alec, I've just thought of something. Have you seen Lady Eva's room?'

'Not yet. You know I just arrived. Unfortunately Sir Leonard had the body removed to the mortuary, but Crummle had everything photographed and the pictures are being developed. Why?'

'There were feathers all over the place.'

'Ah, Sir Leonard didn't mention that.'

'From a ripped pillow. It seems to me the only reason for a pillow seam to split is that the murderer first tried to smother her with it and she fought back. Also, she was hanging off the side of the bed, as if she'd been pulled.'

'He didn't mention that, either.'

'So it must have been someone strong.'

'Not particularly,' Alec said grimly. 'Suffocation is as much a woman's crime as a man's. And when it failed and the stocking came into play . . .'

'It was a stocking? But that doesn't have to mean it was a woman. Anyone can buy a pair of stockings. It could have been either a man who brought one on purpose or a woman who happened to have one in her pocket. But with Lady Eva struggling, we come back to the need for strength.'

'Not necessarily. Half-suffocated, she might be quite feeble. Besides, at that point her murderer couldn't afford to let her live. He – or she – would have the strength of desperation.'

CHAPTER 8

Gloomy, disgruntled and belligerent, Detective Inspector Crummle trudged the length of the library, saying, 'Sir Leonard ordered me to report to you, sir. He's gone to see Lord Haverhill. Sergeant Tring is talking to the servants. Which I've already done.'

'Inspector Crummle? How do you do.' Alec stood up and shook hands. The courtesy invoked no spark of cheer in the local man. 'Daisy, we're just about done, aren't we? I'll see you later. All right, Inspector, let's have your report, and then you can take me up to see the victim's room. Take a seat.'

'Thank you, sir.' Crummle sat down heavily in the chair Daisy had just vacated. 'Pursuant to a telephone call received at—'

'Yes, yes, let's skip all that.' Alec pretended not to see Daisy turn on her way to the door and pull a face at him. 'Tell me what you found when you arrived at Haverhill?'

'I asked to see his lordship. The butler would have left me waiting in the hail, but I wasn't having any of that, letting Lord Haverhill prepare himself. It's no good letting your suspects prepare themselves. I followed the butler up.'

No wonder the Earl had decided to bring in Scotland Yard. 'You see Lord Haverhill as a suspect?' Alec asked. 'Isn't he in his eighties?'

'But a very hearty old gentleman, as I could see the moment I set eyes on him. After interviewing him, I proceeded—'

'Wait a bit. What did you learn from him?'

'Nothing. He told me he had no information to assist me in bringing the investigation to a swift conclusion.'

Alec didn't ask why Crummle had believed Lord Haverhill. He had met this ambivalent attitude to the nobility before, a willingness to suspect them of crimes but not to question their statements. 'So you then proceeded . . . ?' he said.

'I proceeded to instruct the butler, a man by the name of Baines, to show me to the scene of the crime and to send my men to me there.'

Judging by his description of his activities thereafter, Crummle had managed the scene of the crime quite competently. Photographs had been taken, fingerprints dusted for. The local GP had turned up, followed shortly by the police surgeon, who had been forced to agree on the obvious cause of death.

'And I would've left the body where it was,' said Crummle, belligerence to the fore, 'for my superintendent to see, or you as it turned out, but Sir Leonard had it taken away. Said it was upsetting the family.'

'It's a pity I didn't see it as it was found,' Alec agreed, the nearest he could come to criticizing the Chief Constable to the inspector. 'I'll go and have a look in the morgue but it's not quite the same thing. When will the photos be ready?'

Crummle took out his watch. 'My sergeant's developing and printing them quick as he can. With luck he'll be back with them in an hour or so.'

'What did you find in the way of fingerprints?'

'The outside doorknob was a mess, having been used by two

maids, Mrs Timothy Fotheringay, and Mrs Fletcher.' The inspector pronounced this last name with a hint of malicious satisfaction, but went on to admit, 'Not that it'd likely have made much difference if they'd've all used kid gloves. The inside knob, that her ladyship and her ladyship's maid must have used, was wiped clean. Everything else in the room seems to be one of theirs or the housemaid that cleaned. I'll have to wait for the photos of the dabs to be sure.'

'Sir Leonard tells me you've ruled out the servants.'

'The doors between the servants' wing and the rest of the house are locked from midnight till half past six. It seems servants today won't stand for being summoned at all hours. Lord Haverhill's anxious to keep his staff happy, so his household and guests know they can't come if called. The butler has the key. He can be rung for in an emergency.'

'And the exterior doors?'

'All shut and bolted.'

'One wasn't. At least, I understand it was opened and left unlocked for an appreciable time. Miss' – Alec checked his notes – 'Miss Angela Devenish told my wife she went down at one this morning to let her brother Edward in.'

Crummle stared at him with understandable resentment. 'Miss Devenish told Mrs Fletcher?'

It wasn't fair that Alec had an inside source of information, but the inspector would have to live with it. 'Miss Devenish had to wait some time for her brother. I don't know whether she stayed near the door all the time.'

'She'll say she wandered off,' Crummle prophesied, 'so an intruder could have entered. Give us someone else to look at outside the family. These nobs all stick together.'

'What she'll say remains to be seen,' said Alec, beginning to lose patience. He stood up. 'Come on, show me Lady Eva's room. On the way you can tell me what else you've learnt.'

Crummle had not learnt much. The servants had answered direct questions willingly enough, but had not volunteered information, and the inspector had failed to ask the right questions. However, Tom Tring could be relied upon to rectify his omissions.

As Alec and the inspector made their way upstairs, the house seemed oddly deserted. Early afternoon on a fine June day – normally one would expect people to be outside enjoying themselves. But today was not normal. Alec suspected the inhabitants were huddled in bedrooms and sitting rooms, trying to decide alone or in small groups just what they were going to tell him when the questions began.

A uniformed constable guarded the door of the victim's room.

'It's locked and I've got the key,' said Crummle defensively, 'but there's likely another key around somewhere.' He hesitated, then added with extreme reluctance, 'Mrs Fletcher locked the door a few minutes after the body was discovered and gave the key to the butler, and he posted a footman here, too. Apart from me and my men, the only person in there since the maid with the tea started screaming is Mrs Timothy Fotheringay. Seems she was a nurse in the war. Mrs Fletcher sent her in to check whether the victim was quite dead.'

'And the doctors and the ambulance men who took away the body?'

'Well, of course.'

Alec thought it best not to comment. 'Is this the only door?' he asked.

'There's one to a bathroom, shared with the next bedroom, but it was bolted on this side when I arrived. No one could've got in unseen.'

'Good, though the murderer had plenty of time to do what he wanted in the night. What time of death did the doctors propose?'

'Between one and four. They wouldn't commit themselves closer.'

'They never will. Has anyone tried to get in?' Alec asked the elderly constable, who was regarding him with an inexplicable air of approval.

'No, sir. Leastways, a pair of housemaids came to do the rooms and they said the housekeeper told 'em to tidy up this un too, but when I told 'em no, they wasn't going to argue. Relieved, they was, sir, that's the word. Giggling and squeaking like a pair o' mice,' he added benevolently.

'That'll do, Stebbins,' snapped Crummle, unlocking and opening the door and ushering Alec in.

Alec stood for a moment on the threshold. The scene was much as he had expected from Daisy's description. He crossed to the dressing table. 'Any sign of theft?'

'No, sir. There's jewellery in the top drawer there and a purse with a few pounds and change.'

One leather case contained a superb ruby necklace, and another held nearly a dozen elaborate rings. 'Was the deceased wearing any rings?' Alec asked.

'A wedding ring, gold, and another ring on the same finger, a pink stone with pearls around. Her personal maid said she never took it off except to be cleaned. Looked to me uncomfortable to wear in bed but I suppose she'd got used to it.'

'That could explain how the pillow was ripped open. I'd wondered. The ring must have caught a thread.'

Crummle flushed. 'I didn't examine the ring closely.'

'Never mind, it's a minor point and can be checked.' He opened another drawer and found a sachet with several pairs of silk stockings in fashionable beige skin-tones. In a second sachet were more in different colours, presumably to match particular frocks. 'What colour was the stocking around her neck?'

'Sort of brownish.'

'Did you ask her maid whether she ever wore that precise shade?'

'No, sir.' Crummle was indignant. 'I can't see where it matters what colour it is. Sky-blue pink'd kill just as well.'

'True.'

But there might be a clue to the way the murderer thought in whether he brought a stocking with him or, when the pillow failed, used one he found to hand. Alec didn't bother to explain. He was getting fed up with the inspector's lack of imagination coupled with his sense of grievance. He tried to come up with some task which would keep the man out of his way while presenting at least an appearance of usefulness.

'When is the autopsy scheduled, and who's doing it?'

'Dr Philpotts, the police surgeon, said he'd do it this evening if he can't get to it this afternoon.'

'All right, I'll need a written report of all your findings to date, and any theories you've come up with. Try to have it done by the time the photos get here, so we can all go over everything together. This room had better be left as it is until I've seen your photos. And now it's about time I presented myself to the earl.'

As a Scotland Yard detective called in by the Chief Constable, he should be introduced to Lord Haverhill by Sir Leonard. As an invited wedding guest, he should be introduced by Daisy or Lucy. Rather than sort out these competing claims, and unsure of just how his lordship regarded him, he decided to put himself in the butler's hands.

Much better not to involve Daisy, not to suggest to others – to one particular other – that she was involved. He wondered what she had been doing since leaving the library. He hadn't had a chance to remind her to drop a few hints dissociating herself from the investigation.

With Inspector Crummle's inimical glare upon her, Daisy had been only too glad to remove herself from the library. Her business with Alec was unfinished, however. She hadn't had time to pass on her information and opinions about most of the people at Haverhill. She had a nagging feeling there was something both important and urgent she ought to have said, but she couldn't think what, nor even about whom.

The hall was empty, no group waiting for her with anxious questions.

She wasn't surprised. At lunch the taciturn gloom had been thick enough to cut with a knife: the shock and horror of what had happened had sunk in at last. Except for the Haverhills, Lord and Lady Fotheringay, and Sally, everyone had turned up, including the Devenishes and three newcomers who had just arrived by car. The latter were anxious to leave again as soon as possible; in fact, several others had turned around at the station and gone straight home when Lord Haverhill's chauffeur told them what had happened. The rest were resigned to staying. No one seemed to realize the police couldn't actually stop them leaving if they insisted, and Daisy hadn't enlightened them.

On leaving Alec and Crummle in the library, she decided to go up to the family apartments to enquire after Lord Fotheringay's health.

By now she had talked to everyone since the murder, at least briefly, except Lady Haverhill and Maud and Aubrey Fotheringay. Not that she suspected any of the three, but they might know something useful. Lady Eva could have confided in her sister-in-law, for instance, about trouble with a member of her family.

Interrupted by Crummle, Alec had failed to issue his usual prohibition against asking direct questions, but Daisy virtuously resolved not to. On the other hand, he had practically ordered her to drop hints about not knowing what was in Lady Eva's memoranda. If she worded her hints right, they ought to elicit any information available.

When she knocked at the sitting-room door, Lady Fotheringay opened it. 'Oh, it's you, Daisy. We thought it might be your husband. Sir Leonard announced his arrival.'

'He'll be up to make his bow shortly, but he felt he had to smooth the local man's ruffled feathers first. I just popped up to ask after your husband. Lucy said you were concerned about the effect of the shock on his health.'

Lady Haverhill's voice came from within the room. 'Ask Mrs Fletcher to come in, Maud. My son has insisted on taking refuge with his plants, Mrs Fletcher.'

'I'm glad he's well enough.'

'He ought to be in bed,' said Lady Fotheringay. 'Such a terrible shock!'

'I'm afraid the shock has hit my husband harder than was immediately apparent, Mrs Fletcher. Nicholas has not been quite himself for a month or more, as is, I dare say, to be expected at our age. He is lying down at present, but of course he will get up to . . . to welcome your husband.'

'Alec wouldn't dream of disturbing him. He'll have to speak to him sometime, but I'm sure it can wait until he's rested,' Daisy rashly pledged. 'Do you know how Mr Montagu is getting on? I had the impression he was close to Lady Eva.'

'Montagu encouraged Eva in that wretched gossip business,' Lady Haverhill said astringently.

Or had she blackmailed him into passing on rumours heard at his club? Daisy wondered.

'He's taken to his bed,' Lady Fotheringay informed her. 'They were as close as any brother and sister I know, so it's quite understandable. What I cannot understand is why Sally should do likewise. She scarcely knew Aunt Eva. What on earth persuaded my son to marry a girl with such delicate nerves? Not at all suitable for a soldier's wife!'

'Sally is in such a state, Nicholas felt obliged to send Rupert's commanding officer a cable asking that he be released from his manoeuvres.'

'I don't think it's at all surprising that she's upset,' said Daisy, with a glow of conscious virtue earned by sticking up for a person she disliked. 'The very idea of murder is so abhorrent that being involved in a case, however peripherally, is enough to make some people ill.'

'I suppose Mr Fletcher is quite convinced that it's m-murder?'

'Of course he is, Maud, or he'd not have rushed down from London three days earlier than intended. I should say, my dear, that Nicholas is very grateful that your husband is willing to head the investigation.'

Daisy didn't say that Alec was not at all willing and had only come because he'd been ordered to. She wanted to steer the conversation back to Lady Eva's gossip collection. 'There's the London connection,' she said, 'which makes it possible for Scotland Yard to get involved. One of Alec's men is at Lady Eva's house now, going through her files.'

Both ladies flinched, appalled. Daisy had overestimated their *sang-froid*. In the face of the murder of a relative by marriage they managed stiff upper lips, but the prospect of the public washing of the family's dirty linen made them quail.

Clearly they had not considered the ramifications of the crime. Had the murderer? Could he or she possibly have failed to realize that Lady Eva's demise would cause the police to read her memoranda?

'Don't worry, the police will treat the information as confidential.' Unless it was needed as evidence. 'Alec won't even tell me.'

'Do you think she was killed because of something she found out?' faltered Lady Fotheringay, braving her mama-in-law's frown.

'The police must no doubt consider the possibility,' Lady Haverhill conceded, 'since Eva was so ill-advised as to make a hobby of enquiring into other people's private business, and so unwise as to make no secret of it.' She changed the subject. 'Mrs Fletcher, Lucinda appears indifferent to the postpone-ment of her wedding. I confess myself baffled by the flippant manner you modern young women consider *de rigueur*, so I cannot make out whether she is simply putting on a brave face for our sakes. Can you tell me, is she dreadfully upset?'

Daisy hesitated. For a start, she didn't feel she had a secure grasp on Lucy's state of mind – and she wasn't at all sure that Lucy herself did. Secondly, telling Lucy's aunt and grandmother that she had decided to call the whole thing off would only distress them at a time when there was more than enough grief to go around. And in the third place, if they didn't know about Lucy's bequest from Lady Eva, it was not for Daisy to tell them.

'The reason for the postponement is far more upsetting than the postponement can possibly be,' she said guardedly.

'I feel I must take you into my – our – confidence. By the time a decent period of mourning has passed, in today's terms, which I know are very different from those of my young days, I rather doubt that Nicholas will be up to entertaining on the scale presently arranged.'

'Gosh, is he really ill?'

'A degenerative disease which the doctor expects to progress quite rapidly.' The countess's voice caught on the last word, but after passing her hand across her eyes, she continued with her habitual composure, 'Only the immediate family has been told. I need not ask you, I'm sure, to keep it to yourself.'

Daisy's mind raced. It sounded as if Lady Fotheringay would at last become Countess of Haverhill in the not too far distant future. Whether she had the force of character to stop playing second fiddle to her mother-in-law was another question.

In any case, Lady Eva's death had not contributed to the change in her prospects, so there was no reason for Daisy to mention the earl's illness to Alec. 'Of course, Lady Haverhill, I shan't breathe a word.'

'But if you can gently hint to Lucinda the possibility that she

may have to ... to make do with a somewhat less lavish
celebration ...'

'Lucy won't mind, I'm sure. I don't want to make her sound
ungrateful, but it's all been rather a trial to her.'

'I rather suspected this grand affair was more Victoria's
notion than Lucinda's, though, of course, one must make some
sort of show for Lord and Lady Tiverton.'

For a moment, Daisy couldn't think who Lord and Lady
Tiverton were – oh yes, Binkie's parents, the Marquis and
Marchioness. Irrelevant as they were to the present situation,
she had forgotten them.

She wasn't getting very far with the present situation. What
she really wanted was an excuse to talk to the Devenishes,
especially Edward. Just why did young Teddy, Lady Eva's
residual legatee, who had been 'consorting with a divorcée',
turn up unexpectedly at more or less the time the victim was
meeting her end?

Even if Daisy braved Alec's displeasure to ask Teddy
outright, he wasn't likely to give her a straight answer. But
whatever his reason, he must have given his sister some
explanation, true or false, and Daisy was on excellent terms
with Angela.

CHAPTER 9

'I'll tell you one thing, Chief,' said Tom, entering the library with the soft tread of a large man whose mass is more muscle than fat. 'It's going to be quite a job running these people to earth when you want to talk to 'em. The place is a bloody great barracks, excepting in a barracks everyone's got a place where he ought to be. This lot can wander all over. I've asked Mr Baines to loan us a footman to help. He's waiting in the hall.'

'Good thinking. Crummle's detailing a constable to help, too. Ah, here he is.'

'Constable Stebbins, sir.' It was the elderly officer who had been on duty at Lady Eva's door. By no means a large man, he walked with the heavy yet gingerly tread of one whose feet hurt him. 'Mr Crummle said to give you a hand, sir, to round up the suspects.'

'Crummle's revenge,' Alec muttered in an undertone.

Tom stroked his moustache to hide a grin. 'We'll have to keep some of 'em on ice, Chief, or there'll be a long wait between, considering how they're scattered all over. Mr Baines says there's a little sitting room, what he calls an antechamber, across the hall. Suppose we stick them that's waiting in there with Constable Stebbins to keep an eye on them.'

'Good idea, Mr Tring.'

Stebbins breathed a gusty sigh of relief. 'Thank you, sir! Mebbe I did ought to tell you, sir, there's a couple of young chaps Mr Crummle stationed at the front door which there aren't hardly no need for, there being many and many a way out o' this place and the rest not guarded.'

'Thank you, Constable. Sergeant, shanghai one of those young chaps, if you please.'

'Done, Chief!'

'Tell him and the footman I want to see Miss Angela Devenish first, and then Mr Edward Devenish. And after them, let's see, Lucy – Miss Lucy Fotheringay – I think, followed by Sir James and Lady Devenish.'

Usually Alec preferred to question his least likely suspects first, in the hope of eliminating some right away. This time, however, he couldn't separate the sheep from the goats until he had the results of Piper's researches. The chance of anyone's having an alibi, except from a spouse, was minimal. For most of the people on his list he didn't even have Daisy's comments to guide him.

In these preliminary interviews, he might as well start with those few of whose motives he was already aware. Lady Eva had known about Teddy's association with a woman of whom his parents would undoubtedly disapprove, perhaps to the point of cutting off his allowance to force him to live at home. Both young Devenishes stood to gain financially from their grandmother's death. And both had been wandering about the house at about the time she died.

While they waited for Angela's arrival, Tom told Alec what he had learnt from the servants. Though much more detailed than Crummle's report, and with many more opinions voiced, it did not materially change matters.

While the locked doors were not an impassable barrier, Lady Eva had been a generous tipper, therefore always a welcome guest at Haverhill as far as the servants were concerned. Her voracious appetite for aristocratic gossip was well known, as was her lack of interest in the misdeeds of lesser beings, provided they did not directly affect her comfort.

The two servants she had brought with her, her personal maid and chauffeur, had been with her for five or six years. They were satisfied with their positions and did not expect any great recognition in her will.

'Which is just as well,' said Alec, 'as she's left them ten pounds per year of service.'

'People have been killed for less,' Tom rumbled, 'but not by them as'd have to go out looking for a job with the black mark of a murdered mistress against them. I reckon we can rule 'em out, all of 'em.'

'Provisionally, as a working hypothesis.'

'There's one other thing, Chief. Seems Lady I-oh-nee – that's I-O-N-E – Fotheringay went off to London by train after breakfast.'

'Great Scott! Has anyone else sloped off that no one's bothered to tell me about?'

'If so, they haven't bothered to tell me either. I didn't come running, Chief, because she took no luggage and she's ordered a car to pick her up at the station at half past six. I didn't reckon you'd want to put out an all-stations alert or a watch on the ports, not for a Lady.'

'No, you're quite right. Who the devil is she?'

Tom consulted his notebook. 'Lord Haverhill's spinster daughter. Fiftyish, plain, drab, dull. Not that they used those words but that's what it added up to. No money to speak of –

lives at home. They didn't tell Inspector Crummle. He didn't ask.'

'Blast the man! All right, Tom, we'll just have to wait and hope she turns up at ... Ah, here comes Miss Dev— Daisy! What the dickens?'

'This is Angela Devenish, darling.' Daisy's smile had more than a touch of smugness. 'You sent for her and she asked me to come with her. Angela, Detective Chief Inspector Alec Fletcher and Detective Sergeant Tring.'

Exasperated, Alec ran his fingers through his hair. He should have expected this. The way Daisy had talked of Angela suggested they were on excellent terms.

Angela Devenish, having entered with a small, nondescript dog at her heels, seemed not in the least disconcerted by the peculiar introduction. 'How d'ye do, Mr Fletcher,' she said gruffly. 'I hope you don't mind Tiddler. I can't leave him; he howls.'

'Not at all, Miss Devenish.' What he objected to was Daisy's presence, and the whole situation where he was half guest, half inquisitive intruder. 'Won't you sit down?' He indicated the chair by the desk. Then, frowning at Daisy, he pointed to a chair at some distance.

She wrinkled her nose at him but obediently sat, and Tom, his notebook at the ready, took a seat out of Angela's line of vision.

'I regret having to trouble you at such a sorrowful time.' Alec noted that she looked less sorrowful than uneasy. 'Describe for me, please, everything that occurred between midnight and seven o'clock this morning.'

Startlingly, Angela blushed. She didn't look at all the sort of young woman to have been entertaining a swain in her bedroom, but after all, one never could tell. 'Midnight? I didn't go downstairs till just before one.'

'Midnight.'

'I . . . Well, I had to do something to stay awake, to let my brother in, you know, so I started writing an article for the RSPCA magazine. I've never tried it before. I'm not much of a hand at writing, actually, but I thought maybe . . . maybe Daisy wouldn't mind looking at it and giving me a hint.' She sent Daisy a pleading glance.

Daisy opened her mouth. Alec scowled. Daisy shut her mouth but smiled and nodded.

Angela heaved a sigh of relief. That hurdle overcome, she went on, 'At ten to one, I went downstairs. Oh, I ought to say I went by the back stairs, the servants' stairs. I wouldn't have seen anyone even if they'd been about.'

'Did . . . Tiddler go with you?'

'Of course,' she said, surprised. 'I can't leave him; he howls.'

Tom's moustache twitched and Daisy grinned. There and then Alec more or less gave up on Angela Devenish as a suspect. 'Go on.'

'I went to the Long Gallery and opened one of the French doors—'

'Locked?'

'Yes, and bolted top and bottom, but the keys are kept in the drawer of a table. The gold and marble one, you know, Daisy? We went out on the terrace. And hung about and hung about for simply ages.'

'Did you move out of sight of the door?'

'No. That is, I took Tiddler down the steps to the lawn, so I suppose I had my back turned for a moment, but once I reached the bottom I turned round to watch for Teddy. I didn't want him to go in and lock me out. It was a clear night and I could see quite well, though there was only a sliver of moon. Then Teddy turned up at last – the tower clock had chimed the half hour – and we went in and locked and bolted the door . . .'

'You're sure of that?'

'Oh yes. Uncle Nicholas – he's my great-uncle, actually – is very particular about that. There was a tremendous row once when Rupert came in late and didn't lock up. I suppose there's some valuable stuff in the house,' she said vaguely.

Assuming Crummle's men could be trusted to spot any sign of a break-in – and he seemed quite competent at that sort of thing – Angela's evidence meant that Lady Eva had almost certainly been murdered by one of the family.

She didn't seem to realize the significance of her words. Her uneasiness had faded and she continued without prompting: 'We went up to my room and he pinched my counterpane and a pillow. I went to sleep and didn't wake up till a maid brought tea and told me about . . . about Grandmama.'

'You were on good terms with your grandmother?'

'Yes, well, sort of. She didn't like what I do but she liked that I do it. I mean, she approved of me not being a drip, sitting at home knitting, like poor Aunt Ione.'

Daisy gasped. Alec gave her a quick glare and turned back to Angela. Her brow creased in a puzzled frown, she hadn't noticed the interruption.

'That's why she left me some money, and Lucy, too, though of course photography is much more respectable than rescuing badly treated animals. I can't think why.'

'Very odd. Let's just go back to when you at last got to bed. Your brother curled up on the floor with your counterpane around him?'

'Well, after his bath.'

'He took a bath? How long did that take him?'

'I haven't the faintest. I fell asleep right away.'

'Tiddler didn't bark when he came in?'

'Oh no, he's much too frightened. He never barks.' She reached down and gently pulled one ragged ear. 'He was quite badly hurt. I found him—'

'In the morning, Miss Devenish, when you woke, your brother was asleep on the floor in your bedroom?'

'On the other side of the bed from the door, so that the maid wouldn't see him when she brought the tea. He didn't want Mummy and Daddy to know he'd arrived in the middle of the night, you see. When he rang up, he told me not to tell them he was coming or have a room prepared for him. He was just going to turn up after breakfast and pretend he'd left London early.'

'He came from London?'

'No, from a house-party, in Hampshire, I think. That's why he was so late. He couldn't leave there till after dinner.'

'I see. By the way, why on earth did he leave a house-party at that time of night?'

'It was boring,' Angela said simply.

Alec decided he didn't understand the younger generation. Or else he didn't understand the upper classes. One way or another, he felt very middle-aged and middle-class. He glanced at Daisy.

She shrugged and raised her eyes to heaven.

He understood her very well, most of the time, and she was an aristocrat ten years his junior. Cheered, he waited a moment to see if silence would prompt further unsolicited confidences from Angela, but she appeared to have run out of steam.

This was a preliminary interview, he reminded himself, and he had a couple of dozen more people to see. Rising, he said, 'Thank you very much, Miss Devenish. You've been most helpful.'

'Is that all? I knew you couldn't be like Mummy said you would or Daisy wouldn't have married you.'

Alec felt his face reddening. He couldn't remember being put to the blush by a suspect since his early days as a detective constable. Tom's grin was too wide to be hidden by his moustache and Alec didn't dare look at Daisy. He shook the hand Angela held out to him.

'I'll have some more questions for you later,' he warned her.

'Right-oh. Coming, Daisy?'

'In a bit. I want a word with Alec. I'll see you later.'

'Right-oh.'

Tom escorted Angela out.

'Darling, it's too frightful, I quite forgot to mention about Lady Ione.'

'Tom found out from the servants. You couldn't have warned me in time to intercept her at the station, could you?'

'No,' Daisy said thankfully, 'you arrived long after.'

'Never mind, then. Quickly, anything else I need to know about Edward Devenish?'

'He's definitely a bit of a blister. But he must be aware of his sister's devastating frankness.'

'Devastating is the word!'

'I advised her – I advised all of them – to tell the whole truth right away. She's probably the only one to take my words so enthusiastically to heart. Because she's inclined that way anyway, so Teddy must know he couldn't count on her keeping the time of his arrival secret. So it'd be stupid to then go and murder Lady Eva.'

'Perhaps he is stupid. He'll be here in a moment, if they've found him. I suppose you'd better stay so that you can tell me about each person before they come in.'

'Darling, may I really?' She stood on tiptoe to kiss him on the nose.

'Daisy! Sit over there, will you? Not exactly hidden; where people are not likely to notice you.'

She obediently retreated to the shadows as Tom ushered in a youth in dark grey flannels and a navy blazer.

'Mr Devenish, sir.'

As Teddy Devenish crossed the room towards him, Alec was struck by the resemblance of his expression to Crummle's: disgruntled and belligerent. A closer view, however, revealed not Crummle's gloom but a spark of apprehension behind the façade. Teddy was batting on a sticky wicket and he knew it.

'How do you do, Mr Devenish. I'm sorry to have to trouble you on such a—'

'I'm not saying anything.' Teddy leant with both hands on the desk and glowered. 'Not without a solicitor.'

'That is your privilege, sir. No doubt your father has summoned his solicitor?'

'Er, well, no, actually.'

'Perhaps he is unaware of precisely at what o'clock this morning you arrived?'

'I'm of age. I don't have to tell him everything I do.'

'Of course not,' Alec said soothingly as if to a fractious child. 'Family solicitors tend to be rather stuffy. I dare say you'd rather have your own.' He noted with satisfaction that he'd flummoxed the boy. 'Won't you sit down, Mr Devenish?'

Teddy subsided on to the chair with a groan. 'I suppose my sister told you everything.'

'Everything she knows. There are gaps to be filled. Let's start at the beginning. Where were you staying before you came to Haverhill?'

'Why the devil do you need to know that?'

'Routine. Ah, I see my sergeant frowning at me. We'd better start with your full name and address, if you please, just as a matter of routine.'

'Edward Granville Devenish.' He gave the address of his flat in town, on the wrong side of Oxford Street, but not by much. 'The family place is Saxonfield, in Leicestershire.'

'Thank you. And your friends in Hampshire?'

As Alec anticipated, Teddy found it much less perturbing to give his friends' address once he had given his own. 'The name's Hetheridge. Danesbury House, near Nether Wallop. The chap who invited me is Bill Hetheridge.'

'Thank you. What was your reason for leaving Danesbury House late in the evening for a long drive?'

'I can't see that it's any business of yours!'

'Mr Devenish, you went to a good deal of trouble to arrive in the middle of the night, unexpectedly, and to conceal the time of your arrival. At roughly the time of your arrival, your grandmother was brutally murdered. You are one of her heirs. Let me assure you, it is my business to find out why you left Danesbury House and came to Haverhill in such curious circumstances.'

White-faced, Teddy cried, 'I'm not telling you! I won't have you twisting my words!' He stumbled to his feet. 'Leave me alone. Leave me alone, damn you!'

Blundering towards the door, he narrowly missed a couple of chairs. Alec let him reach for the handle before saying in a voice like the crack of a whip, 'You are not to leave Haverhill, Mr Devenish.'

Without speaking, Teddy went out into the hall, leaving the door ajar.

'You think he's our man, Chief?'

'I wouldn't go quite that far, Tom, but young Teddy is definitely in hot water.'

'Waist-deep,' said Daisy soberly.

'I'll ring up these Hetheridges and see what explanation he gave them for leaving. But later, I think. Let him stew for a while. I'll see Lucy next, Tom.'

'Right, Chief.' Tom went out.

'Darling, you're not going to make me sit in this corner while you give Lucy the third degree?'

'No, you can come over here, if you promise not to interrupt.'

'Cross my heart.'

He moved a chair close to the desk for her, at the opposite end from the suspects' chair. 'I won't ask you about Lucy. Tell me about Sir James and Lady Devenish.'

'I don't know much. He rather goes in for killing things – huntin', shootin', fishin' – to Angela's distress, but I can't honestly see him doing in his mother. More likely his wife. Lady Devenish is a shrew, and I'd say she wears the breeches.'

'The London house reverts to the estate. He might see it as a refuge, or as somewhere his wife might be persuaded to stay frequently, now that his mother's not there.'

'Occam's razor,' said Daisy.

'Great Scott, Daisy, I didn't know you'd ever heard of Occam.'

'I know my education was deficient and I didn't understand all the philosophical stuff about nominalism, but I read about his razor the other day and it makes sense. Why should Sir

James get rid of his mother in order to escape his wife, rather than simply doing in his wife?'

'Wider field of suspects. Hush, here's Lucy.'

'Good afternoon, Chief Inspector.'

Alec's relationship with his wife's dearest friend had been mixed, to say the least. To start with, she had strongly disapproved of Daisy consorting with a policeman. Later, involved on the periphery of a murder case, she had been furious at his taking her fingerprints and chiding her for careless storage of dangerous photographic chemicals. His support of Daisy's writing career had met with her grudging approval, and he had learnt not to let her sardonic remarks irk him. At best she was mildly antagonistic, but they had been on Christian-name terms for ages.

He matched her coolness. 'Good afternoon, Miss Fotheringay. I'm sorry to have to trouble you at such a sorrowful—'

She cut him off with a gesture and her own brand of devastating frankness: 'I'm not exactly shattered, I'm afraid. Aunt Eva wasn't a bad old bird, as great-aunts go, but then, great-aunts do go, don't they? At least, most of mine have popped off by now. You mustn't think, because she left me some money, that we were close. And I avoid the rest of her family like the plague.'

'Ah yes, the money. I understand you profit considerably from your great-aunt's death.'

'Are you about to arrest me?'

Alec leant back in his chair and ran his fingers through his hair, a gesture he was wont to employ when exasperated. 'No, I'm not about to arrest you, Lucy. But you must realize I can't overlook the fact.'

'The money would have come in very handy anytime in the

past five or six years, but now I'm getting married, I shan't actually need it. Not that I shan't be glad to have it and I'm grateful to Aunt Eva for leaving it to me, of course.'

From the corner of his eye, Alec caught a glimpse of a perplexed expression on Daisy's face. Whatever was troubling her, he didn't expect her to tell him. She was quite convinced of Lucy's innocence, naturally. He himself couldn't quite see her as a murderer.

He regarded Lucy thoughtfully. 'We may have to go into Lord Gerald's finances.'

'My dear Chief Ins— Oh, what the hell, Alec! I'm sure you'll solve the case long before you have to resort to such expedients. That's why I persuaded Grandfather to try to get you down here. I wouldn't have if I'd done her in. I didn't, you know. And now, if you'll excuse me, I have a rendezvous with my intended.' Standing, she turned to Daisy. 'Coming, darling?'

'Is it tea-time already? Yes, coming. Alec, darling, I've told you all I know about your next two victims. I'll be back as soon as I can. I'll make sure Baines sends in tea for you and Tom.'

'Very welcome it'll be, too, Mrs Fletcher,' said Tom, studiously avoiding Alec's eye.

With brisk steps, the two young women departed.

The library door closed behind them. 'So you've decided to marry him after all?' Daisy enquired as they crossed the hall, already emptied of trestle tables.

'I'm not sure. I simply can't make up my mind. I've a feeling I'll know as soon as I see him. You'll extract Uncle Aubrey from the conservatory, won't you, if he's still there?'

'I'll do my best.'

'Tea's in the drawing room today – Grandmother's got some frightfully Victorian notion that tea on the terrace is inappropriate in a house of mourning.'

'I haven't actually noticed much in the way of mourning.'

'No. Sad, isn't it? Poor old Aunt Eva didn't have the knack of making herself loved.' Lucy grimaced. 'I don't suppose I do, either.'

'Except by Binkie.'

'Maybe that's why I'm not sure. If he's mad about me, there must be something wrong with the poor fish.'

'Oh, Lucy, you're much too hard to please!'

They entered the dining room and, skirting the table, made for the glass doors on the far side which opened into the conservatory. From beyond them, Daisy heard what sounded like a muffled shout, rhythmically repeated. As Lucy pushed the heavy door open, the sound resolved into a yell: 'Help!'

'That's Binkie!' Lucy hurried forward between the palms and heavy-scented datura, Daisy at her heels.

'Help!'

Binkie was kneeling on the slate floor, his back to them, leaning forward, half concealed by luxuriant foliage and pink and white blooms. He straightened.

'Help!'

'Darling, what's wrong?'

'Lucy, go and send for a doctor. Quickly!' Swinging forward again, he pressed down.

'Uncle Aubrey!'

Between Binkie's legs, Lord Fotheringay lay prone, arms outstretched, head turned aside. 'One ... two ... three.' Binkie straightened. 'Go! One ... two.' He leant forward, compressing his lordship's lower ribs beneath his powerful hands. 'One . . . two . . . three.'

'Go on, Lucy,' Daisy urged. 'I'll help here if I can. We all had to learn artificial respiration at the hospital.'

'But what's wrong with Uncle Aubrey?'

Daisy turned her around and gave her a push. 'Run. A heart attack, I imagine. Shall I take a turn, Binkie?'

'That's all right . . . two . . . three . . . I can go on forever. One . . . two . . . But I'm awfully afraid it's too late.'

CHAPTER 10

'I'm afraid it's my job to be suspicious, Lord Haverhill. Your son's death may well be perfectly natural, a heart attack induced by the strain of your sister's murder. But if I were to take it for granted, I should be derelict in my duty.'

'Cardiac arrest,' muttered Dr Arbuthnot, 'well, we all go by cardiac arrest in the final analysis.'

'He was ill.' Lady Fotheringay's face was blotched with tears. 'You said yourself he had a weak heart.'

'Yes indeed. After-effect of rheumatic fever. Though I would have expected a more gradual decline – breathlessness, angina, and so on. I confess I am not familiar with the effects of tropical poisons.'

'But what conceivable motive could anyone have for murdering Aubrey?' Grieved and bewildered, the earl was now unmistakably an old man, his voice quavery. 'He was the mildest, most inoffensive of men!'

'I hadn't had a chance to talk to him yet. Presumably he saw or heard something which could give us a clue to Lady Eva's death, possibly something he didn't recognize as significant. Or the murderer may simply have feared he'd seen something.'

'No, not Aubrey!' Lady Fotheringay sobbed.

Sally Fotheringay patted her mother-in-law's shoulder. 'It

was probably just a heart attack, all the same. It could have been, couldn't it, Dr Arbuthnot?'

'Yes, of course, Mrs Fotheringay, quite possibly.'

'Lady Fotheringay,' Sally corrected him. 'I'm Lady Fotheringay now.'

Lady Haverhill, pale and drawn but still very upright and steadfast, said sharply, 'It is usual to wait until after the funeral to assume a new title, out of respect for the deceased.'

Sally flushed. 'I'm sure no one could respect Rupert's father more than I did. I didn't mean to upset anyone. I'm so upset myself I don't know what I'm saying.'

A smart young woman Alec couldn't place said, 'Oh, pull yourself together, Sally, or go back to bed till Rupert arrives to hold your hand. Mr Fletcher, if you truly have reason to believe Father may have been murdered, I for one will do anything in my power to help you find out who did it.' She bit her lip as if struggling to hold back tears. 'He was a dear. I've never found another to match him.'

'Oooh,' wailed Lady Fotheringay.

The young woman – Flora? – crossed to her side. 'Come along, Mumsie darling, you ought to be in bed. Doctor, can you give her something?'

Flora and Dr Arbuthnot supported the weeping widow from the room, followed by a silent young man in a clergyman's collar.

Alec turned back to Lord Haverhill. 'I'm sorry, sir, I hope I haven't given the impression that I'm certain your son's death is not natural. But nor am I asking your permission to investigate it as murder. If it is so, it can hardly fail to be connected with your sister's. I am in charge of the case, and Sir Leonard agrees that I must continue as I see fit.'

The Chief Constable, hovering unhappily in the background, nodded and muttered, 'Terrible business, terrible
business.'

'We are extremely grateful to you, Mr Fletcher,' said the earl,
'are we not, my dear? I shall make sure everyone under my
roof understands that they are to give you the utmost
cooperation. I only wish your first visit to Haverhill had been
under happier circumstances.'

'Believe me, sir, so do I!' A relaxing country weekend, Daisy
had promised him.

Alec went back down to the conservatory. The police
surgeon had arrived. A young man, he sprang up from his
crouch beside the body with enviable ease.

Tom introduced him. 'Dr Philpotts, Chief.'

'No external trauma,' Philpotts said briskly, 'barring slight
signs of contusion from when he fell forward out of his chair.
He was as good as dead when he hit the floor. Either a heart
attack or you're looking at a case of poisoning, I'd say.'

'That was my feeling.'

'I recognized two poisonous plants as I came in here: datura
and oleander.' He glanced around. 'And I believe that's
another, over there: poinsettia. I can't say I'm up on the
symptoms; have to go look them up. But the garden's bound
to be full of deadly stuff too, foxgloves, lily of the valley,
narcissus, rhododendrons, autumn crocus, hydrangeas, you
name it. I have to warn you, I haven't the facilities for detecting
exotic poisons.'

'No, I think this is a case for Sir Bernard Spilsbury, the
Home Office pathologist. Great Scott, Tom, what happened to
the teapot? Bincombe said the victim was drinking tea when
he died.'

'None here when we came in, Chief, Miss Lucy was more concerned to get the doctor here and it was a while before Mrs Fletcher decided we ought to take a look.'

'But there was someone here all the time. What happened to the teapot? And he said Lord Fotheringay's cup broke. Where the deuce have they gone?'

'Only person I can think of could take 'em away and no one 'd notice is a parlourmaid.'

Alec groaned. 'Damnation! The pot will have been washed out by now. We'll have nothing to give Sir Bernard.'

'They'll have thrown out the broken cup. May be some dregs left. I'll go see what I can find out.'

'Do that, Tom. In the meantime, all these plants seem to be labelled, Doctor. Would you mind making a list of all those you know to be poisonous, and another of any you are not sure about.'

'Willingly, Chief Inspector, but the second list may well be a long one.' Dr Philpotts turned to a fresh page of his notebook. 'I have little knowledge of tropical plants, of which this conservatory holds a great many.'

'It will be something for Sir Bernard to begin with. Incidentally, did my sergeant tell you Bincombe tried artificial respiration when Lord Fotheringay fell and he could find no pulse? Schafer's method, I understand. Would you consider that appropriate?'

'Certainly; in the case of simple cardiac arrest he had a chance – however remote – of resuscitating the victim.' As he answered, the doctor stooped to peer at plant labels and scribbled on his notepad. 'If it was in fact poison, induced vomiting might have been more useful. But that depends on the poison, and if Lord Fotheringay was already dead it would be impossible in any case. In the circumstances, I'd say Bincombe acted with commendable common sense.'

'Thank you.' Alec was relieved to have one less reason for suspecting Lord Gerald of doing in his fiancée's uncle. In fact the only reason he was aware of was the young man's presence on the spot. 'I take it you haven't done the autopsy on Lady Eva yet, or you'd have mentioned it.'

'No. The cause of death is pretty obvious, though.'

'Is the stocking still around her neck? I'll need that. For pity's sake don't throw it away, and send over any rings she's wearing, too. Now I'd better go and put in a call to Spilsbury. Thank you, Doctor.'

He spread over the corpse the sheet Philpotts had drawn back to make his examination, then made for the library to telephone. With any luck Sir Bernard would prove quickly and indisputably that Lord Fotheringay had died a natural death. Alec didn't need any more complications to the already complicated investigation of Lady Eva's murder.

Daisy went to the library to wait for Alec. She wanted nothing more than to be told she was an idiot for suggesting Alec ought to look into Lord Fotheringay's death. Of course it wasn't another murder. People simply didn't go around doing in the members of a noble family, however recently ennobled.

But if they did, who was next?

Before she had time to follow up this horrifying train of thought, Alec came in. Striding towards the desk he didn't notice her until she said, 'Darling?'

'Daisy! Wait a moment.' He sat down, pulled the telephone closer, and clicked impatiently until the operator responded, when he asked for a London number. 'Yes, I'll hold the line. What is it, Daisy?'

'I just wondered. About Lord Fotheringay.'

'No answers yet. The local man doesn't feel competent to do the autopsy so I'm trying to get hold of Sir Bernard Spilsbury.'

'Then you think he was murdered? Someone's decided to do in the Fotheringays, one by one?'

'*If* it's murder, which I don't yet know, I'm sure it's because he knew something which might lead to Lady Eva's murderer. For pity's sake don't go putting it into people's heads that someone has it in for Fotheringays in general.'

'I wouldn't dream of it, darling. But Inspector Crummle is putting—' She stopped as Alec held up his hand.

'Hello?' He spoke for some time, waited, impatiently told the operator that yes, he'd have another three minutes, spoke again, and finally hung up. 'Between the interest of the case and the lure of the peerage, he's agreed to do it as soon as we can get the body to him.'

'I think I saw the mortuary men waiting in the hall.'

'Yes, hold on just a minute.' He went to the door, which opened as he reached it. 'Tom, you've got something already?'

'Easy, Chief. Seems Lord Fotheringay told Mr Baines he'd take his tea in the conservatory today, and the parlourmaid carried in the tray at a quarter to five and then went to help in the drawing room, where the rest had theirs. She set it on the table near the garden door, in the middle there. His lordship was off at the far end messing about at his potting bench.'

'So the teapot was sitting there for up to a quarter of an hour before Bincombe arrived on the scene and found him drinking.'

'She said sometimes he was so busy with his plants he let it grow cold. She usually went in after a bit to see if he needed more hot water, but she had to take up a tray to Mr Montagu too, then service in the drawing room kept her running, there being so many guests. Later, she went to clear up Lord Fotheringay's tea-things, just like normal. That's her job, she says, and that's what she did, though extra quiet and quick seeing he was lying there dead. That was before Mrs Fletcher started wondering if it was suspicious and came and told us.'

'I dare say there was a bit of morbid curiosity in it.'

'Likely. But just because he was dead, she didn't see why she shouldn't dump the tea-leaves on his plants, like he always said to do. Seems it's good for 'em. And she showed me which plant she dumped them on and I took a look. There's some cut-up leaves that don't look like tea to me. Dr Philpotts thinks it could be oleander.'

'You've taken a sample?'

'Sealed in one of them nice little jars with a label they put in the Murder Bag. Didn't I always say we needed something like it? Just over a month we've had 'em and how many times have we used 'em already?'

'You were dead right, Tom. Now give the jar to those mortuary men and I'll leave you to persuade them they have to take it and the body to London post haste. Spilsbury's agreed to do the autopsy this evening.'

'Right, Chief.'

Alec came back. 'What were you saying about Crummle, Daisy? What is he putting where?'

'Not where. He's busy putting the wind up all and sundry.'

'Damnation! Sorry, love. What is it Arbuckle used to say? Tarnation! All the man is supposed to be doing is checking everyone's whereabouts at tea.'

'He seems to be leaving people with the impression that

there's a homicidal maniac about, or alternatively that they're about to be hauled off to the police station to be grilled. Dire warnings in all directions. Sir Leonard's madly trying to pour oil on the troubled waters.'

'Oh . . . heck! Useful language, American. I'd better go and see what . . . Piper!'

Detective Constable Ernie Piper came into the library with a jaunty step, waving his notebook. 'Got the goods, Chief. I'd've been here ages ago but the car that met me had a burst tyre. Afternoon, Mrs Fletcher.'

'Good afternoon, Mr Piper. Let's hope you can at least narrow the field of suspects!'

'Off with you, Daisy. This is not for your ears, remember. Go and help Sir Leonard with the soothing oil.'

'Right-oh,' said Daisy reluctantly.

In the hall, Tom Tring was arguing with two men in white coats, who held respectively a roll of canvas and two poles. Daisy lingered, lurking beside a pillar, to listen, in case she might be able to put in a decisive word.

'Who's a-goin' to pay for the petrol, that's what I want to know,' said the man with the canvas in the voice of one repeating himself for the umpteenth time.

'Us come to fetch a corpus to the morgue in Cambridge,' said the other obstinately, 'not Lunnon.'

'Plans have changed,' said Tom with monumental patience. 'Your orders—'

'My orders is what the guv'nor told me afore us set out.'

'May I be of assistance, Sergeant?' Sir Leonard came out of the antechamber where Crummle was interrogating and infuriating Fotheringays and Devenishes and twigs of their family trees.

'Mr Fletcher has arranged for Sir Bernard Spilsbury to do the post-mortem, sir. Lord Fotheringay's body must be taken to London. These gentlemen are concerned about having the proper authorization to go so far beyond their usual bounds.'

'What I want to know,' said the man with the canvas, 'is who's a-goin' to pay for the petrol?'

Taking out his note-case, Sir Leonard said, 'I am the Chief Constable of this county. I authorize and order you to follow Detective Sergeant Tring's instructions. Here, take this.' He handed over a five-pound note. 'I shall want an accounting.'

'Us'll be on the road come supper-time,' said the man with the poles suggestively.

'A shilling apiece for supper,' spluttered Sir Leonard, 'after you make your delivery. Be off with you before I change my mind!'

The stretcher-bearers scuttled away.

'Thank you, sir,' said Tom.

'I suppose this mean Mr Fletcher is convinced of foul play?'

'No, sir, this is to find out. I understand the local police surgeon feels the determination is beyond his resources.'

'I'm afraid my people are letting you down right and left,' said Sir Leonard, pulling a rueful face. 'I've just removed Inspector Crummle from the case. I really can't have him upsetting so many people of standing. Luckily HQ rang through with news of a new case I was able to transfer him to.'

'Most fortunate, sir,' said Tom blandly.

'It'll mean more work for you and Mr Fletcher, I'm afraid, but I'll leave you several constables.'

'I'm sure Mr Fletcher will be very grateful, sir. As it happens Detective Constable Piper has just joined us, so Mr Crummle's . . . ah . . . assistance is no longer of such importance.'

'Excellent, excellent. I have all Crummle's notes with me here, so I'll just hand them over to Mr Fletcher now, then I'm off home for dinner. In the library, is he?' The Chief Constable limped towards the library.

Following the mortuary men, Tom winked at Daisy. He'd known all the time she was there, of course. Nothing much escaped Tom Tring's small, brown, twinkling eyes.

Giving him a wave, she was about to head for the drawing room when the wicket in the great front door started to open.

Curious as to who would come in that way without ringing the bell and waiting for a servant, Daisy paused. In stepped a very smart middle-aged woman, her hair marcelled beneath a cockaded cloche Lucy would not have disdained, her face unobtrusively but perfectly made-up. Her navy linen costume, piped in pale yellow and worn over a pale yellow pleated blouse, was the last word in elegance. Beneath a hem barely covering her knees, slim legs in skin-toned stockings ended in navy glacé shoes with Cuban heels.

A wedding guest, Daisy assumed, and one sufficiently closely related to the family to walk in unannounced. John Walsdorf must have failed to reach her with the message about Lady Eva.

Reluctantly, Daisy decided it was up to her to break the horrible news before the newcomer dropped a brick. She moved towards her.

The woman met her with an amused smile. 'Don't you recognize me, Mrs Fletcher?'

Daisy stared. She felt her mouth drop open and closed it abruptly. 'Good heavens,' she said, 'Lady Ione?'

'In the flesh, and a lot of new clothes.'

'Lady Ione Fotheringay,' said a loud male voice, 'it is my duty to warn you that—'

Crummle! Daisy swung around. 'Don't be an ass, Inspector. Lady Ione has returned, hasn't she?'

'Wanted for questioning,' said Crummle doggedly.

'By Alec – the Chief Inspector – not you. I believe you have been urgently summoned to take over a new case.'

He scowled. Without another word, he stalked to the front door. Daisy heaved a sigh of relief as he disappeared, with luck for good. Alec would get on much better without him.

'Thank you,' said Lady Ione gaily. 'I suppose he wanted to arrest me for Aunt Eva's murder?'

'I'm not sure that he was actually contemplating an arrest, but you must admit it looked a bit fishy when you departed so abruptly. Especially after your pronouncement at breakfast.'

'Yes, when you put it like that, I can see I ought at least to have told someone where I was going. When one is suddenly and unexpectedly released from prison, one rather loses sight of common sense. I should have held my tongue in the first place.'

'You'd have had to give Alec some explanation in any case. Of your transformation, I mean. He'd hardly credit that it's unconnected with the murder.'

'Alec?' Lady Ione's cheerful insouciance began to give way to uneasiness.

'My husband, Detective Chief Inspector Alec Fletcher. Of course, you don't know, your father had Alec called in to head the investigation.'

'He won't think I killed her, will he? Just because I went shopping?'

'Not exactly "just because",' Daisy pointed out.

'I didn't do it, you know. After twenty-five years, why should I choose this moment?'

'If you didn't do it, you have nothing to worry about, but you must see you'll have to explain.'

'I can't! For twenty-five years, I've danced to Aunt Eva's tune to stop her telling! How can I turn around now and bare my soul to a policeman?'

'Well,' said Daisy doubtfully, 'I dare say he doesn't actually need the details. You could try just saying she knew something you didn't want broadcast to the world. Not that he'd broadcast it if he did know. Policemen have to be frightfully discreet.'

'And policemen's wives likewise, no doubt. Oh, they're taking her away. The endless nightmare is really over.'

Daisy looked round. The stretcher-bearers had put their canvas and poles together and were stolidly carrying their burden across the hall under Tom's vigilant eye.

'Oh, that's not Lady Eva,' she said. 'Gosh, I forgot, you don't know about that, either.'

Behind the delicate cosmetics, Lady Ione turned alarmingly pale. 'What? . . . Who? . . .'

'I think you'd better come and sit down.' Daisy led her unresisting to the anteroom.

Opening the door, she saw that it was a small room only by Haverhill standards, but crammed with furniture, massive Victorian stuff perhaps moved out of the family sitting room upstairs. She was well inside before she saw Constable Stebbins, sitting bootless, tenderly massaging one foot in its darned regulation sock.

Daisy hastily turned Lady Ione to face away from him, while gesturing at him behind her back to get out. Her ladyship didn't seem to have noticed him.

'Who?' she asked again, sitting down and looking up at Daisy, all the newfound animation gone from her face.

'I'm afraid it's Lord Fotheringay.'

'Aubrey! No! But why would anyone want to kill poor Aubrey?'

'That's what Alec is trying to find out.' Daisy failed to mention the possibility that Lady Ione's brother had died naturally. 'Which is why it's so important for you to tell him everything you can bear to. One can never guess which details may turn out to be vital.'

'All right, for Aubrey's sake I'll talk to him. But . . . would it be too much to ask you to come with me?'

'Not at all,' said Daisy. 'I'm sure you'd like to get it over with. Shall we go right away?'

CHAPTER 11

Daisy and Lady Ione, entering the library, met Sir Leonard leaving. Standing aside, he bowed to Daisy and gave Lady Ione a curious look. As they went on, Daisy glanced back to see him staring after her ladyship with a puzzled frown.

No doubt half her relatives would be equally confused the first time they saw her. Alec, never having met the original Lady Ione, merely regarded Daisy with irritation.

Before he could snap at her, she said, 'Darling, I've brought Lady Ione to see you. She just arrived home. Lady Ione, my husband.'

'How do you do, Mr Fletcher.' Her ladyship's composure was admirable.

'Good evening, Lady Ione.' Alec was icily polite. 'Won't you sit down? I trust you intend to explain . . . What is it, Baines?'

The door that had just closed on the Chief Constable opened again to admit the butler. As he crossed the room, he said, 'His lordship's compliments, sir, and he hopes that, although he himself will not come down to dinner, you will dine with the family.'

'Please convey my thanks to Lord Haverhill, but if it will not inconvenience the staff, I and my men will dine in here. We have much to discuss.'

'As you wish, sir.' Baines had come close enough to get a

good look at Lady Ione. Without a twitch of an eyebrow he continued, 'Does your ladyship wish me to inform his lordship of your ladyship's return?'

'No, Baines, I'll go up to Father before dinner?'

'Very well, my lady.' The butler bowed himself out. Alec raised his dark eyebrows at Lady Ione and she rushed into speech.

'I'm sorry. I was too excited to think about anything but going up to town to do some shopping. I didn't realize the police would want me to stay.'

'Let me get this straight. Your aunt is murdered and your only thought is to go shopping?'

Her tone hardened. 'Should I have pretended to grieve? Aunt Eva ruined my life. I was nineteen when I . . . made a mistake. She found out about it and threatened to tell if I . . . didn't behave as she thought I ought. And she never really explained what she wanted so I had to measure up to an invisible ideal.'

'A mistake?'

'I cannot see that the details matter. I've admitted to hating and fearing my aunt. Isn't that enough? I didn't kill her. Perhaps I should have, twenty-five years ago?'

Alec's voice gentled. 'Lady Ione, you are the only person so far who has had the courage to admit to being blackmailed by Lady Eva. We have her memoranda, so there are no secrets. We haven't had time yet to go as far back as twenty-five years. If we knew exactly what your offence was, in her eyes, and what use she made of the information, we would have a much better idea of how others might have been affected?'

'And thus, who might have had a motive for killing her? But I don't particularly want you to find her murderer.'

'Already there has been another death.'

'My poor brother!'

'We don't know for certain whether it was foul play, but once a person has killed to solve a problem, he often finds it immeasurably easier the second time. Are you willing to risk a third?'

'N-no. But I can't . . . !' Lady Ione looked from Alec to Tom, to young Piper in his inconspicuous corner, notebook and pencil in hand. 'Suppose I tell Mrs Fletcher? That wouldn't be half as bad. Then she could tell you.'

Knowing Alec so well, Daisy could see him suppressing a sigh of resignation. 'Very well.' He smiled at Lady Ione. 'It's past time we had women detectives on the force.'

Daisy and Lady Ione retired to the other end of the room. A couple of comfortable reading chairs enveloped them. Lady Ione leaned back with a weary sigh.

'I had forgotten how tiring a day of shopping for clothes in London can be. Or perhaps I never knew. I was young . . . As you are undoubtedly aware,' she said dryly, 'I am not accustomed to spending time or money on my dress.'

'That's part of the story, isn't it?'

'Yes. The easy part.'

'Would it help if I pointed out that my generation doesn't have quite the same view of life as Lady Eva's? The war . . .' To her annoyance, Daisy found herself blinking back tears. 'The war changed things.'

'You lost someone.'

'Gervaise – my brother. And my fiancé, Michael. When someone you love is going off into such deadly danger, you never again have quite the same view of the rules.'

'I was in love. He was an artist, handsome, dashing, charming, and definitely not out of the top drawer, as the current phrase has it, but one met him everywhere. He was beginning to make a name for himself as a fashionable portrait painter.'

'He painted your portrait?'

'A cliché, isn't it? But no, as it happened he painted a friend of mine. Her aunt was bringing her out, and perhaps was not as careful a chaperon as her mother would have been. At any rate, the two of us went to a sitting without her one day when she had some other engagement. Needless to say, my mother was under the impression that she was with us.'

'It must have been simply frightful,' said Daisy, with a shudder, 'never going anywhere without a chaperon.'

'In those days, we took it for granted. But for my friend's sittings, we continued to chaperon each other, without her aunt. By the time the portrait was finished, I was besotted. My mother had become accustomed to my regular meetings with my friend and did not realize when I started to go alone. That, of course, was when . . . things happened.'

'Of course.'

'To cut a long story short, we pretended to have met at a party, he asked my father's permission to marry me, and Father said no. That would have been the end of that, if Aunt Eva had not put two and two together. She heard Mother mention that I was accompanying my friend to sittings after she had seen the finished portrait. No one else would have put those two scraps of information together, but it was grist to Aunt Eva's mill.'

'She didn't pass on her discovery to your parents, though?'

'No, that would have been to give away her power over me.'

'What on earth did she say when she tackled you?'

'I was not fit to be a decent man's wife. If I made any attempt to attract a suitor, she would tell my parents. And if any gentleman should pursue me with serious intentions, she would warn him, even though it would bring disgrace on the family.'

'Gosh, I am glad times have changed. Not that I'm in favour of promiscuity,' Daisy added hastily, 'but to be damned for ever for one slip . . . And not being able to marry a man because your parents disapprove! Mother disapproved of Alec, but I just took no notice. So that's why you retired from the world and went all dowdy.'

'I couldn't think what else to do. Everyone assumed I was pining because Father banned the marriage.'

'Were you? Are you? No, sorry, it's frightfully impertinent of me to ask.'

'When you've been so kind as to listen . . . You're the first person I've ever been able to talk to about this. I did pine for a little while, until I heard that he had got another girl into trouble. He went on to lead a very wild life and die young. So, you see, my father was right.' Lady Ione sighed. 'All the same, if not for Aunt Eva, I might have found someone else to love.'

'Her behaviour was infamous! I wonder how many others she has treated as badly.'

'I hope I'm not the only person suspected of her murder.'

Looking over to where Alec and Tom were poring over Ernie Piper's sheaf of notes, Daisy said, 'Not by a long way. Don't worry, I'll give Alec a very abbreviated version of your story, but I'm sure he'll be more interested in people with more immediate reasons to wish Lady Eva dead. You'd better wait in case he has any further questions.'

'Your husband – What will he think of me?'

'Oh, Alec's somewhere in the middle. He winces when Lucy swears but doesn't believe in the concept of the "fallen woman".'

Lady Ione smiled faintly. 'That's the very phrase Aunt Eva used.'

'Believe me, he sees much worse all the time.' Daisy patted her shoulder and went over to the desk. In a couple of sentences, she gave Alec the gist of Lady Ione's story.

'Great Scott, if that's the sort of use Lady Eva made of her collection, I'm surprised she wasn't done in years ago.'

'Ah,' said Tom ruminatively. 'It's one thing to bully a young girl. Some of these others wouldn't stand for it. Well done, Mrs Fletcher.'

'Yes, thanks, Daisy. It's a great help to know that Lady Eva didn't always just sit on her information. And now you'll be wanting to go and change for dinner.'

'How diplomatic of you, darling. I know when I'm not wanted.'

She went with him over to Lady Ione, Piper following with his notebook. Alec thanked her for her cooperation and asked for information about her movements that afternoon. 'We'll check,' he said, 'but assuming what you say is corroborated, we can at least acquit you of your brother's death, if he was in fact murdered.'

'All the same, I hope the poor old boy went naturally. Aubrey was the best of my brothers.'

Behind them the telephone bell rang. Tom unhooked the receiver. 'It's your call, Chief.'

'That was quick. Excuse me, ladies.'

Daisy and Lady Ione went out into the hall. Lucy was lurking, unconvincingly gazing at one of the non-ancestral portraits. Hearing their steps she swung round.

'Darling, I've been waiting . . .' Mouth open, she stared at Daisy's companion. 'Good Lord, Aunt Ione?'

'In the flesh,' said that lady dryly. She turned to Daisy.

'Thank you for everything, Mrs Fletcher. I hope it helps your husband. I like him.' With a nod to Lucy, she went off, her Cuban heels tapping on the marble floor.

Lucy looked after her. 'But Aunt Ione always wears lace-ups! And frumpy frocks with crooked hems and those ghastly mud-coloured cardigans she knits herself. What on earth has come over her?'

'You might say she's growing young.'

'But why?'

Daisy didn't choose to answer. 'You've been waiting for me?' she asked.

Fortunately Lucy was not really interested in her aunt. 'For ages. I've told Binkie I'm not going to marry him. The poor lamb can't believe I mean it. Will you try to explain to him that it's not his fault, I just don't want to be married?'

'I'll talk to him.' Daisy carefully avoided specifics of what she would say. 'Where is he?'

'In the drawing room, doing the polite.'

'Have you told anyone else the wedding is off?'

'No. It would be too much for the parents and grandparents on top of everything else. Don't spread the word, will you?'

'Of course not.'

'Daisy, why would anyone kill Uncle Aubrey? I can understand Aunt Eva, sort of, but why Uncle Aubrey?'

'Alec thinks he may have seen something which could lead to Lady Eva's murderer. Or at least, the murderer may think he saw something.'

'How frightful! The murderer might imagine the same about any of us.'

'Yes. Which is why you must give Alec any help you can, instead of being so offhand about the whole thing.'

'I don't feel at all offhand about Uncle Aubrey.'

'Good. Once you've made a clean breast of everything you know, there's no further reason to do you in.'

'Beast!' Lucy shuddered. 'Now I don't want to wait till he sends for me again. Not that I know anything useful, but shall I go and see him now?'

'He'll need a proper statement sometime, but I shouldn't disturb him just now, not if you haven't anything in particular to tell him.'

'I'll try my luck. After all, I'm one of his chief suspects, because of the will. Make sure everyone knows I'm spilling the beans, will you? I don't fancy a poisoned cup of tea.'

'You don't want me to hold your hand?'

'No, thanks, darling. Go and hold Binkie's.'

She turned towards the library and Daisy went on towards the drawing room.

Of course Lucy hadn't killed Lady Eva. Unlike a Victorian 'young girl', in Tom's words, a modern young woman wouldn't meekly put up with such browbeating, but she would ignore it, not resort to murder – unless Lady Eva had discovered something a whole lot more serious than a brief *affaire*.

CHAPTER 12

In the spacious drawing room, Daisy found many of the family assembled in gloomy huddles. Perhaps there was a feeling of safety in numbers. Alec had forbidden them to leave, yet after two deaths, tennis or bridge would hardly be decent. The dressing bell, still customary at Haverhill, had not yet rung. The hour was too early for cocktails, which Daisy was sure many were longing for.

Binkie was being talked at by Angela. He hastily extricated himself and came to meet Daisy. His usual calm taciturnity was not now in evidence. 'Daisy, what's this maggot Lucy's got into her head about not marrying me? What have I done?'

'It's not anything you've done. She just—'

'I've managed to get hold of the latest prototype Leica camera for her, to prove I mean to let her go on with her photography. Now I daren't give it to her in case she thinks it's a bribe. Can't you persuade her to give me another chance?'

'I'm sorry, Binkie, I—'

'Don't call me Binkie!' he said wildly. 'Please don't. It's an asinine nickname. How can she take me seriously when people call me Binkie?'

'I'm sorry. Gerald, then. Look, we can't talk here.' She saw

Sally approaching from one side and Flora from the other, with Jennifer hovering nearby. 'Later.'

'Meet me in the conservatory after dinner.'

'Right-oh.' Daisy wasn't keen on returning to the scene of Lord Fotheringay's death, but on the spur of the moment she couldn't think of anywhere else almost certain to be private.

She turned to Sally, whom she hadn't seen since breakfast. The new Lady Fotheringay was pale and drawn. Her black frock was the sort that can be dressed up for any occasion with the right scarf, belt, and jewellery. Worn plain, for mourning, it didn't suit her at all.

'It's disgraceful!' she snapped before Daisy could express condolences. 'My mother-in-law and Lord and Lady Haverhill are distraught over this ridiculous suggestion that my father-in-law's death was not natural. The police have no business making such unfounded assertions, just to make themselves look more important.'

'I assure you, Alec would not—'

'Do dry up, Sally!' Flora's discreet make-up could not hide the angry flags flying in her cheeks. No love lost between the sisters-in-law, Daisy noted. 'You're only making a dreadful situation worse. The police are doing all they can, and if they weren't, Mrs Fletcher's not to blame.'

'It's all very upsetting,' said Daisy soothingly. 'I shan't take offence.'

'Well!' Perhaps Sally had intended to give offence. At any rate, she flounced off.

'How can anyone with such an impeccable pedigree be so thoroughly ill-bred?' said Flora. 'You'd think my brother had picked her up at some music hall's stage door. I wish he would hurry up and come home to keep her under control.'

'He rules the roost?'

'Oh, yes, absolutely. Rupert is quite prepared to exert himself for his own comfort. I think at first he found her shrewishness amusing, but when she started alienating the wives of his fellow officers, he put his foot down. She definitely dances to his tune. Mind you, he can't be easy to live with.'

'No?'

'He's very expensive, and he finds it humiliating to keep coming with his hand out to Grandfather. He likes to entertain, so Sally has to keep up appearances, but I know for a fact that she has to do more than her share of scrimping and saving. I doubt her family helps. It's one of those ancient lineages with lots of blue blood but no money.'

'Did Lord Haverhill help you when you started your business? Not that it's any affair of mine, but I was thinking I'd like to write an article, maybe even a series, about women running their own businesses.'

'There are plenty of us since the war. I'll be happy to talk about it, but not just now.'

'No, I'm sorry, it's the wrong moment. I haven't had a chance to say how sorry I am about your father.'

'Daddy of all people!' Flora was once again furiously angry. 'He was the kindest, gentlest person I've ever known. Your husband *is* going to find out what happened, isn't he? I told him I'll do anything in my power to help.'

'Do you know anything that might help?'

'Not that I can think of. Oh Lord, here comes Rupert.'

The new Lord Fotheringay was tall, broad-shouldered, with the sweeping moustache and the ramrod-straight swagger expected of a Household Cavalry officer. The crown and star of a lieutenant colonel adorned his khaki battle-dress, presumably donned for the regimental manoeuvres he had abandoned to rush home. He was young for the rank, but so many officers of the Life Guards had died in Flanders that those who survived advanced rapidly.

'Do you know him, Daisy?' asked Flora, watching in disgust as Sally ran to her husband and flung herself into his arms, sobbing.

'I met him when I came to visit with Lucy from school. We thought he was the last word in dashing young men. I'd be surprised if he remembered me.'

Rupert bowed his head to speak softly in his wife's ear. When he looked up, his great-uncle Montagu was bearing down on them. With an impatient gesture, Rupert said something to the old gentleman, then steered Sally out of the room with a hand under her elbow.

Montagu turned away, flushed and crestfallen. Daisy was surprised to see him after his distraught state in the morning. He seemed to have recovered his equilibrium, so much so that she couldn't help wondering whether his earlier shock and horror had been real. Suppose he had been so assiduous at passing on his club gossip to Lady Eva only because she was blackmailing him?

Daisy wished she had access to Ernie Piper's notes, just so she could narrow down the field of suspects. For all she knew, the murderer could be absolutely anyone who had been in the house last night.

'Rupert is the absolute pink limit!' said Flora, exasperated. 'I'd better go and see if I can smooth Uncle Montagu's ruffled feathers without suggesting my brother's rudeness is my fault.'

As Flora left, several possible murderers converged upon Daisy.

Nancy: no, she couldn't believe Lucy's sister-in-law had a guilty secret she'd kill to protect. Tim was probably still providing his suddenly widowed aunt Maud with the consolations of religion.

Lord and Lady Carleton: Daisy still hadn't worked out just what their relationship to the Haverhills was. She was simply not well enough acquainted with them to hazard a guess as to whether they might have any guilty secrets.

Mr and Mrs Bancroft: as Lady Eva's granddaughter and grandson-in-law, they must be high on Alec's list, but they claimed not to have expected an inheritance. Daisy disliked Mrs Bancroft because of her scorn for her sister Angela, but her dislike was not enough to brand the woman a murderer, alas. How easy that would make a murder investigation!

Jennifer Walsdorf reached her first. 'Lord Gerald says he's going to stay the night. I take it your husband will share your room?'

'If he's not up all night interviewing people.'

'What about the sergeant and the young man who just arrived? Mrs Maple, the housekeeper, has never had to provide accommodations for the police before and she's twittering about where to put them.'

'They usually stay at the nearest inn.'

'Oh, I'm sure Lord Haverhill would want to give them a bed.'

'Then consider Mr Tring on a level with a visiting valet, I should think, and DC Piper as a footman. Though I don't suppose they'd mind sharing a room.'

'A valet wouldn't lower himself to share with a footman!' Jennifer said with an effortful smile. 'But in any case, they can have a room each. We've plenty of space as John has managed to stop most people turning up. Those who arrived in time for lunch have already buzzed off again, with the permission of the police.'

'John's very efficient.'

'I wish Rupert would recognize that fact. Still, we've always known we couldn't stay here forever. Poor Uncle Aubrey's death has just hastened the inevitable.'

Nancy Fotheringay had come up in time to hear Jennifer's words. 'You and John and the baby will always be welcome at the vicarage,' she said tranquilly. 'It's a huge old place, far bigger than we need.'

'We don't want charity.'

'We're not too far from London. John is bound to find work quickly. And you can help me with the children and the parish work, if you like. There is always too much to do.'

'You're an angel, Nancy!' Jennifer kissed her on the cheek. 'It will be a big relief to have somewhere to lay our heads, however temporary, when the moment comes. Now, I know you want to talk to Daisy, and I must go and confer with Mrs Maple.'

'Will Rupert really turn them out when he inherits?' Daisy asked Nancy as soon as Jennifer was out of earshot.

'It wouldn't surprise me. Rupert has a mean streak in him. But Timmy would say I'm being un-Christian. Daisy, Tim asked me to ask you whether your husband can say with any certainty whether Uncle Aubrey died a natural death or not. It might be some consolation to his poor aunt to know that he was not cut off before his time.'

'Alec doesn't tell me much,' Daisy said cautiously, 'and he won't commit himself till he has the post-mortem results, but I believe he has evidence that points to murder.'

'Oh, we're none of us safe!' Lady Carleton moaned. The others had crowded around by now, and Nancy slipped away. 'Denzil, you must insist that the police let us take Ursula home.'

'Mr Fletcher might be persuaded to let us have Tomkins drive her home,' said Lord Carleton, a sallow, long-faced man at least twenty years older than his wife. 'We'll have to stick it out, though, old girl.'

Her ladyship's lips pursed, whether at this form of address or at the notion of letting her daughter go off with their chauffeur. 'I suppose you don't care if *I'm* murdered,' she said sulkily.

'What we must do,' said Peter Bancroft, 'is stick together. Never go anywhere alone, then the devil can't get you.'

'The devil is one of us, old boy,' Lord Carleton reminded him.

'It must have been an intruder,' said Veronica Bancroft petulantly. 'The police ought to have found traces of someone breaking in by now.'

'One murder might have been an intruder, Ronnie.' Angela and her faithful shadow had joined the group. 'Two must be one of us.'

'I keep telling you not to call me Ronnie! And if it's one of us, you have the best motive I know. You only care about those wretched curs of yours, not about people. I wouldn't put it past you to murder Grandmother to get her money for the horrid beasts.'

'Now, Veronica!' Peter remonstrated weakly.

Astonishingly, Tiddler summoned up the courage to snarl at his rescuer's sister, from his safe haven behind Angela's ankles.

Veronica backed away. 'Get rid of it!' she shrilled.

Teddy Devenish, arriving, stooped to give the little dog an approving pat. 'Know thine enemy,' he said with a grin. 'Clever little scrap, Angie.'

'Peter!' Veronica appealed to her husband.

'Nothing to do with me. He's your brother.'

The Carletons and Daisy abstracted themselves from the brewing sibling strife. Daisy was immediately pounced upon by Lucy's mother.

'Daisy dear, do you know where Lucinda is? I simply can't find her anywhere.'

'Yes, Aunt Vickie, she's with Alec.'

'Oh!' Mrs Fotheringay turned white. 'Oh no! They've arrested Lucinda?'

When Lucy entered the library, Alec was annoyed. He hadn't yet had a chance to telephone Teddy Devenish's friends in Hampshire, and if he was ever granted a moment's peace to study Ernie's list of names, he'd want to interview those on it, not Lucy, whom he'd already seen. She had not been cooperative, and he wouldn't be surprised if she had now come with a complaint. He wasn't at all sure he could summon up the politeness to deal with her as he ought.

'What can I do for you?' he asked impatiently.

'I've come to see if I can do anything for you,' she said with her customary aplomb. 'You didn't really ask me any questions before.'

Because she had walked out, as Alec managed to refrain from saying. 'You had a rendezvous with your intended.'

'Who found Uncle Aubrey. Aunt Eva was one thing – you may think we're all frightfully callous, but no one mourned her much. Uncle Aubrey was different. Besides, two murders . . . Suppose there's a third? So if answering your questions will help you find out who it was, ask away.'

While they spoke, Ernie Piper had reached for his list and turned to the second page. Now he replaced it on the desk in front of Alec, his finger pointing at a name. Alec glanced down.

'What's that?' Lucy demanded. 'You know now I'm not the murderer. I was with you when Uncle Aubrey died.'

'Lord Gerald was with him.'

'But Binkie wasn't here when . . . Oh Lord, you think we're hand in glove? That I killed Aunt Eva and he killed Uncle Aubrey?'

'I have to consider the possibility. Why did he turn up today when he was not expected until Friday?'

'I telephoned and asked him to come.'

'You see, you could have told him you were afraid Lord Fotheringay knew something which might lead us to suspect you.'

'But I didn't. I just wanted to tell him something I couldn't say over the phone.'

'What?' Alec asked bluntly.

Lucy bit her lip. 'If you must know, that I wasn't going to marry him after all.'

Startled, Alec made a quick recovery and shot back, 'Why not?'

'Because with Aunt Eva's legacy, I'll be able to . . .' Her voice tailed off and she pressed her fingers to her lips.

'To live comfortably without him?'

'Yes,' she whispered, but with a defiant lift of her chin. Then she caught sight of her fingertips and stared in horror at the lip-rouge smeared there, the bright crimson of blood.

Alec forebore to state the obvious, that her admission confirmed a financial motive for Lady Eva's death. 'Lord Gerald is devoted to you,' he said, 'and when he arrived at Haverhill, he didn't yet know of your change of heart.' He paused, but she made no comment. He picked up the list of Ernie's gleanings from Lady Eva's files. 'I have here evidence of an additional reason for your wishing to rid yourself of your great-aunt.'

'Oh? What's that?' Lucy leant forward, interested, unalarmed.

'Something you most certainly wouldn't have wanted broadcast to the world.'

'It wasn't Aunt Eva's way to broadcast scandal to the world. I haven't done anything desperately wicked, and she never mentioned anything to me. What is it?'

Ernie bowed his head over his notebook. Tom took a sudden interest in his fingernails.

'You spent a night with Lord Gerald in his rooms.'

A tinge of pink crept into Lucy's cheeks, the first time Alec had ever seen her blush. 'Well? This is 1924, not 1884. We're ... We were going to be married shortly.'

'Were. I rather doubt you'd want your parents or grandparents informed.'

'Oh, as to that, Mummy would have been upset, but everything I do upsets her. Grandfather would have refused to finance a grand wedding. I never wanted one.'

'You claim Lady Eva never spoke to you about her knowledge?'

'She didn't. I suppose, compared to some of the things she dug out about people, it was a minor peccadillo.'

'Because you were going to be married shortly. But you

changed your mind. She might have written you out of her will.'

'I didn't change my mind until after she died. Oh hell, Alec, you don't really believe I killed her? Just to avoid marrying Binkie? I'm actually quite fond of him.'

Alec sighed. 'It's not for me to believe or disbelieve. The evidence is all that counts. All I can say is that you're not the only person with more than one possible motive. What do you know about the plants in your uncle's conservatory?'

'Not much.' Lucy looked slightly puzzled, not at all alarmed. 'I took the tour whenever I came to stay, but just to please the old boy. I'm afraid I paid very little attention.'

'So you didn't know that some of the plants are poisonous.'

'Oh, yes. It was drummed into us very thoroughly as children, by Uncle Aubrey, nannies, parents, aunts and uncles. No one who visited as a child could possibly fail to know. But I'd be surprised if many of us remember which particular plants are poisonous. I certainly don't. Was Uncle Aubrey poisoned with his own greenery? How vile! It seems crass, somehow.'

'Murder is always vile and generally crass, whether the victim is an inoffensive person like Lord Fotheringay or . . .'

'Or an offensive person like Aunt Eva. She really was a nasty old busybody, wasn't she?' Lucy said with an air of detachment. 'I wonder how she found out about me and Binkie. It's not terribly surprising someone got fed up enough to stop her prying for good.'

'Your room is close to hers. Did you hear any sounds in the night – footsteps, a cry, a door opening or closing?'

'Not a thing. I've been sleeping badly, because of this blasted wedding, and Mummy was worried I'd look haggish on Saturday so she made me take a powder last night.'

'Great Scott, Lucy,' Alec exploded, 'why the deuce didn't you tell me right away?'

'That I took a sleeping powder? Oh, I suppose I couldn't have been creeping around murdering great-aunts after taking a bromide.'

'Did your mother watch you swallow it?'

'She mixed it with milk and practically poured it down my throat.'

At last a chance to knock one suspect off his list. Alec jumped up. 'Right-oh, you stay here and answer Mr Tring's questions while I find Mrs Fotheringay.'

'Mummy's known as Mrs Oliver here,' corrected Lucy obligingly. 'Too many Mrs Fotheringays.'

'I couldn't agree more. Where is Mrs Oliver likely to be?'

'The drawing room or upstairs, I expect.'

Alec strode across the hall and entered the drawing room to find a crowd in the middle of the room, the outer members craning to see over the shoulders of those in front. Amidst a confused babble, someone said clearly, 'Stand back, for heaven's sake, and give her air.'

His heart stood still. Another murder?

CHAPTER 13

'What's going on here?'

Daisy heard the question, recognized Alec's voice, but at the same time she was patting Aunt Vickie's hand while Binkie – no, Gerald – fanned her with a magazine, beseeching, 'Daisy, Fletcher hasn't really arrested Lucy, has he?' Oliver knelt on the floor on the other side of the chair where the limp, white-faced woman slumped, patting her other hand.

'I keep telling her,' Daisy said, 'she went to see him entirely off her own bat.'

The crowd parted and Alec came through.

'Thank heaven!' said Daisy. 'Aunt Vickie, here's Alec now. Darling, tell her you haven't arrested Lucy!'

'Mrs Fotheringay, I have not arrested Lucy. I have one question to put to you.' With his dark, fierce eyebrows lowered in one of his most forbidding frowns, he gazed around the faces all agog surrounding them. 'Privately.'

The surplus population melted away, going to stand about the room in twos and threes muttering together with many a sidelong glance.

'I shall stay with my wife,' declared Oliver, rising creakily from his knees.

'By all means, sir.'

'Daisy!' said Mrs Oliver faintly, gripping Daisy's hand.

'I shan't leave you, Aunt Vickie.' Daisy looked up at Alec with a lively interest mixed with a trace of concern. He had not arrested Lucy, but that didn't mean he was not about to.

Alec raised his eyebrows at Gerald.

'Oh, righty-ho,' said that gentleman in confusion, and retreated to hover in no-man's-land.

'Mrs Fotheringay, did you go to your daughter's bedroom last night?'

'Why, yes.' A tinge of colour was returning to Aunt Vickie's face, to Daisy's relief. Nancy appeared with a glass of brandy, pressed it into her hand, and discreetly retreated. 'Lucinda hasn't been sleeping well, you see, so I got a powder from my sister-in-law—'

'Your sister-in-law?'

'Oliver's sister-in-law, really. Marjorie, Henry's wife. She suffers from neuralgia – hardly surprising, the way those girls of hers squabble – and always has bromides by her in case she can't sleep. I took one to Lucinda, and a glass of warm milk. She didn't want to take it, but I mixed the powder into the milk and made her drink it, to the last drop.'

'What did you do with the glass?'

'I rinsed it at the basin in the bathroom and left it there.' She sniffed the brandy, wrinkled her nose, and handed it to Oliver, who took a gulp.

'I saw it this morning!' said Daisy. 'I share a bathroom with Lucy. I was going to use it to brush my teeth but it looked sort of murky, you know, the way a milk glass does if it's not washed thoroughly. Darling, this means you can cross Lucy off your list.'

'I must have a word with Mrs Henry. Is she here?'

'Yes, I'll fetch her over, shall I?' Oliver offered.

'No, point her out to me, if you don't mind.'

Alec went off to confirm the story.

'Does this mean he doesn't suspect Lucinda any longer?' Aunt Vickie asked, hopeful yet fearful.

'He just has to ask Mrs Henry about the dosage and that sort of thing. You're all right now, aren't you? I'd better go and put poor Gerald out of his misery.'

Gerald was on tenterhooks. 'Fletcher doesn't really believe Lucy's involved in this beastly business, does he?' he demanded.

'What he believes has nothing to do with it. He has to look at the facts, and Lucy is one of Lady Eva's heirs. He's delighted to clear her, I promise you.'

'She's in the clear, what?'

'As good as. I doubt Alec's suspicions would stretch as far as a conspiracy between Lucy, Aunt Vickie, and Mrs Henry.'

'Must have suspected Lucy and me of conspiring,' Gerald pointed out. 'Lucy couldn't have killed her uncle. I couldn't have killed Lady Eva.'

'True.'

'If Lucy's cleared, so am I. Here he comes. What-ho, Fletcher?'

'What-ho, Bincombe,' Alec returned genially. 'You and Lucy are out of it, I'm glad to say. I don't suppose you've remembered seeing anything out of the ordinary when you entered the conservatory?'

'Sorry, old chap. Told you, I saw Lord Fotheringay lying there and as soon as I realized he was not breathing I concentrated on trying to revive him.'

'But you've had time to think about it since. Even the slightest impression of some small detail might help.'

Gerald flushed. 'Other things to think about,' he muttered.

'Well, put your mind to it, there's a good fellow. If anything occurs to you, come and see me right away.'

Over Alec's shoulder, Daisy saw Sally and Rupert approaching. 'Watch out, darling,' she murmured, 'the fire-breathing Lieutenant Colonel is upon us.'

'My husband, Mrs Fletcher,' Sally introduced him. She looked nervous and Daisy wondered whether she had felt the rough side of his tongue.

'How do you do, Colonel. I don't suppose you remember me, Lucy's friend? I was Daisy Dalrymple when I last visited Haverhill.'

'Afraid not.' Cold, arrogant eyes passed over her indifferently. 'How do you do.'

'This is my husband, Alec Fletcher. And do you know Gerald Bincombe?'

'Bincombe.' Rupert gave Gerald a cursory nod of recognition, which was returned in kind, without cordiality on either side. He turned to Alec. 'Well, Inspector,' he said with a sneer, 'I see you are hard at work hunting down my great-aunt's murderer.'

'And your father's,' Alec responded levelly.

'Oh, as to that, you're wasting your time. I'm sure you'll find it's a mare's nest. My father was in poor health. But I suppose the kudos is greater if you can claim to have solved two murders rather than one.'

'On the contrary. Two murders are often easier to solve than one. A second death by the same hand is apt to provide clues which aid in solving the first.'

'Ah, so that's why you're hoping Father was murdered.'

'I never hope for any man's damnation.' Alec's grey eyes were icy. The look that made subordinates shiver, suspects shudder, and malefactors wish they were at the North Pole had its effect on the Lieutenant Colonel, who blinked, visibly taken aback. 'And now, if you'll excuse me, I have work to do.'

Daisy went out to the hall with Alec. 'That was a ripping line,' she congratulated him, 'though I'm not absolutely sure what you meant by it.'

'Nor am I!' he admitted with a rueful laugh. 'I suppose I had it in mind that disposing of Lady Eva might conceivably be viewed as a form of self-defence, but there's no possible justification for Lord Fotheringay's murder.'

'So doing him in would damn the murderer.'

'Something like that. Not a suitable conjecture for a policeman. My job is to make a present of him to the courts for judgment, not to St Peter. Daisy, now you've had a chance to think about it, you're quite certain no one was about here in the hall when you and Lucy went to the conservatory? You didn't catch a glimpse of anyone on the terrace?'

Daisy shook her head regretfully. 'Sorry, darling. Whoever put the stuff in the tea had plenty of time to get away. Gerald had been working on the poor old chap for several minutes before we arrived. I'm sure he was too engrossed in his artificial respiration to notice much else.'

'If he did see anything, it's been driven from his mind by this nonsense of Lucy's,' Alec grumbled. 'She's not serious about calling it all off, is she?'

'Just at present, yes. Tomorrow, who knows?'

'It's not like her to be so indecisive.'

'She's just confused.'

'No doubt that's why she didn't mention having taken a bromide until I asked whether she'd heard any sounds in the night.'

'She's not used to being involved in police investigations,' Daisy excused her friend.

'At least I've eliminated her and Bincombe, which is about all I've accomplished so far!'

'Cheer up, darling. It may seem like forever but you've only been here a few hours, and you've had an extra murder on your hands.'

'Which, according to what I told the gallant Lieutenant Colonel, will make my job easier. I should have kept my mouth shut.'

'Impossible!'

'Yes.' He gave her a rueful grin. 'But a policeman ought to find it possible. You're giving me ideas above my station. I shan't be able to expect any cooperation from him now.'

'You couldn't have anyway. Luckily, he wasn't here, and his grandfather is still in charge at Haverhill.'

'True. I'd better go and see if Tom has managed to retrieve any further information that Lucy didn't think to give us. And you'd better go and lie down for a bit before dinner, love. You're looking a little worn.'

'Two murders in one day is a trifle wearing,' Daisy admitted, standing on tiptoe to kiss Alec on the nose. Then she went upstairs to put her feet up and try to work out how she was going to explain Lucy's state of mind to Gerald after dinner when she didn't understand it herself and wasn't sure Lucy did.

Alec returned to the library. Lucy looked round and raised elegantly arched eyebrows.

'All confirmed,' he said. 'It's not that I doubted you, Lucy, but . . .'

'I know, Sergeant Tring has explained to me that you'll have to explain to the Chief Constable why you haven't arrested me.

I'm afraid I haven't remembered seeing or hearing anything or anyone. We've been trying to work out what Uncle Aubrey could have observed that might have led you to Aunt Eva's murderer. It's a bit of a puzzler.'

'We haven't had time to put our minds to it, Chief, but Lord Fotheringay slept in the family wing, the other side of the house from the scene of the crime.'

'Your uncle wasn't a nocturnal rambler?'

'For all I know he came down every night to make sure his plants were tucked up cosily in their beddy-byes. But the straightforward way would be down the main stairs and across the hall, not round by the guest bedrooms.'

'Hmm, it's something we'll have to consider later, when I can talk to Lady Fotheringay. In the meantime, I have a long list of people to see this evening, so . . .'

'So I'll take my leave, before you change your mind and bring out the handcuffs.' Lucy rose, then hesitated, the flippant manner dropping away. 'It has to be one of my relatives, doesn't it?'

'I'm sorry.'

'I don't hold you to blame,' Lucy said wryly. She gestured at the list on the desk. 'If that's what I assume it is, we have enough secrets between us to furnish a dozen motives.'

She left and Alec had peace at last to delve into her family's secrets. He resumed scanning the list where he had left off, then started at the top again.

'Edward Devenish and his divorcée.' Alec reached for the telephone. 'I must put in a call to his pals in Hampshire.'

Tom flipped through his notebook, but Ernie Piper beat him to it. 'Hetheridge, Chief, Bill Hetheridge, Danesbury House, Nether Wallop.'

Alec asked the operator to find the number, ring through, and call him back. He went back to the list. 'Sir James Devenish, prosecuted for assault and battery for horse-whipping a farmer who shot a fox ravaging his hen-house.'

'Five pounds or sixty days,' said Piper. 'He paid, of course. Hefty damages, too.'

'Actual bodily harm, that's aggravated assault,' said Tom. 'He should have done time for that.'

'Brother magistrates on the bench, no doubt, all sympathising with the chastisement of a dastard who dared to shoot a fox. As all his county friends would have heard about it, and he didn't actually go inside, it's not much of a secret. In fact, he's probably quite proud of himself. But even if he'd done something he didn't want known, he'd surely not believe his mother would tell the world.'

'Ah,' said Tom, 'but it shows a propensity to violence, towards people as well as dumb animals, and he gets the London house back, remember. Maybe he wants to sell it. These landowners sometimes get desperate for ready cash.'

'Maybe. I hope we don't have to go into his financial position. Who's next? The present Lady Devenish.'

'Josephine Devenish, Chief, but Lady Eva mostly calls her "that woman" in the records. Looks like they didn't get on.'

'She's been selling off family heirlooms and giving the proceeds to her son? So young Teddy comes in again.'

'Won't the stuff be his in the end, anyway?' Piper asked.

'I imagine so, but it's not yet. It's certainly not Lady Devenish's to sell. I don't know what Lady Eva's interest in it would be, if any, but Sir James might well kick up a dust if she told him.'

'Wouldn't he have noticed things disappearing?'

'Judging by what Mrs Fletcher told us, laddie,' said Tom, 'not unless she sold his guns or his fishing rods. But, Chief, if he's as hen-pecked as Mrs Fletcher told us, likely she wouldn't care if he found out.'

'On the other hand, with theft to hold over her, perhaps he wouldn't be so hen-pecked. Whether she'd murder her mother-in-law to keep the upper hand with her husband, though . . .'

'They didn't get on, Chief,' Piper reminded him. 'The two ladies, I mean.'

'It's still pretty thin, even if you add that misappropriating the family jewels is frowned on in the best circles. We'll have to tackle her about it, though.' As Alec spoke, the telephone bell rang. He unhooked the receiver. His call to Danesbury House came through, and a moment later he was speaking to an incredulous Bill Hetheridge.

'Scotland Yard? Detective Chief Inspector? You're pulling my leg. Who is this? Is that you, Freddie?'

'This is Detective Chief Inspector Fletcher,' Alec repeated patiently. 'If you doubt it, you may ring up Scotland Yard and enquire as to my credentials, but that would waste our time, both of us, and I'm engaged in a murder investigation.'

'Murder! I say, chaps, listen to this! It's a detective chappie wants to know about a murder.' A confused noise of several excited voices came down the wire. 'Right-oh, Chief Inspector, fire away! Who's been murdered? Are we all suspects? How jolly!'

'If that were the case, Mr Hetheridge, I should be on your doorstep. I'm seeking information about the movements of Mr Edward Devenish.'

'Haw, haw, haw, he wants to know about Teddy! No,

Ginger, you can't talk to him. I say, Chief Inspector, Teddy's not here.'

'I'm aware of that. Can you tell me exactly when he left your house?'

'Anyone know when Teddy left last night?' Bill Hetheridge's companions could be heard arguing, as could the clink of bottle and glass. 'Sorry, Chief Inspector, it was after dinner but no one knows exactly when. You might say he did a moonlight flit, didn't say goodbye to anyone. Who's he done in?'

'I'm checking on the movements of a large number of people. Why do you suppose Mr Devenish left without saying goodbye?'

'Hang it all, no suppose about it, haw, haw! Teddy was all broken up, hopes dished, fed up, abso-bally-lutely pipped at the post. You see, the young chump was dashed keen on our Ginger, and she'd been leading him on a bit . . . yes, you did, Ginger, it's no good denying it. Persuaded me to invite him, didn't you?'

'And Miss . . . er . . . Ginger handed him his hat?'

'That's it in a nutshell. Don't know how you Scotland Yard chappies do it, damned if I do. What made it worse was, his grandmother told him to stop seeing Ginger, said she'd tell the parents if he didn't. You see, he defied the old bird, swore he didn't care if he was disinherited, and Ginger told him he might not care but she jolly well did and she hadn't any use for a halfling with empty pockets. Brutal, eh, what? Haw, haw, haw!'

Alec hung up on the sounds of general merriment. 'Fatuous ass.'

'Disappointed in love?' Tom asked.

'It's more complicated than that,' Alec said grimly. 'Young Devenish is in the soup right up to his chin.'

CHAPTER 14

Daisy was feeling guilty. Instead of enjoying basking in the evening sun in the comfort of her chair and footstool, she couldn't help wondering whether she was responsible for Lucy's broken engagement. She had questioned Lucy's love for Gerald, practically suggested she was only marrying him because his father was a marquis. With the wedding preparations in full swing, Lucy hadn't the nerve to cry off, but as soon as the excuse of a postponement appeared she seized her chance.

Which was all very well if she didn't love him, but if she did and only doubted because of what Daisy had said . . .

The knock on her door was a welcome distraction, even if whoever it was just wanted to pump her about Alec's progress. 'Come in,' she called.

Lucy stormed in. 'Darling, that foul little beast my cousin Erica's going around saying Binkie's family will refuse to let him marry me, because of the murders.' She plopped into the chair opposite Daisy's, not at all in her usual languidly graceful way.

'Have you told her you've already called it off?'

'Good Lord, no! That will only confirm what she's thinking.'

'She'll have to know sooner or later, though.'

'Unless I marry him after all.'

'Just to scotch rumours that he's dropped you? I wish you'd make up your mind, Lucy. I'm meeting him after dinner to try to explain you to him, but I don't think I can even attempt it.'

'If you're asking me to explain myself, I can't. I've never been so confused in my life. I didn't know I was capable of feeling so confused. I can't marry him just to spite Erica, but I don't want to turn into a dreary spinster like Angela or Aunt Ione. Daisy, what on earth has come over Aunt Ione?'

'I can't tell you, but I will say that she wasn't a dreary spinster by choice. Come to that, I don't suppose anyone exactly chooses to be dreary, though they may choose not to marry. But Angela isn't what I'd call dreary?'

'Darling, her clothes!'

'We can't all have your sense of style. Instead of fashion, Angela has passion.'

'For those ghastly, dreary mongrels of hers,' Lucy objected.

'She's doing something she cares deeply about. That's not a dreary life. Anyway, look at your cousin Flora. You can't call her a dreary spinster. If you don't marry, you'll be like her, with both fashion and a passion – for photography.'

'Are you trying to persuade me not to get married now?'

'Not at all, I'm just saying there are worse fates. By the way, darling, your ex-intended asked me not to call him Binkie any longer. He said no wonder you don't take him seriously when you think of him as Binkie.'

'It's not that I don't take him seriously! Gerald's a nice name, though, nice and solid. I thought he liked being called Binkie,' Lucy said plaintively.

'I expect he did at school. I don't expect the people he sells stocks to – if that's what he does – call him Binkie.'

'Unless they were at school with him?'

'True,' said Daisy laughing. 'So can I at least tell him— Is that someone knocking? Bother!'

'Shall I see who it is?'

'Would you?'

Lucy went to open the door. 'Oh, hello, Angela. Daisy's resting.'

'Gosh, sorry, I won't disturb her.'

But Tiddler, after a doubtful sniff or two, had recognized Daisy's friendly scent and came scurrying to see her. He grovelled on the floor beside her chair, tail beating madly. Daisy reached down to scratch his head.

'Come in, Angela,' she said resignedly.

'Gosh, sorry, I'll get him . . .'

'No, that's all right. Come and sit down. I'll see you later, Lucy.'

Behind Angela's back, Lucy rolled her eyes and departed.

'He likes you,' said Angela, her tone congratulatory. She dropped into the chair, with even less grace than Lucy had, and sighed. 'I'm sorry to interrupt, honestly, but things are so awful and there's no one else I can talk to.'

'Just in general? I mean, with your grandmother's murder and all. Or is there something new?'

'It's Mummy and Daddy. Your husband called them in, one at a time, and neither of them will tell the other what was said and now they're not speaking to each other.'

Lady Devenish had entered the library already on the offensive: 'I don't suppose you would know about such niceties, but it's time I was changing for dinner. I can't spare you more than a couple of minutes.'

'In that case,' said Alec, 'we'll dispense with the polite amenities and get right down to business. Please sit down. You are Josephine, Lady Devenish?'

'If you don't know who I am—'

'I do, madam. This is a required preliminary. I should warn you that your words will be taken down and may be used as evidence in a court of law. You will be asked to sign a statement. I repeat, is your name . . . ?'

'Yes,' she said grudgingly, 'I'm Lady Devenish.'

Nothing short of shock tactics was likely to work, Alec decided. 'What exactly did your late mother-in-law have to say to you regarding your conversion to cash of a number of family heirlooms?'

'She didn't know! I mean, I don't know what you're talking about. You're supposed to be investigating murder, not whatever unfounded rumours you may have picked up by snooping into private affairs.'

'Madam, in a murder investigation no affairs are private. What did Lady Eva say?'

'She didn't. She couldn't have known. Anyway, the things were mine as much as anyone's. Don't you know the Prayer Book? "With my worldly goods I thee endow!" It wasn't anything James cared about. He didn't even notice the miniatures were gone. It's not as if they were family portraits. And what does it matter to him if I wear paste jewellery? Besides, it wasn't for me, it was for Teddy. Edward, my son. Everything will be his one day, after all.' She stared at Alec with sullen defiance.

He had never dealt with a case involving such larcenous

depredations on an entailed estate and he didn't know the precise legalities of the situation. At present that was not what interested him. 'Did you explain your point of view to Lady Eva?' he asked.

'It was none of her business. As dowager, she had her settlement and the use of the London house. The rest was no longer any of her affair?'

'I rather doubt she saw matters in quite the same light. And if she had told your husband, he—'

'She didn't. She didn't tell him. He would have said something. I suppose she might have found out, the way she was always snooping into everything, but she didn't say anything to me or to James.'

Alec changed his angle of attack. 'Presumably finding out the proceeds went to her grandson mollified her.'

'Perhaps, if she found out. I would have told her if she'd accused me.'

'How would you describe his relationship with his grand-mother?'

'They were devoted to each other. He often called on her in town. She didn't like his friends, though. She complained that they were a fast set, but a young man needs to sow his wild oats, after all.'

'Have you met these people?'

'No. Of course Teddy could have brought them to Saxon-field at any time. I'm sure he will one of these days.'

'I take it his allowance from his father was insufficient for him to keep up with them.'

'James doesn't like him living in London. He says it's far too expensive and rackety. I'm sure it can't be half as expensive as his hounds and horses and guns and such,' Lady Devenish said resentfully. 'And spaniels and retrievers and pointers and beagles.'

No wonder Angela was dog-mad. 'You have no money of your own?'

'A few pounds a week. All my bills and the household bills go to his agent to be paid, so I can't just take money from my pocket to give to Teddy.'

'No doubt Sir James is worried about the family's financial position.'

'Rubbish! He's just selfish.' Her ladyship's lips tightened, as if this outright criticism of her husband made her realize to what extent she'd been led into indiscretion. 'But none of this has anything to do with my mother-in-law's death. You ought to be looking for a murderer, not digging for gossip.'

Alec proceeded to ask her the sort of questions she had probably expected. 'Where were you between the hours of midnight and four this morning?'

'Asleep in my bed.'

'I see your room is on the floor above Lady Eva's. You didn't get up for any reason and leave the room or go downstairs?'

'No.'

'Do you take sleeping pills, powders, or draughts?'

'Never.'

'Did you hear any sounds, usual or unusual?'

'Ha! James snores constantly. I couldn't have heard anything else. I never get a wink of sleep.'

Alec was tempted either to point out, 'You said you were asleep,' or to advise, 'Perhaps you ought to try sleeping pills.' He resisted the double temptation. 'So you would have known if Sir James left the room?' he said instead.

'Indubitably. And he did not.'

'Were you surprised, this morning, to find your son had arrived in the middle of the night?'

'Not at all,' she claimed, uneasily. 'He promised to be here by Friday but I didn't know exactly when to expect him.'

'Thank you, Lady Devenish. What you have just told me will be typed in the form of a statement which you will be asked to sign.'

For the first time, she was alarmed. 'What, everything?'

'Yes. I warned you that your words would be written down and might be used as evidence. I may say that the police are not at all likely to prosecute you for disposing of items not strictly belonging to you. That will be up to your husband to decide, and possibly your son, as heir.'

She gave him a malevolent look. 'I suppose you're going to tell him.'

'Only if it appears necessary to my investigation. I shan't if I can help it, but I make no promises.' He stood up, and she followed suit. She would have liked to threaten to report him to his superiors, he thought, but under the circumstances, she hadn't a leg to stand on. 'Piper,' he said as she stalked towards the door, 'I'll see Sir James next.'

Piper followed her out. As the door closed behind him, Tom said, 'Can't sleep for his snoring, won't take pills: if you ask me, she likes being a martyr.'

'A larcenous martyr.'

'Holds it over him, I shouldn't wonder. Not that I believe she didn't sleep a wink, and I bet he could have slipped out for a while.'

'Very likely. What do you make of her otherwise?'

'Sounds to me like Mrs Fletcher got one wrong for once, Chief. Maybe Sir James lets himself be hen-pecked but he keeps the whip hand.'

'Yes, the hand that holds the purse-strings rules the roost.' Which sounded like a line from Little Buttercup's song in 'that infernal nonsense, *Pinafore*.'

'Lady Devenish is all bluff and bluster. Besides, I'd be surprised if she had the strength to do in Lady Eva, even if she had confronted her about the larceny, and I don't think she had.'

'I'm inclined to agree. Perhaps Lady Eva was saving the confrontation for after the wedding. She had already called Teddy to heel. She might not have wanted another disgruntled face at the feast.'

'Poor Miss Lucy!' said Tom unexpectedly. 'I'm glad at least we've knocked her and Lord Gerald off the list.'

'Yes, she's having a thin time of it.'

'If you ask me, Chief, young Master Teddy's the one we're after for the strangling. Creeping in in the middle of the night like that, with a grudge against his grandma. His ma could've poisoned Lord Fotheringay, to protect him. You going to bring him in again after his pa?'

'No, he can wait till after dinner. A little more stewing won't hurt him, especially as he'll be wondering what his parents are saying. We've all the rest of Lady Eva's list to go through.'

'That's going to put the cat among the pigeons! I mean, everyone'll know she had something on those people.'

'Can't be helped. We'll interview everyone in the end, but with so many people here, the obvious suspects must come first.'

'It was bad luck we couldn't write any of them off for the poisoned tea. Not what I'd call a proper tea-time, everyone popping in and out and turning up when they feel like it.'

'Shockingly lax,' Alec agreed with a grin. 'At least Lady Haverhill, Lady Fotheringay, and Mrs Walsdorf stayed put pouring tea. But we really must speak to absolutely everyone this evening before they forget who they saw and talked to in the drawing room and when. Here's our next suspect. If I don't ask about the finances, Tom, you ask about the London house.'

'Right, Chief,' Tom agreed as Piper ushered in Sir James.

The baronet strode across the room with the long pace of a countryman and offered Alec his hand. 'How do, Fletcher.' His resounding voice also was that of an outdoors-man, used to hallooing to hounds. 'Hope you're gettin' near to arrestin' the bastard who killed my poor mother. Anything I can do to help!'

'Allow me to express my sympathy, Sir James. Do take a seat. Let's clear up the formalities first.'

'By Jove, yes, must do everything all right and proper.'

'Good. First, I should remind you that what you say will be written down and you'll be asked to sign a statement which may be used in evidence. Your name and address, just for the record.'

'Sir James Devenish,' said Sir James solemnly, 'Sixth Baronet, of Saxonfield, Leicestershire. Master of Fox Hounds. Used to be Justice of the Peace, but I had a bit of a dust-up with one of my tenants and they asked me to resign. Thought I'd better tell you. Your wife – demmed fine young woman, Mrs Fletcher – she advised us to tell the whole truth right away and I quite see you won't find the bastard who killed my poor mother if people keep things from you.'

'Very true, sir. Tell me a bit about this "dust-up".'

The Baronet's ruddy face grew redder. 'Silly business, dare say I went too far. Fact is, the fellow shot a vixen, demmed bad form. Said she raided his hen-house. Fact is, the fellow's been complainin' about the hunt tramplin' his corn or I shouldn't have lost my temper. Can't have it both ways, what? Don't like us huntin' across his fields, naturally foxes are going to get out of control. Shouldn't have horse-whipped the fellow, though, I realize that. A pretty penny in damages it cost me, I can tell you.'

'Did your mother know about this incident?'

'Gad, yes! She has . . . had the local paper sent to her every week and they put the case on the front page. Demmed scribblers! She saw a paragraph about it in *The Times*, too. Gave me a proper tickin' off.'

'When was that?'

'Oh, a month ago or so.'

'How did you feel about the scolding?'

'Made me realize I'd made a demmed fool of myself. I mean, gettin' in the papers, demmed bad form, what?'

'Were you angry with Lady Eva?'

'Gad, no! She was angry with me, don't you see.'

'Would you say you have a violent temper, Sir James?'

'Who, me? Peace at any price, that's my motto. Ask anyone! This business was a . . . a thing with a berry in it.'

'Aberration?'

'That's it! I mean, stands to reason, if I was always taking a whack at fellows, Mother wouldn't bother to rake me over the coals. She'd know there was no point. Good gad, man, I never even raised a hand to the children. Though, mind you, it might've been a good thing if I'd taken a cane to the boy now and then. Let his mother raise him and she's spoilt him.' Sir James shook his head sadly. 'Useless sort of chap, shies at a fence, even caught him spoutin' poetry once, though he don't write it, thank God.'

'Were you surprised this morning when you found out he'd arrived in the night?'

'Can't say I thought about it. Other things to think about, you know. My mother, and all that. Quite fond of her.'

'Yes, I'm sorry. If I tell you that we have evidence that she forced him to come, by threatening to tell you something that might well cause you to withdraw his allowance . . .'

'What the devil has the boy been up to?' Sir James demanded.

'I see no need to tell you, as Lady Eva effectively put a stop to it. Of course, it's possible it may come out in court . . .'

'You think Teddy killed his grandmother? Gad no, the boy wouldn't have the guts! Fact is, Angie, his older sister, she's got more spunk in her little finger. Mind you, we don't always see eye to eye, Angie and I. She doesn't like me hunting, or cubbing, or shooting or even fishing. But demme if she isn't willing to fight for what she believes in.'

'Fight?'

'Not with her fists! Angie wouldn't hurt a fly. Not unless it was bitin' a horse, that is.' He grinned at his own wit, then remembered the situation and sobered. 'Veronica, my other girl, she'd want my mother to live forever if only so Angela wouldn't get her inheritance. Spiteful. And Peter Bancroft, her husband, he's a wet dishrag. I've two more daughters, one in Australia, t'other in the North Country, can't get away for the wedding. No sense wastin' your time suspectin' any of them, any more than Angie or Teddy.' Standing up, he leant on the desk with two massive fists.

Alec saw Tom – who had two massive fists of his own – preparing for intervention and gave a tiny shake of the head.

Staring down at Alec, Sir James said earnestly, 'Whoever killed my poor mother, it wasn't one of my family.'

'I hope not.'

'Well, I just hope you catch the bastard, that's all. I just hope you catch him.'

'We'll do our best, sir. I promise you that. Just a couple more questions, if you please. I understand from the butler that you were among the last guests to go to bed, shortly before midnight.'

'That's right. It was just midnight when I climbed into bed. We had the window open and I heard the tower clock chime. Our room's up on the second floor and sometimes it sounds as if the demmed clock is in the room with us.'

'After that, did you leave your room for any reason before seven o'clock this morning?'

To Alec's surprise, once again the baronet's brick red face turned a brighter shade. 'Er-hem,' he said, sitting down. 'Well, er, yes, matter of fact I did. Twice, or maybe three times. Had to . . .' He glanced at Piper, diligently taking down his words, and went on in a hoarse whisper, 'You know, go to the you-know-what. Sawbones says it happens as you get older. Demmed nuisance, what?'

Tom's moustache twitched. With difficulty, Alec managed to preserve his countenance at this evidence of a prudery worthy of a Victorian spinster of uncertain years. 'Did you, on any of these . . . visits, see anyone or see or hear anything out of the ordinary? Footsteps, a door closing?'

'Gad, no! I'd have told you right away.'

'You didn't even see Miss Angela and her brother? See a light in the bathroom or hear water running?'

'No, nothing.'

'Pity. Can you pinpoint the times of your . . . excursions?'

''Fraid not. Fact is, I only wake up halfway, just enough to . . . er . . .'

'To get you there and back. Sergeant, did you have a question for Sir James?'

'Yes, sir. What are your plans for the London house, sir, now that Lady Eva is no longer in residence?'

'Good gad, man,' Sir James exploded, 'my mother was horribly killed this morning and you want to know about the London house? I haven't given it a thought! Well, Fletcher, if that's all, I'll be off.'

'Yes, thank you, Sir James.' Rising, Alec offered his hand, which the baronet shook. 'I appreciate your cooperation.'

'Just find the bastard who killed my mother.' With a glare at Tom, Sir James departed.

'The Bancrofts next, Piper. We'll take them together. Thank you for drawing his fire, Tom.'

'Under orders!'

Alec grinned. 'Since he appears to be cooperative, I don't want him angry with me. What do you think?'

'I dunno, Chief. He certainly doesn't have any illusions about his kids. Seems like a straightforward kind of chap, but there's that temper to consider, and you can't overlook killing being as you might say his way of life.'

CHAPTER 15

Dinner time was dismal.

Daisy and Lucy went down together. Daisy was wearing her black georgette, unadorned by its usual bright-hued scarf or necklace. Without that visual distraction, she felt exposed, but Lucy swore her pregnancy was not showing. Nancy, whom they met with Tim on the stairs, concurred.

'You're only a few weeks, aren't you?' she said. 'Five months is when you really start to notice, and if you wear the right clothes, other people may not till seven months.'

'Wait till you're eight months and big as a blimp,' said Lucy callously.

'A pregnant woman is a beautiful sight in the eyes of God and man,' the Rev. Tim said in his gentle way.

Lucy snorted, but quietly.

In the drawing room Rupert, with Sally at his side, was dispensing drinks with a lavish hand and a sort of uneasy geniality. His position was difficult, Daisy acknowledged. He was standing in as host for his suddenly incapacitated grandfather after the death by murder of his father. A host ought to be affable but, in the circumstances, Rupert rather overdid the affability.

Daisy had known more than one survivor of the hell of

Flanders unable to summon up more than token respect for his elders who had never seen action. Perhaps Rupert had never much respected his somewhat old-maidish father, so busy pottering about his greenhouses. If he had ever held him in affection he was concealing it well – but then, an officer and a gentleman was expected to hide his emotions.

'Dry martinis all round?' Rupert offered as his cousins and Daisy approached. 'I'm rather a dab hand at dry martinis, though I say it as shouldn't.'

Lucy accepted. Daisy asked for vermouth without the gin. She had read enough Victorian novels to be certain gin was not good for babies, born or unborn, and besides, she didn't like it much. Nancy and Tim had sherry, one sweet and one dry.

Handing over the sherries, Rupert said, 'I want to thank you, Tim and Nancy, for being so good to Mother and the grandparents. Sally's told me how you rallied round.'

Tim and Nancy made modest noises.

'You were marvellous,' Sally interjected. Having signally failed to rally round earlier, she had rallied amazingly with her husband's arrival. There was no sign of her previous nervous agitation. 'No, honestly, Nancy . . .'

Lucy and Daisy moved away. 'She's too sickening!' Lucy whispered.

'She is rather.' Daisy looked around. Except for the Haverhills and Lady Fotheringay, just about everyone was there. In spite of the drinks, they were a funereal crowd; the women had all found black frocks to wear to match the men's dinner jackets. The second murder had more than doubled the impact of the first. Those who had been merely irritable at the interruption to their lives now wore appropriate expressions, from downcast and anxious to mournful and fearful. People gathered in small groups, presumably of those they trusted, and looked askance at the rest (Sir James Devenish and his wife, notably, were at opposite ends of the room, Sir James with Angela and Lady Devenish with Teddy). Voices were subdued.

'Grim!' observed Lucy.

'Here come your parents, darling. You simply must talk to your mother. I can't go on fending her off for you.'

'Grimmer! No,' Lucy sighed. 'Poor Mummy! What a beastly daughter I am.'

As Lucy went to meet her parents, Daisy was waylaid by Jennifer Walsdorf. 'Daisy, I'm not sure what to do. Your husband called in the Bancrofts and they went up late to dress, so dinner will be late. Well, that's all right, I've told Baines to announce as soon as they come down, but now he's got Lord Carleton. Is he going to keep sending for people throughout dinner?'

'It wouldn't surprise me. He has an awful lot of people to interview and I'm sure he'll want to speak to everyone tonight while their memories are fresh. The second murder confused everything. If I were you I'd warn Baines that people may be coming and going, so that he can make arrangements to keep their dinners hot. Are Rupert and Sally aware of what's going on? It's really for them to work out what to do, isn't it?'

'They've certainly taken over quickly enough,' Jennifer said resentfully. 'I suppose they're in charge as long as the Haverhills are incapacitated, but don't expect them to do anything that requires any effort. And if I go and explain the situation to them, Sally will say it's all my fault.'

'I don't see why you should have to. Surely it's for Baines to ask them what they want him to do.'

Jennifer's face lit up. 'Yes, it is, isn't it? I'm so used to being an intermediary between him and Mrs Maple on one side and Lady Haverhill and Aunt Maud on the other, I hadn't thought. You know, we've been very comfortable here and I'm terribly grateful to Aunt Maud and the Haverhills, but in a way it will be wonderful to leave and make a life of our own.'

'That's the spirit!' said Daisy.

John Walsdorf joined them. 'For so long,' he said, linking his arm through Jennifer's, 'I have heard about the Scotland Yard detectives, how clever they are. I look forward to see for myself.'

'I have no doubt you'll get your chance, Mr Walsdorf. Alec's bound to want to see everyone, at least briefly.'

'I'm not looking forward to it,' said Jennifer with a shiver. 'John, I must go and speak to Baines?'

'Be sure Sally does not watch, *Herzchen*.' For a moment Walsdorf looked almost malignant.

'I will. I'm just going to tell him to ask her what to do about dinner.'

'Excellent.' He turned back to Daisy. 'Jennifer's cousin Rupert and his wife do not like us. My country was invaded by the Germans and occupied throughout the war, yet Rupert considers me as a German. Sally, she resents that Lady Fotheringay and Lady Haverhill rely on Jennifer. Please, it is true, as Jennifer tells me, that the Reverend Timothy offers us to stay at his house while I seek for a position? I cannot speak to him in case that she has misunderstood, but you were present, I believe?'

'Yes, Tim and Nancy will give you a place to lay your heads if you have to leave Haverhill.'

'These are very good, excellent people! I must go and give to them my thanks.'

As he scanned the room, Daisy saw Lord Carleton come in, scowling. Behind him came Baines, who spotted Walsdorf and came over. 'Mr Fletcher, the detective officer, wishes to see you in the library, sir.'

'My turn for the high jump, as the English say,' Walsdorf observed to Daisy, 'or perhaps your husband wishes only to know what arrangements I have made to stop the guests who will otherwise arrive for the wedding.' He bowed and went to the door. There he met his wife. They exchanged a word and he patted her on the shoulder before going out.

The butler had continued on his stately way to Rupert and Sally. Daisy saw Rupert nod. At the same moment she became aware that Lord Carleton was bearing down upon her in no amiable frame of mind.

To her relief, Binkie – Gerald – reached her first, and Baines immediately announced that dinner was served. Gerald was far too gentlemanly to insist on talking about Lucy at table, whereas Lord Carleton, for all she knew, might have insisted on giving her his opinion of Alec over the soup. She and Gerald joined the procession through the Long Gallery to the dining room.

'Dash it,' he said in a low, gloomy voice as they entered the dining room, 'I'd forgotten the conservatory opens out of this room. Do they keep up that silly business of the ladies withdrawing to leave the fellows to drink port here?'

'The Haverhills do. I don't know about Rupert and Sally.'

'Still the custom in the officers' mess. When they have ladies to dine, I mean.'

'If so, we'll have to wait till everyone's gone. I don't suppose anyone will linger long tonight.'

'Servants'll be buzzing about afterwards. Tell you what, you wait in the drawing room and I'll come in when it's all clear. Then you can join me there.'

'Right-oh,' said Daisy, 'as soon as I can get away from whomever I'm talking to when I see you.'

'You're a jolly good sport, Daisy,' he muttered in her ear as he seated her at the table.

He was not the only silently gloomy diner. Rupert, in his grandfather's chair at one end of the table, kept a conversation going around him, though in the circumstances it could not be expected to be lively. Sally, at the other end, was less adept but managed to rouse Montagu Fotheringay to one of his interminable anecdotes. The club-man had revived somewhat from the shock of his sister's death and, between sentences, he managed to eat with a good appetite.

So did Daisy. She had missed tea.

Soup and fish had been cleared away and footmen and maids were handing around veal with roast potatoes, asparagus and new peas by the time John Walsdorf reappeared. Jennifer had saved him a place beside her. Everyone watched as he sat down and they conferred anxiously together in an undertone. Daisy remembered Lucy's father's suggestion that Lady Eva might have discovered evidence that Walsdorf had been a German spy during the war.

Meanwhile, Ernie Piper had come in and spoken briefly to Baines. The butler went to Montagu Fotheringay. Though unable to hear, Daisy knew exactly what Baines was saying: 'Mr Fletcher, the detective officer, wishes to see you in the library, sir.'

Paling, Montagu expostulated. He gestured to his plate, which already contained veal and potatoes and was only waiting for vegetables. Baines was firm. He reached down and removed the plate. More than one mouth fell open, among diners and servants, at this unprecedented action by a normally irreproachable butler.

Baines had nailed his colours to the mast. He was clearly on the side of the police. No doubt, thought Daisy, he had been sincerely devoted to Lord Fotheringay.

Montagu Fotheringay struck his colours. He lumbered to his feet and every eye followed him out of the room.

CHAPTER 16

Alec, Tom and Ernie, expecting the dull, skimpy sandwiches which were usually their lot in similar situations, had been agreeably surprised by the contents of the tray a footman bore into the library. Fragrant steam rose from generous slices of pork pie. Each plate was adorned with a heap of colourful pickles: onions, beetroot, cucumber, cauliflower and carrot. A bowl of cherries and a sponge cake awaited their pleasure. A pitcher of lemonade and several bottles of beer completed the provisions.

Ernie Piper, about to go in search of Lord Carleton, sat down again and rubbed his hands together.

'That's something like!' said Tom approvingly.

'Cook says there's plenty more where that came from, Mr Tring.' The footman turned to Alec. 'And Mr Baines said to ask you, sir, would you be wanting wine with your dinner?'

'Thank you, no, this will do us very well.'

'These big places,' said Ernie, 'they usually seem to think coppers live on air.'

'We don't hold with police in the house,' the footman informed him, 'but no more don't we hold with murdering Lord Fotheringay, as pleasant and harmless a gentleman as you could ask for. 'Sides, anyone can see Mrs Fletcher's a real lady.'

'The best,' Ernie agreed blithely, reaching for his plate. 'Always right, Mrs Fletcher is.'

The footman looked interested and hopeful.

'That will be all, thank you,' Alec said firmly. 'Piper, in precisely five minutes you will be going to fetch Lord Carleton.'

'Yes, Chief!' said Ernie, his fork already on its way to his mouth.

Denzil, Viscount Carleton was married to a niece of Lord Haverhill. According to Lady Eva's papers, he did not take his marriage vows very seriously.

He was nothing loath to admit as much. 'Oh yes, I have a mistress. Charming woman I've kept for many years. Should have married her years ago and be damned to the bloodlines, but by the time I realized I ought to be thinking of providing an heir, she was a bit past child-bearing. So I married Adela, and she's given me children. Thing is, she hasn't a thought beyond them. I'm not complaining, mind. These days, my dear friend provides companionship and not a lot of the other, if you know what I mean.'

'Are you saying you wouldn't have minded Lady Eva making your liaison public, sir?'

'I'd have been extremely angry,' Carleton said coolly. 'All she'd have accomplished would have been to humiliate both my wife and my friend. But, to do Lady Eva justice, I don't believe she'd have done it. I've never heard of a rumour emanating from her. She's . . . she was like one of those inland seas – everything goes in and nothing comes out.'

'You couldn't be certain of that.'

'No, but if you're suggesting I killed her to stop her talking, you're wide of the mark. I didn't know she knew. Since, apparently, she did, I can't imagine why she should publish the news now after holding her tongue for decades.'

'She found out quite recently.'

'Oh, she did, did she?' For the first time, the viscount lost his lackadaisical air. 'That new maid of Mabel's! I said she had a sly look. I wonder how—'

'However Lady Eva's discovery came about, you claim she never spoke to you on the subject?'

'Not a murmur, and her manner towards me yesterday was no different from the last time we met, which, I may say, we did rarely. She had many nieces and nephews and no especial feeling for my wife. Poor Adela is much too dull to have caught her interest.'

On this point Alec could not shake him, and questions on his whereabouts at the times of the two deaths yielded nothing either to damn or to exculpate himself or anyone else.

As Carleton stood up to leave, he said, 'I'm sure I can count on your discretion. What I have told you is in confidence and must not reach my wife.'

'We shall do our best, but I can make no promises.'

'But—'

'I need hardly remind you, sir, that this is a murder investigation. And that our information came in fact from Lady Eva, not from you. I shall not reveal it to your wife unless it proves absolutely necessary.'

'Under what circumstances . . . ?'

'I cannot foresee possible circumstances,' Alec said firmly. 'Again, thank you for your help, Lord Carleton.'

The look the Viscount gave him was acrimonious, but he left without further protest.

Piper did not. 'Have a heart, Chief, just a quick bite of cake! Sarge'll've finished it before I get another chance.'

'You watch your cheek, young fella-me-lad,' Tom advised him indulgently.

Alec relented. Since the second murder he had been driven by a sense of urgency, a dread that yet another victim would perish beneath his nose, but Ernie was working hard and the ninety seconds it would take him to scoff a slice of cake was neither here nor there.

'What d'you reckon, Chief,' said Tom, 'did he know she knew?'

'I think not. But I think he'd be capable of turning quite nasty if she had threatened him in any way.'

'Yes, he started off as if butter wouldn't melt in his mouth, but he was definitely hot under the collar when he left. Still, he seemed to me too to be telling the truth. And you never know, what he said about who he talked to at tea-time may help when we put it together with what the rest say.'

Ernie, having demolished his cake in thirty seconds flat, quickly returned escorting John Walsdorf. A small, slight man, he gave an impression of neatness despite ill-fitting and slightly shabby evening dress. His eyes, behind steel-rimmed glasses, were wary. Alec did not regard the wariness as a sign of guilt. He had dealt with plenty of honest, well-behaved foreigners who feared the police, often with good reason: either the police in their own countries were repressive and violent or they had had an unfortunate experience with a xenophobic British officer.

'For the record,' he said, 'your name is John Walsdorf?'

'For the record, my name is Johan Walsdorf. I have not legally changed.'

'Call yourself what you want, sir,' said Tom, in much the same indulgent tone he had used to Ernie Piper. 'It's a free country.'

Walsdorf flashed him a smile of singular charm. Perhaps that was what had attracted Lady Fotheringay's niece to the penniless refugee, Alec reflected. Which wasn't to say the man had no other good qualities, nor that the shortage of young men in England since the war had no part in her decision to marry him. Alec had long ago faced the probability that Daisy would never have given a middle-aged, middle-class copper a second glance if so many young men of her own class had not been killed in the trenches.

He started with the usual questions about sounds in the night.

Walsdorf explained that he and his wife slept up at the top of the house, near the nurseries, as Jennifer liked to be near their daughter. 'Also, because we are not quite family, you understand. It is better to be out of the way. Thus it is not likely we will hear someone who goes to Lady Eva's room. I sleep soundly always and get up early.'

'At what time, sir?'

'At six-thirty.' Too late to see anything useful. 'At seven I go downstairs.' He hesitated, and Alec was sure he was pondering whether to give or withhold some piece of information. 'In this house,' he went on, 'the library is not much used, especially when the weather is good, but I like to write letters while all is quiet. I did not know of the death of Lady Eva until Mrs Fletcher came to the library to telephone to the police.'

'I gather you helped her with that, for which I thank you.'

'It is nothing. Such is a job for a man, I think.'

A sentiment Daisy would have heartily disagreed with

though Alec suspected she might have been glad of it in practice.

Walsdorf had not come down to tea. He had still not succeeded in notifying all the wedding guests of the changed circumstances, so he had stayed in Lord Haverhill's study making phone calls and sending wires. Lucy, at the instrument in the butler's pantry, had broken in upon one of his calls to send for the doctor, when Lord Fotheringay was taken ill.

'I cannot believe one would be so foolish as to kill Lord Fotheringay,' Walsdorf said angrily. 'To me is unconceivable – is this correct? – is not possible to want Rupert in place of his father, who was a sympathetic, innocent – no, no, this is the wrong word – a *harmless* man. If you find next Rupert dead, you may arrest me. Lord Fotheringay I would never hurt. For Lady Eva, I do not care one fig.'

'Lady Eva seems to have been interested in you, however.'

'Lady Eva was interested in everyone, but in me not much, because I am not of the society.'

'Nonetheless, she made a note of your having been born in Germany.'

Walsdorf looked at him in astonishment. 'But how the deuce did she know this?'

'It's true?'

'It is true,' he said quite calmly. 'My mother was not well. My father took her to Baden to try the waters and there I was born. My birth was registered in Germany, then my parents returned to Luxemburg and registered my birth there also. I am a citizen of Luxemburg. I have lived always in Luxemburg. Yet when the Germans invaded my country, they wanted to make me fight for them. This is why I have come to England.'

'Lady Eva could have made it very awkward for you if she'd told people you were born in Germany.'

'During the war, perhaps. Some might have imagined that I was a spy – this is why I told no one but Jennifer. Now it matters little. To the English, a foreigner is a foreigner. In any case, Lady Eva has not told. Someone would have mentioned to me.'

'Lady Eva never mentioned to you that she knew?'

'Never a word. I wonder how she found out? It is very strange, this.'

'It is odd,' Alec agreed. 'Piper, any hint of how she found out?'

'I think she got it from some diplomat, sir, but it wasn't very clear.'

'Your Foreign Office investigated all aliens in England during the war,' said Walsdorf. 'This is natural, but it is wrong that they gossip. The police are more careful, no?'

'Much more careful, though in a murder case we cannot promise to keep secrets. I'm afraid you will be uncomfortable if word of your country of birth gets about.'

Walsdorf shrugged. 'Now it is nothing. We cannot stay here longer with Rupert and Sally giving the orders. The Reverend and Mrs Timothy offer to us a home, Jennifer and Emily and me. I do not think they will withdraw only because I was by chance born in a German spa town. These are good people.'

Alec wondered whether to enquire about the antagonism between Walsdorf and Lieutenant Colonel Rupert Fotheringay. He decided to wait and see if Daisy could elucidate. If it was genuine, it gave Walsdorf a strong motive for *not* murdering the late Lord Fotheringay.

Walsdorf innocent might be a good source of information. As an outsider with an inside view, and a shrewd kind of chap, he must see the family more clearly than its own members could. His present disgruntlement made him the more likely to talk. But Alec decided to postpone that, too, until he had spoken to everyone and formed his own impressions. He sent Walsdorf off, followed by Piper in search of Mr Montagu Fotheringay.

As soon as the door closed behind the two, Tom said, 'He's shielding Mrs Reverend Timothy.'

'What? What do you mean?'

'Remember, Chief, we were a bit puzzled about her turning up outside the victim's bedroom – as Mrs Fletcher reported – seeing she slept on the floor above – according to Mrs Walsdorf – and likely couldn't hear the maid screaming. I know you noticed Mr Walsdorf hesitated when he talked about coming down here early. It's my guess he saw her then. If she was up and about, she could have heard the racket, and maybe it was a guilty conscience kept her up and about. Then she bribed him to keep quiet about seeing her by offering him and his family a home.'

'What a nasty, suspicious mind you have, Tom! I dare say a vicar's wife is used to early rising. And aren't their children here? She probably went to check that they weren't raising Cain. Besides, neither she nor the vicar is on Ernie's list.'

'Ah,' Tom ruminated.

'We'll have to ask her, of course. But Daisy did say, if I recall correctly, that she asked Nancy to check that Lady Eva really was dead and offered the key to her room to the Rev. Timothy. Obviously she trusted them.'

'You know how Mrs Fletcher is, Chief. She takes a liking to someone, she sort of overlooks anything that points in their direction. And the vicar is Miss Lucy's brother.'

Alec sighed. 'Yes, Daisy does tend to take people under her wing. I thought this time it was just Lucy and Bincombe . . .'

'And Miss Angela.'

'. . . But you could be right. It's just possible Lady Eva had found out something very recently and approached them about it although she hadn't yet put it in her books.'

'Clergymen and choirboys,' Tom said darkly.

'I trust not! The Reverend Timothy has a wife and children. He's not one of those High Church celibates. Apart from that, how did Walsdorf strike you?'

'Truthful. I don't think he knew Lady Eva knew, and I don't think he was too worried that she did. But if we find Rupert lying dead . . .'

'We'll know where to look,' Alec agreed with a grin.

CHAPTER 17

'Mr Montagu Fotheringay,' Ernie announced, ushering in a bulky gentleman dressed with an almost foppish elegance that ill-became his stoutness. His sister and his nephew lay dead, yet he had a camellia in his buttonhole which must have come from the conservatory, and two or three gold charms dangled from his Albert watch-chain. Perhaps he hoped they would protect him against becoming the next victim.

According to Daisy, he had virtually collapsed at the news that his sister had been murdered. Overcome with relief? Horrified? Or acting horror?

As he lumbered the length of the room, Mr Montagu didn't appear to be in any condition for so vigorous an activity as strangling a hefty, healthy woman. Not that his size was necessarily a disadvantage: he was no larger than Tom Tring, who could move with a speed and efficiency that always took malefactors by surprise. Yet the Honourable Montagu Fotheringay was breathing heavily by the time he sat down in front of the desk, his cheeks mottled and his forehead bedewed with perspiration, which he blotted with a large silk handkerchief.

Of course, that could be nerves.

His well-manicured hands were incongruously small. But Lady Eva had been strangled with a stocking, not by hand.

He gave his address as his club. 'Until today,' he added morosely, 'I'd have said "and Haverhill", but Nick and I have never got on, and with Rupert taking charge I shan't feel free to come down anytime without an invitation. What's worse, Rupert has no family feeling and he'll probably discontinue my allowance when he inherits. Thought I'd be dead by the time that happened. Might as well be, with the pittance I'll have left.'

'"Nick" is your brother, Lord Haverhill, sir?' Alec asked to clarify matters in Piper's notes. 'You don't get on with him?'

'Always been a damned Puritan prig, even when we were boys.'

'So you wouldn't have been happy had he found out that you suffer from . . . a social disease, shall we say.'

'Got a dose of the clap. And she was such a nice girl, too. Nick would hit the roof if he knew, but there's no reason he should find out. Hi, how do you know? Don't tell me Eva wrote it down in her blasted book? Well, if that don't take the biscuit! She might have known someone would read it if she dropped dead of a seizure. That cloddish son of hers, likely as not, if he can read.'

'But Lady Eva died of strangulation, not a seizure, and we have read her files.'

Unexpectedly, the Hon. Montagu grinned. 'Juicy reading, eh? She'd never let me take a peek.'

'She told you about her records, though?'

'Years ago.'

'And that she was aware of your . . . ailment?'

'No, no, I told her about that. You see, I'm afraid it wasn't the first time, but my faithful old doctor had died and I didn't know where to turn. Thought Eva, with her interests, might be able to give me the name of another man who specialized in such ... ailments. Which, I may say, she did. Not easily shockable, my sister. Marvellous fellow she sent me to.'

'You weren't afraid she'd pass on the information to your brother?'

'Good gad, no. Thick as thieves, Eva and I. Always was my favourite sister. Don't mind admitting, I'm going to miss her like the devil.' Clearing his throat noisily, he blinked hard. Alec felt in his pocket for a handkerchief, but Montagu pulled himself together. 'Poor old girl, what a way to go!'

He admitted to having left his room 'more than once' during the night, to visit the lavatory, which was opposite his room at the far end of the passage from Lady Eva's. He had noticed nothing out of the ordinary. If he had for a moment supposed that his sister was being foully done to death, he would have gone to the rescue. 'Not as limber as I was, but I can put a good deal of weight behind a fist, these days. Dare say I could have given a decent account of myself. Funny, I'd have expected Eva to fight off the beast who attacked her. Very active, she was, always buzzing about hither and yon. She used to say, "I'm not going to be one of those old ladies who put up their feet and wait to die. I'll go with my boots on." And so, in a manner of speaking, she did.'

Best not to tell him the theory that Lady Eva had fought off an attack with a pillow before succumbing to the stocking, Alec decided. Where was that damned stocking? Surely Dr Philpotts had completed the autopsy by now? He glanced at his wristwatch. Only quarter to nine. It had been a long day, and showed no sign of ending.

Montagu Fotheringay, still shattered by his sister's murder, had not gone down to tea. His nephew Henry had brought the news of Aubrey's death. He had dressed and gone to present his condolences to his brother and sister-in-law and the grieving widow, and to offer his services to act as host. Nick had told him that Rupert was expected.

'So, of course, I had to go down to dinner. I couldn't let that young whippersnapper think I was running shy. He was extremely rude to me, I may say, when I offered my sympathy on the loss of his father. But then, he never had much time for Aubrey, since Nick holds the purse-strings. Rupert gets a good allowance, besides his pay, but he's always coming with his hand out and Nick always shells out. Whereas if I run a little short, I might as well go begging to the man in the moon. Matter of fact, Eva used to oblige me occasionally, another reason why I'm going to miss her like the very devil!'

Daisy had said Montagu was the only person who seemed genuinely to mourn Lady Eva's death. Alec saw nothing in the man's rambling to contradict her judgment. If the maid confirmed that he'd been undressed when she took up his tea and when she fetched the tray, and if no one had seen him about, he could be crossed off the list for the murder of his nephew if not for his sister.

The Hon. Montagu went off to resume his interrupted dinner. As he left, a footman came in with an envelope and a small brown-paper parcel.

'I didn't want to interrupt, sir. These came a few minutes ago, by messenger. From Dr Philpotts, he said.'

As expected, the packet contained a stocking and a ring. The ring was gold set with an oval rose quartz, blush pink, surrounded by seed-pearls, of no great monetary worth. Its value must have been sentimental, perhaps an early gift from the late Sir Granville. Flattish, it would not have been too awkward to wear in bed. One of the prongs holding the stone in place had been bent back and on it was caught a wisp of thread.

'Let's have the lens,' Alec said to Tom, whose precious Murder Bag contained a magnifying glass among its treasures.

But Tom had picked up the stocking and was delicately rubbing it between his fingertips. 'Artificial silk, Chief,' he said. 'You're not telling me any of the toffs in this house wear artificial silk stockings. Looks like it must have been a man who bought it specially for the job.'

By the time Montagu came back to the dining room, everyone else was eating rhubarb and strawberry tart with whipped cream. The horrible events of the day didn't seem to have put Lord Haverhill's cook off her stride. The pastry was flaky, its contents succulent, with just the right amount of sugar. Daisy hoped the baby was enjoying it as much as she was.

For ten minutes or so the diners were left in peace. Then Teddy Devenish was summoned to the library.

'But he's already been questioned!' cried Lady Devenish, anguished.

'Don't fuss, Mater. I expect they just want to check that I locked the door behind me when I arrived last night.' In spite of his bravado, Teddy was pale and obviously anxious.

'Go with him, James,' his mother begged.

'Not me,' said Sir James. 'He's got himself into a mess, he can get himself out of it. Perhaps it'll make a man of him at last.'

Teddy flushed furiously and marched out.

'James! You must send for a lawyer.'

'Nonsense. What's the point of wasting money on a lawyer if you're innocent? You don't think Teddy killed his grandmother, do you?'

'Oh, James!'

People started whispering to their neighbours. Many hadn't yet seen the police, so for one to be called in a second time must be significant.

'Do you think Fletcher's going to arrest him?' Gerald muttered to Daisy.

'How should I know?' Daisy raised her voice a bit and went on, 'I expect it's just that Alec's thought of a question he forgot to ask before.'

Angela gave her a grateful look, but the whispering didn't stop.

Though Montagu was still eating, Sally, keeping an attentive eye on Rupert, took his cue to rise, saying, 'Shall we take our coffee in the drawing room, ladies?'

But whatever the custom in the Household Cavalry officers' mess, Rupert was forced to bow to the refusal of several ladies to be parted from the protection of their spouses.

'No!' Lady Devenish exclaimed. 'I know Teddy didn't do it, so the killer is still on the loose. I'm not going anywhere without James.'

This was curious, Daisy felt, when not so long ago the two had not been on speaking terms. But Sir James meekly followed his wife.

'Denzil, you'll come with us, won't you?' pleaded Lady Carleton. 'We can't be sure . . .'

'It's all right, Vickie,' said Oliver, 'I'm right behind you. Come along, Lucy.'

'Come along, Peter,' ordered Veronica Bancroft. 'We'll stay together.'

Flora went out with her aunt Ione, and Angela collected Daisy on her way. Daisy glanced back to see Gerald glumly moving to sit beside Rupert. He had to wait and make sure everyone was gone before he and Daisy met in the conservatory. Baines set decanters of port and brandy before Rupert, who was looking distinctly annoyed at the general resistance to his plans.

Montagu allowed a footman to serve him a large slice of tart with lashings of cream. Daisy wondered whether Rupert was sufficiently willing to be rude to his great-uncle to leave before the old man had finished his meal.

Sally had led the way through the door to the Long Gallery, followed by most of the others, but a few had gone through into the hall. This was the way Angela took Daisy. The reason was apparent as soon as they stepped through the door. Tiddler, banned from the dining room, dashed out from behind a pillar and launched himself at Angela's knees with a squeak of relief and joy.

'Down!' she said hastily. 'Don't ruin my stockings, this is my only decent pair. Good boy. If you were just a bit bigger and a bit braver, you'd make a good watchdog.'

Daisy stooped to pet the little beast. 'Alert, loyal, but not quite fierce enough. You don't really feel as if you need a watchdog, do you?'

'Don't you?'

'No. Alec knows everything I know, so why should anyone attack me?'

'I told him everything, too, which was little enough. I didn't see or hear anything to help him. But after all, I was up and about last night and the murderer could think I might remember something significant. Who knows?

I think whoever did it is mad. What could Uncle Aubrey have seen, tucked away in the family wing?'

'Perhaps it wasn't anything he could have seen last night but something he might have noticed before or after. We'll never know, now. But there wouldn't have been any point at all in killing him if other people might have had the same information.'

'I suppose not. Well, I'd better take Tiddler out for a few minutes. Coming?'

'Not just now. I'll see you later.'

'Right-oh.' Angela turned towards the Long Gallery and the gardens beyond.

Daisy made for the lavatory in the downstairs cloakroom. After the vermouth before dinner she had stuck to water instead of wine, but an attentive maid had kept refilling her glass and these days it didn't take much liquid to make her run.

As she approached, Lady Devenish came out, with that furtive look peculiar to the well-bred woman caught answering a call of nature. She ignored Daisy in a pointed way which could have been due to modesty or dislike or the two combined.

Emerging a couple of minutes later, Daisy glanced towards the library, wondering what Alec was up to. A movement caught her eye. Someone – Lady Devenish? – had hurriedly withdrawn into the shadows behind a pillar near the library door. She must be waiting for her son, or perhaps nerving herself to interrupt his interrogation. Though her dislike was mutual, Daisy couldn't help pitying her. If Teddy was still in there, Alec must have good reason to suspect him of killing his grandmother.

Grand-matricide? What was the Latin for grandmother?

Daisy's school had not considered Ancient Languages suitable for fragile female brains.

Sir James, though he had heeded his wife's plea to leave the dining room with her, was not visibly present to protect her. Daisy could think of several possible explanations. He might believe her safe because he knew his son was the murderer; or he might know she was safe because he himself was the murderer; or he might not much care if she was murdered.

With a shiver down her spine, Daisy made for the drawing room. She didn't want coffee, which had a tendency to keep her awake now that she was pregnant, but that was where Gerald would look for her. And there was a certain amount of comfort, if not safety, in numbers.

The numbers in the drawing room were not as great as she expected. Several people were missing, including Sir James. No sign of the Carletons, nor of Tim and Nancy. John Walsdorf was absent, though Jennifer was pouring coffee from a Thermos bottle. Apparently Sally had decided that this was a menial task unworthy of the lady of the house. She was talking to her sister-in-law, Flora. Judging by her gestures, they were discussing redecorating the old-fashioned crimson-and-gold room. Flora looked less than enchanted at the prospect, hardly surprising when her father had been poisoned just a few hours earlier. Sally might be trying to conciliate Flora after their earlier flare-up, but really, she had no sense of tact whatsoever.

Lady Ione was sitting alone near the window, sipping coffee in her self-contained, self-possessed way. Daisy had noticed her black frock earlier. If not a Paris model it was a copy, undoubtedly a new purchase. The glossy satin crêpe, jet-beaded and fringed, was adequate for mourning an unloved aunt but perhaps rather too decorative and lustrous for a beloved brother.

Daisy went over to her. 'May I join you?'

'Of course. Don't you want coffee?'

'No, thanks. What a beautiful evening it is.' The electric lights were on in the house but outside the rosy glow of sunset lingered in the dusk. 'It seems frightfully inappropriate.'

'Yes. Poor Aubrey! I'm afraid I'm very selfish, I've been thinking of myself. You know, I don't think I can bear to stay at Haverhill with Sally running rampant, but I can't come up with any practical alternative. I'm far too old to start a career. I don't suppose you have any ideas?'

'Not off the cuff, but I'll put my mind to it.'

'On the other hand I can't envision Rupert mouldering away here at Haverhill. He'll probably live expensively in town and bring dashing house-parties down for long weekends to interrupt the quiet mouldering away of the rest of us. You know, you're an extraordinary person, Daisy.'

'Me?' Daisy queried in ungrammatical astonishment.

'You. After my impulsive dash to London I was absolutely terrified of coming back to this house, to the family.'

'You didn't show it.'

'I'd decided bright and breezy was the only way to carry it off. Then I was faced with Aubrey's death and a police interrogation. Without your support, I suspect I'd have disintegrated entirely. I'd have been a mass of sodden hand-kerchief by the time I had to deal with the family, quite unable to cope with their questions. You pulled me through.'

'Oh, rubbish.' Daisy felt her cheeks grow hot. Blast! she thought. Nearly a mother and still blushing like a Victorian debutante! 'You'd have managed. And you'll work out how to cope with Sally if you decide to stay, or how to get along on your own if you decide to leave.'

'That's part of it. You have faith in people and they rise to your expectations.'

'I expect to like people, and usually they turn out to be quite nice. Not always,' she added, her eyes on Sally, whose condescending manner to Flora was obvious even from a distance. Beyond the two, she saw Binkie – Gerald – stop in the hall doorway and look around for her. She gave him a little wave. He nodded and left. 'There's Lord Gerald,' she said, relieved at the excuse to quit this embarrassing conversation. 'Will you excuse me? I promised to try to explain Lucy to him, though it's a hopeless case.'

'That's another part,' said Lady Ione, with a trace of amusement. 'You not only like people, you care.'

Already on her way, Daisy managed to pretend she had not heard.

Lucy's mother intercepted her on the way to the door. 'Daisy, I've heard you're meeting Lord Gerald in the conservatory. Of course I know you mean nothing wrong by it, dear, but don't you think it presents a rather odd appearance?'

'Sorry, Aunt Vickie, it can't be helped.'

'If he has information for the police, why does he not go straight to your husband instead of using you as an intermediary?'

'But it's nothing to do with the police. Nor is it exactly a clandestine assignation, since apparently the whole world knows, but we need privacy if I'm to persuade him to be patient with Lucy's asininities.' Was there such a word? she wondered.

'My dear, it's very kind of you to take so much trouble for Lucinda. But the conservatory! In my youth, a rendezvous in a conservatory bore such implications . . .'

'Not any longer.'

'I realize times have changed, but you don't think your husband . . . ?'

'Good heavens, no! Alec won't mind, since Lord Gerald has been crossed off his list.'

Mrs Oliver looked blank.

'His list of suspects. He'd be furious if I went to meet someone who might be a murderer, naturally. The thing is, the family isn't likely to interrupt us there after Lord Fotheringay died there so recently. Not that I'm frightfully happy about lingering there myself, but it was the first place that sprang to mind on the spur of the moment.'

'I see,' said Mrs Oliver doubtfully.

'I have to do all I can, Aunt Vickie, to sort Lucy and Gerald out. We can't just let them fall apart.'

'Heavens, no. As it is, I simply can't think what I'm going to say to Lady Tiverton. I'm sure the Tivertons have never had a murder in the family.'

'Most people haven't,' said Daisy. 'They can hardly blame you or Lucy.'

'I wish I could be certain of that.' Aunt Vickie went on for a while longer about the respectability of the Bincombe family before she said, 'But I'm keeping you, Daisy. Do your best to bring Lucinda and Gerald back together, and I'll worry about Lady Tiverton later.'

'That's the spirit, Aunt Vickie.'

Daisy went on towards the door but this time was headed off by Sally. She seemed to be in a conciliatory mood, for she said, 'You haven't had coffee, Mrs Fletcher. I'm afraid it's very remiss of me not to have made sure you were given a cup. I'll have to have a word with Jennifer. Come along now and we'll get you some.'

'Thanks, but I didn't actually want any this evening. It doesn't agree with me in the evenings at present.'

'Oh, I do understand! When I was carrying Dickie, I couldn't bear coffee. But there's no reason you shouldn't have a cup of tea, or cocoa if you prefer. Jennifer ought to have asked what you would care for. Would you like her to squeeze some orange juice for you?'

'No, truly, I don't want anything.'

'I hope your husband drinks coffee. I told Jennifer to have some sent in for him and his men.' The blasted woman seemed to be obsessed with making sure Daisy understood that Jennifer Walsdorf was an inferior in spite of being Rupert's first cousin.

'I expect they'll be glad of it,' Daisy said. 'They've had a long day and it will help keep them awake and alert.'

'Oh, but surely they're arresting Teddy Devenish?'

'I couldn't say. But even if they do, there's all sorts of things still to be done, getting an arrest warrant and charging him and carting him off to prison. Alec couldn't leave all that stuff to Tom and Ernie.'

Sally's eyebrows rose. 'Tom and Ernie?'

'Detective Sergeant Tring and Detective Constable Piper. They're friends of mine.'

While Sally was absorbing this facer, Daisy escaped.

She hurried across the hall, careful not to glance towards the library in case poor Lady Devenish was still anguishing there over her son's detention. The dining room was in darkness but for a shadowy area by the windows at the far end. Why hadn't Gerald left the lights on for her? Daisy felt for light-switches on the wall just inside the door, found a row and flipped one. Crystals sparkled as one of the elaborate gasoliers, converted to electricity, burst into life.

On the far side of the room, the glass doors to the conservatory reflected the light, the table and chairs, and Daisy as she approached, circling the table. Beyond the glass panes, the conservatory looked dark. Daisy was afraid she had been too long delayed and Gerald had given up waiting, but when she came closer she saw a dim yellow light, half obscured by foliage. She remembered that Lord Fotheringay had mentioned using only oil lamps. The brightness of electricity upset the plants' growth patterns, he had said.

She pushed open the door. 'Gerald?'

Silence.

The atmosphere was muggy, full of exotic fragrances. He had probably stepped out for a breath of fresh air. Daisy made her way along the winding path between the bushes and trees, some grouped in beds, some in individual pots: plain clay pots, decorative Chinese pots, hideous Victorian pots. The tap of her heels on the slates rang loud in her ears.

Ahead, the lamp burned steadily, in the open space where Lord Fotheringay had sat down to drink his cup of tea and never arisen. Her memory full of the sight of that innocuous gardener dead on the slate floor with Gerald bending over him, she did not for a moment recognize what now lay before her eyes.

The crumpled black heap was Gerald. A palm tree lay across his shoulders. Daisy's eyes, flicking away from the sight she didn't want to see, followed the dark, hairy palm trunk to the shattered pot and spilled soil, dark and rich.

She made herself look at Gerald. On either side of his head was a pool of bright red liquid, spreading, spreading.

CHAPTER 18

Another death? It couldn't be a coincidental accident! The back of Gerald's head was matted with blood and a steady stream trickled down on each side to drip into the growing puddles. Did that mean he was still alive? Daisy was not sure. What she could see of his face was bone white.

She needed to feel for a pulse and stanch the bleeding and go for help and, above all, not be sick. Her gorge rose as she knelt beside him, but she'd had a lot of practice recently at fighting down nausea. She conquered the turbulence in her stomach.

Her trembling fingers failed to find a pulse. She'd never been much good at finding pulses, not even her own. Stop the bleeding. She fumbled in her evening bag, dangling from her wrist, and pulled out her handkerchief. Belinda had hemmed the dainty little square of muslin for her for a Christmas present, and embroidered daisies in the corner. She hated to ruin it and it was far too small to be much use, but she had nothing else to use. Gerald's own handkerchief would be more adequate, but she couldn't reach it. Even if she managed to lift the palm and shift his large, muscular body, she knew people with head injuries had to be moved with extreme care.

If he wasn't already dead.

Could she use his socks to bind her folded hankie to the wound? No, her own stockings were more accessible. But what if his skull was fractured? She didn't dare put any pressure on the spot.

Maybe she ought to run for help. She couldn't bear to leave him. Suppose he wasn't yet dead and the murderer came back for another try?

'Hullo!'

Daisy jumped a mile. 'Angela, thank heaven! Gerald's hurt and I don't know what to do. Go for help.'

Angela strode forward from the garden door. Tiddler stayed cowering on the threshold, his quivering nose uneasily testing the air. 'No, you go. I'll deal with this.'

'You were a VAD?'

'No, Land Army.' Angela dropped to her knees, pulling a large linen handkerchief from her sleeve. 'But you wouldn't believe what some of the girls did to themselves with sickles and scythes. Besides, I've treated animals with similar injuries. Go on, quickly. Send Nancy and get Dr Arbuthnot here on the double.'

And Alec, Daisy thought. For a moment she hesitated. Was Angela the murderer come back for another try? No, she had to trust the lover of all creatures great and small, or Gerald would bleed to death anyway while she looked on, afraid to act.

'Don't touch or move anything you needn't,' she said, and ran.

Entering the hall, she saw between pillars a footman about to disappear through the baize door to the servants' wing.

'Stop!' she cried. He swung round so abruptly several cups slid off his tray and smashed on the marble floor. 'Lord

Gerald's hurt, badly. Find Mrs Reverend Timothy and send her to the conservatory. Hurry!'

He dropped the tray on top of the broken china and was already dashing off as he said over his shoulder, 'She's upstairs with Lady Fotheringay.'

Daisy sped on to the library and burst in. 'Alec! Lord Gerald – he's been attacked.'

He looked up in annoyance, then took in her words and her face and jumped up. 'Dead?'

'I don't know. He's bleeding horribly.'

'Where?' he snapped, coming around the desk towards her.

'In the conservatory. Oh, Alec ...' Realizing tears were pouring down her face, she dabbed at them ineffectually with the hankie still in her hand, then ran into his arms.

'Tom, conservatory,' he ordered over her head. Tom picked up the Murder Bag and dashed off. 'Ernie, telephone. Both doctors. Devenish, you're in the clear, for this one. Hop it. No, wait a minute, go and find one of the local bobbies Sir Leonard left us and send him to the conservatory. Then keep your mouth shut. Daisy, I can't stay. Are you going to be all right?'

'Yes,' she sobbed into his chest. 'Go, Alec. Don't let him die. Angela's looking after him. I didn't know what to do! How am I going to tell Lucy?'

'Calm down, love. Coming for me was the best thing you could possibly do.' He picked her up and deposited her on a sofa by a window. 'There, keep your feet up. I take it you didn't see anyone.'

'No, only Angela. Darling, what if ... ?'

'She knows you saw her. She's not going to harm him now. If Bincombe can be saved, we'll save him.' He strode out after Teddy Devenish.

Drying her eyes, Daisy was aware of Ernie watching her with concern as he talked on the telephone. Seeing she was once again more or less *compos mentis*, he asked, 'What sort of injury, Mrs Fletcher?'

'His head. Someone hit him on the head with a palm tree. There's blood everywhere.'

'Head injuries always bleed like a pig,' the young DC said comfortingly, and relayed the information into the phone. A moment later he was asking for another number and reporting to the police surgeon. 'Yes, sir, Dr Arbuthnot's coming, fifteen minutes he said. I'll tell the Chief Inspector you're on your way, sir. Thank you.' He held down the hook, cutting off the call, and said to Daisy, 'What d'you reckon, Mrs Fletcher, should I ring the CC? The Chief didn't say.'

Daisy thought. Sir Leonard hadn't been much help but he hadn't been a hindrance, either, and he had neatly disposed of the abominable Crummle. 'He might take offence if he's not notified at once. Yes, better ring him up. But don't wait for him to come to the phone. Leave a message. I'm sure the Chief needs you in the conservatory.'

Piper left a message with Sir Leonard's butler, hung up, and gathered up all the papers the Yard men had scattered over the desk. Stuffing them into his pockets, he came over to Daisy. 'You going to be all right now, Mrs Fletcher? Can I get you anything?'

'No, thanks, Ernie, I'll be all right. I don't know why I came unstuck like that.'

'He's a friend of yours, isn't he, Lord Gerald. It's different from a stranger, or even someone you know just a bit. And then, if someone's dead you can't help them and you can take your time to . . . to get a grip on yourself. But if they're not, and you're all in a rush, like, trying to decide what to do for the best . . . well, it's different.'

'Very,' Daisy agreed fervently.

'And you did the best thing you could, coming for the Chief, like he said.'

'I sent a footman for Nancy Fotheringay, too. She was a nurse during the war. Oh, blast! What one servant knows they'll soon all know, and what all the servants know can't be kept from anyone else. I must go and find Lucy.' She started to swing her legs off the sofa.

Piper fielded her ankles neatly. 'You stay put,' he said, then blushed and hastily put his hands behind his back. 'Sorry, Mrs Fletcher, but you didn't ought to get up yet. You looked like a ghost when you came running in. I'll see Miss Lucy comes to you.'

He left Daisy trying desperately to decide how on earth to break the news to Lucy.

She hardly had time to begin to fret herself to flinders before the elderly housekeeper bustled in. 'Oh dear, madam, this is a very nasty business!' She came over to the sofa and stood gazing down at Daisy, hands on her hips. 'Cocoa,' she announced. 'That's what you need, madam. Very soothing, cocoa is, made with milk and nice and sweet. I'll bring you some in a jiffy, with my own two hands. You just lie there and rest.'

Before Daisy could do more than murmur, 'Thank you, Mrs Maple,' she was trotting out again.

Cocoa did sound soothing, but Daisy was dismayed by how quickly word of the attack on Gerald had spread. Lucy must have heard by now – unless by chance Mrs Maple had been coming down the back stairs as the footman ran up to fetch Nancy.

Something of the kind must have happened, because when Lucy entered the library a few minutes later she obviously had no idea that her ex-fiancé was lying hurt, dying, perhaps dead. At her most languidly graceful, she crossed the room saying, 'Has he talked you into pleading his case? Quite useless, I'm afraid, darling, unless he's come up with something Mummy hasn't already said.'

Behind her came her parents. Daisy silently groaned. Their presence was going to complicate her revelation no end and make the effect on Lucy much harder to gauge.

'Sit down, Lucy. Aunt Vickie, Oliver, I've got some . . .'

'You're looking frightfully seedy, Daisy,' Lucy said, frowning. 'Are you feeling ill?'

Aunt Vickie clucked anxiously.

'I'm perfectly well,' Daisy said, 'but Gerald isn't. I wanted to break it gently but I don't know how. He's the latest victim.'

Lucy and Aunt Vickie both sat down very suddenly. Lucy's face was as still and inexpressive as a mannequin's in a shop window, carved in celluloid.

'Dead?' asked Oliver, pale-faced, his hand on his wife's shoulder.

'I don't know. Maybe not. He was . . . he was hit on the head and b-bleeding dreadfully.'

'Daisy, dear, don't talk about it.' Given someone to succour, Aunt Vickie pulled herself together. 'Try not to think about it. Think of your dear baby!'

'I'll go and see what I can find out,' said Oliver. 'In the conservatory?'

Before he reached the door, Constable Stebbins creaked in. 'Mrs Fletcher? Oh, there you are, madam. The Chief Inspector sent me to tell you the young chap's still alive. Hanging on by a thread, if you ast me, but he ha'n't passed on yet.'

Daisy let go a long breath she hadn't known she was holding.

'Thank you, Officer.' Oliver's calm manner was no different from what it would have been had Stebbins announced the recovery of a parcel dropped in the street. That was how an English gentleman behaved in the presence of minor official-dom. But when Lucy faltered through stiff lips, 'Is he . . . ?' and was unable to continue, her father read her mind and asked, 'Is Lord Gerald conscious?'

'That he's not, sir, nor like to be soon, and just as well. If you was to see the crack he took on his noddle . . .'

'Thank you, Officer,' Oliver repeated firmly.

'Thank you, Mr Stebbins,' said Daisy, earning a beam for recalling his name. 'I should think you'd better hurry back to see if the Chief Inspector needs you.'

Stebbins gave his agonizing new boots a meaningful glance, as if to say, 'I'm not hurrying nowhere in these.' But he saluted and tramped off, meeting Mrs Maple in the doorway.

Daisy was pleased to see the housekeeper, less because of the tray she carried than because her arrival postponed the moment when they'd have to talk about Gerald.

'Dr Arbuthnot's come,' Mrs Maple announced. 'I don't know what the world's coming to, Mr Oliver, and that's a fact. Here's your cocoa, Mrs Fletcher. Will you take something, Mrs Oliver? Miss Lucy?'

'I'm going to bed,' said Lucy, and walked out. Her mother burst into tears.

'The girl is quite impossible!' said Oliver angrily.

'Don't cry, Aunt Vickie! It isn't that she doesn't care. But there's nothing she can do for Gerald – I'm sure Alec wouldn't let her near him anyway – and she can't face explanations just now. Don't you understand?'

'You just listen to Mrs Fletcher, Mrs Oliver,' the old retainer advised. 'That's good, sound, common sense. I've seen bad news take people like that before. Miss Lucy just needs to be let alone to take it all in, that's all.'

'They're right, my dear. Best leave her alone for the moment. And I think the best thing for you would be to go up, too, with one of Marjorie's powders to help you sleep. We'll go and find her right away. You're going to be all right, Daisy?'

'To tell the truth, I've a very good mind to go to bed, too. This seems to have been an extraordinarily long day. I'll just finish my cocoa and write a note to Alec – I don't want to disturb him. Then I'll follow you up.'

Oliver led Aunt Vickie out, while Mrs Maple fetched a pencil and notepaper for Daisy, and a blotter to lean on. 'You keep your legs up for a bit before you go facing the stairs,' she advised. 'Not but what there's a bit more colour in your cheeks now, madam.'

'That's the cocoa. Thanks! Mrs Maple, I've been thinking.'

'Well, I'm sure I can't think when you've had a chance to do that, madam!'

'No, but this is a pretty easy think. Assuming Lord Gerald doesn't . . . doesn't die in the next little while, they're not going to want to leave him lying on the cold, hard slates. But I'm sure he should be moved as little as possible, certainly not carried upstairs. Is there somewhere you could have a bed made up?'

'Why yes, the little room near the front door – the antechamber some call it. I'll go and ask Mrs Walsdorf . . . No, then, I won't. It'll only make trouble. And ask Mrs Rupert I won't neither! Nor call her my lady till his poor father's properly buried.'

'I'm sure no one can possibly mind your putting Lord

Gerald in there. After all, he's the son of a marquis. Oh dear, someone's going to have to break the news to Lord and Lady Tiverton!'

'Not you, my dear,' said Mrs Maple firmly. 'Leave it to Mr Fletcher, who's a gentlemanly man, for all he's a policeman, and well up to the task.'

'And the Haverhills . . .'

'I'll go and speak to the Reverend about that this minute.'

'Oh yes, Timothy's the one for that. Poor Tim! Everyone's counting on him and Nancy.'

'And who better, madam? There's two that'll have their reward in Heaven, sure enough, bless them.'

The housekeeper left and Daisy, sipping the cocoa, pondered just what she needed to say to Alec. In the end, she wrote: 'Darling, I can't think of anything else I can do to help, so I'm going to our room. I shan't sleep, though, until I hear how Gerald is, and I have things to tell you, so please come up when you can. All my love, Daisy.'

She folded the paper in three and three again, tucked the ends in, and wrote 'DCI Fletcher' on the front. Then she thought of Belinda, who would have come home from school to be told by Mrs Dobson, the cook-housekeeper, that her daddy had been called away. Bel was used to such eventualities, and she had been going to stay with a school friend for the weekend while both Alec and Daisy were away for the wedding. But, reliable though Mrs Dobson was, Bel would be happier if she could go to the Prasads a day earlier, or if that was not possible, to the Germonds.

Daisy set down her cup on the tray, picked up the note to Alec, the blotter, the unused paper and the pencil, and went over to the desk. Lying on it was the beginning of a letter, in some foreign language she didn't recognize. Even the handwriting looked foreign.

She remembered the sheet of paper John Walsdorf had slipped under the blotter when she came in that morning to ring up the police. He must have family or friends still in Luxemburg. It was quite natural, of course, but the fact that he had not cut all ties made him seem somehow more foreign. Perhaps he had foreseen such a consequence from the insular English and that was why he had hidden his letter. There was no reason to see anything sinister in it.

Daisy wondered if Alec knew. Walsdorf was one of the few he had already seen, before calling Teddy Devenish in for the second time, which suggested that Lady Eva had discovered something about him.

Actually, it was irrelevant whether his continuing connections in Luxemburg were what Lady Eva had ferreted out. Everything she knew was known to Alec. Anything she didn't know had nothing to do with her murder. So Daisy had no reason to tell Alec about the letter, thank heaven. Not that she had exactly read someone else's correspondence, as she couldn't understand a word, but just looking at the thing made her feel guilty. One simply didn't nose into other people's letters. She set down the blotter squarely on top of it.

What a pity Ernie had taken all the police notes with him! She hardly knew a thing about the investigation. Alec hadn't had time to talk to most of the residents and guests at Haverhill, let alone to listen to her opinions of them, and now he had two murders and an attempted – so far – murder on his hands.

Daisy shivered. No one knew how Lord Fotheringay had posed a threat to the murderer, but when he died Gerald was the first on the scene. And when Gerald was attacked, Daisy herself had been first on the scene. She would lock her bedroom door when she went upstairs.

In the meantime, she sat down at the desk and wrote briefly to Melanie Germond, Sakari Prasad, and Belinda. In a drawer she found stamps and envelopes. If the letters went out first thing in the morning, they should be delivered in time for Bel to spend tomorrow night with one of her friends. Sighing, she sealed the envelopes. On the whole it was a definite blessing that Alec's mother had moved to Bournemouth, but there had been a few advantages to having her living with them.

She didn't feel at all like walking down the drive to the letter-box by the gates. Wondering where to put the letters so that they would be posted as early as possible, Daisy went out into the hall.

John Walsdorf came towards her from the direction of the stairs, a sheaf of envelopes in his hands. He had not come to the drawing room for coffee after dinner, she recalled. He must have been upstairs writing letters – not in the conservatory hitting Gerald over the head. She hoped.

'You have letters to post? I may take them for you? I have written to those wedding guests I failed to reach by telephone or telegraph, and some explanations to others. To those I spoke to only briefly or left messages. I go to walk to the letter-box now. We have missed the last post but thus without fail they will catch the early post.'

'Thanks!'

'I hope you did not consider to walk down yourself. This is too dangerous at this time. Already are two persons lying dead.'

He didn't know about Gerald? Daisy decided to leave it to

someone else to break the news. 'Thanks,' she said again, handing over her letters. 'Do you think you'll be safe?'

'I know nothing dangerous to anyone. And besides . . .' He pulled the butt of a pistol just far enough from his pocket for Daisy to see it. 'If the murderer attacks me, Mr Fletcher may not have to arrest him.'

'But if you killed him, he'd have to arrest you. Be careful.'

Walsdorf bowed and went on his way.

If he was the murderer, he could shoot someone and claim self-defence, Daisy thought. He could have shot her. No, too much chance of someone coming through the hall, and Alec, for one, would never credit that she had attacked him.

She shouldn't have stayed alone in the library. Not that she had been alone for long, with everyone popping in and out, but the point was that they had all, in the end, left her alone there, even Ernie. Maybe they all unconsciously believed she was safe because she was the wife of the great Detective Chief Inspector from Scotland Yard. She had no such faith in her own immunity.

The stairs looked long and lonely. Someone could push her down them and claim she had turned dizzy and fallen.

Not likely, she assured herself, hurrying up. If she was only hurt, not killed, she'd know who had done it. She went into her bedroom and turned the key in the lock. Then, realizing it was probably not the only key, she shot the bolt, too.

That was when she realized she had given John Walsdorf the note for Alec, saying she had something to tell him.

CHAPTER 19

'Daisy?' Lucy's voice came from the bedroom next door. Daisy stopped brushing her teeth and spoke through a mouthful of toothpaste: 'Ung-huh?'

'Come in for a minute, when you're finished?'

'Ung-huh!'

She finished her teeth, gave the enormous bathtub a longing and regretful look, washed her face, and went through the connecting door. A glance reassured her that Lucy's door to the corridor was bolted. She turned to Lucy. Sitting up in bed, without make-up, she was pale and wan, her hair tousled.

'I tried to go to sleep but it's much too early and . . . How is he?'

'I don't know, darling. I couldn't go and interrupt them to find out. I wrote a note to Alec to ask him to come up and tell me, but I've gone and given it to John Walsdorf and he'll be putting it in the letter-box right at this very minute.'

'Silly ass. Why on earth?'

'He was going to the post and I didn't want to walk down the drive. I wrote to Belinda and to her friends' mothers to propose her going to stay tomorrow as well as Friday and Saturday.'

'I'd have been a terrible mother, you know.'

'Why? You'd have a nanny, and then they go to school.'

'Darling, it's simply not done to let a nanny bring up one's offspring these days. One is expected to take an interest, kiss the little dears good night and so on. Did your mother ever kiss you good night?'

'Not that I remember,' Daisy admitted. 'I sometimes didn't see Mother for weeks on end.'

'Did you want to?'

'Well, no. But if I had, maybe we'd be on better terms now.'

'You could hardly be on worse,' Lucy said candidly.

'Don't rub it in! You and Aunt Vickie don't exactly make a practice of falling into each other's arms.'

'No. Mummy was usually at home, and we were usually taken down for tea, unless there were guests. But I've always been the cuckoo in the nest, and cuckoos don't make good parents.'

'Rubbish,' Daisy snorted. 'You can carry analogy too far, you know. Is that why . . . ?'

'Partly, maybe. I've never much cared for children. I simply can't bring myself to swoon over Tim's offspring, or George's.'

'Other people's are different, though I must say I adore Violet's. Or rather, one's own are different. Even if Bel isn't strictly speaking my own . . . Well, let's not get soppy. But when she's not happy, I mind.'

Lucy was silent for a moment, then she said, 'I wish I knew how he is! I feel as if it's all my fault. If I hadn't been so beastly to him, he wouldn't have been meeting you in the conservatory. In fact, if I hadn't called him down from town, he wouldn't even have been at Haverhill, let alone walking in on poor Uncle Aubrey's death.'

'Of course it's not your fault, darling. It's the murderer's fault. You're not going to go all weepy on me, are you?'

'No.' Lucy summoned up a sort of smile. 'Though some-times I wonder if the weepy sort have the right idea and we stiff-upper-lip types . . . What's that?'

Daisy listened. 'Someone knocking on my door, I think.'

'Don't open it!'

'I expect it's Alec. If not, I won't.' She went through the bathroom to her and Alec's room, and over to the door. 'Who's there?'

'It's me, love.'

'Darling!' She slid back the bolt, unlocked and opened the door. 'How is he?'

'Still breathing, but Arbuthnot doesn't like the look of him at all. Severe concussion and considerable loss of blood. The latter might have done for him but for your friend Angela.'

'Thank heaven! I was so afraid of leaving her with him – she'd been outside since right after dinner and I'm sure she's strong enough to have bashed him with that tree.'

'I don't see you had much choice. You'd likely have killed him through ignorance. Angela had every chance to finish him off undetectably before Tom arrived, so I've crossed her off my list. That clears Teddy, too. I know I let him go before, but there was still the possibility that he and his sister had con-spired. The trouble is, he was easily my best suspect.'

'I can tell you who wasn't in the drawing room for coffee.'

'I thought that must be it when I got your note. You didn't see any clue that might lead us to the murderer?'

'It was murder, then? Attempted murder?'

'Looks like it.'

'Why?'

'Daisy . . . !'

'All right, I won't ask. But, darling, I'm afraid this time I'm a terrible witness. A dead body is one thing, and bad enough, but someone who might die if you do the wrong thing rather takes your mind off anything else. I saw a broken flower-pot and a small palm and spilled soil. And him.' She wasn't ready to think about it in any more detail than that. 'No sign of anyone else.'

'You haven't told anyone what he was hit with, have you? Someone may be hoping we think it was an accident.'

'Give me credit for a little common sense!'

'Well, don't mention it. To anyone at all.'

'I won't. You said you got my note? John must have checked what I gave him before he went out.'

'Never mind that,' Alec said impatiently. 'I've only got a minute. First, who knew you were meeting Bincombe?'

'Everyone. I mean, I can probably remember who was nearby when we arranged it, if I try, but at least one of them must have talked about it afterwards because Lucy's parents knew.'

'They knew why you met?'

'No. Actually, Aunt Vickie was afraid it would give people the wrong idea but ... Gosh, I'd forgotten! She actually assumed it was because Gerald wanted me to pass on some tidbit of information to you. So the idea was current, not just in the murderer's mind.'

'Great Scott, Daisy!'

'Darling, I don't know how to stop people thinking it's a good idea to tell me things they want you to know.'

'Are you trying to tell me you don't encourage them?'

'Look at Lady Ione. You were right there and I didn't say a word. Anyway, that's got nothing to do with it. Gerald just wanted to talk about Lucy and the rest was a misconception for which I accept absolutely no responsibility!'

Alec sighed. 'Never mind that, then. Who wasn't in the drawing room?'

'Right-oh. Angela, of course. She took the dog out right after—'

'Just names, Daisy, at least for the moment.'

'Lady Devenish. I saw her lurking in the hall outside the library when— All right, darling! Sir James wasn't there, nor were the Carletons. Mr Walsdorf. Tim and Nancy. Darling, it couldn't have been—'

'Nancy Fotheringay was extremely helpful with Bincombe until the doctor arrived. They'd both been up with Lady F and the Haverhills, easy to check.'

'Thank heaven! This is difficult, thinking who wasn't there. Maybe I should tell you who was.'

'Make a list, please. You can add any explanations that come to mind, but underline the names so I can pick them out. Is Lucy fit to do the same?'

'I think so. She's in a funny mood, blaming herself. Doing something positive will probably help. Shall I bring the lists down?'

'No, I'll send someone up for them in about half an hour. Unless it's Ernie, slide them under the door. You stay here and keep the door bolted. I'll probably be very late, so I'll just go and doss with Tom and Ernie.'

'Oh no, darling, tap on the door and wake me up, even if it's three in the morning. If I'm asleep. Not knowing about Gerald . . .'

'You need your sleep, love, for the baby.'

'I'll try,' Daisy promised. 'I'm tired enough, but I rather think Macbeth hath murdered sleep.'

Alec kissed her. Raising his head, he looked towards the bathroom door and frowned. Daisy turned her head.

Leaning against the door jamb, Lucy said sardonically, 'Sorry, didn't mean to snoop.'

But despite her cool tone, her hands were clenched in the pockets of her kimono, Daisy saw. Perhaps Alec also noticed, because he said quite gently, 'I have to run. Bincombe is still among the living. Daisy will tell you about him. Don't forget to bolt the door after me, Daisy.'

Daisy did so.

'Does that mean he thinks we're really in danger?' Lucy demanded.

'I doubt that you are, darling, but presumably Gerald was bashed because he was first on the scene, and this time I was.'

'Gerald didn't see anything. He would have told Alec hours ago. Why shouldn't he?'

'Very likely he didn't see anything, but you know how sometimes something you hardly noticed at the time strikes you later. I suppose the murderer was afraid of that, especially when Gerald arranged to meet me. People do tell me things when they're not sure they want to bother the police.'

'Because the police make them feel silly if it's unimportant.'

'Because they're afraid they'll look silly,' Daisy said firmly. 'Quite another matter.'

'Sorry. What did Alec say about Gerald? It's not good, is it?'

'Bad concussion, and he lost a lot of blood. Alec said he would have bled to death if Angela hadn't . . . I didn't know what to do, Lucy!'

Lucy came and put her arms round Daisy, but she said, 'Buck up, darling. We can't all be medical experts. Wait a minute, did you say *Angela? Cousin Angela?* The one with the dogs?'

'She said she'd saved animals with similar injuries.'

They looked at each other and burst into whoops of laughter.

Their mirth did not last long but Daisy, at least, felt better. 'Come on,' she said, going over to the writing table, 'there are things we can do to help. I told Alec we'd make lists for him of who was in the drawing room after dinner. Pity we can't do the same for tea-time.'

'Angela!' Lucy was still marvelling. 'I'll have to start being nice to her. Too humbling! I'd have thought he'd want to know who wasn't there, not who was.'

'Try and remember who wasn't, and you'll see how much easier it is to say who was. One might simply not have noticed someone.'

'I see what you mean. Right-oh, let's give it a go.'

Alec uttered a silent blasphemy as he came down the flight of stairs to the hall and saw the small group of people watching him, all too obviously waiting for him. Rupert strode forward to meet him.

'Inspector, what the deuce is going on here?' he demanded contemptuously. 'How many more murders are we to expect? If this is the best Scotland Yard can do, we might as well have left the investigation to the local dolts!'

Stopping on the bottom step, where he had an inch or two advantage, Alec looked him up and down in silence for a moment, then said, 'So you agree that your father was murdered, Lieutenant?'

Rupert's lips tightened. 'Lieutenant Colonel.' His sudden smile, as sardonic as it was unexpected, strongly reminded Alec of his cousin Lucy. 'No, Chief Inspector, I do not believe anyone would harm my father.'

'Well, we'll see when the autopsy results come back. As for the rest, if you wish to return the case to Inspector Crummle—'

'Crummle?'

The Reverend Timothy joined them. 'Believe me, Rupert, you do not want Crummle back on the job.'

'Are you speaking ill of your neighbour, Timmy?' Rupert jeered. 'All right, I'll take your word for it. No, Chief Inspector, we don't want Crummle.'

'Just as well. It would take not only the Chief Constable's approval but my Commissioner's. And at this time of night . . .'

'Say no more. No doubt you are doing your best.'

'You could help, if you were to ask your guests not to retire until they have spoken to me. I haven't yet had time to see everyone, though I have just had a long talk with Daisy, who has told me everything she observed on entering the conservatory. Every new attack provides new clues. Now, if you'll excuse me, I must return to Lord Gerald.'

'How is he?' Rupert asked with concern, and the rest of the group, who had been listening at a little distance, gathered closer.

Whatever Alec said was bound to reach the murderer's ears. He knew what he wanted the murderer to believe. Unfortunately it was far too near the truth for comfort. 'Lord Gerald is still unconscious,' he said. 'I'm afraid Dr Arbuthnot does not expect him to survive.'

'Oooh!' The wail came from Lucy's mother. 'How am I going to tell the Tivertons?'

The Rev. Timothy put his arm around her shoulders. 'You don't need to, Mother. Uncle Nicholas has said he's going to telephone Lord Tiverton. He's just waiting for me to take him the latest news. I only wish it were better!'

'Mr Fletcher,' said Lucy's father, 'I don't want to ask for special treatment, but if you could see your way to interviewing Victoria first, so that I can put her to bed with one of my sister-in-law's bromides . . .'

'I'll see what I can do, sir, but it won't be for a while yet, I'm afraid.'

'Good enough. Come along, Vickie.'

'Well! I don't see why Vickie should have priority! I'm sure I'm just as upset about Ursula as she is about Lucy.'

'Come now, Adela,' said Lord Carleton dryly, 'why should you be upset when Ursula all too obviously is not?'

'I think it's all too thrilling for words!' exclaimed a gawky girl of sixteen or so.

In the midst of the general disapprobation this remark engendered, Alec escaped.

At the door from the dining room to the conservatory, he had posted Stebbins. Seeing him, the elderly constable lurched to his feet and saluted. 'I hope as you don't mind me sitting down, sir,' he said anxiously.

'As long as you don't drift off.'

'Not likely, not with retirement coming up. 'Sides, I'm not sleepy. It's me feet, you see. These here new boots hurts something chronic.'

'Anyone try to come through?'

'Nossir. But here comes summun now, sir.'

Alec swung round to see the door to the hall, which he had shut behind him, begin to open. It was too late to duck into the conservatory and leave Stebbins to deal with the intruder. 'Please, not Lady Carleton!' he muttered.

'It's the CC, sir,' the constable reassured him unnecessarily, saluting again as Sir Leonard entered, followed by Dr Philpotts.

Philpotts, black bag in hand, dodged past the Chief Constable and came striding round the table, saying, 'Still living? Arbuthnot's with him? Head injury? Right, we'll see what can be done.' And he disappeared into the conservatory.

'The Curse of the Conservatory,' said Sir Leonard. 'It's like one of those thrillers, isn't it? I don't want to get in your way, Fletcher, but I thought I'd better turn up. Show willing, don't you know. Can you give me an account of what's going on in a few words?'

'Of course, sir. Lord Gerald Bincombe arranged to meet my wife in the conservatory after dinner, to talk about his intended. She arrived to find him badly hurt, apparently struck on the back of the head with a palm tree.'

'By Jove, there's an original weapon! I suppose it couldn't have been an accident?'

'No, sir. I said "apparently". The tree lay across his body but had not actually been in contact with the injury. The pot's been smashed and the soil spilled, and among the debris is a clear spot roughly five inches wide, of indeterminate length, and roughly rectangular with rounded corners at one end. The other end could be any shape – it fell clear of the debris – or rather the debris did not fall on it. We think the murderer must have flung the weapon away after hitting Bincombe, shattering the pot. Then he picked it up and took it away.'

'Hmm, about five inches wide, with rounded corners? Cricket bat?'

'That's an idea. Certainly a cricket bat could be wielded with sufficient force to cause such a nasty injury. Dr Arbuthnot considers that ninety-nine people out of a hundred would have been killed instantly.'

'Hard head, what?'

'Bincombe played Rugby football for one of the universities. I gather a thick skull is a prerequisite,' Alec said dryly.

'Jove, yes, wouldn't last long in a scrum otherwise. Bincombe – he's the one who was with Lord Fotheringay when he died? Connected?'

'We can only assume so, sir. We're working on the premise that the murderer believed Bincombe had recalled something of significance which he hadn't mentioned to us. I'm afraid people seem to have a tendency to confide in my wife matters they had far better bring to us . . .'

'It's those blue eyes of hers,' Sir Leonard said shrewdly. 'Noticed it myself, matter of fact. Competent little woman, though,' he added in a congratulatory tone, 'and there's not many you can say that about.'

Alec managed to keep a straight face while resolving to pass on the compliment. 'Apparently there was general speculation that this was why Bincombe had asked Daisy to meet him privately.'

'And the murderer acted to forestall the revelation! Just as he killed Lord Fotheringay to prevent his talking about Lady Eva's murder.'

'So it would seem, sir.'

'Dammit, man, does this mean Mrs Fletcher is now in danger?'

'I sincerely trust not, but she's upstairs with her door bolted. I've done my best to spread word that she's told me all she saw, and to emphasize the fact that each new attack gives us more to go on. Not that I've had time to gather facts, let alone to consider them.'

'And I'm keeping you from your work now!' Sir Leonard apologized. 'Is there anything I can do to help?'

'Yes, sir, two things. First, Constable Stebbins here has been extremely useful, but he's been on duty all day and deserves a rest. There's also a constable on duty at the gate who ought to be relieved. If you could arrange to have reliefs for them and a couple more men come out to take the night watch, and possibly to help search for the weapon, I'd be very grateful.'

Stebbins was heard to mutter, 'Me too!'

'Certainly, certainly. And?'

'I'm hoping to interview this evening everyone I haven't seen yet. I can't keep them from their beds if they choose to go, but if you were to go and mingle and give them a pep talk . . .'

'Pep talk?'

'Sorry, sir, bit of slang I picked up in America. Encouragement, let's say, to stay downstairs and do their duty as citizens. I've asked Lieutenant Colonel Fotheringay to do the same, but your word might carry more weight.'

'I'll see what I can do,' Sir Leonard promised. '"Pep talk", eh? I like it! And you can count on me to make sure everyone knows you've wrung Mrs Fletcher dry.'

An infelicitous image, and inaccurate besides, Alec thought, continuing into the conservatory. He would never be able to wring Daisy dry of her endless theories. Nor would he want to, for now and then they actually proved valuable. He must remember to send Piper up for her and Lucy's lists of names. Daisy's was certain to come with plenty of comments. A 'competent little woman' indeed.

He allowed himself a grin, only to meet Tom's eyes and raised eyebrows. Sobering, he shook his head.

By the light of an oil lamp, several lanterns, and a large electric torch, he surveyed the scene of the latest crime. The fallen palm had been moved aside. The two doctors knelt on either side of Lord Gerald, who lay now on a spread quilt which Tom and Ernie had managed to slide beneath him with minimal disturbance. At his head knelt Nancy Fotheringay. With gentle, capable hands she was removing the bloodstained bandage covering his injury, while Angela prepared a fresh dressing at the table which earlier had held the fatal cup of tea. His hair had been shaved around the ugly wound.

Pointing, Dr Arbuthnot was explaining to his colleague what he had found and what he had done about it. Ernie Piper stood by with his notebook, taking down their consultation. Alec looked just long enough to see that blood still seeped, slowly now, from the mashed area at the back of Bincombe's resilient cranium.

He turned to Tom and they moved aside, out of the way.

'I've done some photographs and a sketch of that clear shape, Chief.'

'The Chief Constable suggested a cricket bat.'

'Could be! What I don't get is why he threw it, and why he picked it up afterwards.'

'Who can fathom the mind of a murderer? Perhaps he's beginning to be disgusted at the lengths to which his first murder is leading him. Can you imagine him standing over Bincombe, the bloody bat in his hands, satisfaction turning to horror. He flings the weapon away from him, then realizes he must take it away to polish off his fingerprints.'

'All the crooks know about dabs these days,' Tom said grumpily.

'But they don't always remember to act on the knowledge. Perhaps he thought there was a chance of our believing the whole thing was an accident.'

'What, with no blood on the bloody tree-trunk? And the pot exploded through spontaneous combustion, I suppose!'

'Who can fathom the mind of a murderer?' Alec repeated. 'He was hurried, remember. Too rushed to make sure Bincombe was dead. Daisy might arrive at any moment.'

'Good job she didn't arrive too soon.'

'Yes.' Alec's agreement was heartfelt. 'At any rate, we'll have to have a look for the weapon in case it has prints on it. I've asked Sir Leonard for a couple of extra men. If we don't find the damn thing tonight, at least we can stop up the holes so no one's sneaking out in the small hours to drop it in the lake.'

'If it's a cricket bat, it'd float. Even that drip of a Devenish boy would know that.'

'You *are* feeling contrary this evening, Tom!'

'Three murders in one day, two of 'em while we were here. It's enough to make anyone contrary.'

'True. Anyway, Teddy Devenish is already out of the picture for this one.'

'Worse luck. I fancied him for doing in his grandma,' Tom said with regret, then brightened. 'That's still possible, though, unless his ma's got an alibi for Lord F and Bincombe.'

'His mother protecting him? Conceivable, though I rather doubt she'd think of using a cricket bat, or know where to find one. We're going to have to do it the slow way, asking everyone whom they were talking to at tea and after dinner, whom they saw and who was missing. With luck at least we'll eliminate the majority. Two at a time will speed things up, and there's plenty of room in the library for one of us at each end.'

'Right, Chief. Just make sure I get the ones without handles to their names!'

'If you like, though I think you're quite capable of coping

with any of them, with what Ernie calls your "posh vocab". First, though, as he's busy with the medicos, would you go up and get Daisy's and Lucy's lists? Maybe we'll be able to cross off a few names before we start. I'd send Stebbins but . . .'

'Those new boots of his! It'd take him half an hour. Right, Chief, I'll be back in a trice.'

Alec returned to the doctors. Arbuthnot was closing his bag.

'I'm handing over to Philpotts, Chief Inspector. I'll send out a nurse to sit with him overnight. He's not likely to regain consciousness.'

'We'll take care of him tomorrow,' said Nancy Fotheringay, 'won't we, Angela?'

'I'm not a trained nurse,' Angela said in alarm. 'I wouldn't know what to do if he gets worse.'

'If he gets worse, he'll be dead,' Arbuthnot told her.

'Oh, I wouldn't say it's that bad,' the police surgeon contradicted him quite cheerfully.

'Time will tell. Anyway, I'll send another nurse in the morning. I'm sure Lord Haverhill is not going to quibble at the expense. May I say, Fletcher, that I most sincerely hope you will not have to call me out again tonight. Or tomorrow, come to that.'

'Believe me, Doctor, you can't wish it any more than I do. Thank you for turning out so promptly and for ministering to the victim.'

'Only sorry I couldn't do anything for the previous two. Good night.'

'Good night, sir. Oh, by the way, please don't mention to anyone, anyone at all, Dr Philpotts' comparatively optimistic opinion of the case.'

'I shouldn't dream of raising false hopes.'

As Arbuthnot trudged away through the greenery, Alec looked down at Lord Gerald's pallid face and bloodless lips, almost as white as the fresh bandage Nancy was applying with Angela's assistance. 'Do you really see cause for hope, Dr Philpotts?' he asked quietly, drawing the police surgeon aside.

'Certainly. His pulse isn't good but it's better than it was when Arbuthnot first took it. We agree that a blood transfusion is not called for. His breathing is shallow but regular. His heart is strong. We find no apparent indentation in the skull, so we may hope that no fragment of bone is compressing the brain. There may be a crack; I can't tell without taking him to a hospital for an X-ray, and it would be most unwise to move him.'

'Not even to a bed? I gather a bed has been prepared for him on the ground floor.'

'Hmmm.' Philpotts took Lord Gerald's pulse again, listened to his breathing and his heart with a stethoscope, thumbed back each eyelid in turn and shone a light into his eyes. 'Pupils equal in size,' he grunted. He glanced around the conservatory. 'This is a dashed inconvenient place to care for him. He'll do better in bed if we're very careful getting him there. He was hit with a flat object, by the way, or there might have been more damage. Less extensive but more concentrated force. The blow missed the spinal column, thank heaven.'

'Yes, it's high, isn't it. Tall attacker?'

'From Arbuthnot's description of his original position, I'd say he might have been stooping or crouching, to tie his shoe perhaps.'

'That's what we thought. Glad to have you confirm it, Doctor.'

'Good job, too. He didn't have too far to fall. I wouldn't give much for his chances if there'd been a second blow on the opposite side of the head.'

'All in all, our murderer botched this one,' Alec said thoughtfully. 'Either he's getting nervous or he's so over-confident he's not taking pains. Either way, he's making mistakes, and that makes our job easier.'

'I can only hope,' said the doctor, 'that he's made enough mistakes this time for you to catch him before he has another go!'

CHAPTER 20

The knock on the bedroom door made Daisy jump. 'Who's there?' she called.

'It's Jennifer.'

Jennifer had been pouring coffee when Gerald was attacked. But her husband had been wandering about the house. Did Jennifer pour tea at tea-time today, as she did yesterday? Had she perhaps prepared the pot that went to Lord Fotheringay? John Walsdorf was one of the few interviewed so far – because Lady Eva's notes had revealed some secret he might be ready to kill for?

Daisy looked at Lucy, who shrugged. There were two of them, after all. Walsdorf was still on his way to the postbox. Or was that pretence? After handing over Daisy's note, he could have watched as Alec went up to talk to her and came down again. He could be lurking just outside the door, waiting to rush in when she opened it to Jennifer.

'Daisy, are you all right?' Jennifer asked, her voice worried.

'Yes,' she said for the umpteenth time that evening. 'Half a mo.'

Lucy stuck her pen in the inkstand, went over to the fireplace, and picked up the poker. Daisy turned both their half-done lists facedown and went to slide back the bolt.

'I'm sorry, are you in bed already?'

Daisy opened the door. 'No, not yet. What's up?'

'Sally asked me . . . No, let's be accurate, Sally told me to come and see if you'd like a drink, alcoholic or otherwise, or an aspirin or anything. Hello, Lucy! I'm so sorry about Lord Gerald. Are you feeling chilly? A shock takes some people that way, I know. I'll have a fire laid.'

'No, I just feel safer with a poker in my hand,' Lucy said with brutal frankness.

Jennifer's quick, nervous glance behind her did much to persuade Daisy of her innocence. 'I keep forgetting. I suppose I can't really believe all this is going on. Here, at Haverhill! It's such a staid place. The wedding would have been the biggest excitement we'd had in ages.'

'Sorry to disappoint you. But you have plenty of excitement to make up for it.'

'It's not exciting, it's horrible. People getting hurt and killed, and not knowing whom you can trust, and not even being able to get away. We all have to stay up till we've seen your husband, Daisy, but I don't suppose anyone will be able to sleep, anyway. Oh, Lucy, your mother asked me to give you this. It's one of your aunt's powders.'

'I shan't take it. Keep it for yourself.'

'Thanks, but I never take anything, in case Emily wakes in the night. It wouldn't surprise me if all the children have nightmares tonight. The nurserymaid told Tim and Nancy's boys, silly girl, and of course they told Emily and Dickie. Luckily they haven't properly understood. I think I'll go up now and make sure they're asleep. Daisy, is there anything you'd like?'

'No, thanks. Mrs Maple gave me cocoa earlier, which was just what I needed.'

'Oh, good. Good night, then.'

Bolting the door after Jennifer, Daisy noticed that she had dropped the paper of bromide powder on the little table by the door. She picked it up. 'Better not take this, darling.'

'I wasn't going to. But I must say, she didn't appear to be frustrated at being deprived of the opportunity of slipping oleander into your bedtime drink.'

'No. I quite like Jennifer.'

'She's all right. She was a fool to marry a penniless foreigner.'

'Oh, Lucy, don't be so narrow-minded! You don't like Alec because he's a policeman and not out of the top drawer, and—'

'I do like Alec, Daisy, now that I know him.'

'I dare say you'd like John Walsdorf if you got to know him. Does he still have family in Luxemburg?'

'I've no idea. Why?'

Daisy was thinking of the letter she'd seen in the library. 'I just wondered,' she said. 'There's something frightfully romantic about those little tiny countries like Luxemburg – Andorra and Liechtenstein and Monaco.'

'Ruritania,' agreed Lucy, who had adored Ramon Novarro in *The Prisoner of Zenda*.

'Transcarpathia.' Daisy giggled, remembering the fiery young ex-Grand Duke she had met last year. 'Only that's part of Russia now. Maybe I could persuade an editor to pay me to go and write about the others, the real ones. The Walsdorf family could be a useful connection.'

'I doubt it. If they were anybody, he'd have talked about them.'

'True.' But she didn't care if they were 'anybody' or not, and it would give her an excuse to ask Walsdorf about them. 'We'd better get on with our lists. Alec will be sending someone to pick them up.'

'With Mummy jawing away at me, I didn't really notice anyone else.'

'At least that lets Aunt Vickie out! Picture the scene, yourself sitting there, Aunt Vickie—'

'And Daddy. Poor Mummy, she's having a rotten time of it. I wish someone would come and tell us how Binkie is!'

'Gerald.'

'Gerald. It's a nice name, isn't it? But he's always been Binkie, I'll never remember.'

'Do concentrate on your list, darling. This isn't a game. It may help Alec catch whoever hit Gerald.'

'That horrible brat Erica was sitting near us, smirking. I'm sure she was listening to every word of Mummy berating me for spoiling my chances.'

'Write her down.'

'I'd rather Alec gave her a hard time.'

'Write her down.' Daisy buckled down to her own list.

Entering the drawing room after dinner, Daisy had seen Jennifer already pouring coffee. Daisy had talked to Lady Ione for some time, and she remembered watching Sally and Flora. On her way out to meet Gerald, when Aunt Vickie stopped her, she'd noticed Oliver in the background in confab with his brother Henry. Then Sally had caught her and drawn her attention to Jennifer, still busy at the coffee-pot.

Whom had she not seen?

Sir James Devenish had not been there; of that Daisy was sure because out in the hall had been Lady Devenish, lurking in a most suspicious manner. Would she go so far as to hit Gerald over the head to save her beloved Teddy? Because Teddy had the best of all possible alibis for that particular attempt at murder.

Angela had been out in the garden. True, she had apparently saved Gerald's life, but could that have been to divert suspicion from both herself and Teddy? Suppose she had killed her grandmother for the money, done in Lord Fotheringay because he knew something dangerous to her, then attacked Gerald although he knew nothing, just so she could then save him? Daisy didn't believe she had so misjudged Angela, but she'd better suggest the far-fetched possibility to Alec.

She hadn't noticed the Carletons or the Bancrofts in the drawing room, but she hadn't particularly looked for them. Not evidence, Alec would say.

She read over her short list and comments with dissatisfaction, then glanced at Lucy's, which was no longer. About to suggest comparing them, she was interrupted by another knock on the door.

'Who's there?'

'It's Montagu, Mrs Fletcher.' He was wheezing slightly, as if he'd come up the stairs in a hurry. 'Could I have a word with you?'

Daisy and Lucy exchanged looks and both shook their heads. Lady Eva's brother was on neither list. The last time Daisy had seen him, he was still eating dinner while Rupert, irritated by the defection of most of the men, poured a brandy for Gerald. Assuming Gerald had waited until they all quit the dining room before he came to signal to Daisy, Montagu Fotheringay could easily have watched him go and nipped back to the conservatory to lie in wait.

'Uncle Montie?' breathed Lucy.

Daisy shrugged. 'It's possible. I wish I'd had a chance to ask Alec who's still on his list!'

Lucy reached for her faithful poker. Daisy went to the door.

Uncle Montie stood there, a massive figure in his crimson dressing-gown. Daisy recalled Lucy's telling her that the doors between the house and the servants' wing were kept locked because of his depredations among the housemaids. Was his wheezing caused by excitement, not exertion? Had he non-lethal designs upon her person?

At least, beneath the dressing-gown, he had on all his clothes except for dinner jacket, black tie, and shoes. His loose, bunion-bulged carpet slippers looked most inappropriate for a seduction scene.

'Er, beg you'll excuse the undress,' he said with obvious embarrassment. 'Just came to me a moment ago, perhaps you can give me a hint.'

'A hint, Uncle Montie?' Lucy sauntered to join Daisy, the poker hidden behind her.

'Oh, you here, Lucy?'

'As you see. What sort of hint are you after?'

'Advice. Call it advice.' He gave a hunted look back into the passage and added in a hoarse, urgent whisper, 'Not out here, don't you know!'

'Come in,' said Daisy, resigned.

Lucy slipped around behind him and stuck her head out into the hall. 'All clear,' she reported. 'Your reputation is safe, Daisy.'

Her great-uncle turned on her an affronted stare. 'Nothing of that sort, dash it! Thing of it is, Mrs Fletcher, the Chief Inspector seems to think I had a hand in doing in poor Eva. Assured him I wouldn't have harmed a hair of her head, but I can't say I'm sure he believed me.'

'I'm afraid the police can't go by what they believe or disbelieve. They have to have evidence.'

'What did Aunt Eva have to say about you in her notes, Uncle?'

'Dash it, Lucy, that's none of your business! Nothing,' he added without conviction.

'So what advice did you want from Daisy?'

'Thought she might be able to give me a hint about how to persuade Fletcher I was dashed fond of Eva. But if it's proof he's after, there's nothing to be done.' His shoulders slumped despondently, he turned to leave.

Daisy bolted the door after him. 'The trouble is,' she said, 'when they see you standing guard over me, they have to abandon whatever plans they may have for biffing me on the head, so we can't tell if they actually had plans.'

'Shall I go back to my room and pop through now and then to see if you're stretched lifeless?'

'You wouldn't know who did it. No, but next time someone knocks you could hide in the bathroom with your poker, keeping watch.'

'I might not be quick enough. It's all very well putting a name to the murderer, but I'd rather you survived the experience.'

'There must be a way—' Daisy started, only to be interrupted again by a knock on the door. 'Who is it?'

'Tring, Mrs Fletcher.'

Tom's rumble was infinitely comforting. Daisy opened the door, to find the sergeant staring after the Hon. Montagu. 'What's up?' she asked.

'Wearing his dressing-gown over his clothes, wasn't he?'

'Yes, thank heaven.'

'So if a maid took a tea-tray to him in his room and saw him in his dressing-gown, he could be out and about in a few seconds.'

'Yes, I suppose so.'

'You're labouring under a misapprehension, Sergeant,' Lucy drawled. 'It couldn't happen that way. All the maids have strict instructions not to enter Uncle Montie's room alone.'

'Ah!'

'She'd leave the tray outside, knock on the door, and tell him it was there, then buzz off.'

'And when he's done?'

'He'd put it out to be fetched.'

'So all the while he's thought to be taking tea in his room, he could quite well be nipping downstairs to mess about with Lord Fotheringay's tea!'

'I can't picture Uncle Montie "nipping",' said Lucy, 'but otherwise, you're absolutely right.'

'Ah,' said Tom profoundly. 'What about after dinner? Was he in the drawing room?'

Lucy shook her head. 'If so, I didn't notice him.'

'Nor did I,' said Daisy. 'He was still eating when everyone else except Gerald and Rupert left the dining room. He'd been with you and Alec, remember. Gerald was going to wait until everyone was gone before he came to the drawing room to fetch me, so ... Oh, no, I'd forgotten, he had to wait till the servants had finished clearing up, too. But that would have given Montagu time to go round by the corridor to the conservatory to lie in wait for Gerald.'

'But anyone who left earlier and didn't come to the drawing room had plenty of time,' Lucy pointed out.

'True. Montagu knew he wouldn't have to hang about too long, though.'

'I'll pass it on to the Chief, anyway,' said Tom. 'Have you ladies finished your lists?'

Daisy handed them over. 'Can you tell me who's still under suspicion, Tom? It's rather anxious-making not knowing.'

'Easier to tell you who's not, but aside from Miss Lucy here and Lord Gerald of course, the earl and countess, and Lady Fotheringay, there's none I can think of we're absolutely sure of, because of the possibility of conspiracy. These lists of yours may clear some, and we've just got to check that the Reverend and his missus were up with the Haverhills to clear them. Time is what we haven't had enough of!'

'I know. We won't keep you any longer. Just tell us how Gerald is.'

'Not good,' said Tom gravely. 'Not good at all. And still unconscious.'

Daisy was bolting the door behind him when Lucy said, 'I'm going to bed. If anyone else wants to consult you, you'll just have to talk through the door.'

'Darling!'

'I'm not a nurse. I can't help him, any more than you can. Good night.' She turned towards the bathroom door, then swung back as another knock sounded. 'Oh, hell! Why can't they leave us alone?'

'Mrs Fletcher? It's Adela Carleton.'

'What can I do for you, Lady Carleton? I'm just going to bed.'

'Oh, please, you simply must make your husband let us take Ursula home!'

'I'm sorry, I have absolutely no influence over his investigation. Wouldn't he let you send her home with your chauffeur?'

'I couldn't do that. She's at just the age when girls fancy themselves in love with chauffeurs and footmen and . . . and that sort of person.'

'Your maid —'

'We only brought one between us, and I can't possibly spare her.'

'Well, I'm sorry, but there's nothing I can do. Good night, Lady Carleton.' Daisy moved away from the door.

Lucy was still in the room. 'I can't think why Mummy insisted on my having that brat for a bridesmaid,' she said waspishly. 'Ursula's only a second cousin, like Julia and Erica. They needn't have been invited at all.'

'I seem to remember someone falling for the art master when we were sixteen or so.'

'He was a jolly good photographer, even with the ghastly equipment available then. He taught me a lot.'

'And that's why you kept sneaking off to the Art Room?' Daisy held up her hand as Lucy opened her mouth to retort. 'No, I'm sorry, don't let's quarrel. Things are bad enough without that.'

'It's been an absolutely foul day altogether, hasn't it? Tomorrow can only be an improvement. 'Night, darling.'

Lucy went through to the bathroom and closed the door. Daisy sank into one of the easy chairs. She felt she had let Lucy down, not understanding her feelings about Gerald, not knowing what to say to help. She hadn't been much help to Gerald either, she thought mournfully, nor even to Alec. And now she was too weary even to think about the case.

Before she could fall into a decline, there came yet another knock on the door. Daisy heaved herself to her feet and went over. 'Who's there?'

'It's Sally.'

Sally couldn't possibly have hit Gerald. She had been under Daisy's eye in the drawing room all the time. On the other hand, Daisy was tired and she didn't like Sally. 'What is it, Sally? I'm just going to bed,' she said through the door.

'Oh, I'm sorry to disturb you, but Rupert's grandfather is awfully disturbed about what's been going on.'

'Understandably.'

'Yes, of course, but would you mind awfully coming to tell him how the investigation is going, reassure him that everything's being done that can be done?'

'I don't know how it's going. Alec doesn't tell me what he's doing.'

'But you were there when—'

'I've told Alec all I know, which is practically nothing, and he's told me practically nothing, which is all I know.' Did that make sense? 'But you can tell Lord Haverhill I'm quite sure everything's being done that can be done. I'm sorry, I really am too tired now. Say I'll come and see him in the morning.'

'Well, if that's how you feel . . .' Sally sounded offended.

'It is,' Daisy said bluntly. 'Good night.' Ungracious, she supposed, but even if she had been up to date with Alec's investigation, she honestly wasn't up to a harrowing account of the horrors of the day, not even for the Earl.

Any subsequent knocking on her door went unheard. Within a very few minutes she was in bed, and she didn't have time before she dropped off to wonder whether she'd be able to sleep.

CHAPTER 21

Tom came into the library while Ernie Piper was reading back to Alec his shorthand notes of the two doctors' comments on Lord Gerald.

'You're doing very well with the medical terminology,' Alec said with approval.

'Once I've got it straight, I don't forget it, Chief. 'Sides, it's the same things over and over, isn't it? Not the oleander poisoning, but strangling and bashing people on the head. Pity more people don't have heads as hard as this bloke's.'

'You can say that again,' Tom agreed, setting two sheets of writing paper on the desk. Alec recognized Daisy's hand-writing on one.

'A thick skull seems to be the only thing that saved Bincombe from instant death,' he said. 'I wonder . . . Ah, there you are, Doctor. I was just wondering if you'd completed the post-mortem on Lady Eva before we called you out again.'

Dr Philpotts entered the library at a brisk stride, followed by Sir Leonard. 'All but tidying up. Death was by strangling, of course, by means of that stocking I sent you. She was, as you surmised, half suffocated first with a pillow. I found a few small feathers in the trachea and lungs, which she must have inhaled gasping for breath after the pillow tore. You noted the thread caught in her ring?'

'Yes. With a magnifying glass, it appears to match the pillow ticking.'

'I cut off a snippet and made a microscope slide. If you can let me have a bit of the ticking, I'll make sure of the match. Not that there can be much doubt.'

'It's up in her bedroom. Here's the key, Piper.'

Ernie dashed off.

'How is the latest victim, Doctor?' asked Sir Leonard.

Philpotts glanced at Alec, who gave a tiny shake of the head. The fewer people who knew of the police surgeon's comparatively hopeful prognosis, the better.

'In a bad way,' Philpotts answered. 'We've tucked him up in a makeshift bed in the anteroom near the front door. Mrs Fotheringay – Mrs Reverend Timothy, a highly competent woman – is to sit with him until Arbuthnot's night nurse arrives.'

'And Constable Stebbins is on guard outside the door until his relief arrives,' Alec added.

'Yes, yes, I telephoned for four fresh men. I've spoken to a number of people, Fletcher, impressing on them that they must not retire until you have interviewed them and asking them to spread the word. I suggested they should gather in the drawing room, where you can find them.'

'Excellent, sir.'

'I told the butler to direct people there, also. I thought I'd go and sit with them, show willing, don't you know, and keep an eye on things, as it were.'

'That will be most helpful, sir.'

'And I've just been up to see Lord Haverhill. He's shockingly distressed, of course. He asked whether you might spare him just a few minutes. I know you're pressed for time, but I think it would be a good idea if you had a word with him, assure him the police are doing their best, and all that sort of thing.'

'I'll go up to him at once. There are one or two questions I must put to him, anyway. Sergeant Tring, you can make a start on collating those lists and deciding whom we should call in first. After Mrs Oliver – I see no reason why we shouldn't take her first.'

'She's on both lists, sir, Mrs Fletcher's and Miss Lucy's. Out of the picture.'

'Good. Piper can help you when he gets back, but I shan't be long.'

Alec, Sir Leonard and the doctor went out to the hall, where Sir Leonard made for the drawing room. As Alec turned towards the stairs, the doctor put his hand on his arm.

'Just a moment, Fletcher.' He waited till the Chief Constable had nearly reached the drawing room door before continuing softly, 'The palm tree left a bruise on the victim's back. It was definitely not the cause of the head injury. I kept my mouth shut in front of Sir Leonard . . .'

'Thank you. He's a gregarious soul and might let something slip in front of the wrong person. Here comes your specimen.'

Ernie Piper came racing down the stairs with a strip of blue-and-white striped ticking in his hand. He gave it to the doctor, who went for a last look at his patient before going back to the mortuary to finish off the autopsy. Alec went upstairs, hoping he remembered the way to the family wing.

He wasn't at all happy about facing Lord Haverhill. The Earl had every right to be annoyed, not to say furious, that since he called in Scotland Yard, one murder had become three. Not quite three. Bincombe still clung to life. Should Alec tell Lord Haverhill that Dr Philpotts by no means despaired of his recovery? Better not. The fewer who knew, the less likely that the murderer would hear and perhaps decide to try again.

Alec came to what he thought was the family sitting room. A footman lounging against the doorpost straightened as he approached.

'I'm s'posed to keep people from bothering his lordship, sir,' he said uncertainly.

'Have many people tried to bother him?'

'Lots. Lady Carleton and—'

'That's all right, I don't need their names just now, but if you could write them down for me, I might find a use for them at some point.'

The footman spread empty hands. 'I don't have nothing to write on, sir.'

'I'll bring you a piece of paper and a pencil from in there. Lord Haverhill asked to see me.' Alec knocked, opened the door without waiting for a response, and went in.

Lord and Lady Haverhill sat on either side of the hearth, where a small fire burned. They both looked round when Alec entered, and the Earl started to rise, stiffly, levering himself with both hands on the arms of his chair. His cheeks were sunken, his eyes hooded as if the effort to keep up his eyelids was more than he could manage.

'Mr Fletcher . . .'

'Please don't get up, sir.' Alec moved forward as the old man sank back.

'How is Lord Gerald?' asked the Countess anxiously. She looked in better shape than her husband, but her eyes were red-rimmed. She had wept for her quiet, eccentric, amiable son.

'Not good, I'm afraid, ma'am. He's still unconscious and may remain so.'

'That such a thing should happen to a guest in my house!' exclaimed Lord Haverhill. 'I hardly knew what to say to Tiverton. The Tivertons are coming, of course, first thing in the morning. They were on their way, in any case, for the wedding.'

'Poor Lucy! She must be heart-broken.'

Alec assumed Lucy's decision not to marry Bincombe had not reached her grandparents' ears. He had seen her only briefly since the attempted murder and she had looked tense but not heart-broken. Daisy said she was in a 'funny mood, blaming herself'. He couldn't pass that on to her grandparents.

He said, 'I'm afraid events keep overtaking me. No sooner have I begun to work out how to tackle the case than a new disaster presents itself. However, we have accumulated considerable information, though we've had no time to analyse it, and I expect what I learn this evening to narrow the field of suspects.'

'All members of my family,' the Earl said unhappily. 'I can scarcely credit the whole business. I keep expecting to wake up and find it's been a nightmare.'

'Do you expect anyone else to be assaulted, Mr Fletcher?' Lady Haverhill asked with more than a touch of acerbity.

'My dear, how can Mr Fletcher possibly know?'

'Assuming our reasoning to be correct, I doubt it. I'm confident that I know the reasons for the first and third attacks. The second puzzles me.'

'You're convinced now that Aubrey was murdered?'

'I have no proof until I hear from the pathologist, but the attempt on Lord Gerald's life . . .'

'Yes, of course. He saw something.'

'Or the murderer was afraid he had seen something.'

'But how could Aubrey have posed a threat to Lady Eva's murderer?'

'That's the question. I suppose he wasn't in the habit of leaving his room at night, perhaps to check on his plants or make sure the conservatory doors were closed, or something of the sort?'

'Certainly not,' said Lady Haverhill. 'He was engrossed in his plants, not obsessed.'

'Whatever he learnt, however he learnt it, we'll never know now. But why didn't he come to you with the information, Mr Fletcher, after Eva's death?'

'People have all sorts of reasons for not telling us things, sir,' said Alec. 'Often they don't realize the significance. Sometimes they just don't like to talk to the police. Or they decide to ask the person they suspect for an explanation. Perhaps that's what Lord Fotheringay did.'

'That doesn't sound at all like Aubrey,' said his mother.

'No,' Lord Haverhill agreed, 'but this is idle speculation and we are keeping you from your investigation, Mr Fletcher. If there is anything at all we, or the household, can do to help, please don't hesitate to ask.'

'Thank you. I have one more question for you. Were the Reverend and Mrs Timothy with you at tea-time and after dinner?'

'With us and with Maud,' Lady Haverhill said, adding disapprovingly, 'My daughter-in-law is under sedation.'

'You can't suspect Timothy and Nancy!'

'It's my job to suspect everyone, Lord Haverhill. Can you give me times for their visits to you?'

Consulting each other, the Earl and Countess provided times which excluded Timothy from both attacks and Nancy from that on Bincombe, though she had visited their children in the nursery at tea-time. So Nancy could have put the oleander in the teapot. However, Alec couldn't conceive of her conspiring with anyone but her husband – nor with him, come to that! He had been sure enough of his judgment to leave her to watch Bincombe. Now he was ready to cross them both off his list.

He went downstairs to tackle Daisy's and Lucy's lists. The vast house was so still, every footstep sounded loud in his ears as he crossed the hall. If Sir Leonard had managed to gather everyone in the drawing room, they were too subdued for the sound of their voices to carry. So much the better. Alec had rather expected more vociferous complaints.

In the library, Tom and Ernie had put together a list of those who could not have been in the conservatory when Bincombe was attacked.

'Both Miss Lucy's parents,' said Tom.

'Thank heavens!' said Alec.

'Erica Pendleton and Julia Lasbury – they're the two bridesmaids who came early, before their parents.'

'I suppose the parents will turn up any moment, to complicate matters.'

'Lady Ione – but she was already out of it – and Miss Flora F. Mrs Rupert F. Mrs Walsdorf. All four Henry Fotheringays: ma, pa, and two bridesmaid daughters. Edward Devenish, who was here with us. And that's it, Chief. Miss Lucy has a feeling there was someone else, a couple, in the further reaches of the drawing room, but she didn't notice who.'

'Pity. But that's a good lot knocked out. Which leaves?'

'Lady Devenish,' said Piper. 'Mrs Fletcher spotted her skulking about outside the library after dinner, waiting for sonny-boy.'

'Yes, she told me.'

'But she needn't have stayed there,' Tom pointed out. 'She could have gone to the conservatory and come back.'

'Daisy didn't notice her when she came to tell us about Lord Gerald?'

'She didn't say so, Chief, but she wasn't in a state to do much noticing.'

'True.'

'I wouldn't have said Lady Devenish was strong enough for a blow like that. I could be wrong, though.'

'Never, Sarge!'

'You watch your lip, my lad! I was just thinking, Chief, ladies aren't the delicate plants they were in my young day. All this tennis and golf and whatnot. I've heard they even play cricket and hockey at some schools for young ladies!'

'Not Lady Devenish.'

'No, I s'pose not,' Tom said reluctantly. 'The younger ladies.'

'Most of the younger ladies seem to be accounted for. I'll include Miss Angela – she could easily have finished him off while she was alone with him. We'd never have managed to prove she could have saved him.'

'Pity. I bet she could hit a ball for six. Cricket bat or not, we're going to have to search the place for the weapon, right, Chief?'

'Not you and I, Tom.' Alec grinned at Piper's horrified face. 'The CC has sent for some extra constables and Ernie shall organize them. The house is huge, but being Victorian, not mediaeval, it's comparatively simply laid out. They can start on the public areas as soon as everyone has gone to bed and if necessary search the bedrooms tomorrow after everyone's up.'

'Chief,' said Piper, suddenly excited, 'the murderer wouldn't take the weapon to his bedroom, would he? Don't you reckon there must be a cupboard somewhere where they keep bats and balls, and croquet stuff, tennis racquets, all that sort of stuff? If it was a cricket bat, wouldn't he stick it in there with all the rest?'

'Good point, young 'un.'

'Yes,' Alec said, 'good idea, Ernie. I must be tired. Go and find out, from a servant, not one of the family. And then go and look.'

Piper dashed off.

Alec and Tom returned to the lists. 'What about Sir James Devenish?' Alec asked. 'He can't claim to have been with his wife if she was seen alone in the hall.'

'No,' said Tom with grim satisfaction, 'and he strikes me as almost as likely as young Teddy. He's certainly strong enough.'

'But is he clever enough?'

'Clever enough to hang on to the purse-strings. I can't see him using poison, though.'

'Hmm. Out of character, perhaps, but in spite of Smith and his brides in the bath, a multiple murderer can't be counted on to behave in a normal fashion, even normal for himself. What about the other daughter, Mrs Bancroft, and her husband? They may be the nameless couple Lucy thought she saw in the drawing room.'

'Someone will know. Mrs Walsdorf'll know, I expect. Mrs Fletcher said she was pouring coffee.'

'She must have noticed everyone, then. Good.'

'Walsdorf was out and about though. I wouldn't put poisoning past him.'

'Because he's a foreigner?' Alec asked dryly.

'No, Chief! Because he's a smooth, mild, soft-spoken sort of chap, like Dr Crippen.'

'Not at all the sort, in fact, to hit someone over the head.'

'You've got me there, Chief. I'll give you Sir James poisoning Lord Fotheringay if you'll give me Mr Walsdorf bashing Lord Gerald.'

'Fair enough. Who's left?'

'The Carletons. Unless they were the couple Miss Lucy saw. How about he did in Lady Eva because of the mistress, and she did in Lord Fotheringay to protect him so her darling daughter's daddy wouldn't be hanged, and he tried to do in Lord Gerald because if she was caught, so'd he be.'

'Ingenious!' Alec said admiringly. 'And not beyond the bounds of plausibility.'

Tom preened his moustache. 'Then there's the Honourable Montagu Fotheringay. Personally, I agree with Miss Lucy he's not up to the physical exertion required, but Mrs Fletcher fancies him. He came to talk to her in her room just before I was up there.'

'She didn't let him in!'

'Yes, but Miss Lucy was standing right behind her with a poker.'

Alec laughed. 'Lucy brandishing a poker! I wish I'd seen it.'

'She told me the maids are forbidden to go into Mr Montagu's room alone. So the maid who took up his tea-tray wouldn't have seen him. He might have answered when she knocked. I didn't ask.'

'What makes Daisy suspect him?'

'Oh, just that he was one of the last out of the dining room, so he'd have known pretty near when Lord Gerald would go to the conservatory and that he wouldn't have long to wait.'

'It's a point. The longer the murderer hung about in the conservatory, or watching to see when Bincombe left the dining room, the more chance he'd be missed or seen. Is that the lot?'

'Well, there's always Mr Baines.'

'The butler?' Alec asked in surprise.

'He had the key to the servants' wing door,' Tom pointed out defensively. 'And he's always buzzing about. The nobs wouldn't notice him or think twice if they did. I'm not saying he's likely, mind, but he's possible.'

'Quite right, we must take him into account. Now, before we have anyone in, let's go over the people in Lady Eva's notes. With any luck, Ernie will return bearing a cricket bat with blood on one end and a nice, clear set of fingerprints on the other.'

Before they had finished running through the suspects with known motives for killing Lady Eva, Ernie Piper returned. He bore in triumph a cricket bat, holding it carefully with a handkerchief wrapped around the upper part of the blade.

'Blood on the end all right,' he announced. 'And soil stuck to it. There's a big closet – more like a box-room – down that corridor behind the conservatory, between the gun room and the billiard room. Full to busting of tennis stuff, croquet, cricket, golf clubs, badminton, anything you can think of. Pushed in right at the back, this was.'

'Well done, young 'un.' As he spoke, Tom extracted his fingerprint kit from the Murder Bag. 'Let's hope he was too rushed to think of wiping off the dabs.'

But the bat bore not a single fingerprint, old or new.

'Pity,' said Tom, 'but at least I shan't have to take the dabs of a couple of dozen nobs all screaming blue murder.'

CHAPTER 22

Jennifer Walsdorf came into the library warily, like a mouse hoping the cat is not in the kitchen. Piper directed her to where Alec stood behind the big desk at the far end. He had decided to leave Lucy's mother to Tom, being himself rather too close for comfort to that branch of the family.

While Tom, with impeccable courtesy and his most re-assuring manner, seated Mrs Oliver Fotheringay at the long table, Alec watched Mrs Walsdorf approach down the long room. Her black frock looked slightly out of date and as if it had been made for someone else. Of course, all the female guests were wearing makeshift mourning, but she was a poor relation, probably making do with cast-offs at the best of times. Very likely she wore cheap artificial silk stockings. Under pressure of events, Alec had neglected to follow up the artificial silk stocking.

Anyone could have bought a pair, he reminded himself, bowing slightly to the anxious young woman. 'Do take a seat, Mrs Walsdorf,' he said. 'I believe you're in an excellent position to help us.'

'John didn't kill anyone! That business of his being born in Germany, it doesn't mean anything. I don't know why Lady Eva wrote it down.'

'He told you about that.'

'Oh yes. He told me before we were married that he was born in Baden-Baden, and he told me today that Lady Eva knew. He found out only this afternoon, from you. It really wouldn't have made any difference to us if she'd told people.' She sounded as if she was trying to convince herself. 'Some people already dislike and distrust him just because he's a foreigner, and the others don't care exactly where he was born. There's simply never been any reason to mention it. After all, he left Germany when he was only a few days old. He hates the Germans for invading his country.'

'Who can blame him? Actually, what I want to ask you about is whom you saw in the drawing room after dinner, where, I gather, you were pouring coffee?'

Mrs Walsdorf confirmed all the names Daisy and Lucy had provided, and added Mr and Mrs Bancroft. 'John didn't come,' she said reluctantly. 'He didn't want to stay and drink port with Rupert, of course, but he still had one or two letters to write and then he was going to take them to the letter-box. He went up to Lord Haverhill's den again, as you were in here. Surely Lord Haverhill must have seen him.'

Alec hadn't thought to ask. Anyway, he doubted the Haverhills had been in any state to notice. 'Did any of the others come in late?' he asked.

'Just Rupert and Lord Gerald, and Lord Gerald didn't stay for coffee. Is he . . . is he going to die?'

'I'm afraid the doctor thinks he'll just slip away without regaining consciousness.'

'It's awful! Who's doing it, Mr Fletcher? Is it a maniac? He might kill any of us next. I'm so afraid for Emily!'

'Your child? I don't think you need be, Mrs Walsdorf. These

are not random murders.' Alec could only hope he was right. The last thing he wanted was a house full of panic-stricken people. They had held up pretty well so far, he acknowledged. For the most part, the 'nobs' were being stiff-upper-lip, while the servants went on with their work as if none of the horrors had anything much to do with them, in which belief they seemed to be justified. So far. 'What about tea-time?' he asked. 'Where were you then?'

'Pouring! In the drawing room. We usually have it on the terrace in the summer, or in the Long Gallery if it's not nice out, but Lady Haverhill sent word to serve it in the drawing room.'

'Why is that?' So that she was less likely to be seen going to the conservatory? No, surely Lady Haverhill had not strangled her sister-in-law, poisoned her own son, and hit a noble guest over the head!

'Because of what had happened. Because it's more formal. I'd expected Sally to want to play hostess, but she sent a maid to tell me to pour. Not that I mind pouring. I always do it for Lady Haverhill. But that's because her wrist and hand tire easily and she doesn't want Aunt Maud to get ideas about taking over. I'm sorry if that sounds catty, but it's true. Poor Aunt Maud has been looking forward for decades to being Countess of Haverhill, and now she never will. Of course, Sally just enjoys telling me what to do and watching me do it. Never mind, it won't be much longer.'

'Tell me whom you remember coming to tea.'

Almost all the guests had turned up at tea-time. Unfortunately, there had been considerable coming and going, and Mrs Walsdorf couldn't remember who had come when, nor how long they had stayed. 'I'm sorry, but there are three doors,' she pointed out, 'to the hall, the Long Gallery, and the French windows to the terrace. I couldn't have watched them all even if I'd known it was important. I was kept pretty busy, too.'

Alec let her go. He and Tom went on to interview all those who had been cleared of the attack on Bincombe by her, Daisy's, and Lucy's evidence.

Asked about tea-time, several people mentioned a row between Sally and Angela over the latter bringing her dog into the drawing room. Flora Fotheringay had overheard Lord Carleton speaking most disagreeably, not to say cuttingly, to his wife – making her glad not to be married. Mrs Bancroft had drawn her husband's attention to her mother, Lady Devenish, observing that she looked quite haggard. Sally had had to speak sharply to Jennifer, who seemed distracted and had slopped some tea into a saucer. Mrs Henry Fotheringay had noticed Teddy Devenish, because she had had to admonish her elder daughter to stop making eyes at him.

Unfortunately, no one had any idea when these events had occurred. Most had not arrived on time and all agreed that people had been coming and going constantly.

The only two who had anything useful to report were Erica Pendleton and Julia Lasbury. They had wasted (Erica's word) twenty minutes on Teddy Devenish before his disillusionment with women ceased to be provocative and became boring. They had ambushed (Tom's word) the unhappy young man on his arrival in the drawing room a couple of minutes before the servants brought in the tea-things, prompt at quarter to five. Teddy Devenish could not have poisoned Lord Fotheringay, nor assaulted Lord Gerald.

'But he still could have strangled his grandma,' Tom pointed out, 'and Lady Devenish could have done the rest to protect him.'

Lady Devenish and Sir James, Lord and Lady Carleton – the latter with no known motive, Mr Montagu and John Walsdorf all still belonged on the list.

Meanwhile, on one of his trips back and forth to fetch people, Piper reported that the night nurse had arrived. The patient's condition was unchanged, he said, Mrs Reverend looked dead on her feet, and he had told her the Chief wouldn't mind if she went straight to bed. Considering what Nancy Fotheringay had done that day, Alec was surprised she was capable of standing. Her stamina was as remarkable as her kindness.

A little later, Piper had brought in Sir Leonard. His four fresh constables had turned up at last. One at the lodge gate, one outside Lord Gerald's room – what were the other two to do?

Alec tried to recall what he had wanted them for. Search for the weapon? Piper had found the cricket bat, for all the good it did them. 'It would take an army to cover all the outside doors,' he thought aloud.

'Luckily these aren't the sort of people who can sneak off across the park and disappear into the populace,' Sir Leonard offered. He was looking a little glassy-eyed.

'No. We'll station one of your men in the conservatory. The doors are locked but there may be other keys around. I want it thoroughly examined in daylight. We could easily have missed something. The other chap had better patrol the house, to reassure people.'

'Most of them have gone up to bed, except those few you haven't seen yet.'

'It's past one o'clock, Chief,' Tom murmured.

'Lady Carleton, Ernie,' said Alec wearily. 'She's going to be upset if we've kept her up for nothing. All the rest we saw earlier. They can wait till morning, but give them my apologies.'

Lady Carleton entered accompanied by Ursula. 'Since you won't let me take my daughter home, I'm not letting her out of my sight,' she announced, wilted but still militant, 'until you catch this maniac. She should have been in bed hours ago.'

Behind her back, Ernie Piper shrugged and rolled his eyes.

Alec gave him a resigned nod. 'As you wish, Lady Carleton. Perhaps Miss Ursula can help us too.'

'I won't have her badgered. She's very sensitive.'

'I don't mind, Mummy. It's all too frightfully exciting for words,' Ursula enthused, not at all wilted. 'The girls at school will be wild with envy when they hear I've been questioned by a real Scotland Yard 'tec!'

'Let's start with you, then,' Alec said with a smile. 'Tell me what you did at tea-time.'

'Mummy didn't want to go down, because of there being a murderer on the loose. She didn't want to go to lunch either, but Daddy made her. He said everyone would think one of us had killed Aunt Eva if we didn't appear.'

'What nonsense, Ursula! As though anyone could possibly suppose such a thing.'

'That's what he said,' Ursula persisted. 'Anyway, I was simply starving again by tea-time, and I'd just persuaded Mummy to ring for a servant and ask to have tea brought up to the room – hers and Daddy's – when Daddy came in and said not to be ridiculous, we must go down. Mummy wouldn't go without him, so we all went. We were so late I thought there might not be any cakes and biscuits left, but it was all right, there was plenty for everyone. Sally even told Mrs Walsdorf to send a maid for more hot water for the tea.'

'Aunt Sally,' her mother corrected her.

'She told me to call her Sally, Mummy, because Aunt Sally sounds like a funfair – you know, the thing you throw things at – and we're the same generation even if she is a bit older than me.'

'Thank you, Miss Ursula,' Alec said, cutting off whatever Lady Carleton was about to say. 'Now, what about after dinner?'

Ursula pouted. 'Mummy made me go upstairs with her. It's not fair, Alice and Mary stayed down for coffee with the grown-ups. Then after a bit, Daddy came and said Lord Gerald had been attacked, and Mummy said she was going to try again to get you to let her take me home. Then you said everyone should wait in the drawing room, so we did.'

'Is that correct, Lady Carleton?'

'Yes, yes, but it really is most improper for a girl not yet out to call a woman ten years her elder by her Christian name.'

'Never mind, Mummy, we'll be calling her Lady Fotheringay after the funeral.'

'Ursula! And when have you attended a funfair, I'd like to know?'

'Never,' her daughter lied promptly. 'Some of the other girls talked about them. Is that all, Detective Chief Inspector? You see, Mummy, there was nothing to it. But what a story I'll make of it when I get back to school!'

'Ursula, it is *not* a story we want spread about!'

Piper ushered them out, Lady Carleton expostulating all the way.

In spite of the girl's obvious untruthfulness when it suited her, Alec believed her report. It exonerated her mother, but left her father completely unaccounted for at the crucial times.

Lord Carleton, Sir James and Lady Devenish, Montagu Fotheringay and John Walsdorf, Alec thought as he climbed the stairs towards bed, hoping Daisy was not sleeping too soundly. She'd be pleased to hear the long list had shortened to five. No, six. He kept forgetting Teddy Devenish, because the boy had been in the library when Bincombe was attacked. He was still very much in the picture for his grandmother's murder.

Alec could only trust it would not take another murder to narrow the six down to one.

CHAPTER 23

'Are you awake, darling?'

'I am now.'

'Sorry!' Daisy kissed Alec's ear in a most unsorry fashion.

He rolled over and took her in his arms. The ensuing interlude was entirely satisfactory to both.

The tower clock chimed eight. Alec sat up abruptly.

'I asked you to wake me at seven thirty!'

'I did. There's no hurry. No one will be up for ages. You'll think better if you're rested. Lie down, darling, you're letting a draught in.'

He obeyed, muttering, 'I bet Tom and Ernie are up.'

'Haven't they got things they can do without you?'

'Yes, as a matter of fact. I told Tom to have another go at the servants this morning, and to see if he can find the gardener who assisted Lord Fotheringay in the conservatory. Thank heaven I have a sergeant I can rely on to ask the right questions without detailed instructions! And Ernie's to go over the conservatory with a fine-tooth comb. We couldn't do a thorough job by oil lamp and electric torch.'

'That made it even beastlier finding him.' Daisy shivered, and Alec put his arm around her. 'The gloom and shadows, I mean. I hope he's survived the night. Or maybe I don't, if he's going to die anyway.'

'I shouldn't tell you this, love, and you are absolutely not to repeat it to a soul, not even Lucy: the police surgeon is actually quite hopeful that Bincombe will come round.'

'Thank heaven! But why . . . Oh, you're afraid the murderer might have another go at him if he's afraid he's recovering. Have you any idea who it is? You must have knocked a few people off the list, at least.'

'Just six names left. Last night that seemed an awful lot, but this morning it seems not too bad, considering how short a time we've been on the case and how many suspects we started with.'

'Good going. Who are they?'

'Daisy, you know that's another thing I shouldn't tell you.'

'Yes, you should,' she argued. 'Otherwise how can I know whom to beware of? After all, it's me he's likely to come after next.'

'I hope not. It should be obvious that you've told me all you know.'

'That's what I told people last night. But still, I'd be much more comfortable knowing, darling.'

With a sigh he gave in. 'Lord Carleton. Sir James and Lady Devenish and Teddy – at least for Lady Eva's murder, assuming conspiracy. And Montagu Fotheringay and John Walsdorf.'

'Not John Walsdorf. I was alone with him long before I had a chance to tell you everything. In fact, he could easily have read my note to you saying I had things to tell you. He wasn't even one of the people who came up here and insisted on talking to me.'

'No? Who was? Tom only told me about Montagu.'

'Jennifer . . . Oh!'

'Oh indeed,' Alec said grimly. 'Don't write off John Walsdorf yet.'

'She left a bromide for me, in case I couldn't sleep.'

'What did you do with it?'

'Come to think of it, she actually brought it for Lucy, who didn't want it. But she left it on the little table by the door.' Daisy sat up. 'Yes, it's still there. Are you going to have it analysed?'

'Most definitely.'

'Jennifer may not have known anything about anything John did.' She snuggled down again. 'I suppose Lady Eva knew something about him?'

'Yes, and I'm not telling you what.'

'I wonder if it had anything to do with his letter.'

'His letter? Daisy, what have you been keeping from me now?'

'Nothing, really. I keep forgetting about it. Only when I went to the library first thing to call the doctor and police about Lady Eva, he was already there and writing something. He shoved it under the blotter when he saw me. Then this evening, after I found Gerald, Ernie Piper gave me the blotter to lean on when I wrote you that note. When I put it back on the desk, I saw Walsdorf's letter lying there.'

'Did you read it?' Alec demanded.

'Darling, one simply doesn't read other people's letters.'

'Great Scott, Daisy, this is a murder investigation!'

'Actually, it was in a foreign language,' Daisy confessed. 'I can't see what it could possibly have to do with the murders.'

'We can't tell unless we read it.'

Alec swung his legs out of bed, running his fingers through the crisp dark hair that never looked ruffled. He rubbed a hand over his chin. 'I'll have to shave.'

'And dress, darling. You don't look very official in your pyjamas.'

'No?' he said in mock disappointment. 'I thought you got me the dark blue for when I'm called out in the middle of the night.'

'Bel chose them, remember. You look very handsome in them, but not official. I'll dig out your clothes while you wash and shave.'

'Thanks, love.'

A maid had unpacked his bag, the one that was kept in constant readiness at the Yard, and tucked the clean shirts and underwear and the large supply of handkerchiefs away in the chest of drawers. Even before they were married, Daisy had learnt that he always carried extra hankies for weeping witnesses and sobbing suspects.

She ferreted out vest, pants, socks and shirt. Finding his tie where he had discarded it the night before, she rolled it up tightly in an attempt to smooth it, as she didn't want to waste time summoning a maid to iron it. He always wore his Royal Flying Corps tie when dealing with the upper classes. Not having a public school or club tie, it was the best he could do to put himself on a level with those who cared about such things, and it often helped.

He had hung up his suit neatly in the wardrobe, and the tie came out of its roll looking quite respectable, though the narrow end had a tendency to curl inward.

'Thanks, love,' said Alec, coming through from the bathroom to find all his clothes neatly laid out for him. 'I think I'll keep you.'

'What a relief! I assume all the people left on your list are on Lady Eva's, too.'

'Yes, but I really am not going to tell you what for.'

'No, but you can tell me whether they've admitted knowing she knew.'

'Some have. Let me think: Montagu and Sir James, oh, and Teddy. Lady Devenish equivocated but I'm pretty sure of her. Walsdorf and Carleton adamantly deny Lady Eva ever spoke to them.'

'That's interesting. Her son, daughter-in-law and brother on one side and distant relatives by marriage on the other. It wouldn't surprise me if they were telling the truth. Why should she care if Walsdorf and Carleton misbehaved? The others might bring scandal on her family.'

Alec stopped buttoning his shirt and stared. 'You may have a point there, Daisy. If I can just remember which of the others . . . Teddy Devenish, her grandson, had been spoken to severely. Lady Ione you know about – she was her niece.'

'There you are, then. If she hadn't spoken to Walsdorf and Carleton, they had no motive to do her in.'

'It's only a theory, but I must say it's quite persuasive. I'll keep it in mind. By the way, there's one other suspect I forgot to mention. Tom thinks we ought to add Baines to the list.'

'Tom thinks the butler did it?' Daisy asked in astonishment.

'No, but he is the only servant with a key to the connecting door.'

'He might have had a chance to poison Lord Fotheringay's tea, too, but I bet he was in the housekeeper's room after dinner, drinking port and discussing the shocking doings. The coffee was in a Thermos. Servants expect to have time off in the evenings these days, even when people are being murdered right, left and centre. Gosh, I do hope Dr Philpotts is right about Gerald!'

'No more fervently than I do. Quite apart from his being a good chap, I dread to think what Superintendent Crane and the AC are going to say about this débâcle.'

'There's absolutely no need to worry about that, darling,' said Daisy. 'They will undoubtedly blame the whole thing on me.'

Downstairs, Alec went first to enquire after Lord Gerald. The young uniformed constable on guard came to attention and saluted smartly.

'Anyone asking after him?' Alec asked.

'Just the one toff last night, sir. Gentleman, that is. Came when everyone else'd just gone upstairs.' He consulted his notebook. 'Lieutenant Colonel Fotheringay. Said he's by way of being acting host and besides, he needed to know in case his grandfather asked, which is Lord Haverhill, he said, which owns this place.'

'And you told him . . . ?'

'Lord Gerald Bincombe is unconscious, sir, and like to stay that way till he dies. That's what the nurse says, anyways, sir. She come out a couple of times to the cloakroom, and that's what she told me. PC Jones, he's the man patrolling the house, he stopped here for a minute a couple of times so I could go piss, sir, and he said no one came while I was gone. Then this morning, the butler came to ask and I told him the same.'

Both entirely natural enquiries, Alec thought.

'And DS Tring, he came by, too, an hour ago maybe. Said to tell you he'd be talking to the servants and DC Piper was in the conservatory.'

'All right. I'll arrange for someone to take over here as soon as I can.' He knocked gently and went on into the room.

Mrs Maple had provided a Chinese-painted rattan screen to keep draughts from the door off the patient. The nurse came around it, finger to her lips. A plump, middle-aged woman, in a white cap and starched apron, she looked almost as crisp and alert as when Alec had spoken to her briefly last night, explaining what he wanted her to say about her patient's condition.

'He's moving his hands about, sir,' she said in a low voice, 'and once or twice I've thought I heard him muttering.'

'A good sign?'

'Compared to what he was. Likely he'll come round, I'd say. But whether he'll make sense and whether he'll recover or relapse, your guess is as good as mine.'

Alec went round the screen. Bincombe lay still as a log, but it was possible to imagine that he had a touch of colour in his face. Alec felt hope rising.

'If he says anything you can make sense of, make sure you write it down and let me know at once. You're all right until someone comes to relieve you?' he asked the nurse.

'Not to worry, sir, I'm good for as long as it takes. There's many a time I've been on my feet all night. This was nothing.'

He thanked her and went to join Piper in the conservatory. He found his detective constable helping a grizzled gardener repot the fallen palm.

'It's what his lordship would've wanted,' the old man said doggedly, tears rolling unnoticed down his ruddy, seamed cheeks. 'Just done it a couple o' days ago, us did, him and me, seeing it was getting cramped in the old pot. Very slow grower, this here tree, and a rare 'un. Us've had it a dunnamany years. It grows leaning, see, on a slant like, and the top o' the trunk's thicker nor the bottom. And the loose soil in the new pot didn't help none, else it wouldn't've fallen. The rest o' the palms, the rootball gets that tight and heavy they'd just go on standing there, was you to break their pots. Mebbe you can tell me, sir, seeing this young fella can't, who killed his lordship, that never did none any harm?'

'We don't know yet, but we will. Have you finished with my young fella?'

'Ay, sir, I can manage now. My thanks to you, lad, and there'll be more when you lay hands on who killed his lordship.'

'Well?' Alec asked as they moved away.

'I finished going over the place,' Ernie said, 'before I lent the old chap a hand. It was a wash-out. I know a lot more about growing palms than I used to, though. And he confirmed what Miss Lucy said, that children visiting are warned about the poisonous plants over and over.'

'I'd forgotten that. But it would add weight to Daisy's latest theory.'

'What's that, Chief?'

'That Lady Eva was more likely to speak to close relatives about their misdeeds than to those who wouldn't bring scandal on her immediate family. I don't for a moment believe she never spoke to Lady Devenish about the snapping up of unconsidered trifles. Walsdorf and Carleton also both denied she'd mentioned her discoveries to them, remember, and I'm more inclined to believe them. Neither would have visited as a child. It's not definitive, of course. Either might happen to know about poisonous plants, or Lord Fotheringay might have pointed them out. Dammit, nothing is definitive! I assume the gardener wasn't anywhere near here at the crucial times?'

'No, he was working in the kitchen garden in the afternoon and he'd gone home to his cottage before the nobs' dinner time. And I asked him if Lord F had mentioned anything odd he'd noticed about anyone staying here, which he hadn't. Seems all they ever talked about was potting soil mixes and fertilisers and watering schedules and such.'

'The only thing I can think of is that he might have seen a man with a stocking or pair of stockings the day before Lady Eva's murder. If it was a married man, he wouldn't think much of it, until he heard how she was killed. If he heard. We'll have to find out whether it's general knowledge. Daisy saw her, and Mrs Reverend Timothy, but neither would have talked about the details. Who else?'

'The two maids, Chief.'

'If they talked, all the servants will have heard, and Tom will know about it. Let's hope he has come up with something useful.'

But the only remotely useful information Tom had was an alibi for the butler. As Daisy had surmised, Baines had been in the housekeeper's room when Bincombe was attacked, taking a glass of port – which Mr Tring would kindly not mention to them as might object – and discussing the murders. The two maids had noticed only Lady Eva's horrifying face, not what was around her neck.

'The murderer'd know it would come out once we started asking questions, though, Chief. I reckon Walsdorf'd be the most likely to have been seen by Lord F, seeing he lives in the house.'

'But Mr Montagu'd be the one that'd look oddest carrying stockings,' Ernie argued, 'seeing he's not married.'

'What about the artificial silk end, Tom? Any of the ladies wear them?'

'Miss Angela, Mrs Reverend, Mrs Lieutenant Colonel, Mrs Walsdorf, just who you'd expect from what we've found out about their financial situations. They all had an odd stocking or two, but they ladder so easy that's not surprising. The colour didn't help. It's the most popular shade at Woolworth's and most of the maids have a pair for their days out. So it doesn't really mean anything. Anyone could get hold of them easy enough.'

'Walsdorf, Sir James, Lady Devenish, Lord Carleton, Montagu,' said Alec. 'Or conceivably Teddy Devenish with his mother covering up for him. Maybe someone will have an explanation for his whereabouts that we can disprove. That would seem to be our only remaining hope.'

CHAPTER 24

John Walsdorf was the first of the remaining suspects to come down. Alec had already looked under the blotter on the desk in the library and failed to find there the letter in a foreign language. He couldn't see what bearing it could possibly have on the case, but he asked about it first.

'It is a letter to my mother in Luxemburg,' Walsdorf said calmly. 'I can show if you wish, but you will not understand. It is in *letzeburgesh*. I forgot about it yesterday because I was very busy. When I went to the letter-box I remembered and I came to get it, after I gave Mrs Fletcher's note to you.'

'Why did you hide it in the first place?'

'Some tell me, since I wish to be English, I must give up my family in Luxemburg. It is better that they do not know I write. But it is no crime, I think.'

'No crime at all. Where were you at tea-time and after dinner?'

'Writing letters. Yesterday I wrote many letters, to all those who were to come to the wedding. Even those I reached by telegraph or telephone, they must have a letter also. It is etiquette. Because you were using this room, I wrote in Lord Haverhill's study. He can tell you I gave him many, many letters to sign, but he did not watch me write them. I have no alibi, as you say.'

'You don't seem worried about it.'

'I am not. I have killed no one, and I trust the British system of law. It is fairer, I believe, than the *Code Napoléon*, though everywhere justice is better for the rich than the poor.'

Alec was not inclined to argue. As further questioning elicited no new information, John Walsdorf remained on his list.

As he was leaving, Alec said, 'Oh, by the way, I need to send a constable into Cambridge with something to be analysed by a chemist. Do you think Lord Haverhill's chauffeur could give him a lift?'

If Walsdorf knew of the powder his wife had offered Lucy and left for Daisy, his face showed no sign of it. 'His lordship wishes every effort to be made to assist you. I shall tell Baines to send the chauffeur to you immediately,' he said.

By the time he left, Lord Carleton was up and about. He was perfectly prepared to account for his late arrival at tea and absence after dinner.

He never drank tea, he said, disliking the beverage, and he felt no need to eat between luncheon and dinner. 'Having written a letter, and not wishing my wife to see the name and address on the envelope,' he continued blandly, 'I decided to walk down to the letter-box at the end of the drive. I'm sure the constable stationed there can confirm seeing me.'

'We'll ask him.' Whether the constable had been bright enough to note the time was another matter. The postman might remember Carleton's letter and when he had picked it up from the box. It would all have to be checked. 'But you did in the end turn up at tea in the drawing room.'

'When I returned, I found Adela and my daughter still in the bedroom, where I had counted on a half hour of peace and quiet. Adela did not want to go down. Ursula was complaining bitterly of being deprived of cake, and I was ... irritated enough to insist on their making an appearance. Adela refused to go without my 'protection', so down we all went.'

'When you came in from the post, you crossed the hall to the stairs. Did you see anyone?'

'Not that I recall. Oh, wait a minute, the butler was just disappearing through the baize door.'

No help there, unless Baines had chanced to turn his head and see Carleton enter the hall from the corridor or dining room or Long Gallery. Alec looked at Tom, who shook his head.

Of course, Carleton could have come through the front door after going round the house from the conservatory.

His explanation of his whereabouts after dinner was equally impossible to prove or disprove. Going out to the terrace to smoke a cigar, he had seen Angela crossing the lawn below with her dog, her back to him. Even if she had seen him – and she said she had seen no one – he could easily have gone from the terrace to the conservatory by way of the Long Gallery and dining room and returned before Daisy reached the conservatory. People had kept stopping her to talk, and several minutes had passed between Gerald's appearance in the drawing room to summon her and her escape. Long enough, at any rate, for the murderer to assault him and make himself scarce.

Like Walsdorf, Carleton again denied that Lady Eva had taxed him with her discovery of his secret.

When he left the library, the chauffeur came in.

'Mr Baines said to tell you, sir, Lord and Lady Tiverton are here. They had a peep at Lord Gerald and they've gone up to

see his lordship – Lord Haverhill, that is – and then they want
to talk to you.'

A complication he didn't need, Alec thought, though an
inevitable one. He had impressed upon the day nurse that
everyone was to be told Bincombe's condition was unchanged.
He could only hope she had managed to convince the Marquis
and Marchioness of the wisdom of this course.

He had Piper telephone the Cambridge police headquarters
to ask what chemist they used to analyse evidence and to
request that the postman and the constable who had been
stationed at the gate yesterday evening should be questioned.
The chauffeur went off with the paper of supposed bromide.
Meanwhile, Tom went out to the flower bed below the terrace
outside the drawing room, where he found the stub of a cigar
of the make Carleton said he smoked.

''Course,' Tom said gloomily, 'it don't prove he spent long
enough out there last night to smoke the whole thing. Could
be one he smoked earlier and saved.'

A footman came in to report that Sir James Devenish had
just returned from a fishing expedition to the stream in the
park and was willing to be interviewed while his catch was
cooked for his breakfast.

'Bad form,' the Baronet said guiltily, 'with Mother just
popped off yesterday, but a morning like this is irresistible. I
sneaked out before Josephine woke up. What can I tell you?'

'Tea-time yesterday. You weren't there.'

An extraordinarily furtive look crossed Sir James's ruddy,
open face. He even glanced behind him before saying
confidentially, 'Fact of the matter is, I popped down to the village
shop. There's a footpath across the park. Know you fellows said
no one was to leave, but I just went to get the Pink 'Un.'

'Buying the *Sporting Times* is not a crime, sir, though it might have been a good idea to let us know before you went. No doubt the shopkeeper will be able to tell us when you were there.'

'Fact is, I didn't get there till nearly six, just before they closed. I went for a walk through the woods.'

'You don't care for tea, perhaps?'

'Nothing against tea, though I'd rather have a whisky and soda any day.' He glanced back again. 'What I don't care for is these demmed family gatherings. Mean to say, at home everyone knows Ruby and wants to hear about her latest litter. Here, no one gives a damn if I tell 'em Admiral's lame in the left foreleg! What am I supposed to talk to people about? Must say, your wife put up a demmed good show when they stuck the poor girl next to me at dinner, but I could see her eyes glazing over.'

'Why did you come to Haverhill, then?'

'Oh, Mother insisted. Big family wedding. Duty to turn out and all that twaddle. Besides, the stream is well worth fishing.'

'Did you meet anyone on your walk?'

'Not a soul.'

'That's a pity. What about after dinner last night? I assume you were once again escaping the family . . .'

'Escaping Rupert.'

'. . . But where did you escape to?'

'Suggested a game of billiards to Henry – m'cousin, don't you know – but he seemed to think he should be protecting Marjorie and the girls.'

'You didn't feel it necessary to protect Lady Devenish?'

'Gad no! I mean, there may be times when I'd like to put her out of her misery, but why should anyone else? Besides, she said she was going to wait in the hall for Teddy and I'll be demmed if I was going to stand around with her like a silly ass.'

'You didn't, by any chance, decide to put your mother "out of her misery"?'

'Mother? Good Lord no! Mother enjoyed life. Josephine don't seem to a lot of the time. Not that I'd touch a hair of her head, of course.'

'So, when Mr Henry failed to cooperate, where did you go?'

'The gun-room. I like guns. Uncle Nick has a good collection. Not been out shooting in years though. Not being properly taken care of. Aubrey not interested.' He brightened. 'Young Rupert might be, come to think of it. Soldiers – guns. Anyway, just went to potter around. Thought I might go out today, pigeons, rabbits, whatnot. But fishing seemed less disrespectful, somehow.'

'The gun-room is opposite a door to the conservatory which we have reason to believe was used when Lord Gerald was attacked.'

'Devil take it,' Sir James roared, 'I can see why you might suspect me of doing in poor Mother, but why the deuce should I go for Bincombe? Perfectly decent fellow!'

Alec ignored the roar and the question. 'Did you hear footsteps, doors opening and closing, anything like that?'

'Matter of fact, I did. Thought I heard a door close, and damme, I nearly looked out to see who it was. Then I remembered there wasn't anyone I wanted to talk to and hoped he wouldn't come in. But it had caught my attention and I heard footsteps in the corridor, then another door opening and closing.'

'A man's footsteps?'

Sir James's forehead creased. 'My dear chap, demmed if I can say. I assumed so – gun-room, billiard-room, what? – most likely to be a chap. In a hurry, that's all I can tell you. Then I didn't hear anything for a bit, then another door opening and closing, and footsteps going away. Damme, you mean if I'd stuck me head out the door, I'd've caught the murderer practically red-handed?'

'I would say it's a great pity you didn't, except that you would undoubtedly have been attacked too.'

'Dare say I can give as good an account of myself as anyone.'

'Who knew you were going to the gun-room?'

'No one. Stands to reason, don't it, if you want a bit of peace and quiet you don't tell people where you're going!'

'If your wife was in the hall, she'd have seen you turn down the passage.'

'Nipped along while she was in the cloakroom,' Sir James said in a tone of self-congratulation. 'Not a soul saw me.'

And equally, he had seen no one. Alec found it hard to believe that the baronet was capable of making up such a story and presenting it in a credible manner.

'Ah,' said Tom. 'Seems a pretty straightforward chap, but remember how Mrs Fletcher thought he's under the cat's paw while all the time it's him that holds the whip hand. And Mrs Fletcher isn't easily fooled.'

'You're right, in spite of the mixed metaphors. We'll have to dig into his financial situation, find out how badly he needed the London house and whatever the estate was paying out to Lady Eva. Ring the Yard, will you, Tom, and get them going on that. Strictly speaking it's not Fraud Squad territory, but see if you can get Fielding. I'd better go and find Lord and Lady Tiverton and find out if they're after my blood.'

* * *

Daisy and Lucy went downstairs together and headed straight for Gerald's room. The constable on duty refused point-blank to let them go in and could not be budged. His lordship's condition was unchanged, he said. Lucy unhappily believed the statement; Daisy rather doubted but she didn't dare reassure Lucy after Alec's absolute prohibition.

'Breakfast,' said Daisy.

'I'm not hungry.'

'Come on, darling. It won't help Gerald if you fade away.'

'It's nothing to do with Gerald. I'm just not hungry.'

'Come and keep me company, then. I don't expect anyone will be there. Alec kept them up very late last night.'

'Did it help?' Lucy listlessly accompanied her breakfast-ward.

'He's narrowed it down to five people who had motives to murder Lady Eva and no alibis for tea-time or after dinner.'

'Who?' Lucy demanded.

'Darling, Alec would kill me if I told you. What's more, he'd never again tell me anything.'

Lucy didn't argue, and that, more than anything, worried Daisy.

Angela was the only person already at breakfast. 'Awfully sorry, Lucy,' she said gruffly. 'Wish I'd arrived just a couple of minutes earlier and nabbed the brute, or even stopped him. Any news?'

Lucy shook her head. Going to the sideboard, she poured herself a cup of coffee. Her back to Angela she said, 'Daisy says you saved his life.'

Angela flushed. 'Oh, it was really Nancy. And that big detective, Sergeant Tring. All I did was stop the bleeding. Anyone could have done it.'

'I couldn't.' Daisy was filling a plate with scrambled eggs, two sausages, and two triangles of toast. 'I've never been so glad to see anyone in my life.' That was somewhat of an exaggeration, considering she hadn't been at all sure Angela wouldn't finish Gerald off as soon as she left. But she had to make up for Lucy's ungraciousness.

At least Lucy sat down at the same end of the table as Angela, though she just stared into her coffee, stirring it.

'Someone had to go for help,' Angela said. 'Daisy was jolly efficient. Lots of people would have just broken down in tears.'

'I waited to do that until after I'd summoned help,' said Daisy, joining them. 'Are you going to take Tiddler for a walk this morning, Angela? A stroll down to the lake is just what I need.'

'Yes, right after breakfast.'

'Why don't you come, Lucy?'

'I can't. Binkie's – Gerald's – parents are bound to turn up and they'll want to see me. I can't think what I'm going to say to them.'

'Darling, would you like me to stay and face them with you?' Daisy offered.

'No, thanks.' Lucy returned to contemplation of her coffee.

Later, walking down the track with Tiddler bouncing around them, daily more self-confident, Daisy said, 'I'm sorry Lucy was so unappreciative.'

'Oh, I didn't mind. Just saying what she did was as much as she could manage in the way of gratitude at present. She's too confused to know how to respond, like a dog that's been hurt or abandoned and doesn't quite dare trust anyone. They're usually snappish to start with, you know, until they learn what to expect.' Angela hesitated. 'I sort of know how she feels. Daisy, does your husband still suspect Teddy?'

'He couldn't have . . .'

'Not of bashing Lord Gerald. But my grandmother . . . ? I'm awfully afraid Mother might have poisoned Uncle Aubrey to protect Teddy, except that I can't see how he could possibly have known anything about Teddy. I mean, I don't know which way his bedroom faces, but I suppose he could have looked out in the night and recognized Teddy. Only how could Teddy or Mother know about it? Uncle Aubrey wasn't really interested in anything but his plants. He wouldn't have mentioned seeing Teddy to anyone.'

'No, it's quite a puzzle.'

'Besides, by the time he was killed everyone knew Teddy had arrived in the middle of the night. The police did, anyway. And I absolutely can't imagine Mother hitting Lord Gerald.'

'I shouldn't think she'd be strong enough to do so much damage,' Daisy said.

'No, but what if . . . what if Daddy did? I know he doesn't seem to care much for Mother or Teddy, but for the sake of the family. There have been Devenishes at Saxonfield forever, and Teddy's the only son and heir. Oh, Daisy, I don't think I could bear it if all three of them were arrested!'

'That sounds most unlikely,' said Daisy, but she wondered if Alec had considered the possibility.

CHAPTER 25

The moment Lady Devenish walked into the library, Alec dismissed the possibility of her having hit Bincombe. She was too short and too flabby. Last time he saw her he had considered her a credible poisoner but doubted her ability to strangle her mother-in-law. Now he was quite sure she hadn't the strength or the reach to wield a cricket bat in that near-deadly fashion.

But now they knew more of the circumstances surrounding the poisoning of Lord Fotheringay's tea, and no one had reported seeing her in the drawing room at tea-time.

She claimed to have stayed in the sitting room set aside for the Devenishes when Lady Eva's murder was discovered. 'I had expected that tea would have been sent up,' she complained, 'in the circumstances. I dare say it would have been if the rest of my family had not gone to the drawing room.'

'The rest of your family?'

'James, Teddy, Veronica, Angela. None of them came near me or thought to have tea sent up. Not being a Fotheringay, it would hardly have been proper for me to ring for it. So I went without.'

'Not being a Fotheringay,' Alec picked up, 'had you ever visited Haverhill as a child?'

'No,' she said, surprised, 'I met James in town. My mama-in-law was the only Fotheringay I met before our marriage.'

'Lord Fotheringay must have been pleased to have someone new to show his conservatory to.'

Lady Devenish sniffed disapprovingly. 'In those days, it would have been considered most improper for a young married woman to meet a man in a conservatory!'

One in the eye for Daisy! Alec avoided looking at Tom but was aware of the twitching of his moustache. 'Are you saying you were never given a tour of the conservatory?'

'Oh, James and I strolled through it now and then, but I never had the least interest in plants.'

She admitted her children had mentioned to her that some of the plants in the conservatory were poisonous. She had simply forbidden them to go in there. It was disgraceful that Aubrey – who had children of his own! – should grow such stuff.

Alec could not get her to budge from her assertion that she had no idea which plants were poisonous, nor from her claim of remaining in the upstairs sitting room at tea-time. She admitted waiting in the hall for Teddy after dinner. What else was to be expected of a mother whose only son had been dragged away from his meal by the police and might be coerced into confessing to things he had not done because they needed to make an arrest?

'Whom did you see in the hall while you were waiting?' Alec wished he had thought of this line of questioning earlier.

Lady Devenish flushed. 'I wasn't watching,' she said evasively. 'I remember Montagu coming out of the dining room and going upstairs. A couple of footmen went in, to clear the table. When they left, Lord Gerald came out of the Long Gallery and watched them cross the hall. He went to the drawing room door, looked in, then turned back to the dining room. And a few minutes later, Mrs Fletcher went running after him. Then, of course, she came tearing out like a hoyden, bumped into a footman and made him drop his tray, and dashed into the library. Teddy came out, so I didn't stay any longer.'

She insisted she hadn't noticed anything else. Alec let her go.

'These mealy-mouthed women!' Tom exclaimed. 'Mrs Fletcher met her coming out of the cloakroom, so she must have seen Mrs Fletcher going in, but not a word of it! I wonder who else she saw go in there and can't bring herself to mention, coming or going?'

'It doesn't help,' Alec agreed. 'If necessary, we'll ask her point-blank. We'll see Montagu first, though it looks as if he just went upstairs and stayed there. Then it's past time we went over everything we've learnt so far. Let's hope we'll find something significant in our notes that we've been over-looking!'

Ernie Piper was sent off to enquire after Lord Gerald and then go to find Montagu Fotheringay. He came back after a couple of minutes.

'Dr Philpotts is here, Chief, and he'd like a word with you in Lord Gerald's room.'

The police surgeon greeted Alec with a grin. 'Pity I didn't bet on my prognosis against Arbuthnot's,' he said in a hushed voice. 'The patient is sleeping normally now, not unconscious.'

'You're certain?'

'Ninety-nine per cent. All the easily visible signs are present. I don't want to wake him by doing a more thorough examination. The longer he can sleep the better. He's going to have one hell of a headache when he wakes up and he may very well not remember much, if anything, of what happened. He is not, I repeat not, to be pestered with questions.'

'For how long?'

'Hm. My surgery is at six. I'll try to drop in at about five to have a look at him. I'll tell you then.'

Philpotts departed on his rounds and the nurse allowed Alec past the painted screen to take a peek at Bincombe. Normal colour had returned to his face and the flickering of his eyelids suggested that he was dreaming. Alec silently wished him happy dreams.

'Don't tell anyone his condition has improved,' he impressed upon the nurse. 'His parents understand the need to keep it quiet.'

'Not to worry, Mr Fletcher. As if I'd do anything to endanger any patient of mine! We don't want the nasty brute that hit him having another go.'

Returning across the hall, Alec was intercepted by Baines. 'Beg pardon, sir, but Mr and Mrs Pendleton arrived half an hour ago and they're asking to see you.'

'Pendleton?' Alec asked blankly, his head ringing with Fotheringays and Devenishes.

'Miss Erica's parents, sir.'

'Oh yes. I expect they want to take her home. If that's all, tell them that will be all right as long as she remains available at a known address for questioning, should it prove necessary. And the same goes for the other girl, Miss . . . Miss . . .'

'Miss Julia Lasbury, sir?'

'That's the one. If her parents turn up, she may leave. And if you can get rid of them all without my seeing them, Baines, I shall be exceedingly grateful.' Alec handed over a ten-shilling note, hoping it would be reimbursed as a necessary expense. It was worth it anyway, though interviews with the Pendletons and Lasburys could not possibly be half as painful as the one with the Marquis and Marchioness of Tiverton.

'I dare say it can be managed, sir,' said the butler suavely as the note vanished.

Piper caught up with Alec as he attained the haven of the library. 'Mr Montagu says if you want to talk to him you'll have to come upstairs to his room, Chief. Says he's not well, and I must say he looks like death warmed up.'

'Did you ask him what's wrong?'

'Rheumatism in his hip. The pain kept him awake all night. I asked did he send for a doctor. He said the quacks just prescribe aspirin and a hot water bottle and a reducing diet.'

'And I bet he follows the first two and won't have anything to do with the third. All right, Ernie, I'm going to leave him to you. If he tells you anything other than that he was in his room at the relevant times, come and get me. Otherwise, when you have his statement, find Lady Devenish and see if you can get her to describe how he went upstairs last night without putting the words in her mouth.'

'Right, Chief!'

Ernie Piper's return coincided with the arrival of a footman bearing lunch. As they ate, he reported exactly what Alec expected: Montagu Fotheringay continued to claim to have stayed in his room at tea-time yesterday ('He was still upset about Lady Eva, like he told us, and he felt an attack of rheumatism coming on so he thought he'd better try slimming'), and returned thither immediately after his interrupted dinner ('Missing tea didn't work, just made him hungrier at

dinner'). Lady Devenish, asked to describe his gait, said he had
walked heavily from the dining room to the stairs and ascended
one step at a time, favouring his left leg.

'So it looks like he's out of it,' said Piper.

'We can't cross him off the list,' said Alec, spreading butter
on a crisp roll to go with the cold chicken and salad. 'But I
don't like the look of him. The trouble is, for one reason or
another I don't really like the look of any of them.'

Their lunch was interrupted by a telephone call from Sir
Bernard Spilsbury's assistant. The Home Office's Chief Pathologist confirmed that Lord Fotheringay had ingested a fatal
dose of oleandrin and associated glycosides. The lack of
evidence of gastrointestinal distress might be explained by the
victim's weak heart, which could have failed before the devel-
opment of other visible symptoms.

In a way, the confirmation of poisoning helped: if he had
died naturally after all, then the attack on Bincombe made no
sort of sense and they would have had to reconsider the whole
situation. On the other hand, it was absolutely no help in
trying to guess what Lord Fotheringay could possibly have
known that Lady Eva's murderer considered a threat.

After lunch, Alec sent Piper to ask after Bincombe. The
nurse said he had roused enough to drink a glass of water,
and then gone back to sleep. She had told Lady Tiverton
when she looked in on her son. Her ladyship had promised
to tell no one but her husband. They were keeping to the
suite of rooms Lady Haverhill had put at their disposal,
attended by their own servants, so none of the household
would witness their relief.

'I asked the nurse if Lady Tiverton didn't want to sit with
him,' Ernie said. 'She thought it was natural that a grand lady

who could pay for a nurse wouldn't want to take care of her sick child, but if you ask me it's unnatural.'

'I shouldn't worry, young 'un,' said Tom. 'You won't be marrying a grand lady.'

Ernie blushed, and Alec wondered briefly if his latest flame was turning serious. That was all well and good as long as it didn't take his mind off his work.

The thought made Alec wonder what Daisy was presently up to. It was not like her to keep her nose out of an investigation once she was involved, however peripherally. She hadn't even come to ask after Bincombe. She must realise that he wouldn't tell her, that he was serious about her not meddling in his cases.

He mustn't let her take his mind off his work.

The three of them set to work collating statements. It was Ernie who realised that the Cambridge police had not yet responded to their enquiries. He telephoned. The constable stationed at the gate yesterday evening had seen two gentlemen come to post letters. He had made sure they returned up the avenue but had not thought to take their names or note the times. The postman had picked up such a mass of letters he couldn't possibly recall any particular one.

The collating went on. They made out schedules of the reported movements of all the suspects, which mightily impressed Sir Leonard when he came to check on their progress but which by no means added to their progress. When a footman brought a tea-tray into the library, they were still stuck with the same list of unsatisfactory suspects.

Daisy arrived five minutes after the tea-tray. 'I've been thinking,' she announced, perching on a corner of the long table and helping herself to a chocolate biscuit.

Alec sat back with a sigh. 'What have you been thinking?'

'Well, tell me first how you're doing.'

'We don't know who the murderer is, or who the murderers are. We still have six names on the list. We still have no idea what Lord Fotheringay could have observed, unless he saw a man wandering about with a stocking hanging out of his pocket. In which case, why the deuce didn't he come to us as soon as he heard of his aunt's murder?'

'Well, he was the vaguest of men except where his plants were concerned. But I don't believe that need worry you.'

'What? Daisy, what do you know? What have you been doing?'

'I've been talking to people and, as I told you, I've been thinking. And I think we've been looking at everything backwards. What if—'

Dr Philpotts came in. 'You can talk to him now,' he announced. 'No more than ten minutes. You leave at the least sign of agitation. You obey the nurse implicitly.' He helped himself to a chocolate biscuit. 'I've got to run.'

Daisy stared after him. 'You mean Gerald is all right? You beast, Alec, you might have let me know!'

'Could you have kept it from Lucy?'

'Of course! Probably. I think so. I haven't told her Dr Philpotts was hopeful.'

'Good for you,' Alec said ironically. 'Now what's this about looking at everything backwards?'

CHAPTER 26

The walk with Angela and Tiddler had sparked Daisy's reappraisal of the murders, or rather Angela's comment when they reached the gazebo 'ruins' and turned to look back at the house.

'It's so enormous. It must cost a fortune to run. Just think of all the animals I could save with all that money!'

Lucy had said something similar when Daisy arrived at Haverhill just two days ago. Rescuing dogs had not come into it, but she had mentioned her grandfather's enormous expenses and the 'pots of money' which allowed him to pay for Lucy's wedding as well. Daisy was sure Lucy had said something else even more significant, but she couldn't quite pin it down.

'When Angela and I got back to the house,' she told Alec, 'people were practically queuing up to talk to me. Everyone was sure I must know what you were up to and what you'd found out. I didn't have to go looking for people, honestly. All I did was sit in the sun in the Long Gallery and they came to me. I could do without the rest of the house, but I really do covet the Long Gallery. It's a wonderful room.'

'Great Scott, Daisy, if you have something to say, get on with it!'

'Sorry, darling. You haven't had a chance yet to appreciate it. Anyway, people asked me what was going on, and of course

I didn't tell them even what very little I know. But they also wanted to tell me their own ideas. Lucy was right, some of her relatives really are poisonous! The one thing that puzzled just about all of them was what Lord Fotheringay could have discovered that threatened Lady Eva's murderer.'

'I hope you weren't asking questions,' Alec said ominously.

'Oh no, darling. I may have just sort of nudged one or two people in that direction, but mostly I just looked at them.' Daisy widened what Alec persisted in referring to as her 'misleadingly guileless' blue eyes. 'And out it came.'

'Ah,' rumbled Tom, 'so you see Lord F's murder as a stumbling block, Mrs Fletcher?'

'The more I learn about him, the more it doesn't make sense. His only interest was his plants, and he went through life blissfully unaware of anything else. I started to wonder what other motive Lady Eva's murderer could have had for killing him. And that was when I started to think we'd got it all backwards.'

Alec, Tom and Ernie all sat up straight and looked at her. It was most satisfactory. 'Go on,' said Alec.

'Suppose the original plan was to murder Lord Fotheringay and Lady Eva had information that would give away the murderer. After all, she was in the business of nosing about, so to speak. It's far more likely than the other way round. It would have to be some clue that was meaningless at the time but which would have become significant after Lord F's death. Yet it had to be something the person she saw knew she knew— Sometimes the English language is most inadequate!'

'We know what you mean, Daisy. Get on with it!'

'Then I remembered that she went to the conservatory at tea-time the day before, the day I arrived. Incidentally, darling, may I have some tea in your cup? I'm parched.' While Alec passed his cup and saucer to Tom, who presided over the pot, she continued. 'Lady Eva realised Lord F hadn't turned up to tea on the terrace and she decided he ought to be more sociable on such a grand family occasion. She marched off around the side of the house to fetch him. Thanks.' Daisy took a long draught of tea.

'You think she saw—' Alec started.

'Wait! Let me tell this in order or I'll get muddled and miss things out. Any detail could be significant,' she quoted him. 'The thing is, Lord and Lady F came out together just a moment later, from the Long Gallery. He had left the conservatory before Lady Eva arrived. It was the perfect opportunity for someone to pick a few oleander leaves unobserved.'

'Which Lady Eva observed,' Piper put in. He had started taking notes.

'Which Lady Eva observed. My feeling is, if she had seen a family member, who ought to have known better, picking the stuff, she would have scolded and quite likely mentioned it when she came back. But if it was a relative by marriage who might never have been told about the poisonous plants, she'd just warn them and leave it at that.'

'Ah,' said Tom ruminatively. 'Sounds reasonable.'

'Pure speculation,' Alec said, 'but it doesn't really matter. If she saw this person, this person probably saw her. Assuming your theory has anything in it.'

'Well, I think it's logically consistent. This person – can I call him or her X?'

'Do.'

'Right-oh, X has to dispose of Lady Eva before he – I can't go on saying he or she so I'll stick to he – before he can safely administer the oleander to Lord F. So there's the motive for her murder, nothing to do with her collection of scandal.'

'And it also served very nicely to muddy the waters,' said Alec. 'But we come back to the question of who had a motive for killing Lord F? As far as I've gathered, he had very little at his disposal before succeeding to the estate on Lord Haverhill's death.'

'Precisely,' said Daisy triumphantly, 'and that's where what Lucy said comes in. Death duties!'

'Great Scott!' Alec exclaimed, properly impressed. 'You may have something there.'

Tom and Ernie looked puzzled. Death duties were not of compelling interest to anyone on the salary of a detective sergeant or constable.

Alec let Daisy explain. She thought it very noble of him, since he deplored anything which reinforced Ernie Piper's belief in her infallibility.

'Aubrey Fotheringay had had a weak heart for years. His father, on the contrary, was an exceptionally healthy, vigorous man. In the normal course of things, Lord Haverhill might have been expected to outlive his son. But Lord Haverhill reached the ripe old age of eighty and there was still no sign of Aubrey popping off. Instead, Lord Haverhill started to go downhill. It began to look as if he would be the first to go.'

'A very natural course of things,' Tom observed in a rather disapproving voice.

'Yes indeed, but very much more to the government's advantage than the estate's. Lord Haverhill dies, enormous death duties are levied on his enormous estate. What remains goes to his son, who becomes Earl of Haverhill. The new Lord Haverhill dies, somewhat less enormous death duties are levied on his no longer quite so enormous estate. The much reduced residue goes to his son in turn.'

Piper was quick to grasp the implication. 'But if Lord Fotheringay dies first, he has no estate, so no death duties. So when the present Lord Haverhill dies and death duties are paid, the estate is still pretty enormous.'

'And it goes to Rupert,' said Tom. 'He wasn't here.'

'No,' Daisy agreed. 'But his wife was.'

Alec let Daisy stay while they discussed her new theory, which was only fair, she considered. She was quite surprised, though, that he didn't even once remind her it was pure speculation.

'We didn't even consider them,' he said in self-disgust. 'The Lieutenant Colonel was vouched for by his senior officer. We didn't find anything in Lady Eva's papers that suggested he or Sally had anything to hide.'

'I don't think they did,' Daisy said. 'I heard that he was expensive and she had to scrape and save . . .'

'She wears artificial silk stockings,' Tom put in. 'That's what Lady Eva was strangled with.'

'There you are, then. I bet her pearls are artificial too.'

'But whenever Rupert wanted anything his pay and his allowance wouldn't cover,' Alec said, 'he came to Haverhill and his grandfather shelled out. Who told us that?'

'Mr Montagu,' said Ernie.

'Flora told me the same,' Daisy observed. 'Lucy said Rupert found it humiliating to beg from Lord Haverhill. He's bored with the Army. Lady Haverhill told me that.'

'Why on earth . . . ? Why do people tell you these things, Daisy?'

Daisy fluttered her eyelashes at him. 'I didn't ask, I promise you. I had no interest in Rupert whatsoever then. She also said he doesn't want to come and live here at Haverhill either, to help run the estate. And I think it was Lady Ione who told me he wants to live a life of expensive, luxurious idleness in town, just bringing house-parties down for the odd weekend to his country place. It wouldn't be half so luxurious after two lots of death duties, if he could even afford to run Haverhill.'

'And Mrs Rupert wants real silk stockings,' said Tom. 'Not to mention real pearls. Do you think it was all her doing?'

'She couldn't have attacked Gerald,' Daisy reminded him.

'No, but she could have done the others and talked him into that, to protect her.'

'I don't think so. I don't see her as a Lady Macbeth. I think he's firmly in command and he told her to poison his father while he had a perfect alibi, just in case anyone suspected it wasn't a natural death. Which would have been unlikely if she hadn't murdered Lady Eva first. I think she panicked when Lady Eva saw her pick the oleander.'

'It certainly couldn't have been part of the original plan,' Alec agreed. 'They might well have got away with just Lord Fotheringay's death.'

'Sally was in a dreadful state this morning,' Daisy went on. 'Everyone thought she was being rather feeble, affected more strongly than was quite decent by Lady Eva's death, but it makes much more sense if she was the one who killed her. And remember, she'd hoped for a nice, quiet suffocation with a pillow and then had to strangle her after a fight.'

'She must have taken the stocking with her in case,' said Piper. Then he blushed. 'Or what d'you think, Mrs Fletcher?'

'It could have been in her pocket. Assuming she was wearing

a dressing gown, it's quite possible she stuffed her stockings in her pocket for some reason when she took them off at bedtime. I've done it on occasion.'

Piper's face was scarlet, his gaze glued to his notebook. As far as he was concerned, discussing a lady's stockings with her was far less decent than throwing a fit at the murder of one's husband's great-aunt.

'So Sally is in a state,' said Alec. 'So much so that Lord Haverhill sends for Rupert. In spite of which she goes ahead and poisons her father-in-law?'

'I wouldn't be surprised if she was afraid he'd be frightfully angry if he arrived and found she hadn't done it. Bang goes his alibi, or they have to postpone the real murder until he goes back to the Army, risking Lord Haverhill dying in the meantime.'

'Possible,' Alec conceded, more grudgingly than Daisy considered quite decent.

'He must have been frightfully angry anyway, when he arrived and found out she'd botched it. And then she tells him she's afraid Gerald saw her . . .'

'If he did see her, it'll be a big help. Which reminds me,' said Alec, standing up, 'I'd better go ask him before he falls asleep again.'

'Darling, I'm coming too.'

'No, you're not. What if someone saw you going in?'

'No one will. They're all at tea and I bet you everyone is there, giving themselves an alibi in case someone else is poisoned, if you see what I mean. If there's anyone in the hall, I'll pretend I was on my way to the cloakroom. Let me see him, darling. I have to tell him Lucy's worried sick.'

Alec gave in. 'Tom, Ernie, go over the notes again. See if there's anything to confirm or contradict Daisy's fantasy.'

'Fantasy, ho!' said Ernie not quite sotto voce.

Tom winked at her as she rose to follow Alec.

They found Gerald not only awake but sitting up. He was drinking lemonade.

'Dying of thirst, poor lamb,' said the nurse with proprietory pride. 'Making up for loss of blood, you see.'

'No one was to know he's awake!' Alec exclaimed in annoyance.

'I asked for it for myself,' the nurse explained placidly.

Gerald set down his empty glass on the bedside table, beside a nearly empty pitcher. 'That's better! Daisy, how's Lucy?'

'Desperately worried. Alec won't let me tell her you're recovering. Are you really well enough to sit up?'

'Nothing wrong with me bar a bit of a headache. To tell the truth, I feel just as if I went on a bit of a bender last night. I promised the doctor I wouldn't get up till tomorrow, though. Fletcher, can't Lucy be told I'm all right? She's not going to spread it around, any more than my parents will.'

'Have you talked to them?'

'No, but Miss Robbins here told me they came when I was sleeping.'

'The fewer who know, the safer you are.'

'You still don't know who it was? Who killed Lady Eva and Lucy's uncle and hit me?'

'No. I take it you don't remember seeing whoever hit you, nor whoever poisoned Lord Fotheringay's tea?'

'Not a thing. I don't think it's that I don't remember, I just didn't see.'

'I've been thinking, darling.' Daisy ignored Alec's groan. 'Surely the oleander must have been put in the teapot soon enough to give it time to steep. Gerald only just got there when he drank it, so he couldn't possibly see who did it.'

'Then why the deuce did he hit me?' Gerald demanded.

'We didn't tell anyone exactly when you arrived,' Alec said. 'For all the murderer knew you could have arrived in time to see her – or him – leave the conservatory and then waited around for your appointment with Lucy until he drank the tea. You see the importance of not revealing more information than absolutely necessary.'

'Except,' Daisy pointed out, 'in that case it led to Gerald being hit on the head.'

Alec turned his most fearsome frown on her, but before he could speak, Gerald said, 'Listen. I have an idea.'

Alec turned the frown on him. Daisy could read his mind: wasn't it bad enough her coming up with ideas without someone else starting?

Needless to say, Gerald was uncowed. 'You're afraid the murderer will have another go at me. Why not let him?'

Daisy burst into the drawing room in a manner her mother would have stigmatized as thoroughly unladylike. 'Lucy? Oh, there you are, darling. Alec says Gerald's not going to die after all!'

Already pale, Lucy turned white. Fortunately she was seated, with her parents and Tim and Nancy. Daisy forced herself not to glance at Rupert or Sally, keen though she was to see how the news affected them.

Nancy beamed. 'He's going to be all right?'

'Well,' Daisy temporized, a little more loudly than was strictly necessary as she had by now crossed the room to the group, 'the doctor came to see him. He's still unconscious but Dr Philpotts is pretty sure he'll come round within the next twenty-four hours.'

Giving her a surprised look, Nancy opened her mouth. Daisy sent her a desperate if silent appeal and hurried on, 'He'll have a frightful headache and he may not remember what happened, but there's a chance he will be able to say who attacked him. Then everything will be cleared up and we can all go home.'

'Daisy, dear, do the Tivertons know?' Lucy's mother asked anxiously.

'I think Alec was going to tell them, Aunt Vickie. But I expect they'd be happy to see you.'

'Yes, of course. Come along, Lucy.'

'Not me,' Lucy said grimly. 'You forget, Mother, I'm not going to marry him.'

Several people gathered around. Daisy managed to slip away. Lucy joined her before she reached the door.

'Did you have to tell me in front of everyone?' she demanded irritably as they went out into the hall. 'Of course I'm glad he's going to be all right, but it's really nothing to do with me now.'

'No, I'm sorry,' Daisy said in her most soothing tone. 'I was so pleased I just didn't think. Isn't it wonderful news?'

Lucy's mouth trembled. 'Yes. Yes, of course it is. I'm so glad for his parents.' She turned away towards the stairs and Daisy let her go.

Nancy caught up with her. 'Daisy, the doctor—'

'Sshh!' Daisy drew her farther from the drawing-room door, into the middle of the hall where no one could possibly listen without being seen.

'The doctor couldn't possibly be certain Lord Gerald will recover consciousness, let alone within a given period. You must have misunderstood, and it's a great pity you told Lucy.'

'Oh, blast! I shouldn't have told her with a trained nurse sitting beside her! Alec will be furious. I think you'd better come to the library and talk to him.'

Alec managed to obfuscate the issue so that Nancy went away confused but reluctantly willing not to contradict Daisy's story.

When Alec returned to the desk from escorting Nancy to the door, Tom said, 'I don't want to be a wet blanket, Chief, but all this isn't what you might call according to Hoyle.'

'Nothing ever is once Daisy gets involved.'

'Darling, that's unfair! It's entirely Gerald's idea.'

'Yes, and that's our excuse: the police surgeon himself told us not to agitate the patient, so we dared not contradict him. All the same, Piper, make a note of Tom's objection, please. If anything goes wrong, it's my responsibility. You two are following orders.'

'Nothing's going to go wrong, Chief,' said Ernie, 'not with Mrs Fletcher involved.'

'Ah, but this is where she ceases to be involved. Daisy—'

'Wait, I've got an idea. Stebbins!'

'Stebbins?'

'If you have a bright young officer on duty, like the chap who's been guarding Gerald's room all day, it's going to look a bit fishy if he drowses off. If it's Constable Stebbins with his creaky feet, no one will wonder at it if he snores his head off.'

'You've got a point there, Mrs Fletcher,' said Tom.

'Yes.' Alec sighed. 'Ernie, ring them up and say we want Stebbins for night duty.'

'They're not going to believe it, Chief!' Ernie reached for the telephone.

'Fortunately, it doesn't matter what they believe.'

'Stebbins is perfectly all right,' Daisy said indignantly, 'as long as you don't make him walk too much. This is the perfect job for him and I bet he doesn't really fall asleep. He'll be there to help if you need him. And I might have another bright idea, Alec, so you'd better let me stay.'

'For the planning, all right,' Alec conceded, 'but you are to be tucked up cosily in bed when the lights go out.'

CHAPTER 27

Not according to Hoyle, Alec thought ruefully as he sneaked down the back stairs. Tom was all too correct, he was breaking rules written and unwritten. He would never have suggested such a course of action, but when Bincombe urged the plan upon him, he had not resisted very hard.

The investigation was at an impasse. Bincombe didn't know who had attacked him or poisoned Lord Fotheringay. He hadn't seen where Rupert went after dinner since he himself waited in the Long Gallery for the servants to finish clearing. He did recall Rupert saying he was going up to the nurseries to look in on his little boy. So late in the evening, the child would have been asleep, the nurserymaid on duty within call but not within sight.

That Lady Devenish said she had not seen Rupert in the hall proved nothing. While she was watching Montagu go up the main stairs, Rupert could have cut through behind the pillars to the very service staircase Alec was now making use of, which debouched in the corridor between conservatory and library. Or he could claim to have done so while actually going to the conservatory.

Daisy's theory was attractive, more so than the other possibilities, but they had no proof, only possibilities. An

attempt by the murderer – or one of the murderers –
to eliminate Gerald tonight would settle the matter. If no
attempt took place, they would be no worse off.

At the bottom of the stairs, Alec turned off his electric torch.
Feeling his way along the dark corridor was easy and his
rubber-soled shoes made no sound on the parquet floor.

The first step he took on the hall's marble squeaked. He
froze. Not a sound reached his ears. Across the hall, a dim light
was visible near the door to Gerald's room, and there was
another at the head of the main stairs, but they only made the
great space seem darker. Shoes in hand, Alec crept around
behind the pillars and into the blackness under the stairs, where
he stopped again to listen.

Tom and Ernie had had it easy. Baines gave Tom the key to
the servants' wing door, close to Gerald's door. They had only
to wait until all the residents had gone upstairs to nip around
the corner. Alec had to pretend to retire with Daisy and come
down again, hoping the murderer had not preceded him, was
not already lurking, watching for an opportunity. Tom
suggested leaving the ambush to him and young Piper, but
Alec wouldn't let his men break the rules unless he was there
breaking them too.

The murderer wouldn't go down until Stebbins had had time
to drift off to sleep, Alec reassured himself. He went on from
pillar to pillar, approaching that dim electric light.

One last glance around, and he slipped past the elderly
constable into the room. Stebbins, alert at present though
seated on a hard chair, winked at Alec as he turned to close the
door gently behind him.

Here a light glowed behind the screen sheltering the bed
from the entrance, where the night nurse, persuaded into

cooperation, was waiting anxiously. The electric lamp was turned away from Gerald, who lay on his back, arms laid neatly at his sides on top of the bedclothes. With his eyes closed he would look as if he was still unconscious, if it weren't for the fresh colour in his cheeks. As it was, he looked fit enough to tackle any number of murderers, especially when he grinned at Alec.

'Have you any white face-powder?' Alec whispered to the nurse.

She produced a compact from her handbag and, lips pursed, toned down Gerald's bloom while Alec moved the lamp to a table further off, beside a sofa. He looked down behind the sofa to see Ernie lounging on a couple of cushions.

'Don't you dare fall asleep.'

'I wouldn't, Chief!'

Tom was seated behind the second screen, intended to shield the patient from the window's daylight and draughts. Beside him a chair awaited Alec.

'Most comfortable vigil I've ever kept,' Tom whispered.

'Better than a street corner in Whitechapel,' Alec agreed.

Settling down to wait, he wondered who was lurking out there in the shadowy hall hoping for a chance to find Bincombe unattended. Daisy's latest theory was credible, but Alec still favoured the Devenishes, one, two, or all of them in league, though for Daisy's sake he hoped Angela was not involved. Or would John Walsdorf creep through the door, bent on murder? Somehow he couldn't picture Montagu either lurking or creeping – there was simply too much of him.

Alec looked at his watch. An hour to go before Stebbins was to start snoring, and another quarter before the nurse would hurry to the cloakroom, clutching her belly as if she had eaten something that disagreed with her. With luck, the watching murderer would expect her to stay there for a while.

The whole thing depended entirely on luck. But then, one way or another, most investigations did.

Daisy undressed but she was wakeful. It was useless trying to go to sleep while Alec and Gerald and Tom and Ernie were downstairs waiting for a murderous attack. Not to mention Constable Stebbins with his tortured feet.

She put on her dressing gown, went to the writing table and started a letter to Belinda, telling her about Angela's Tiddler. Then she wrote to her mother, who would be furious if she found out from Daisy's sister, Violet, that Daisy was staying at Haverhill. She wouldn't write to Alec's mother until she got home, in case Mrs Fletcher decided to return to St John's Wood to look after poor, deserted Bel.

The article she had hoped to offer her American editor, describing an aristocratic English wedding, had gone down the drain, but she could make a start on planning one about Angela's work. That kept her occupied for some time, until her eyelids began to droop. Maybe she would sleep after all.

She went to brush her teeth. Indistinct sounds from Lucy's room suggested she hadn't been able to fall asleep either.

Then a door clicked shut.

Daisy dropped her toothbrush, spat foam into the basin, and flung open the connecting door. The bedside lamp was on. No Lucy.

Had she got it all wrong? Was the murderer for some obscure reason aiming at Lucy and Gerald all along? Heart in mouth, Daisy looked behind the bed, under the bed, in the wardrobe.

No Lucy.

There seemed no conceivable reason to remove her body. Perhaps she had been stunned and carried away to be murdered at leisure. Daisy hurried to the door and cautiously peered out. She was just in time to see Lucy's peacock kimono turning the corner of the passage towards the stairs.

Lucy was on her way to where her erstwhile fiancé lay supposedly helpless. She didn't want to marry him. Her family were pressing her to relent. In her state of mental disturbance, could some aberration have made her believe her only way out was to kill him? What if she had killed Lady Eva for the money which would enable her to live comfortably without him?

Creeping barefoot along the passage after her dearest friend, Daisy tried to bring logic to bear. Lucy couldn't have poisoned Lord Fotheringay. Someone else had done that. But her great-aunt? She could have pretended to swallow the powder her mother gave her that night. Aunt Vickie was not difficult to deceive. And Lucy had not been in the drawing room after dinner last night, when Gerald was attacked.

Lucy strangling Lady Eva and whacking Gerald over the head – the idea was ludicrous! Wasn't it?

Daisy peeked around the corner. Lucy was standing at the balustrade separating the gallery from the vast, murky gulf of the hall, gazing down. From below came the hurried tap-tap of heels on marble. The nurse must be on her way to the cloakroom, as arranged.

The tapping ended with the firm closing of a door. For a couple of minutes, Lucy stood still. Daisy hoped she had come to her senses and would go no farther, but, soundless in soft slippers, she moved to the head of the stairs and paused again, staring down. Then she started to descend.

* * *

Once the nurse had left, the dimly lit room was so still that Alec could hear Stebbins snoring on his chair outside the door. The constable was a willing, not to say overenthusiastic, conspirator.

Most of the bed was visible through chinks in the rattan screen Alec was hiding behind, though the door was hidden by the other screen. He had only to turn his head to see Bincombe's bandaged head, calm, relaxed face and closed eyes. His nearer hand lay open, palm up, fingers slightly curled, on top of the blue blanket. His feet beneath the bedclothes lolled slackly to either side. He was the very picture of an unconscious patient neatly arranged by his nurse.

Though Alec neither heard nor saw the door open, he was instantly aware when it happened: Tom Tring, who had a view of an upper corner, stiffened. The soft click of the closing latch was only audible because Alec was expecting it.

Someone had entered the room stealthily. Someone was standing just inside, straining every sense. But if accosted now, that someone could say he had just come to see how Bincombe was doing, very quietly so as not to disturb him. They had to wait until the murderer's intent was clear beyond question – yet not allow him to further harm his victim.

A dark figure approached the bed, silhouetted against the shaded lamplight. A man, tall, with a pillow in his hands . . .

. . . come to make sure Bincombe was well taken care of, had every comfort the house could supply . . .

With startling swiftness the pillow descended on Bincombe's face. Alec and Tom sprang forward, flattening the screen. Piper erupted from behind the sofa. Quicker than any of them Lord Gerald's fist flew up and connected with the intruder's chin.

Rupert Fotheringay flew backwards, toppling the other screen, landing heavily on his back in its ruins, dazed.

As Piper pounced with jingling handcuffs, the door was flung open.

'Gerald!' cried Lucy.

'Hello, old thing,' said Bincombe sheepishly, sitting up in bed and massaging his knuckles.

Lucy took in the scene at a glance and turned into an avenging Fury. 'How dare you!' she yelled at Alec. 'How dare you use Gerald as bait in your filthy trap!'

'It was his own idea,' Alec said mildly.

'Lucy, you will marry me, won't you?' Bincombe pleaded.

'No I . . .'

'Don't be an ass, Lucy.' Daisy's barefooted arrival on the threshold, with Constable Stebbins looming behind her, added the crowning touch to turn drama into farce. 'After lashing out at Alec like that because he put Gerald in danger, you can't pretend you don't love him.'

'I can't go through all this again!' Lucy wailed.

'Darling, if you're talking about the family wedding, just follow our example and tie the knot at a registry office while the family is looking the other way.'

'Which they will be for some time,' Alec said grimly, standing over the handcuffed Lieutenant Colonel. Tom and Piper had sat him up against the wall, where he leaned groggily. 'The trial for murder of the heir to the earldom is liable to keep the Fotheringays' attention occupied for the foreseeable future.'

'Murder!' Rupert sat up straight. 'I haven't killed anyone. It was—'

'It is my duty to inform you,' Tom intoned as Piper whipped

out his notebook and a pencil, 'that you are not obliged to say anything, but anything you do say will be taken down and may be used in evidence.'

'I haven't killed anyone,' Rupert repeated urgently. 'It was my wife, and she was never supposed to do in Aunt Eva. And then to bungle it and have to strangle her, so no one could possibly believe it was a natural death! Just like a woman – she couldn't even manage to pick a few leaves without being seen and then she panics and . . .'

Alec bundled Lucy and Daisy out of the room and closed the door firmly behind them.

'What a revolting specimen!' said Lucy in disgust.

'I hope you're referring to your cousin, not to Alec.'

'Rupert always was a bit of a cad but I never thought he was such an out-and-out rotter, trying to blame the whole thing on Sally. He won't get away with attempted murder, will he?'

'I shouldn't think so. He seemed to be anxious to implicate himself as a co-conspirator or accessory to murder or something. Lucy, you are going to marry Gerald, aren't you?'

Lucy sighed. 'I suppose so. I really do love him, but I don't know what sort of wife I'll make. A shrewish one, I expect. If we settle for a registrar, will you and Alec be our witnesses?'

'Then all is forgiven?' said Daisy. 'We'll be delighted!'